enjoy "Degrees of
Guilt."

Regards,

Degrees of Guilt

by Jim Bennett

 FriesenPress

Suite 300 - 990 Fort St
Victoria, BC, V8V 3K2
Canada

www.friesenpress.com

ISBN
978-1-4602-9596-0 (Hardcover)
978-1-4602-9597-7 (Paperback)
978-1-4602-9598-4 (eBook)

1. FICTION, WAR & MILITARY

Distributed to the trade by The Ingram Book Company

Acknowledgements

Looking back three years to when I sat down to write my first novel I am reminded of an ancient explorer. I knew I wanted to travel to a faraway, mysterious place, where others had gone, but I hadn't. I had a general idea of where I wanted to go, but little idea of how to get there, and no idea of what I would encounter along the way.

That you're reading these words means I reached the destination and returned, but not without help from many people. Where this story works, it is with the assistance of the people acknowledged, and others who encouraged me. Where it doesn't work so well, it will be entirely my fault.

My wife of 13 years, Sandra Pupatello, who lives in Ontario, 3000 kilometres away, listened to every word as I read the unfolding story to her, and at the end of each reading, said, "That's it? That's all you wrote?" Or, if I hadn't read to her for a few days, "Do you have enough to read to me again?"

If Marco Polo's wife had had a cell phone, he would not have turned around at China. He would have circumnavigated the earth, discovering America from the east.

My brother Paul, an accomplished commercial bush pilot before joining the Federal Department of Transportation as an inspector, read the manuscript with the precision of a regulator. He pointed out my early errors, but mercifully, not all at once, and in a most constructive manner.

My parents, Trevor (90) and Mildred (86) and my children, Stephen and Victoria, in their 40s, who claim to like the story, perhaps indicating intergenerational appeal. My friend, Ward Samson, outdoors activist and retired teacher, who phoned regularly, to say, "I didn't call for any reason. I just want to know how the book's going."

Paul Butler, an accomplished novelist and editor, whose recommendations greatly improved my manuscript, and shortened it. The cuts are now the genesis of a sequel and two unrelated stories.

Kevin Miller and Genevieve Penny, from FriesenPress, neither of whom I have met. Kevin's detailed and insightful review and recommendations have made it a much better read. Genevieve came through on every timeline committed, and more. She has insisted, for which I am grateful, that I reread, reread and reread, looking for flaws, and outright errors, when I wanted to be writing another manuscript.

To all of you I am deeply grateful.

Prologue

The helicopter came up fast. Billy, the gunner, positioned in front of the wheelhouse, was so intent on the seals he did not hear it approach. From the back of the boat, sixteen-year-old Jeff Wheeler watched in anger as the approaching helicopter caused the seals to dive off the ice pans and disappear.

Frozen, he watched as Billy looked skyward, lifted his rifle, and triggered a shot straight into the cockpit.

A small, white puff appeared on the helicopter's Plexiglas windshield, and then the hollow-point .223 slug pierced the pilot's chin, went straight through his brain, and exited through the top of his head, lodging in his helmet. Death was instantaneous.

The helicopter plummeted into the water between two ice pans. Its main propeller ripped into one of them, twisting it away from the aircraft and sending up a shower of ice crystals, snow, and water. Moments later, the roiling water was the only evidence of the crash.

Inside the helicopter, the three dazed passengers struggled to free themselves as the icy water of the Gulf of St. Lawrence rushed into the cabin. Their frantic efforts were in vain, and they drowned before most of them could unfasten their restraints.

It took nearly ten minutes in the strong ocean current for the helicopter to settle six hundred feet to the bottom, where it tumbled slowly along the ocean floor before coming to rest in an area favoured by local crab fishermen.

Back on the surface, on the main deck behind the cabin of the small, converted scallop dragger, reactions were mixed. The older man, Riley Wheeler, nearly deaf, and bent over skinning a seal, had not heard the helicopter engine until his grandson, Jeff, had tapped him firmly on the back. Now shocked, he stood there quietly. But not Jeff. His reaction was precisely the opposite.

"Oh my God, oh my God, oh my God! Uncle Billy shot it down! Fuck, fuck, fuck! What do we do now?"

Billy, as if in a world of his own, smiled. "I guess I taught those ragheads a lesson!" he said to no one in particular. "They won't fuck with us again."

The two sealers on the main deck were joined immediately by the fourth member of the crew, the skipper, retired Master Warrant Officer Josh Short. He had been in the wheelhouse steering the small vessel through pans of broken ice so Billy could shoot the seals through the head. Josh was accustomed to assuming command.

"Okay, men, we've got to figure out exactly what happened here," Josh said.

"What do you mean what happened here?" Jeff cried. "Uncle Billy just shot down a fucking helicopter! It sank. It's gone. Whoever was on board is dead. We've got to do something. We've got to call the cops."

"Young man, sit down and be quiet," Josh said sternly. "We'll decide what to do. You have nothing to worry about."

Billy came back from the front deck, around the wheelhouse, to join the others. His expression changed when he took in the scene of the three men on the main deck. "Warrant? What are you doing here? I thought you retired. Don't tell me you signed up again. And why did you bring Dad and young Jeff? They should never be in a place like this."

Josh took the rifle carefully from his brother-in-law's hands. "Soldier, coffee is on in the mess. Let's have one while we plan our next move."

Leaving the freezing air behind, the four stepped into the small cabin that served as wheelhouse, galley, and sleeping quarters.

"Riley would you mind pouring up the coffee?" Josh asked his father-in-law. "Jeff, reach into the locker and got the Coffee-mate. Your Uncle Billy and I got to have a chat."

Inside, the heat from the engine room, combined with the recently lit gas stove, warmed the men's bodies after a long morning outside in freezing temperatures.

"How's it going with you today?" Josh asked casually as he and Billy sipped on hot coffee.

"I think it's going okay, but I keep having those dreams," Billy said, shaking his head. "They won't go away. Sometimes it's Bosnia. Sometimes it's Afghanistan. And last night, I dreamt we were out sealing, and I shot down a helicopter."

"That wasn't last night, Billy," Josh said quietly. "And it wasn't a dream. That just happened. You just shot down a helicopter."

Billy's tanned face turned white. "O Lord, that's awful. How are the people?"

"They're all gone, Billy. Dead. The chopper fell into the water and sank.

That's one hundred fathoms down. They're gone. Now we've got to figure out the best way to handle it."

The wheelhouse fell silent.

"I'll tell you the best way to handle it," Billy said calmly, tears in his eyes. "Give me your rifle. I'll go up on the bow again. In a few minutes, it'll be over. That'll be easier for everybody. Then radio ashore and have them contact the RCMP in Port Saunders and tell them there's been an accidental shooting aboard the *Reuben and Naomi*. When they show up, tell them what happened, and give them the GPS coordinates so they can drag for the chopper."

"I can't let you do that," Josh replied. "You didn't mean to shoot down that chopper and kill those people, but that won't help much, and you got to think of your family."

"You don't get it, Josh," Billy said. "You were with me in Bosnia. You know the stuff I did over there. I had a hard time dealing with that back when I had Emma. Afghanistan was worse, and now I'm all alone. I'm keeping it together for the sake of the kids. What if they find out about this?"

"Billy, I'm not going to argue with you," Josh said. "We're going to lock up all the guns and ammunition right now. Your dad can take the wheel. We're heading home, but not on a straight course. We've been stopped too long in one position, so first we're going to put some distance between us and that chopper before we go ashore."

He turned to his father-in-law. "Riley, take the wheel and work your way through that loose ice in front of us. First, go westerly, and then work your way southward. Pause every fifteen or twenty minutes like we're still hunting seals. We've got to kill some time so we don't get home too soon. If we do, people will ask questions."

"I'm sorry I panicked, Uncle Josh," Jeff said. "I see what you're doing. After all Uncle Billy's been through, we've got to look after him."

"It's okay, Jeff," Josh said, putting a hand on his shoulder.

The dull thud of an ice pan against the ship's wooden hull ended their discussion.

PART 1

THE ACTIVIST

Chapter 1

Seventeen-year-old Ruth Winters was worried. She was pregnant, and she had not told Glenn. She hoped he would be okay with it.

Since they arrived in San Francisco in late July, he had been different than he had been in Ontario. He still believed in social justice and equality, but there was an edge to him she had not seen before, particularly with drug debts. She convinced herself that was just business. He had to be tough.

Glenn Holmes believed in free love, and he practised it. He said it was hypocritical to claim you believed in something and not do it. He told Ruth he did not mind if she had sex with others, but she did not. He had lots of partners, so she had herself tested from time to time at the free clinic.

Now into her third month, and soon unable to conceal her increasing size, she had to tell him. She hoped they could stop living in the van and move to a commune, where she had friends. Life would be wonderful.

She procrastinated.

Then one morning as she filled a duffel bag with dirty clothing to take to the Laundromat, trembling, she blurted it out.

"I'm having a baby!"

"Not with me you're not. I don't want kids," he replied.

"It's too late for that."

"What do you mean?"

"I'm pregnant," she said, tears welling in her eyes.

"You stupid fucking bitch! How can you be pregnant? I thought you were on the pill!"

"I was," Ruth said, sobbing now. "But back in September, after the others returned home and we were stoned most of the time, I guess I must've forgot for a few days. Anyway, we love each other, and some of our friends have

1

babies, so why can't we?"

"Are you out of your fucking mind?" Glenn asked. "I don't love you any more than any of these other freaks love each other. You'll have to find an abortionist and get rid of it. The only downside is that you probably won't be able to have sex for a while afterwards."

Shocked and horrified at what she was hearing, Ruth began to shake visibly. "If you don't love me, then we're finished, but I certainly won't be killing this baby, even if you are the father. I'm Catholic, and that goes against everything I believe in."

"Then I guess you should call Mommy and Daddy back up in Toronto and ask them to send you money to come home."

"What about the money they sent in August?" Ruth asked. "I gave it to you. You said it was mine any time I needed it."

"That's long gone," Glenn said. "It costs money to live down here and keep this van on the road. The bumper sticker says 'Gas, Grass, or Ass, Nobody Rides for Free'. That includes you." He motioned toward a gas station near where they were parked. "You can use their payphone."

Ruth's parents were relieved to hear from her, as she had not called for three months. While willing to pay for her to return, they would not have her embarrass them with an illegitimate grandchild. They arranged for her to live at a church-run home near Hamilton until she delivered the child in June. Only then could she return home and finish her final year of high school.

*　　*　　*

Glenn continued in his hippie lifestyle for several months. Then a tip to the San Francisco police by Ruth's father resulted in his arrest for drug trafficking. Now it was his turn to call home for help.

His father travelled to San Francisco and visited him in jail. Then he arranged a plea bargain with the local district attorney. Glenn would be released and deported back to Canada without facing criminal charges as long as he first went back on the street and became a paid police informant.

He did that for nearly six months. Prodded by the police to keep up a steady flow of arrests, sometimes Glenn would plant drugs in a vehicle and advise the police the owner was a dealer. Eventually, because he was free on bail and still dealing drugs, suspicion grew that Glenn was a rat.

When one of his tips resulted in the arrest of someone dealing drugs for local bikers, the DA feared Glenn would be killed, and their arrangement might become public.

The police re-arrested him, gave him $2,000 in reward money, and told to get in his van and go back to Canada. His prosecution file was shredded. Officially, he had never been arrested.

Chapter 2

From the first time he showed up on campus, Glenn was a big hit with the other students, particularly girls straight out of high school. He was a little older and well travelled. He had been to California, had access to drugs, and was a good talker.

At his father's urging, Glenn registered for business. However, the subject was dry, the professors ancient, and the students far too preppy and uptight. Soon, he switched to arts and decided to major in sociology. It suited him much better.

The professors were laid back; some being draft dodgers from the US. Most did drugs, and they were not that much older than him. In their classes, he discussed his California adventures, soon becoming a BMOC (big man on campus).

The subject area that appealed most to him was mass motivation. Academically, he found it interesting, recognizing it as a tool to get people to do his bidding. With the Vietnam War raging, he was able to whip up groups of protesters to demonstrate in front of the US consulate.

Glenn did not care if the Americans were in Vietnam. He just liked the thrill and the power of being able to motivate groups of people to do his bidding. Being against the US establishment made it even more satisfying, payback for having been kicked out of their country.

His biggest coup in the protest movement came during his final year, in 1973. Most of the department favoured Marxism, so they celebrated when the people of Chile elected Marxist president Salvador Allende. When Allende was overthrown and killed by a right-wing junta, purportedly supported by the CIA, the Marxist professors and students were outraged.

Seizing the opportunity for self-advancement, Glenn put together a group to go to Ottawa and demonstrate against the Americans. The demonstration turned violent. Many were arrested and thrown into jail overnight. Once

released, they returned as heroes, led by their chief organizer and spokes-
man, Glenn Holmes.

*   *   *

After completing a Master of Arts degree, the normal academic track was to
complete a PhD. However, having been so preoccupied with the protest game
and his clandestine, profitable drug business throughout his six years of university, Glenn had a weak transcript. He was in a tough spot if he wanted to
be accepted at any university.

He would have preferred to remain in Toronto, where he had spent his
entire university life, but the competition was far too intense, and he did
not want to be scrutinized too closely by people who might have a score to
settle with him. Glenn researched other universities that might accept him,
knowing his weak transcript would be a problem.

Although he did not realize it at the time, in September of the final year
of his master's program, his solution materialized. While working as a teaching assistant (TA) for Professor Sonia Feltham's Sociology 100 (Introduction
to Sociology) course, he met Virginia Whiteway.

A first-year student, Virginia had just arrived from Winnipeg. Not only
was she naïve, she was new to the city, nearly broke, and had few friends.

She knew Glenn by reputation. He was the guy who organized student
protests. He also loaned money to students who were broke. Most people
liked him, although a few despised him.

She did not know his money-lending activities were anything but chari-
table. Instead, it was a way for him to invest the money he earned from drug
sales, giving him a regular source of freshly laundered cash.

As for his drug business, Glenn had not handled any drug transactions
personally for a few years. Instead, for fifty percent of the profits, he loaned
money to others who wanted to make money selling drugs themselves while
minimizing the risk of him being caught and thrown into jail again.

Virginia knew some people said Glenn was a jerk. When she mentioned
his name, a few rolled their eyes, saying, "Not him" or "You need to be really
careful around him. If he offers to help, it always comes at a price."

She brushed off the warnings, because Glenn was so charming, so helpful,
and so knowledgeable. She thought the other students were simply envious
that he was being so nice to her. She did not realize that every September
brought a new crop of Virginias for Glenn to exploit.

At the end of class, some students tended to hang around and chat. One
day, Glenn suggested his group, including Virginia, go to a nearby coffee
shop, a favourite hangout of many arts students.

Soon, she felt comfortable asking him for help with an initial assignment.
In the course of that meeting, he inquired as to how she was doing.

"Everything's good," she said, "but Manitoba Student Aid is slow, so right now, I'm broke."

"Have you tried emergency student assistance?" he asked. "They may help you. If not, I've got a few dollars. I can spot you a small, short-term loan."

"Thanks. I'll try them."

A few weeks later, she sought his help again.

"How'd it work out for you?" he asked. "With your student loan?"

"It turned out okay, but everything is so expensive. I'm afraid of falling behind again."

"Well," he said, "I'm a bit better off now than I was a few weeks ago. My loan came through. I don't mind helping you in the short term."

"Thanks," she replied. "I appreciate your offer, but I would have to pay you back. What I really need is a job, but I don't know anybody here, and I don't have much experience."

"The registrar's office usually hires students when it's busy," he suggested. "I can mention it to Professor Feltham. She may recommend you for any work that comes up."

Virginia could see why so many students liked Glenn. However, it remained a mystery as to why some students did not.

When Glenn raised Virginia's situation with Professor Feltham, she eyed him sceptically. "Now, Glenn, I know what you're like. What's your real interest in this girl?"

Glenn and Feltham had been carrying on an affair for two years. In her mid-forties, with half-grown children, Feltham was married to an older, now retired professor. Although brilliant, sex was never important to him. Then it had ended completely with his prostate operation a decade earlier. He truly loved his wife, and he was disappointed he was unable to perform sexually, so they came to an understanding. He would not take issue with her looking elsewhere to satisfy her needs as long as the children did not find out and she did not embarrass him.

"She really needs help, and I'm afraid she may drop out if it gets much tougher for her financially," Glenn said. "Besides, given our situation, do you think I would say anything to you if I had any interest in her?"

"I'll see what I can do," Feltham said. "But if I find out there's anything going on between you two, it will be a big issue for all three of us."

A few days later, Glenn took Virginia aside. "Go to student employment and complete an application to work in the registrar's office," he said. "Use Professor Feltham as a reference and give them a reference from somebody in Manitoba. They may not check the second reference, but confirm it in case they do."

A week later, Virginia had a job for ten hours a week and a promise of full-time employment in the summer when classes ended. She invited Glenn out for a celebratory coffee.

"I can't believe how easy you made this for me."

He shrugged. "It was nothing, really."

"I haven't decided on a major. If I went with sociology, what courses would I need, and what are my job prospects after graduation?"

By then, Glenn was thinking he should get to know Virginia better. The next time she asked for help with the course, he suggested she come to his office. After a few visits, he was satisfied she was interested in him, too.

"I would really like for us to get to know each other better, but the university has a rule against fraternizing with students," he said. "I'm sure Professor Feltham would make an issue of it, too."

"Maybe on campus," Virginia replied. "But what about off campus? I don't see how that's anybody's business."

"You may be right, but believe me, if we we're seen together off-campus, it'll be an issue." He paused. "You could drop by my apartment though. It's not far, and it's private."

Knowing what was at stake, they agreed to be discreet.

Chapter 3

As the long Canadian winter dragged on, Glenn worked on his MA thesis. Its title, "Mass Motivation in the Modern Protest Movement", was catchy enough. He could provide ample material from personal experience, but he was a weak writer, so he struggled with his first draft.

Finally, he hired somebody to take the parts he had written and rewrite them for him. The final version, well written and appearing well researched, was a complete fiction. He had faked the research, using pseudonyms to make it appear more convincing. Next, he had to find a way to overcome his weak transcripts.

By then, he and Virginia were secretly living together at his apartment. He was careful, as he was still seeing Feltham a few times a week.

Feltham, knowing Glenn would move on after graduation, had begun to focus her attention on another student. That was fine with Glenn, as he did not want to be forced to explain his relationship with her to Virginia, who was becoming more demanding.

Glenn had applied to a PhD program at four universities. Two were in British Columbia, where he perceived a good chance for acceptance based on his thesis, his well-established protest record, and BC's penchant for left-wing activism. However, there were many applicants, so competition was stiff.

He also applied at a prairie university, but he did not want to go there. The winters were cold, and the right wing seemed entrenched there.

His fourth application went to Atlantic Canada, where he thought his chances were best. The competition was not as fierce, and based on his Ontario reputation, the socially progressive university would consider him an asset.

Glenn was still concerned his transcripts would be his undoing when a solution surfaced. Virginia started work at the registrar's office on the first

Monday in May. That evening, she was excited to tell Glenn the details of the job. She explained that she was the first person to arrive and open the office in the morning and the last to leave in the evening. Her duties included the mail. She received, sorted, and distributed it internally. At day's end, she collected it for delivery to the post office.

"It seems they intend to get their money's worth out of you this summer," Glenn said.

While she also handled reception, filing, clerical work, and general duties, it was the mail that caught Glenn's attention. All he had to figure out was how to intercept it. Overnight, he concocted a solution.

Virginia was concerned about her appearance — in particular, her weight. She had arrived from Manitoba a lean, fit, 5-foot, 8-inch, 120-pound farm girl. For months, she had complained she had gained weight and was no longer fit.

"Do I look fat to you?" she asked often.

"Not at all. You look perfect," Glenn would reply.

At breakfast on Tuesday, he sat back in his chair. "You know how you're always asking me if you're fat?"

"Yes," she replied, her face turning red.

"And I always reassure you that you look perfect. Well, I know you want to stay in shape, so why not take a fitness class this summer?"

"It's a great idea," Virginia said. "We could go together."

He smiled. "Do I look like I need a fitness class?" Neither fat nor fit, he had no interest in exercise. "There's a class from four thirty to five thirty. You're off at four, so you can make the class and be home for dinner."

"I'd love to," she replied, "but I have to take the mail to the post office. That's a fifteen-minute walk each way. I was hoping the walk would help me."

"I know how important this is to you," Glenn said, "so here's what I'll do. I'll drop off the mail for you so that you can go to the fitness class."

"Really?" Virginia asked. "You'd do that for me?"

"Well, it's not just for you," Glenn said sweetly. "It's for us. I want you to feel good about yourself. I insist."

So that is what they did. Glenn came by at four every afternoon and picked up the mail while Virginia went to the fitness class. Before delivering it, he looked for envelopes addressed to the universities where he had applied.

There were not many. The ones he found he took back to their apartment and steamed open, looking for his transcript. After a few weeks, not only did he find his transcript, he also saw the transcripts of every other student.

The only one that interested him, in addition to his own, was that of his archrival. He was applying to the same universities as Glenn, and he had outstanding marks.

Excitedly, Glenn took all eight envelopes containing the transcripts to his friend Al, who produced forged documents.

"Al," he asked, "Can you swap these?"

"What you mean?" Al asked, bewildered.

"Can you make the name on one become the name on the other?"

Finally getting it, Al smiled. "Oh, Mr. Glenn, I do passports, even. I do foreign money. I do driver's licenses. Of course I can do this one. For you, Mr. Glenn, I do anything. When you need done?"

"I need to put this in the mail tomorrow," Glenn replied.

"No problem, Mr. Glenn. I do for you tonight. You pick up in morning."

"Now, Al," Glenn said, "I don't expect you to do this for nothing, but I don't mind a deal. How much does this usually cost?"

"Mr. Glenn, people pay me fifty dollars for one, but you send me many customers. This big honour for me, so is for no cost."

Graduate school admission was very important to the academic community, and rejection was often a source of embarrassment, so that summer, faculty members were impressed when Glenn received offers from four universities. They also whispered privately when their best student was rejected by three and accepted by only a small, western university. Glenn's rival was further humiliated when Glenn mentioned he had declined three offers.

* * *

Glenn arrived in Nova Scotia on September 1, 1976, taking up residence in student housing and familiarizing himself with the campus.

The university's stature came as a shock to him. One of the oldest in Canada, it boasted a world-class reputation. Instead of a quiet, little place to pull off an easy PhD, he found himself in one of the finest universities in North America. To make matters worse, his reputation in the protest movement had preceded him. Combined with his stellar, but forged, academic record, the entire department had great expectations of him.

Instead of being ecstatic, he was dismayed. He had landed in a position where he knew he could not compete. He realized he had to plan his exit strategy. That plan began to gel when he attended a public session by representatives from the Green Earth Society, a British Columbia-based environmental group established to protect the whales and the seals and to oppose pollution.

Glenn attended, ostensibly for research purposes for his PhD based on mass motivation in social activism, but his real motivation involved a mercenary element. The US had withdrawn from Vietnam the prior year. He needed a new cause to remain active in the protest game.

Fewer than a dozen people showed up. The Green Earth representatives were disappointed at the small turnout but excited to meet Glenn, an experienced, committed protest organizer. When they discussed fundraising difficulties, they told Glenn their most successful fundraising drive had been in response to the killing of baby seals. An appeal to donors, containing pictures of dead seals and bloodstained ice flows, had raised large amounts of cash. The two representatives — a US draft dodger and a professor on sabbatical — wanted to establish an east coast chapter. Glenn was their best bet.

Glen saw the potential but did not want to appear too eager. "I may be able to provide a little help, but there are two things we have to be clear about," he said. "First, this is my area of study. For objectivity, I need to appear at arm's length from you, and I'll need a budget for expenses. I don't have any money."

They agreed. Then the subject turned to fundraising.

"Given the previous response, why don't you focus on that?" Glenn asked.

"What did you have in mind?" the professor, Philip Montieth, asked.

"What I propose is we find an international celebrity. Then put together an expedition to watch seals being killed. Lay on some media. If it gets picked up in the US, and perhaps Europe, you could raise some serious coin."

"It's a fabulous idea," said the draft dodger, Horace Appelbaum. "But I don't think we can pull it off. We're in BC, and the seal hunt takes place in Newfoundland."

Glenn smiled slyly. "Well, I can work on it over the next few months. There's no downside. If I can't put it together, we won't do it. I can use the work as part of my research. If it's successful, I can use it — as long as I'm not officially connected. I'll prepare a budget. You decide."

The next day, Montieth and Appelbaum headed west in their VW van, convinced they were onto something big. As for Glenn, he had a new cause, his PhD research being the ideal cover. Unaware of the seal hunt or fundraising components, the department was pleased they would figure prominently in the ongoing activities of Green Earth.

Glenn wasted no time pitching the idea, explaining it as a great opportunity for an exclusive story for both print media and television. For just $10,000 each, a newspaper reporter and a TV reporter could cover the first publicly documented seal hunt protest.

He made the same pitch to celebrity agents. While there was little interest amongst North American celebrities, the outlandish nature of the proposal intrigued a European porn star. Again, the fee was $10,000, paid by bank draft to Glenn Holmes.

Next, he reported back to Green Earth in BC that he been able to put the whole thing together. It would be expensive, but the publicity could generate enormous donations worldwide and raise the group's profile. It was a ground-floor opportunity for Green Earth. If they did not move quickly, another group might seize the initiative, and Green Earth would miss out.

He told them the porn actress had demanded $10,000 for her appearance, and the media would not cover it unless their expenses were paid. He estimated the expenses for each of the three to be in the $2,500 range, and it would also cost $2,500 for his airfare, vehicle rental, and hotel and restaurant bills.

He offered to set up an account at the local bank under "Glenn Holmes, in trust for the Green Earth Society".

Glenn was amazed how quickly he received a $20,000 cheque. As agreed, he opened a trust bank account for Green Earth. Then he rented a safety deposit box and stashed the three US$10,000 bank drafts.

Chapter 4

"So, it's set," Glenn said. "Tomorrow we fly to Newfoundland, and our adventure begins."

There were seven of them. The nominal expedition leader was Davis Wainwright, a twenty-one-year-old university student. From small-town Alberta, he had gone to British Columbia to study journalism and had been attracted to Green Earth. He had been promoting the group in media circles and was the natural choice to represent them.

Andrew Bartlett, from New York's *The World Today*, had recently joined the paper. At thirty-eight, he had worked as a freelance reporter in troubled parts of the world. He had accepted the position because his partner had been hired to do media relations with a New York-based oil company. She was pressuring him to settle down and have a family. He needed work and accepted the position, expecting the job to be uninspiring. His colleagues were junior to him and aggressive. Under pressure to perform or be fired, he needed a big story. He could not imagine this assignment, halfway to the North Pole, would produce it. However, nobody else wanted to go, and his editor pressed him.

"Bartlett, I know you're used to racier work than this, but nobody else wants to go, and you're the elderly junior on the staff," his editor said. "Eventually, we'll send you to cover a war in Africa or a revolution in Central America, but for now, you're doing the seal hunt story."

Los Angeles-based KWOW television sent a cameraman and a reporter. Cameraman, Walt Ledrew, fifty-eight, was originally from Boston. Three years earlier, he had retired and moved to Los Angeles, where he did free-lance work for TV stations and private videos for entertainers. He jumped at the chance to go to northern Newfoundland in the middle of the winter. While living in Boston, he had visited the province a few times in the summer to fly fish for salmon. To him, it looked like a paid winter vacation.

The reporter, Deanna Aucoin, had just joined KWOW from an affiliate in Spokane Washington. Although popular in the Pacific Northwest, Los Angeles was a different market. At thirty-two, she was too old to compete with the pretty bobble heads and too young for the gravitas of a senior reporter. She was working with speech and fitness trainers. She had lost thirty pounds in three months and was experimenting with Botox to get rid of the new lines around her mouth. If she needed to have her molars extracted to make her face look thinner, she would do that, too.

Her biggest obstacle was her education. She took the news seriously, making it difficult for her to present current events as entertainment, but if that was what California wanted, that was what she would give them. She intended to claw her way to the top. She had left behind a failed marriage and a seven-year-old daughter, now living with her ex-husband, an insurance executive in Spokane.

The porn star, Bridget Devereux, was from a village in the French Alps. Her father, Pierre, was the local butcher, while her mother, Nicole, helped out.

Bridget, the middle of three daughters, loved to socialize, learning early how to manipulate men, generally older ones. At seventeen, she headed to Paris with her thirty-year-old boyfriend, the son of an industrialist. Within a year, she was pregnant and had her first abortion.

The boyfriend lost interest in her and moved on, leaving her to support herself. She was hired quickly by a cabaret. Immaculately groomed, young and fit, with blonde hair and blue eyes, she was a male magnet of the first order.

Travelling with Bridget was her manager, Rory Delroy, age fifty-eight. Based in Beverly Hills, he had discovered her ten years earlier. Initially, he hoped she would be a hit in Hollywood. However, the competition was tough. Even with excellent acting skills, she would never be a serious actor unless she improved her English. That was too much work for Bridget. She opted to star in a few B movies, box office flops.

When Delroy suggested she consider erotic films, Bridget jumped at the opportunity. However, porn stars had short careers, replaced quickly by younger bodies and fresher faces. When Glenn approached Delroy, seeking a photogenic actress, Delroy knew no serious actor would accept. He recognized an opportunity to turn a quick dollar, but he did not want to use a newer, more valuable girl. Bridget would fit the bill and for less money.

Glenn explained they hoped to be filming small white seals being clubbed to death. He did not want someone too squeamish. Unsure how she would respond, Delroy raised the subject cautiously with Bridget.

She responded with a laugh. "Oh, Rory, you don't have to worry. My father was the town butcher. I have seen hundreds, perhaps even thousands, of animals slaughtered — cows, sheep, goats, chickens, geese, and more. Whatever people eat, first they have to kill, so I don't mind a little bit of blood."

In Halifax, Glenn briefed the group. "We fly into Deer Lake. It's a small town of three or four thousand people, a hub for local traffic. There, we'll meet local taxi drivers, Abe and Ben Sullivan. We've rented a four-wheel-drive truck, a Suburban, and a large cube van. Abe will drive the Suburban. His son, Ben, will drive the truck. Ledrew will drive the van and haul our stuff. He's been up there before and knows his way around."

"What did you tell him we're doing here?" Delroy asked.

"Working on a documentary about the seal hunt and how important it is for the local economy. Our angle is that the hunt is no more or less humane than the slaughter of any other animal, and there's no danger of seals ever becoming extinct."

"Slick," Delroy said, "really slick. Do you think they'll buy it?"

"I think so," Glenn said. "I telephoned mayors up there and found one in a place called Yankee Point. Isaac Gillett, a teacher. He's seen more of the world than most of them. He's put it together for us."

"What exactly did you tell him?" Bartlett asked.

"That's the best part," Glenn replied. "I told him we're doing a documentary to tell the real story of the hunt. I told him we're on a shoestring budget from the National Film Board of Canada, hoping National Public Radio in United States might buy in. He took the bait."

"What does our itinerary look like?" Delroy inquired.

"We're staying in a motel in a place called Plum Point. It's the only place around there open for the winter. I guess things get really slow, so our visit is a big deal. We'll be there for two nights and then drive on to St. Anthony for two nights. Then back to Deer Lake and head for home."

"I've heard they get lots of storms and mountains of snow," Delroy said. "Is there any chance we might be stuck up there?"

"Sullivan says that's true, but he says we should be more concerned about the cold. He says it can get as cold as minus forty up there when the ocean is covered with Arctic ice."

Bartlett smirked. "Is that minus forty Fahrenheit or minus forty Celsius? You Canadians switched over a few years ago."

Glenn rolled his eyes. "At minus forty, it doesn't matter."

Chapter 5

"Do we need all this?" Glenn asked, seeing red gas cans, shovels, tow ropes, and tire chains in the truck.

"Hopefully not," Abe said, "but it doesn't hurt to be prepared. Speaking of which, you folks aren't very well dressed for winter. You should go to one of the stores and pick up some warmer clothing."

Glenn looked at the Sullivans, who were wearing snowmobile suits, lined boots, fur caps, and oversized sealskin mittens. "I doubt it," he said, "but I'll ask the group."

Four hours later, they arrived in Plum Point and checked in. While the Sullivans made small talk with the staff, the protest group met in Glenn's room.

"I've arranged dinner at six," he said. "The locals call it 'supper'. We'll be joined by Isaac Gillett and his wife, Martha. They'll give us the rundown for tomorrow. He's put it together, so we need to show our appreciation. But be careful what you say. We don't want it to fall off the rails."

The next morning, they awoke to snowmobiles roaring past the small motel. It was a typical late March morning — completely calm with bright sunshine, minus twenty-two degrees. Snow covered everything, rendering the landscape a brilliant, retina-searing, white inferno.

"You'll need a hearty breakfast," Joseph, the motel owner, said. "We've packed your lunches. Ike called an hour ago. He'll be here by seven thirty. I think I just heard his truck come into the parking lot."

Ike entered, smiling. Then he frowned. "Don't tell me that's all you're wearing. You can't go on the ice dressed like that. You'll freeze in half an hour." He turned to Abe. "You've been around here long enough to know they need to be dressed warmer than this. Why didn't you say something before they left Deer Lake?"

"I tried," Abe said, "but they wouldn't listen."

Ike turned to Joseph. "What time does John open his store?"

"Eight, most mornings, but his truck just went up the road. He may be in now."

Ike nodded. "Okay. Let's go over there and get you folks properly fitted out."

They did, and by nine, they were at Yankee Point meeting real-life sealers. Standing by their snowmobiles on the snow-covered ice, the film group looked no different from the locals. It was their first look at snowmobiles close up with sleds attached.

Ike did the introductions. "This is Reuben Short, his two sons, Jacob and Esau, and his grandson, Joshua."

Reuben was sixty. His lean, wiry body could have passed for a man forty, but his tanned, leathery face, with deeply etched lines around his eyes, and full white beard told a different story. Pleasant, though a man of few words, and even more reserved among strangers, his occasional smile showed he was missing four front teeth.

Jacob and Esau were identical twins. They were thirty-eight and virtually indistinguishable from each other. Like their father, both wore full beards, fiery red, like their hair. Larger than him, both were well muscled, standing over six feet tall.

Fully in sync with each other, it was not uncommon for one twin to finish a sentence the other had started. Both were carpenters, having attended vocational school in St. Anthony twenty years earlier. Like a matched set, they were almost always together. The only time they had ever worked apart was during their four-year apprenticeship.

"After we got our carpenters' papers," Jacob said.

"We worked on the mainland for a while," Esau finished.

"It used to be hard," Jacob said.

"To get hired," Esau added.

"But when they saw..."

"How well we work together..."

"They always wanted us..."

"Back again."

"The only thing..." Jacob began.

"That we don't go together..."

"Is sleep..."

"Together," Esau concluded.

Josh chimed in with a laugh. "I'm sure they'd even sleep together if their wives would go for it."

Clearly a standing joke among the group, it elicited a laugh from all four.

Joshua was fifteen. The illegitimate son of the twins' younger sister, Dorcas, he had been raised by his grandparents. A quick study and a good worker, he had been helping his grandfather in the fishery since he was ten years old. He had started sealing at age twelve.

The visitors peppered the sealers with questions. The two women were interested in the twins. Wainwright chatted with Josh. The others turned their attention to Reuben.

Having to practically interrogate the taciturn older man, Glenn started with a simple question. "So, how long have you been killing baby seals?"

"Do you mean just seal pups or do you mean all kinds of seals, including beaters, bedlamers, and old harps, too?"

It appeared as if Reuben was unaware of the emphasis Glenn had placed on the word *baby*. However, the older man had picked up on the exact meaning of the question. Instead of making an issue of the young fellow's obvious ignorance, old Reuben gave him the benefit of the doubt, thinking the kid was from the city. He probably said "baby sheep" and "baby cows" too.

"I mean any kind of seals," Glenn said.

Reuben's white beard hid a fleeting smile at the younger man's discomfort. "I started sealing with my Uncle Noah after my dad drowned. I was twelve. I'm sixty now, so I guess that's forty-eight years."

"How many seals have you killed in forty-eight years?" Bartlett asked.

"I couldn't say, I've never kept track of it, and I've never stopped to figure it out," Reuben replied. "Last year, me and the boys got a little over five hundred. I think it might've been five hundred and seven or five hundred and eight. That was a good year, but we've done even better, between seven hundred and eight hundred a few years ago."

"So you kill between five hundred and eight hundred seals per year?" Bartlett asked, scribbling furiously on his notepad.

"No," Reuben replied thoughtfully. "Some years, we don't get any."

"And why is that?" Bartlett, an experienced interviewer, pressed on.

"That doesn't happen too often," Reuben replied. "When it does, it's usually because the seals are too far off or the ice conditions make it too hard to get them. Generally, we get at least a few hundred every year," he added, as if to provide a reliable answer.

Satisfied the old sealer was being forthright, and having sufficient numbers for his story, Bartlett tried to fill in the details. "How do you kill them?"

"Well, that all depends on whether it's whitecoats or beaters," Reuben replied. "I prefer the gaff for whitecoats and a twenty-two for beaters."

"Why the difference?"

Reuben untied a long pole from the sled and held it up. "This is a gaff."

Thick as a man's wrist, one end tipped with an iron hook and point, it resembled an oversized pike pole used by a medieval soldier.

"Did you make this for killing seals?" Bartlett asked as he examined it.

"No. The gaff is used in fishing boats for reaching into the water to pull up ropes or to reach another boat to pull it closer. For sealing though, the gaff is real handy. When you're out on the water, jumping from one piece of ice to another, it's easy to fall in. If you got a gaff, you can put it across the space between the pans and climb out, and you can use it for a pole to jump from pan to pan."

"But how do you use it to kill the seals?" Bartlett asked.

"Well, a young seal's head is soft. One smack kills 'em right away."

"You said something about using a twenty-two-calibre rifle for beaters," Glenn said. "What do you mean by that?"

"Well," Reuben replied, "a couple of weeks after they're born, the white fur starts to fall out. After six to eight weeks, they get their spotted coats. Then they're called 'beaters'. You've got to shoot beaters through the head on the ice."

"Why is that?" Glenn asked.

"If you shoot them in the water, they sink, and you lose them. If you shoot them on the ice but not through the head, they'll dive into the water, and a shot through the body spoils the pelt."

"Why a twenty-two?"

"The ammunition doesn't cost much, and a bullet through the head does the job. Me and the boys use twenty-two magnums. They're more powerful. You won't see any shooting today though, because it's whitecoats."

Most of the group were beginning to feel the cold and were becoming impatient. Ledrew, having spent summers in Newfoundland, should have known it was considered courteous to make small talk with strangers, but he was tired of the meaningless chatter and the slow pace.

"So, when will I get to shoot some seals?" he asked.

"Sir, there must be a mistake," Reuben replied. "I just said we're not going to shoot the seals. We're going to bat them."

Ledrew was growing increasingly irritated. "I know you're not going to shoot them. I'm here to shoot — to *film* you clubbing them and then skinning them on the ice."

"I think you're both right," Ike said, coming to the rescue. "It's a matter of terminology. When cameramen talk about filming, they say *shooting*. When sealers refer to clubbing, they say *batting*."

"That's right, Pop," Josh cut in. "I was watching television the other day, and they talked about clubbing seals. It's the same thing. It's just a different word. I imagine most of these mainlanders have as much trouble understanding us as we have figuring out what they're saying."

Alarmed a disagreement could sabotage his venture, Glenn jumped in. "Any minor differences that make it difficult for our viewers to follow can be edited out later. Walt has a good point though. We're anxious to get started. Up to now, we haven't seen any seals."

"I wondered if you could see the seals," Reuben said, "because none of you said anything. I can see twenty-five or thirty young ones and a half dozen older ones right now."

The revelation caused excitement among the newcomers, who responded in chorus. "Where? Where?"

"Over there, on the other side of that open water," Reuben replied. He pointed past what looked like a long, narrow lake in the middle of the ice, nearly a mile away. "The small yellow spots are young seals. Most of the dark spots are old ones. The dark spots that don't move are bits of kelp, dirty ice, or shadows. Let's see if this helps you see them any better."

Going to his sled, he opened his old canvas knapsack and removed a scraped and battered leather cylinder. It contained an ancient telescope.

"Try my spyglass," he said. He turned to Josh. "Let them take turns with your spyglasses, so they can all have a look."

The other sealers opened their knapsacks, removing binocular cases. The twins' showed signs of wear, while Josh's were new, a Christmas gift a few months earlier.

Soon, it dawned on the newcomers that it would be difficult to approach the seals they were watching. Not only was the ice outside the long, narrow body of water moving southward as fast as a person could walk, the hole in the ice was getting wider while two smaller holes were opening up.

Visibly discouraged, Glenn turned to Ike. "So, how do we get to them?"

"We won't get to those seals, but we can get to others that these guys will show us. Old Rube won't let us down. He may simply have been making a point."

"And what point would that be?" Glenn asked warily.

"Nothing big," Ike said. "Just that things around here aren't always what they seem. People who don't pay attention miss a lot and don't even know what they missed." He turned to Reuben. "So, where's the patch of seals that you told me about yesterday?"

"They're just down around that small point," he answered. "No more than a half-mile away." He motioned toward a few dozen scraggly, windblown spruce trees with their gnarled, half-dead tops pushing up through the snow.

Ike nodded at some fresh snowmobile tracks. "We may be too late. It looks like somebody is ahead of us."

"Don't worry about that," Reuben replied. "I sent the boys down there a half hour before you showed up. They haven't moved."

"How many?" Ledrew inquired.

"We saw roughly a hundred," Jacob replied. "Including a few dozen old ones."

Realizing they were waiting on him, Reuben took charge. "There's eight of you, counting Ike. Four can ride with us on the snowmobiles. The other four can ride on the sleighs. It's only a short run down across that ballycatter, but to be fair, if you go on snowmobile, you can come back on a sleigh. That will make it even for everyone."

Now Devereaux had a question. "Monsieur Short, please excuse my

English. What is that word you say, 'ballee something'?"

"It's a local term," Ike said. "Ballycatter. It means ice that builds up along the edge of the ocean during winter. We'll be riding over ballycatter to where the seals are."

"But is it safe to drive on?" she asked.

Ike smiled. "Perfectly safe."

Chapter 6

Within minutes, they reached the snow-covered point, stopping to take in the small, frozen-over cove that lay beyond it. At the mouth of the cove was an area of open ocean, a quarter mile wide, which was disappearing quickly as a freshening breeze from the northwest pressed the heavy ice toward the land.

Before their eyes, the ice was covered with seals, both young and old. As the open water narrowed and then began to close, becoming a dark slit and finally a series of waterholes, the adults headed for the water, dived, and vanished.

"Now," Reuben began, "we should wait a little longer and let the holes close up completely. With the old ones gone, we can take our time and walk down to the whitecoats. Mr. Ledrew can set up his movie camera equipment, and the rest of you can take pictures."

"Wouldn't it be easier to go down there on the snowmobiles?" Bartlett asked.

"Yes," Ledrew agreed. "My equipment is heavy. It would be easier to haul it right to the seals and then set up."

"It's only about a hundred yards," Reuben replied. "If we go much closer with the snowmobiles, the noise will scare the seals. We don't want that. The boys will carry your equipment."

"You don't want to scare them?" Glenn asked. "Aren't you planning to kill some of them?"

"We're planning to kill all of 'em," Reuben said, "but that's not the point. There's no reason to be barbarous. If we go over to the seals and bat 'em over the head with those gaffs, most of 'em won't even see it coming. If we drive out among 'em, they'll be scared half to death. That's what we do, anyway."

"Isn't that just your way of justifying killing these helpless animals?" Ledrew asked.

"No," Reuben replied. "Just because we're going to kill 'em is no reason to frighten 'em half to death."

By then, the light wind had caused the holes in the ice to disappear completely.

Reuben turned to Ledrew and motioned toward a seal. "If you want to set up your camera over there, you can. Then you can film me or one of the boys killing that one."

It was a perfect setup, but Glenn wanted more. "Can we start there but after that do a few more? To make it realistic, can we film four of you killing some at the same time?"

Reuben thought for a moment and then nodded. "I suppose so. Let me check with the boys."

Jacob and Esau agreed, as long as they weren't delayed too long. By then, the sky was clouding over, the wind picking up, and a few large snowflakes were falling.

The four sealers went to work, clubbing each seal on the head and killing it instantly. It took nearly half an hour. During that time, they paid little attention to the visitors moving among the animals for Ledrew to film and Bartlett to photograph.

They did not notice the women being filmed and photographed first with a living seal, and then, a few minutes later, repeating the process after the seal had been killed. Finally, the visitors posed on the bloody snow where the seals had been slaughtered.

Before 4 p.m., all of the seals having been dispatched and assembled into piles of pelts and shoulders, Reuben turned to the visitors. "That's pretty much it. All we've got to do now is to haul them back to our shed, where we separate the fat and salt the skins for when the buyers come in April or May."

After a day in freezing temperatures, the prospect of a heated building, even if it was a fishing shed, appealed to everyone.

"I guess we better take you folks first," Jacob said.

"The sleighs won't be so clean a half hour from now after we haul the seals pelts in them," Esau added.

Sharing a laugh, the brothers headed back to the snowmobiles. Keeping the seating arrangements from the morning in mind and then reversing them, they climbed aboard for the ride back to the Shorts' fishing shed.

The place had its own odour, a cornucopia of salt fish, sealskins, tarred twine, motor oil, gasoline, and wood smoke from the forty-five-gallon drum, converted into a stove, which sat in the middle of the floor.

Reuben turned to his grandson. "Josh, you stay here and put on a fire so these people can get warmed up. We'll go back for the pelts."

That suited the teenager just fine. He was happy not to have the stink of seal fat on his new sleigh, at least for the moment. Taking birch bark and kindling, within minutes, he had a roaring fire that turned the stovepipe blood red. The old oil drum took on a pinkish hue, its heat radiating throughout the building.

The visitors, who had been cold, tired, and hungry, began to warm up, digging into beef sandwiches, chocolate bars, and potato chips from the motel. Thermos bottles of coffee, lukewarm and barely enough to go around, could not have tasted better.

Glenn turned to Ike. "Thanks to you and the Shorts, we've had a good day. There's not much more to do here, so we've decided to drive to St. Anthony tonight. Didn't you say it's only a little over an hour from here?"

"In summer, maybe," Ike replied. "But in winter, even with good going, more like two."

"Okay, but it's only five o'clock. If we leave right now, we can make it by seven, except we've got to wait for the Sullivans. Can you go back to Plum Point and ask them to load everything into the van and join us?"

"It's a half hour drive, each way, plus loading the stuff and checking out," Ike said. "You won't leave 'til dark. It's drifting. If the wind picks up, the weather could get really bad, really fast."

"I understand," Glenn said. "We'll ask Abe when he gets here."

"I can phone them from my house," Ike suggested. "What should I tell them about checking out?"

"We paid for two nights when we checked in," Glenn replied, "so there's just the food bill and incidentals. Ask Abe to cover it. I'll pay him back."

Ike called a few minutes later and found the Sullivans in the motel bar. That morning, they had visited old friends Abe knew from thirty years of running taxis up and down the peninsula. Then they spent the afternoon in the bar, shooting pool.

Abe was sober enough to drive, having only consumed a few beers. Ben was not. He had been drinking rum and Coke plus the house specialty, B-52 shooters. The barmaid had his attention. He kept her pouring the layered drinks, tossing them back and tipping generously.

Told of the change of plans, Ben apologized to his father. "Fuck! I don't think I'm fit to drive. I didn't think I'd have to drive until tomorrow. What can I do?"

"Well, you're a bit wobbly, but you'll be okay. Go to the restaurant and have some strong coffee. Then get Esther to make some sandwiches. Throw in some bags of chips, a few chocolate bars, and a half dozen cans of Coke. Pick up a couple packs of gum or cough drops for your breath."

"How much time do we have?" Ben asked.

"Ike said we've got to pack up their stuff. That should kill an hour. I'll drive. You take a nap. When we get to Yankee Point, I'll try to talk Glenn into coming back here for the night. I'm not keen on driving to St. Anthony this late. There's been a low drift all day, and the plows don't operate at night, so the road might not even be open."

Chapter 7

The Sullivans arrived in Yankee Point a little after 7 p.m. Although the snow had stopped falling, the wind had picked up a little and was causing the previously fallen snow to drift across the landscape, filling in dips and accumulating behind trees and anything else it encountered.

Inside the shed, the atmosphere was collegial. A fire was roaring in the oil drum stove. Two kerosene lamps gave off a yellow light. Music blared from an old car radio, powered by a twelve-volt battery. Remarkably, the radio could pick up stations from up and down the east coast. Josh had tuned it to a station in Antigonish, Nova Scotia that was playing a song by Credence Clearwater Revival.

Josh and Davis Wainwright had lots in common. Both were from small rural towns, and while the Shorts made their living from the sea, Wainwright's people were cattle ranchers. As a teenager, Wainwright had helped his grandfather on the ranch — branding, dehorning, and castrating calves — so he was not put off killing seals. Two of his uncles had competed in rodeo — calf roping and chuck wagon driver. One made it to the Calgary Stampede but withdrew when three of his horses were put down after a bad pileup. Wainwright had seen animals die before.

Ledrew, who doubted he would be back again, especially after the airing of their so-called documentary, nevertheless wanted to know if there were any good salmon fishing rivers in the area.

Glenn was agitated. The day had exceeded his expectations, but he did not want to waste any time, and he certainly did not want them becoming too familiar with the locals. He cursed himself for letting the Sullivans stay behind, but he did not want them around during the filming.

Delroy was bored. He had been cold and bored all day. Now he was warm and bored. He would have sent his assistant, Andre Littlejohn, on the trip with Bridget, but he suspected they were having an affair. While Bridget was past her prime as a porn star, he was concerned that if he did not give her enough attention and work, she and Littlejohn might set up their own agency. After two long days in this cold, miserable, empty, uncivilized wasteland and two or three more days to go, he wished he had sent Littlejohn after all.

At the back of the large room, father and twins were preparing the pelts for the buyer. Devereaux, Aucoin, and Bartlett were keenly interested in the process, looking on, asking questions.

Devereaux's interest stemmed came from her upbringing, having been around the slaughter of animals and the preparation of their skins for the local tannery. Aucoin and Bartlett followed with the interest of reporters working on a story, which, of course, they were. Bartlett was keen to know how much the sealers would earn.

"We never know how much we'll make, but it makes up a good part of our living," Reuben explained. "We know how much we got paid last year, so we just try to get as many seals as we can before the quota is reached and we got to stop."

"So," Bartlett asked, "based on last year's price, how much will you get for the seventy-seven you got today?"

"That depends on the cull. Whether they're all whitecoats or not."

"What do you mean? They all look white to me," Bartlett said, examining the pelts.

"If you look at 'em real close and run your hand over 'em," Reuben replied, "the fur will come out of some. The buyer will claim they're raggedy jackets, worth only five dollars a piece."

"Five dollars?" Bartlett exclaimed.

"Yup. Then he'll take 'em back to his place and brush 'em 'til there's no loose fur. Then he'll sell 'em to the tannery in Dildo as whitecoats."

"Where did you say the tannery is located?" Devereux asked, incredulous.

Suddenly, all of the newcomers were focused on the location of the tannery. Everyone in the room, except Reuben, was aware of the connotation.

Josh, listening to the discussion at the back of the room, while chatting with Wainwright and Ledrew at the front, turned and walked back.

"Pop," he said, "*dildo* means something a lot different to these people than it does to us."

While the visitors laughed, Reuben stood there, bewildered and red faced. Jacob helped out, explaining the definition of the word. This time, Esau, mildly embarrassed, did not finish his older twin's sentences.

"What's wrong with their men if the women got to use those things?" Reuben asked.

That elicited another round of laughter. Ledrew, undergoing treatment for erectile dysfunction, blushed.

"Do you suppose the buyer has been telling the truth about seal cocks all this time?" Reuben asked.

"What's he talking about?" Bartlett inquired.

"The seal buyer says he'll buy the cocks from seals," Josh clarified. "He says there's a market for them in China."

"You mean the seal penises?" Bartlett asked.

"Yes," Josh said, switching to the anatomically correct term. "He keeps telling Pop and the uncles they should cut the penises off the males, and he'll buy them. Pop figures the buyer is just trying to make fools of us, and he won't do it. The uncles think there's no harm in taking a chance, just in case he's telling the truth. People around here think that's disgusting, but people in some parts of the world do strange things."

Bartlett thought that seemed like something to follow up. It might be a story.

Chapter 8

Abe was apologetic. "I'm sorry it took so long to get here. It's blowing more. The road was drifted up, and the van isn't good in winter driving."

While true, it had delayed them by only minutes. The real cause for the delay was to give Ben time to sober up. The lie went undetected.

"We had a good day and don't need tomorrow," Glenn replied, irritated but trying to appear congenial. "We want to go on to St. Anthony tonight. What's it like outside?"

"Not great but manageable if you got to go," Abe said, sensing Glenn's determination. "If we leave right away, we can make St. Anthony by nine thirty or ten, if we don't run into trouble."

"What kind of trouble?" Ledrew asked.

"Well, traffic's been coming from St. Anthony all day, so we know the road is open."

"So, what's the problem?" Glenn demanded.

"One guy told me the Department of Highways had to clear some big drifts north of Big Brook," Abe replied. "That's over an hour north, more than halfway to St. Anthony. The weather here might be fine, but up there, it could be bad."

"When you say a big drift, how big is that?" Ledrew asked.

Abe shrugged. "Could be ten to fifteen feet high and perhaps a hundred feet or so long or even longer."

Glenn was anxious to get moving. "But you said the road was open, so it doesn't matter how big the drifts are as long as snow has been cleared from the road. Isn't that right?"

"The thing you have to watch out for with low drifting conditions, like tonight, is some places fill up quickly, even though the rest of the road could be open," Abe replied.

"How can we find out what it's like up there?" Glenn asked, his impatience growing.

"You can only find out by going there," Abe said.

"Well, we're in three vehicles," Glenn pointed out. "All of them won't get stuck. You have tow ropes, tire chains, and spare gas in the pickup, so let's get going. If the lead vehicle gets stuck, we can tow it out."

That seemed to allay everyone's fears. The three-vehicle convoy set out for St. Anthony. Abe, accompanied by Glenn, Bartlett, Devereaux, and Delroy, led in the heavy, four-wheel-drive Suburban, the best of the vehicles in winter driving. Ben and Davis followed in the pickup. Ledrew brought up the rear with Aucoin.

At first, things went well, although the pace was slow. Then, an hour after leaving Yankee Point, near Big Brook, conditions worsened. The wind picked up, and it began to snow heavily.

Saying nothing, Abe started to worry about the snowdrift that he knew was eight to ten kilometres north of Big Brook. A trucker back in Plum Point had told him it was a big one. He hoped it wasn't too big for the Suburban to get through. If he kept his speed up, he knew the vehicle could punch through a high drift if it was not too long and carry through a long drift if it was not too high. It was heavily loaded with passengers and supplies. The weight would help the vehicle power through the snow but would be a hindrance if they got stuck. As they cleared Big Brook, Abe took note of the odometer so he would know when to expect the snowdrift.

For the next eight kilometres, road conditions changed little, although it began to snow even harder. Ordinarily, with such poor visibility, Abe would have reduced his speed, perhaps to a crawl, taking care not to run into any vehicle stopped on the road, while glancing from side to side to avoid driving into the ditch. Now he needed to maintain a higher speed to get through the fast-approaching, unseen drift.

He glanced down at the speedometer. Seventy kilometres an hour. They had covered nine kilometres since Big Brook.

Glenn, looking straight ahead, saw it first. "Slow down! Slow down! We're gonna get stuck."

Instinctively, Abe hit the brakes, slowing the Suburban to less than fifty kilometres an hour. Then, realizing they were entering the big drift, he hammered the accelerator, but it was too late.

Had he seen the drift first and hit the gas, as he intended, they would have probably made it through unscathed. Even if the pickup and cube van had become stuck, they could have pulled them through with the tow ropes. That did not happen. The heavily loaded Suburban barely made it halfway through the drift before stopping.

Having driven with his father all his life, Ben knew what to expect him to do in those conditions. He would maintain a safe driving speed, but if he encountered a large drift, he would accelerate to get through it.

That's why the dim glow from the Suburban's snow-covered brake lights surprised him. His father was stopping without warning. In response, he also slammed on his brakes, then eased up, pumping the brake pedal to avoid skidding.

Behind them, Ledrew had his hands full navigating the cube van. The large vehicle was lightly loaded, and the wind was playing havoc with it. Frequent, sharp turns in the road meant that sometimes he was headed straight into the wind. Other times, going broadside, the van was nearly blown off the road. Unaccustomed to winter driving, in poor visibility or not, he had no intention of being left behind on such a night.

While he could not see the Suburban, he kept the pickup in sight. That was too close for comfort. Suddenly, without warning, the truck hit its brakes. Ledrew swore and jammed on his brakes.

An experienced winter driver would have pumped the brakes and even down-shifted to slow the cube van while maintaining traction. Instead, Ledrew panicked. With the brakes fully applied, he yanked the steering wheel to the left to avoid a collision. He fishtailed, sliding out of control. The rear tires went into the ditch, and the cube van skidded to a stop, blocking both lanes.

Now Ledrew could see that the truck's brake lights were going on and off. Ben, pumping the brakes, had not stopped as abruptly as Ledrew expected.

Inside the Suburban, Abe and Glenn exchanged heated words.

"Why didn't you stop?" Glenn demanded. "Instead of driving into this snowdrift?"

"Why did you yell at me to slow down?" Abe replied. "If I had accelerated, like I would have if I had seen it first, we would have carried all the way through and not gotten stuck." He jammed the Suburban into park. "Stay here. I'll go back and check on the others."

Abe went to get out, only to discover his door would not open. Neither would any other door. Snow was halfway up the side. Undeterred, he put on his fur cap and mittens, opened the side window, and climbed out into the storm.

After assessing the situation, Abe concluded that the Suburban was stuck solid and going nowhere until the snow plow arrived. He hoped the pickup was well behind and not stuck. Even if it was, eight people would be able to push it out. The van should be fine. It would have stopped without entering the snowdrift.

Looking behind, Abe saw the pickup was thirty feet behind, headlights on and engine running. It was in the track the Suburban had created. So far, so good.

The cube van was a different story. At first, in the driving snow, Abe had trouble seeing it. Then he was dismayed to see it was at forty-five-degree angle from the gravel road with its rear tires stuck in the northbound ditch. The front was more than halfway across the southbound lane, leaving no room for vehicles, including the pickup truck, to pass. It would take a tow truck, or a piece of heavy equipment like a snow plow with a chain to pull it back onto the road.

Spending the night in a snowdrift on the highway was not a new experience for Abe. It had happened four or five times in the past thirty years. Ben had also been caught in storms — once with his father and once alone. However, Abe was concerned how the newcomers would fare. He knew they were inexperienced in such winter conditions. He did not think they were in serious danger if everyone remained calm, but people often panicked in such situations. That was their undoing.

Sometimes, they left their vehicle, attempted to walk to safety, got lost, and died of exposure. Other times, they fell asleep with the engine running, and carbon monoxide got them. Other times, they died of carbon monoxide poisoning without falling asleep as snow accumulated around their stranded, running vehicle.

Stopping briefly on the passenger side of the truck, where it was more sheltered, Abe spoke to Ben and Wainwright. "I'm going to check on Ledrew and see how they're doing. It looks like he slammed on the brakes too hard and lost control. I hope nobody got hurt. Then we'll figure out what to do. Hang tight. I'll be back in a few minutes."

He walked the thirty-five feet back to the van. In only a few minutes, his fur cap was covered in snow. Before leaving the Suburban, he had untied the string at the top and tied the flaps around his chin for protection from the weather. Now as he approached the van with its two nearly hysterical occupants, he looked more like a yeti than a man coming out of the storm.

He had to pound on the ice-covered window to gain entry. Aucoin backed up to give him room to climb aboard. He closed the door to keep the heat in.

"How are you two doing on this lovely evening?" he asked. His tone betrayed no concern. Instead, it was as casual as it had been back in Deer Lake a day and a half earlier when they first met. His manner had the intended effect of putting the occupants at ease after their harrowing experience. Ledrew, who have been complaining bitterly to Aucoin about how fast he had to drive to keep up with the Sullivans, was apologetic for having got the van stuck.

"Don't worry about it," Abe said nonchalantly. "Do you mind if I check out the back just in case company shows up?"

Aucoin was accustomed to winter driving but nothing this severe. Furious at the Sullivans for their speed and Ledrew for his poor driving, she calmed down and picked up on Abe's dark humour. "I haven't had time to prepare for guests. What you see is what you get."

The van had no divider between the passenger compartment and the cargo area. Inside access was gained directly from the front while outside access was gained from a large door in the rear. With its rear jammed solidly into the snow, the only way to access the cargo area was through the front. Abe saw it was no longer level but tilted slightly downward, because the rear tires were in the ditch.

"It's not perfect," he said, "but we can all take shelter here until the storm dies down. I'll head back and get the others."

Stopping at the truck, he shouted to Ben over the roaring wind. "Take what you need to the van. And take two cans of gas, the tow ropes, and the snow shovels. I've got to get everyone out of the Suburban before she drifts over. Leave the engine running with the headlights on so I can find my way back."

In the minutes since he had left the Suburban, his footprints had drifted over, and the tailpipe was covered in snow. Wading through the drifts to the passenger side, he banged on the frosted window. After some effort, Glenn managed to get it open.

"This thing will soon be completely covered in snow!" Abe yelled over the howling wind. "We've got to take shelter in the van. Bring any warm clothes you got and follow me."

Bartlett opened the rear passenger window. "Why can't we just stay here and wait it out?" he yelled over the wind.

"She's drifting over!" Abe yelled back. "Soon you won't be able to get out. Fumes from the engine will get you, if the cold doesn't."

The four inside the Suburban complied immediately, donning their winter clothing. Glenn reached over and turned off the engine.

"Leave the key in the ignition!" Abe yelled. "One less thing to worry about tomorrow."

The four climbed out into the storm, joining Abe.

"Hold on to my hand!" Abe yelled to Devereux and then turned to the others. "Follow us!"

They waded through thigh-deep snow toward the truck's headlights. Passing the truck, he looked inside to confirm it was empty. When the five arrived at the van, Ben helped them inside. Even though it had been only minutes since they exited the Suburban, it seemed like much longer. All felt the effects of the cold.

Assembled in the cargo compartment, they brushed the snow off themselves and each other. Although warmer than outside, it was still cold, because the heater could not heat such a large space. Nevertheless, wearing winter clothing, they were relatively comfortable.

Abe volunteered his assessment. "Here's the situation. We're over nine clicks from Big Brook. There's a highways depot in Flower's Cove, roughly sixty to seventy clicks behind us. There's a highways depot in St. Anthony. That's roughly sixty to seventy clicks ahead of us. No equipment will operate in this weather. They can't keep the road open in heavy drifting like this. If they get stuck, they could be out for a while."

After pausing to knock some melting snow from his fur cap, he continued. "Before we left Plum Point, I called St. Anthony to tell them we were coming a day early. They'll expect us tonight. If we don't show, they'll call Plum Point and find out if we left. They'll know we're on the road somewhere. Even so, I don't expect any plows until sometime tomorrow."

As the full impact of his words sank in, Delroy was the first to reply. "What do you mean by 'sometime tomorrow'?"

"Well, they won't operate tonight, as they only plow in the daytime. They won't start plowing until the storm is over. So, if the storm ends by morning, that's when they'll start. With the distance between Flowers Cove and St. Anthony, you're looking at six to eight hours to get the road open. If they have big drifts, it can take two to three days to open a single lane for stop-and-go traffic."

By then, the visitors were beginning to panic. Abe faced a barrage of questions.

"You mean that, at best, we're here until late tomorrow?" Bartlett asked, grim faced.

"That's what I figure," Abe replied.

"What do we do for a bathroom?" the women asked in unison.

"The men can step outside. We've got to go outside to make sure at least one side is clear for exhaust anyway. As for the ladies, I know it's a bit crude, but the tow ropes are in a five-gallon plastic pail. We can put the pail in the back corner of the van. The men will have to look to the other way while you use it."

"But we've got nothing to eat or drink," Delroy said. It was more a statement of the obvious than a question.

"That's right," Abe concurred. "When Ben and I get out, we'll fill the empty pop bottles and any other containers we have with snow. It'll melt inside. It's not perfect, but it's better than nothing. It won't hurt you."

"Why did you say we've got to go outside in the storm?" Wainwright asked.

"Two reasons," Abe replied. "First of all, we have to make sure that the front of the van doesn't drift full of snow. If it does, and the snow melts around the wiring or the air intake, the engine will die. We'll be left in the dark without heat. We've also got to shovel snow away from the sides so the exhaust fumes can escape. Otherwise they'll come inside and gas all of us."

Glenn cursed himself silently for not staying the extra night in Plum Point. He still hoped his St. Anthony plans could go ahead but said nothing, as he was worried the group might turn on him for getting them into this mess. If they did, he intended to blame Abe. He would argue the experienced taxi driver should have insisted they stay in Plum Point. After all, that was why they hired him.

As the reality of their situation set in, an air of gloom settled over the van's occupants.

Chapter 9

An hour later, Ben, dozing in the passenger seat, dehydrated from the alcohol he had consumed, sat up suddenly. "There's somebody outside!"

Through a small section of the side window not covered by frost, he saw two snowmobiles. Each one was towing a sled with a forty-five-gallon drum lashed to it.

Earlier in the day, forty-five-year-old Andrew Sparrow and his fifteen-year-old son, Andrew John (A.J.), had gone to Cook's Harbour to get heating oil. Ordinarily, Big Brook received oil deliveries every two weeks in the winter, but due to the recent storms, the oil truck had not come. On a nice day, they could make the twenty-five-mile run in an hour. Both residents of Big Brook were accustomed to winter travel.

Abe opened the door and yelled to them. "Come in!"

After two hours on the snowmobiles, mostly in a raging storm, they did not need to be asked twice.

Abe introduced himself and the group to the newcomers. "I'm Abe Sullivan. This is my son, Ben. These people," he gestured to the others, "are from the mainland. They're here doing a documentary on the seal hunt. Where are you guys from?"

"I recognize you," Andrew replied. "I've seen you around in a taxi a couple times. I'm Andrew Sparrow, and this is my son, A.J. We're from Big Brook."

"What are you doing out in this weather?" Abe asked.

"On our way back from Cook's Harbour. We thought we would be ahead of the worst of it, but we were delayed. That put us right in the middle of it. How long have you been here?"

"Close on an hour now," Abe replied. "I guess we're stuck here 'til the plow comes through."

"That won't be until tomorrow, at the earliest," Andrew said. "You mightn't be in very good shape by then. Me and A.J. will have to get you out of here."

"How?" Glenn asked, "There's too many of us for to fit on your snowmobiles. Where would we go?"

"Leave that to me," Andrew replied. "It's between five and six miles to Big Brook. That's only a fifteen-minute run in good weather, but in this it'll be two to three times that. We can take the two women. In Big Brook, we'll round up some men to come for the rest of you."

Suddenly, the atmosphere in the van improved.

"What sort of timeframe are we looking at?" Glenn asked, now back in charge. "How much longer will we be stuck here?"

"If we allow a half hour to get there, perhaps an hour to unload, find some men, and gas up, and a half hour to get back, that's a couple of hours," Andrew said. "It's almost ten o'clock now, so around midnight."

His frank assessment dampened the atmosphere in the van once again.

Chapter 10

The men arrived in Big Brook quicker than expected. Upon their arrival, they saw the light was on in the old one-room school that now served as the church. That meant old Reverend Charlie Spencer was still here. He was a legend. He would know what to do.

The two snowmobiles pulled up in front. Andrew jumped off and ran into the building. There, he found the reverend putting on his parka to go home for the night.

He was not actually going home though. Home was the Cook's Harbour rectory. He was staying with Andrew's parents. Old friends, they enjoyed his company and looked forward to hosting him whenever he stayed over.

Before Andrew could finish telling him the situation, the reverend interrupted. "Tell them to come in here and warm up. We'll get a crew together to go get the others."

A.J. and the two shivering, snow-covered women were already coming through the door.

"Your parents are still up waiting for me," Reverend Spencer said. "Let's go."

Outside, over the raging wind, the reverend yelled to Andrew. "You take off! I'll hop on the sleigh behind the oil drum."

Within a few minutes they were at the Sparrow residence. At the doorway, they were met by Margaret Sparrow, a tiny, white-haired, birdlike woman wearing wire-rimmed glasses. Behind her in a heavy plaid shirt, work pants, and suspenders was her eighty-year-old husband, Israel, a tall, still powerful bear of a man.

"Come in, come in, come in," Margaret said, in a distinct, rapid-fire Scottish accent. "If you stand there much longer, you'll catch your death of cold and freeze the house out at the same time."

In the kitchen, Margaret sized the women up. "The first thing you need is some warm, dry clothing, then something to eat. When did you have your last decent meal, anyway?"

"Breakfast, around seven this morning," Aucoin replied, still numb from the cold and shivering as she spoke. "We had sandwiches around four or five this afternoon."

"Good grief, lassies, that will never do, not travelling in this weather, anyway," the little lady replied. She took in their wet, ice-encrusted clothing and then beckoned them to follow her. "Come with me."

They trailed after through a doorway covered by a curtain into a room off the kitchen, behind the wood and oil stove. Originally built as a sitting room, it had been converted into a master bedroom so the elderly couple would not have to navigate the stairs up to their bedroom.

Reaching for a string, Margaret turned on the bulb that shone from a white ceramic light socket in the ceiling. "I don't think you can fit into my clothing," she said, "but you're welcome to try. This is my dresser."

She pointed to another dresser. "That's Israel's. Wear any of his you want."

The women looked at each other.

"Take off what you're wearing," Margaret ordered. "Then give me your clothing so I can hang them behind the stove to dry."

She turned briskly and left the room.

In the kitchen, the four men were engaged in an earnest discussion when Margaret entered.

"This is what we've got to do," Reverend Spencer said, turning to her. "Andrew will round up some men and go back down on the barrens to the big drift for the others. He says there are seven, and he figures they'll be in bad shape if they got to stay there all night. A.J. will stay here. He and I will go around to a few houses and see who can take a couple strangers for the night."

"They can all stay here," Margaret offered. "We can make up some beds on the floor. It's not like we haven't done it before."

"Thanks, Margaret," the reverend replied. "That'll be our backup plan, but I'm pretty sure we'll find places for the others. Anyway, we'll know soon enough."

He turned to Andrew, who was about to leave. "It might be a good idea if one or two snowmobiles take a coach box in case the travelers have something they don't want to leave in the vehicles." He stood up and looked at A.J. "Well, it's too warm in here to be standing around in snowmobile suits, so we better get going."

Margaret looked at the elderly minister. "What about you? When are you going to eat? You're nothing but skin and bones."

"You feed the women. A.J. and I will be back as soon as we can. We can eat then."

The door closed behind them.

Margaret turned to her husband. "It's good thing I cooked that large ham for the minister's visit. There's a lot left. Carve the meat from the bone. Then take the big pot. Fill it halfway with water, put the bone in it, and put it on stove."

"Pea soup?" Israel asked.

Margaret nodded. "Pea soup. Then skin the three rabbits Andrew gave us yesterday and take some moose out of the deep freezer."

By then, the two women, wearing Israel's work shirts, pants, and home-spun woollen socks, were coming out of the bedroom. Strings cinched size forty pants around waists measuring twenty-six and thirty inches.

"The two places are set for you," Margaret said. "Please have a seat. I hope you like ham, boiled vegetables, and homemade bread."

Both women dug into the offered food, their voices returning as they ate.

"These look like beets," Aucoin said. "The kind my grandmother used to make. But what's in the other two dishes?"

"The yellowish one contains homemade sweet mustard pickles. The greenish one is homemade rhubarb chutney," Margaret said. "Please try them. They're very mild. I have deep-dish rhubarb pies in the pantry. We like them warm, so I'll put one in the oven. I like it with canned cream."

Devereux was interested in Margaret's background. "You sound like someone from Scotland."

Margaret laughed. "That's because I am someone from Scotland."

"But how is it you're here?" Devereux asked, interested in the apparent anomaly of someone from Scotland, an eighty-year-old lady, so obviously settled in that remote place.

Margaret laughed again. "It's a long story. If time permits, I'll tell you, but right now, there's work to be done. I'm about to put on a pot of pea soup. Israel is in the pantry, skinning rabbits and shaving frozen moose meat so it will be cooked when your friends arrive. Andrew says that should be one and a half to two hours from now."

As the women finished their rhubarb pie and cream, the outside door opened, sending a draft from the porch.

"That will be the reverend and A.J.," Margaret speculated. She was proven right when she opened the inner door to reveal both of them taking off their outer garments and boots before entering the kitchen.

"I imagine you'll want to change into something dry before eating," she said.

They did. The reverend went upstairs. A.J. headed into his grandparents' bedroom, changing into his own clothing from a supply he kept there. When they finished, they rejoined the four in the kitchen.

"Pull up a chair," Margaret said. "Israel will serve you while I take the ladies upstairs to inspect the sleeping quarters."

Picking up a flashlight, she led them into a small, cold, unlit hallway through yet another door. There, she reached up for a string, a light switch for another naked sixty-watt bulb. They ascended a small, narrow staircase to the second floor, where she turned on another light, revealing four painted, wooden bedroom doors and a bathroom. The upstairs temperature, while above the freezing mark, was bone chilling.

Margaret nodded at the glow from a small electric heater in the bathroom. "When it's really cold, we keep the heater on in the bathroom to keep the water from freezing."

She continued, showing them the rooms. "The reverend's room is the one at the front right, directly over the kitchen stove. Heat rises through a grate to keep it warm. There's another room over the kitchen. It also has a grate to permit heat to rise, but it has only one bed, a double. If you don't mind sharing, you'll be warmest there. The other two rooms only have single beds. A little more privacy but not so warm."

"I don't mind sharing," they answered in unison.

"That settles it," Margaret said. "This will be your room. Now I've got to get downstairs to make sure the soup doesn't burn. Israel's a good cook, but sometimes he doesn't stir it as often as he should. I imagine you're both tired. You don't need to wait up for your friends unless you want to."

"I'm going to stay up for a little while," Aucoin said.

"Me, too," Devereaux added.

By then, Reverend Spencer and A.J. had wolfed down the ham and vegetables and were devouring rhubarb pie. The reverend had found three families to billet the seven men.

"I told them the men will warm up and eat here," he said. "They only need a place to sleep."

"Who are they staying with?" Margaret inquired.

"Israel's sister Rebecca and Henry said they would put up a couple. Cornelius and Isabel Ward will take two, and so will Danny and Jennifer Young. So nobody is billeted alone, I'm hoping you and Israel will take another."

"Of course we will," Israel said. "We'd put them all up if you wanted us to."

Margaret closed the oven door and sat in a rocking chair by the stove. She reached into a cloth bag and withdrew several pure white crocheted squares. Taking a crochet needle and a ball of pink yarn, she began to crochet a raised rose in the center of a square.

Devereaux returned to her earlier question. "So, how did you come to be here?"

"I followed him," she said, nodding at Israel. Then she told how they met. She was born in 1897 in Arbroath, on Scotland's east coast. Her father was a local merchant and fish dealer. Her mother was a fisherman's daughter.

When World War One broke out in 1914, many young men headed south to London to join up, and many girls her age followed them. In London, the far-off European war was exciting, but the excitement did not reach as far north as Scotland.

She pleaded with her parents to be allowed to go to London, but they refused, saying, "You're too young to go on your own" and "This will probably be over in a few months, and you'll have wasted your money going down just to return home."

However, the war did not end early. By 1915, when she turned eighteen, her parents finally relented, permitting her to go as long as she stayed with her mother's sister, Vera, a nurse working in London.

"I met Israel in the late summer of nineteen fifteen at a social for soldiers from the colonies," Margaret said. "There were Canadians, Australians, New Zealanders, and a small group from Newfoundland, all very polite, nice, young chaps from all over the Commonwealth. I was impressed that they were so patriotic. These young men had come from all over to fight for king and country, to protect us from the German Kaiser."

"What did you talk about?" Devereux asked.

"Well, we didn't actually talk."

"You didn't talk?" Aucoin exclaimed.

Margaret shook her head. "No. He was very reserved. I met five lads from Newfoundland, including Israel and his brother Isaac. They believed they were taking a year away from fishing to go to Europe for the war and then returning home to their fishing boats."

Her voice lowered. "The next time I saw him was in nineteen sixteen. The Newfoundland Regiment had been sent to Gallipoli, a disaster for all sides. His brother, Isaac, had been killed in action, and Israel suffered a serious wound to his left arm."

Glancing at him, she continued quietly. "You see that he has a limited range of motion in that arm. It doesn't hold him back though. It never has. In fact, he says being wounded at Gallipoli likely saved his life. Otherwise he would have been at Beaumont Hamel the following July, when the Newfoundland Regiment was nearly wiped out."

"But how did you reconnect with him?" Aucoin asked, impatient to hear about the courtship part of the story.

"This is very touching," Devereux added, equally intrigued, "but what about the two of you? How did you get here? Why all this suspense?"

Margaret got up from her rocking chair, went to a small sewing room off the kitchen, and then returned. Extending her open hand, she displayed a medal. Attached to it was a ribbon, and affixed to the ribbon was a star and a palm branch.

Devereux recognized it immediately. *"Mon Dieu! Cette est une Croix de Guerre.* My grandfather has one of these. Where did it come from?"

"It was awarded to him by the French after Gallipoli," Margaret said in a hushed voice.

"Your husband is a brave man," Devereux replied.

"In some respects, that's true. In others, not so much. That man," she continued, glancing toward the oversized pantry where Israel was washing pots, "can face another army on a battlefield, but when it comes to talking about his feelings for a woman, he loses his nerve completely. Amazing, isn't it?"

"So, what did you do?" Devereux asked.

Before Margaret could continue, they heard the sound of approaching snowmobiles.

"It looks like your friends are here," Margaret said. "I hope everybody's okay." She smiled, a twinkle in her eye. "Israel won't mind if you keep wearing his clothes, but I believe your things are dry, and they're certainly more fashionable."

They did not need to be asked twice. Suddenly, it dawned on them they looked ridiculous in oversized men's work clothes. Fearing their appearance could be tabloid material, they grabbed their own garments and rushed upstairs to change.

Chapter 11

Outside, the wind had lessened. The temperature had fallen further. While there was a low drift, overhead stars were visible. By then, everyone in the tiny community knew about the people who were stuck on the road. They also knew that Andrew and A.J. had rescued two women, who were at Margaret and Israel's house. Several men had gone back to the big drift for the others.

Rumours abounded as to the travellers' identities. Everybody had heard of Abe Sullivan and some of his exploits. Nobody could figure out why he would be taking a bunch of people, mainlanders, up the Northern Peninsula in a snowstorm.

Nothing so exciting had happened in Big Brook since German submarines caught a convoy of ships headed for Europe. In the narrow Strait of Belle Isle, they were sitting ducks. To save his crew, one captain ran his ship ashore at full speed. Knowledge of the engagement was kept out of the media so as not to alarm the Canadian public.

* * *

The rescuers delivered seven cold, tired, hungry men to the Sparrow residence. Delroy was in the worst condition.

Margaret took one look at him and started issuing orders. "This man is dangerously chilled. Israel, you and Reverend Spencer take him into our bedroom. Strip him as fast as you can and dress him in your clothes. Then bring him into the kitchen. We need to get some warm fluids into him quickly. I'll attend to the others."

The two Sullivans and Wainwright were in fairly good condition. The others –Ledrew, Bartlett, and Glenn — were so chilled they were shivering and slurring their words. As she concluded her assessment, Israel and Reverend Spencer brought Delroy out of the bedroom, supporting him by his arms.

"Israel," Margaret said, "take these three men into the bedroom and find them something to wear. Reverend Spencer and I must get something warm into this man, and we need to keep him moving."

She turned to A.J. "Pull out whatever you have here," she said, motioning toward Wainwright and Ben. "They look to be about your size."

She turned to the women. "I hope you two have food-serving experience. As soon as they change, start feeding them. Don't stand on ceremony, just do it. Begin with the pea soup, but be careful, it's hot. Chilled, they may not realize they're scalding themselves. Use any dishes and cutlery you find in the pantry. A.J. will help you."

She went into the sewing room and returned a moment later with a flask of brandy. She poured two ounces into a glass, added a heaping teaspoon of sugar, then poured four ounces of hot water from a kettle. Stirring it to dissolve the sugar, she handed the glass to Reverend Spencer and gestured toward Delroy. "Get him to drink this hot toddy, but be careful, it's hot."

She made four more hot toddies and gave them to A.J. to distribute.

Within half an hour, the Sullivans and Wainwright had finished eating and were in good spirits. Ledrew, Glenn, and Bartlett had also finished their soup and were devouring large plates of baked rabbit and rice, stewed moose meat, and boiled vegetables.

Reverend Spencer was spoon-feeding pea soup to Delroy, who was seated in Margaret's rocking chair by the stove, slowly beginning to recover his senses.

"It's getting late," Margaret said. "I'm sure you're very tired after your long day. We arranged for three families to take in two guests each, so six of you are to go to other homes for the night. I think we should change that.

These three gentlemen, Ledrew, Glenn, and Bartlett, shouldn't go out in the cold again, not yet. As for Mr. Delroy here, we should keep him up for a while. He may have frostbite to his feet and hands. If so, he may need to be sent to hospital when the weather clears. Gangrene is always a possibility.

That leaves Mr. Sullivan, his son, and this young man." She nodded at Wainwright. "The wind is lessening. Otherwise, I would insist everyone remain here for the night."

She motioned to her grandson. "A.J., take them to the families expecting them for the night." Then she turned to her husband. "Israel, after these gentlemen finish eating, bring mattresses from the bunk beds upstairs. Gather up pillows and bedding. Make a bed for them on the kitchen floor."

She smiled at the two women, "Let me know when you want to retire for the evening. I'll give each of you a hot water bottle to take to bed."

Both accepted her offer, heading upstairs for the night.

Nearly finished her orders, Margaret motioned toward a small cot in the corner of the kitchen. "Mr. Delroy will sleep on the daybed."

With everything in place, she glanced at the clock. "It's after two thirty. I think we should call it a night."

Chapter 12

At sunrise, a little after 6 a.m., Israel got up, padded into the pantry, and opened a canister of coffee. Selecting the larger of two coffee pots from the cupboard, he filled the bottom part with water and the top part with coffee and then placed it on the stove.

Then he reached into a small wall cabinet, retrieved an old pipe and a package of tobacco, and sat down at the kitchen table. He tapped the previous ashes from the pipe's bowl and proceeded to fill it.

While Margaret did not exactly approve of his smoking, she did not object strenuously either. He had been smoking for a long time. Since the smoke bothered her, he smoked outside.

On fine mornings, he liked to go outside early to look around, have his morning smoke, and assess the weather.

Overnight, the wind had stopped. The air was calm, and the temperature had risen to a balmy minus ten degrees Celsius.

Israel enjoyed his pipe for several minutes, contentedly sending clouds of white smoke upward. When the tobacco was completely consumed, he put the pipe in his pocket and went back into the house.

Inside, he was greeted by the aroma of fresh coffee. Taking two cups, he put a bit of canned milk in each. Then he added coffee to both, one to the top and the other three quarters full. He added hot water to the second one to weaken it. Then he took it into the bedroom and placed it on the nightstand beside Margaret.

Coming back into the kitchen, he turned on the radio to wait for the 7 a.m. news and weather report. Then he sat to enjoy his own coffee. Gradually, others joined him.

First was Reverend Spencer. A familiar visitor, who preferred tea over coffee, he went to the pantry and retrieved a teabag from a canister. He dropped it into a mug and filled it with hot water from the kettle.

Next were Aucoin and Devereux, fully dressed and well groomed. Like Israel, they had awoken to the rising sun streaming through their bedroom window. That was followed by the sound of somebody moving around the kitchen below. Then came the sound of coffee percolating and its unmistakable, tantalizing smell.

The only bathroom in the home was adjacent to their room. In it, the small electric heater had been on all night. While it may have looked like a museum, it was comfortable with an ample supply of water. The women moved quickly to avoid the rush expected when everyone else woke up.

When they entered the kitchen, Margaret greeted them. "Well, you look no worse for wear. Now, what can we get you? Would you like coffee, or would you prefer tea?"

Both opted for coffee, served black.

Margaret noted that the three men on the floor were awake. "I imagine you'll want to change into your own clothes."

Having slept wearing Israel's clothing while theirs hung in the kitchen to dry, all three nodded in assent.

"Israel will show you to the bathroom. Hopefully you'll find everything to your satisfaction."

All three retrieved their garments and followed Israel upstairs.

Throughout it all, Delroy slept on, dead to the world, on the daybed.

When Israel rejoined them a few moments later, Margaret announced it was time to get breakfast underway.

"What can we do?" Devereaux asked, anxious to help.

"One of you can make toast," Margaret replied. "The other can scramble eggs."

While Devereux cracked eggs at the kitchen table, Margaret took Aucoin to the back of the pantry to a new four-slice toaster.

"A gift from the grandchildren after they were here last Christmas," she said, smiling. "They felt the old two-slicer was too slow. Israel will slice the bread thin enough so it doesn't get stuck. All you have to do is butter it. Keep going until you have two dozen slices."

By then, Israel had sliced a third of the large bologna into a dozen perfectly uniform, half-inch-thick slices, cut them in half, and had them frying in the second skillet.

Margaret put a large measure of rolled oats into a saucepan. Filling it halfway with cold water, she added a pinch of salt and put it on the stove. Then she turned to the reverend and held up a wooden spoon.

"I know you like porridge. Can you stir it to make sure it doesn't boil over while I set the table?"

The old kitchen table could seat only six people, so Margaret went to a back room and returned with a card table. Unfolding the legs, she placed it at the end of the table, providing space for two more. Then she spread a long, plain tablecloth and set eight place settings.

She had just finished when Glenn, Bartlett, and Ledrew came back downstairs. By then, with breakfast preparations complete, she turned to address everyone.

"Please sit in. Israel and Reverend Spencer usually sit at each end. The others can sit anywhere else."

Going to the pantry, she returned with two tall stacks of toast. "It's not every day that we have the clergy and visitors from afar join us for breakfast. This is indeed a rare pleasure. Reverend Spencer, would you be kind enough to say grace?"

They all bowed their heads in prayer.

Afterwards, noting Margaret had not eaten and that there was an unused setting, Devereaux motioned to the empty chair. "Madame Sparrow, you haven't eaten. Won't you join us?"

Margaret smiled. "That place is for Mr. Delroy, when he wakes. There will be time for me to eat after all of you have finished."

By then, Delroy had started to come out of his deep slumber. He sat up on the daybed, stretched, and yawned. "Did somebody say my name?" he asked groggily. "Something smells really good."

"Good morning, Mr. Delroy," Margaret replied. "Welcome back to the land of the living. I trust you slept well?"

"That I did," he said, "but right now, I need a bathroom. Then I'll have coffee."

Glenn volunteered to show him upstairs. He wanted to talk out of earshot of the others, starting before they got to the bathroom.

"Delroy, this is getting all fucked up, and it's all that goddamn Abe Sullivan's fault!"

"Glenn, for the love of God, I'm bursting. Let me piss first!"

Glenn would not stop talking, continuing as Delroy stood at the toilet, relieving himself. "You should be as furious at Sullivan as I am. You almost died. He should've told us how bad it could get. We should have stayed in Plum Point. Besides, I think I smelled booze on that kid of his. Perhaps that's why they got us into this mess."

"Settle down, Glenn. I need a coffee, and what the fuck am I wearing? What happened to my clothes?"

Relieved Delroy was not blaming him for their predicament, Glenn chuckled. "Don't worry about your clothes. They're hanging by the stove in the kitchen. By now they're likely dry. That little, old bat downstairs took our clothes. She had us wear the old geezer's rags until ours dried." Glenn stepped closer and lowered his voice. "I'm concerned the women are getting too friendly with her. We don't want them blabbing. We need to get out of here as fast as possible. Wainwright isn't even here. He slept at another house. Who knows what he's saying."

Returning downstairs, they were congenial and grateful to their hosts.

"Mr. Delroy, your place is right here," Margaret said, directing him to the empty chair. "Would you like to start with coffee or tea? I haven't eaten as yet. I was waiting for you. If you're wondering about your clothing, I hung everything up. They're nice and dry, but eat first. You can change afterwards. If you prefer to bathe before you change, the upstairs tub is available. We have lots of hot water and soap."

Before they finished eating, they heard snowmobiles outside. It was Andrew and A.J. With them were the Sullivans and Wainwright. They had news.

"I was out snowmobiling, and I saw the big highways truck from St. Anthony," A.J. said. "I rushed down to the road to ask him about three machines stuck in the big drift. They had to be towed out of the way, just to get one lane clear."

Seeking to regain control of their situation, Glenn turned to Abe. "What should we do?"

"I think me and Ben and a couple of you guys should go and check them out," Abe replied, happy to be useful again. "If everything is okay, we can come back for everyone else and get on the road."

"What is there to check out?" Glenn asked, anxious to get underway. "Why can't we just go and get them and be on our way?"

Overruled by Glenn the day before, Abe's reply was abrupt. "We don't know what kind of shape they're in. We left the Suburban's windows open. She might be full of snow. The van was facing into the wind, so the engine compartment might be full. Even if she starts, when the engine warms up, melted snow could short out the electrical. We would need to tow her to a garage to be dried out. Nope. We've got to check them out first."

"How long will that take?" Glenn demanded.

Abe shrugged. "An hour, perhaps more. We've got shovels, a broom, and brushes in the vehicles. Ledrew was driving the van. He can come with us. You can join us, too, or send young Wainwright. He seems to know what he's doing."

"I'll go and hook up my sleigh," A.J. said. "Hey, Davis, do you want to help me?"

Glenn decided to let Ledrew, Wainwright, and the Sullivans do the work. He stayed behind to keep an eye on the others.

An hour later, the men returned with the vehicles in good running order.

Abe raised the issue of paying the Sparrows, but the elderly couple refused to accept anything. When Devereux insisted, Margaret finally conceded.

"The church is always struggling. If you want to make a donation, Reverend Spencer will mail you a receipt."

"What about the men who helped?"

"You could cover their gasoline," she said. "Maybe five or ten dollars each. They're unemployed fisherman waiting for spring. Usually, they do well with seals, but this has been a poor year. Next month, when the ice breaks up, they may get some beaters. Then they'll be fishing for cod."

With the issue settled, by 11 a.m., they were headed for St. Anthony.

The group was relieved at having come through the storm unscathed. Coupled with anticipation of what St. Anthony would bring was a growing desire for the trip to end.

Aucoin and Ledrew had more than enough footage, even if they had turned around and gone back after the day at Yankee Point. Bartlett had taken so many notes he had filled his notepad and was using a high school exercise book Margaret had given him. He took photos sparingly to conserve his remaining film.

Devereux was upbeat. Except for being panicked in the van the night before and chilled on the snowmobile ride to the Sparrows, she was enjoying the winter adventure.

Delroy just wanted to turn around. Before the snowstorm, he was bored. His near-death experience from hypothermia had left him paranoid. Keeping his fears to himself, he wondered why they were still driving away from the airport in Deer Lake. What would happen if they were caught in another storm and nobody showed up to rescue them? What would happen if the locals discovered what they were up to? Things could get ugly.

Wainwright, driving in the truck with Ben, had reservations about the venture. These people were not much different from folks in rural Alberta, where he grew up. He was beginning to like them, particularly Josh and Ben. He had started out believing seals were in danger of extinction. Now he knew the hunt was federally regulated, with a quota to ensure sustainability. He had to discuss this with Green Earth, but first, he needed to tell them about Glenn.

While Wainwright was supposed to be in charge, Glenn controlled everything. After a few days with him, Wainwright had reservations about Glenn's moral compass. He intended to discuss the events of the past few days with Glenn, but having watched him pressure Abe into leaving Plum Point the night before and then blame him when they were stuck in the snowdrift, he was not looking forward to challenging him. He knew Glenn was planning some sort of media event in St. Anthony, but they had not discussed the details. That was beginning to worry him.

*   *   *

Travelling along the shore of beautiful Pistolet Bay, Glenn realized he knew little about St. Anthony. Suspecting Abe could fill him in so he could appear informed when he met the locals, he decided to turn on the charm.

"So, what's St. Anthony's claim to fame?"

"What do you mean?" Abe asked warily.

"Is there any kind of industry there? What do the people do? How big is the town? You know, that kind of stuff."

"Well, it's the end of the Viking Trail. It's got a bank, a police station, a big fish plant, and a hospital."

"Anything else?"

"Restaurants, mostly only open in the summer, a drug store, and a groceteria."

"And how many people live there?"

"I don't know for sure, but it's the biggest town up here, so I'd say maybe three or four thousand."

Glenn had no more questions. Abe fell silent, sensing he had heard enough.

The silence was broken as they passed the sign that said "L'Anse aux Meadows Historic Park." The picture of a Viking boat caught Glenn's attention.

"What's that all about?"

"Oh, that's where the Vikings lived roughly one thousand years ago," Abe explained. "They dug up some relics, and there's a little park. They say the feds have plans for it. Are we staying at the Valhalla or the Polar Bear Inn?" Abe asked as they rolled into town.

"We're at the Polar Bear," Glenn replied.

The hotel had twenty-four rooms. Log cabin themed, it included a coffee shop, a gift shop, a small bar with a stone fireplace, and a dance hall for over two hundred people. While only a few locals were drinking beer, the large bandstand, four pool tables, and ten dartboards indicated it was a popular hangout.

"Are there phones in the rooms?" Glenn asked as he picked up his key at the front desk.

"Yes sir," answered forty-something Elizabeth "Betty" Reed. "Just dial nine to get an outside line for local calls. For long-distance, dial zero, and I'll call the operator for you. They'll give us the time and charges for the call." She smiled cheerfully. "The coffee shop closes from two thirty to four thirty in the wintertime. Then it reopens until seven. The gift shop has no set hours this time of year. Let me know if you need anything. I'll open up for you."

"Where I can find Enos Reed?" Glenn asked, impatient at the slow pace.

"Enos is my husband," Elizabeth replied proudly. "Together, we own this place. He's also the school principal. We've been expecting you. He asked me to call as soon as you arrived. I was gonna do that after I checked you in."

"When do you think he'll get here?"

She chuckled. "About five minutes after I tell him you're here."

Leaving their luggage in their rooms, the group headed to the coffee shop, taking up five tables. The Sullivans headed for a corner table. Before even looking at the menu, they ordered drinks — a double rye for Ben and a beer for Abe.

Aucoin and Ledrew sat at a large window overlooking the town. Glenn and Wainwright sat in the far corner by the crackling black and chrome woodstove. Devereaux and Delroy took up positions in the centre of the room.

Bartlett occupied the remaining table overlooking the town. After being confined at close quarters on the drive, most of them welcomed the opportunity to spread out and confer with their respective travelling companions. Bartlett wanted to work on his story. He wanted to get three instalments out of the trip. To avoid being be scooped by Aucoin's television story, he planned to file the first story by telephone or telex from Deer Lake.

Chapter 13

No sooner were they seated than a red GMC Jimmy came barrelling into the parking lot, sliding to a full stop at the main entrance. Out jumped its diminutive driver. He rushed through the front door, spoke briefly with Elizabeth, who was dusting the gift shop, and then headed to the coffee shop.

Smiling from ear to ear, he stretched out his right hand. "You must be Glenn Holmes. I'm Enos Reed. We talked on the phone. I'm glad to see you made it. I hear you had a rough time on the road. I'm happy you're finally here. What can I do to help you?"

Throughout this rapid-fire outburst, nobody else said anything. There was no opportunity. He did not even appear to inhale.

"I thought you were the mayor and president of the chamber of commerce," Glenn said.

"I'm not actually the mayor; I'm the deputy mayor," Enos replied. "The mayor is battling cancer and spends a lot of time in St. John's. He wanted to resign, but council wouldn't hear of it. Quitting would be the kiss of death for him. He's still mayor, but as deputy, I cover his responsibilities. You're right about me being president of the chamber. I got involved when Betty and I bought this place."

"And you're also the school principal?"

"Mr. Holmes, you'll find people wearing many hats in small towns around here."

"No need to be so formal, Enos, just call me Glenn." Then, realizing all eyes were on them, he added, "Please excuse my manners. I haven't introduced everyone."

"Oh, I already know Abe and Ben," Enos replied. "They're regulars. I figured the other people were with you, although I wasn't sure, because you're not all sitting together."

"That's because we're all working on different things. Besides, we're happy to have a bit of space after being cooped up in those vehicles."

After Glenn completed the introductions, he asked Enos if there was anywhere they could meet in private for a few minutes. "I need your help with something," he said.

Enos was happy to accommodate. "Sure, we have an office behind the reception desk. That should work, but your lunch is practically here. Don't you want to eat first?"

Glenn was anxious to enlist him and did not want to waste any time. "We'll only need a few minutes." He turned to Wainwright. "Can you ask the kitchen staff to keep my food warm while I have a word with their boss?"

"Hey, what about me?" asked Wainwright.

"Don't worry, I'll fill you in later," Glenn answered.

Without waiting for a response, both men exited the coffee shop and went straight to the office.

Glenn explained they were doing a documentary on the importance of the seal hunt. He had already told Enos by telephone that they were doing a documentary, but he had not supplied details. Now he repeated the story that had worked so well with the mayor of Yankee Point.

Unknown to Glenn, both mayors were friends and colleagues. They had discussed the documentary in support of the seal hunt. Enos did not share that information with Glenn, but having spoken with Ike Gillett, he was keen to help the visitors.

"We already have some excellent footage from Yankee Point," Glenn said. "What we need now is a big public show of support. Your town is the most northerly and the biggest in the region. We want to say we went to the northern tip of Newfoundland."

"What can I do?" Enos asked.

"We'd like you to orchestrate a large show of public support for the seal hunt."

"No problem," Enos replied. "When would you like to do it?"

"It's probably too late today. How about tomorrow morning?"

"How many people do you want in the demonstration?"

"This is for television, so we should have at least a hundred, but two hundred would be better."

"Here's what I'll do," Enos said. "I'll go back to school and announce we're planning a demonstration. I can't do it during school hours; the board might not approve. I can't make it mandatory either, but there'll be lots of interest. School starts at nine. When there's assembly, we start at ten. I'll treat it as a voluntary assembly. The kids can bring their parents. That will cover transportation and increase the numbers."

"How could we arrange for a police presence if we wanted one?" Glenn asked.

Enos giggled. "You won't need a police presence in St. Anthony. There's hardly any crime — a few driving offenses, the occasional bar fight. There hasn't been a murder in a hundred years. But I can mention it to the sergeant. They may come out of curiosity. The cops around here are bored. Where do you want to have this?" he asked, almost as an afterthought.

"How about in front of this place? Your parking lot?"

"Wouldn't it be better to have it in a bigger place, like the shopping mall parking lot?" Enos asked. "Our parking lot isn't very big. It'll be jammed full of people."

"That's just it," Glenn said. "We need a place that's jammed full of people, so smaller is better, just in case you only get a small crowd. Besides," he added slyly, "you've been so helpful, you should benefit from any television coverage."

Seeing an opportunity to promote his business, Enos agreed quickly. Then he became concerned there was not enough time to prepare for the event. "I wish you'd told me you had something like this in mind. I could have ordered some signs or placards for our demonstrators to hold up. How will anyone know why the group is demonstrating?"

Glenn smiled. "Come with me."

They went outside to the van. Glenn lifted the back door and pointed to two boxes. "Each box contains one hundred placards. Two different sizes. They have a range of messages. Most favour the hunt. Others criticize people who oppose the hunt. Your people can use these or, if they want to, make their own."

Just then he realized Wainwright was watching from the coffee shop. "Bring your Jimmy around, and back it up to the van. You may as well take them now. We don't need them back. The school kids can keep them as souvenirs."

Within minutes, Enos was back at the school, assembling the students in the gymnasium. He explained the demonstration. Then he gave the signs to the janitor to distribute to the students so they could take them home and nail them to sticks for use in the morning.

Gloating, Glenn returned to the empty coffee shop. A note told him his lunch was in the kitchen. He ate alone, enjoying a tasty, if somewhat dry, platter of fish and chips.

As he exited the coffee shop, Betty approached. "Enos was supposed to tell you we're having a social for your group this evening."

Wary of anything that might interfere with his plans but remaining cordial, he smiled. "That's nice. What does he have in mind?"

"Tonight is ladies' darts night. We have twelve teams of six. They play from seven to nine. In honour of you being here, they're combining it with a potluck dinner. Tonight, they'll be here by six. Everyone will bring a dish. When darts finish, an accordion player will fill in until the band starts at ten."

"Really?" Glenn asked. "You arranged all that for us?" He smirked. "And what kind of music does this band play?"

"Well, rock 'n' roll, of course. Enos plays bass guitar. One of the young doctors plays lead. We have a music teacher who sings, and the drummer is a local fisherman."

Visiting each room individually, Glenn explained the night's itinerary. "I know our trip has been challenging," he said. "To give everyone a break, I've arranged for some entertainment. We're starting with local dishes at six. Then you can watch the women play darts. Then there's an accordion player, followed by a rock 'n' roll band. Pass on the word to the others if I don't see them first."

Satisfied none of them had an inkling of the demonstration and everyone would be occupied for the evening, Glenn retired to his room. He put out the "Do Not Disturb" sign and slept until 5 p.m.

The evening was a huge hit, but not in the way Glenn hoped. The locals were so hospitable and entertaining that some of the visitors began to have misgivings about what they were there to do.

Initially, they planned on spending four nights in Newfoundland — two in Plum Point followed by two in St. Anthony. Now they were a day ahead of schedule. They wanted to capitalize by leaving right after breakfast the next morning and driving the five hundred kilometres to Deer Lake, stopping briefly in Plum Point for fuel.

*   *   *

The next morning was a frosty minus thirty-four degrees Celsius. As they finished breakfast in the coffee shop, scores of snowmobiles, pickup trucks, and cars filled the parking lot. Police cars arrived with their lights flashing. Officers began directing traffic.

Before long, hundreds of people dressed in snowmobile suits, their faces covered by balaclavas to protect them from the cold, put on a demonstration. Glenn could not resist a smirk as he watched the others.

Although some placards displayed benign messages, such as "Save Our Seal Hunt" or "We Depend on Seals", many said, "Go Home or Die" or "Protesters Go Home". Others said, "Go Home French Whore." The most provocative showed a scantily clad woman being clubbed over the head, blood running down her face. No words were required to convey the intended message or the protesters' glee.

Except for Glenn, the entire group beat a hasty retreat to their rooms. While the others cowered behind locked doors, Bartlett, the former war correspondent, and Ledrew, the TV cameraman, returned quickly.

Bartlett, who had restocked with film in the gift shop, snapped pictures while Ledrew filmed the demonstration from the motel doorway.

A half an hour after it started, as if on cue, the demonstrators left.

Unknown to the terrorized visitors, it was nearly 9 a.m., and the kids were afraid of being late for school.

Minutes later, the traumatized visitors were in their vehicles, headed away from St. Anthony as fast as they could go. When asked why hundreds of people, so hospitable the night before, had turned into a hostile mob in the morning, the Sullivans had no answer.

Abe suggested that maybe they got their facts wrong and did not know the group was there to do a documentary. That did nothing to calm anyone's fears. By then, some in Glenn's group were beginning to mistrust the Sullivans.

When they arrived in Plum Point two hours later, nobody would leave the vehicles. Fearing they might be pursued or that another mob might be waiting for them, they stopped only briefly for fuel and then continued to Deer Lake.

Arriving at the airport town a day ahead of schedule, they rebooked their flights and got out of Newfoundland.

Chapter 14

For several days, their stories grabbed the attention of newspaper readers and television viewers alike.

While still en route, Bartlett filed a short piece by telephone from Halifax. Being Thursday, without pictures, it was a teaser for Friday's feature story. That story focused on clubbing seals. Complete with pictures from the day spent on the ice at Yankee Point, the glaring headline read, "The Brutal Canadians and the Bloody Hunt." The morning edition sold out before 11 a.m. The afternoon edition, with thousands of extra copies, sold out as well.

Saturday's story, with the headline "News Team Escapes Lynching by Bloodthirsty Canadian Mob", sold more copies than any edition since June 6, 1968, the day after Bobby Kennedy was assassinated.

The most prominent front-page photo was of a balaclava-wearing protester waving a placard that displayed a picture of a sealer clubbing a scantily clad woman. He was flanked on each side by protesters carrying placards saying, "Go Home or Die" and "Go Home French Whore."

Bartlett's coverage catapulted him to the head of New York reporters. Speaking engagements abounded, and job offers flooded in. Realizing their star reporter might be hired by a competitor, *The World Today* doubled his pay, gave him a large office, and guaranteed he could select his own assignments.

In Los Angeles, television station KWOW played teaser telephone audio clips on the Thursday evening news to promote Friday's story.

The coverage was bloody and dramatic. Introduced by a breathless Aucoin, it focused initially on Devereaux, dressed in a snowmobile suit, posing provocatively with young whitecoats, their warm, dark, moist eyes staring into the camera. Then it showed the seals being clubbed to death by bearded, hooded sealers, swinging ten-foot-long, hooked and iron-tipped poles. With each blow, the seal pups' blood and brains sprayed across the snow-covered ice. Then the sealers flipped them on their backs and skinned them.

The camera returned to Aucoin. She explained that after witnessing such carnage, they sought refuge in St. Anthony, the only town in that wild, remote region. Instead of a refuge, they were attacked by a mob and barely escaped with their lives. Then the broadcast cut to the blood-chilling mob scene outside the Polar Bear Inn.

Neither Aucoin nor Bartlett mentioned being rescued from the snowstorm near Big Brook or the hospitality extended by the Sparrows and others in that tiny hamlet. Nor did they mention the party thrown in their honour at the Polar Bear Inn the night before they left.

Any qualms that Aucoin had about having lied to the locals in Newfoundland about the nature of the expedition evaporated quickly when she saw the opportunity to gain media stardom. Within hours of her story airing, she received job offers from other networks. The girl from Spokane had mastered the California news market, and she intended to make the most of it.

The story was also a turning point for the others. Ledrew set himself up as Ledrew Cinematography, offering to accompany any groups shooting exposés in any part of the world. Delroy saw an immediate uptick in the number of nubile young women wanting to join his stable. Demand skyrocketed. He received calls from filmmakers, advertisers, modelling agencies, and big companies who would never have given his two-bit operation a second thought.

The entertainment world also saw Devereaux in a different light. Talented, fully clothed, and with her natural French accent, she became an exotic property overnight. As Delroy had predicted, Devereaux moved on and set up shop for herself. In high demand, she never took off her clothes for money again.

Chapter 15

Back in Halifax, Davis Wainwright was troubled. The expedition had been more successful than they had expected, yet he was uncomfortable about having duped the Newfoundlanders with their documentary charade. He knew he would have to discuss the compromise of Green Earth ethics with his principals when he returned to Vancouver.

He could not understand why and how the mob materialized without warning and then vanished. More curiously, he could not figure out where they had obtained professionally printed placards in an outpost like St. Anthony on such short notice. Seeking answers, he raised the subject with Glenn. The answer shocked him.

"Of course you can't figure it out," Glenn said, his voice dripping with sarcasm. "That's because I set up the whole thing."

"What do you mean?" Wainwright asked, fearing the answer.

"Are you deaf or just stupid?" Glenn snapped. "You know I set it up. You were with me. You went along with everything."

Finally, the enormity of the deception sank in. "Well, at least we had nothing to do with the demonstration," Wainwright said, his voice strained. "They really were out of control. What did they expect? They brought it on themselves. Can you believe some of the signs?"

"There you go again," Glenn said. "You really don't have a clue, do you? We were never in any danger. I brought the signs with us. The protesters were a bunch of kids from the high school where Enos Reed is the principal. We arranged the demonstration as a photo op for the media."

"What?" Wainwright stared at him, aghast.

Glenn roared with laughter. "Just like the locals thought we were doing a documentary for them, those media clowns and that French tart they brought with them bought the demonstration hook, line, and sinker."

Wainwright paled.

"Don't look so worried," Glenn said. "You and me and Green Earth are in the clear. We can cash in on this for years to come!"

Wainwright said nothing, fighting hard to suppress the urge to vomit.

On Sunday, Wainwright left Halifax International Airport bound for Vancouver. The week had been a roller coaster ride. He had arrived, excited to be the Green Earth team leader on an expedition to Newfoundland to do an exposé on the seal hunt. Having spent three years on a student's income, Wainwright had not travelled like some of his classmates from wealthier families had. He had never been east of Saskatchewan, so he was thrilled to go on the trip.

Being named as the leader of an expedition to the ice floes to protect baby seals was beyond his wildest expectations. He could visualize the trip helping him become well known in environmentalist circles. After that, who knew? Maybe he would rise to national or even international prominence.

He knew Glenn Holmes, a PhD candidate at a local university, was handling the arrangements, but he had not met Glenn. They had not even spoken until they met at the Halifax airport.

He understood Glenn was a highly regarded political activist. He had learned that much from Montieth and Appelbaum, who were thrilled to have enlisted him. The reason for their excitement was Glenn would ostensibly, if not publicly, handle their east coast operations. With him, they could claim to have members from coast to coast, a great leap forward for their little-known organization.

From Appelbaum and Montieth, he had also heard stories of Glenn leading anti-war protesters to the US embassy in Ottawa. He gathered their new comrade might be unorthodox, even aggressive, in his approach, but that did not matter.

Green Earth's entire *raison d'être* was to jar the conscience of ordinary people in order to enlist their support for environmental issues. If Glenn's *modus operandi* was unorthodox, even bordering on extreme, he would be a good fit.

As for Glenn's insistence on anonymity, it was perfectly understandable that he would want to keep his distance from them to maintain his academic integrity. The strategy also worked well for Green Earth. They were well schooled in shaping public opinion. They knew that by keeping Glenn out of the fray, they could trot him out later to support them independently.

Upon arrival in Newfoundland, Wainwright believed he would be leading a protest against the killing of baby seals. However, Glenn explained that instead of a protest, they would be doing an exposé. He said they needed coverage of seals being killed — the bloodier the better.

"You know what they say in the media?" Glenn had asked, driving his point home. "If it bleeds, it leads. Reporters aren't going to Newfoundland unless they get a big story, and I intend to give them one."

Wainwright cringed but said nothing.

Glenn went on to explain that because the region where the seal hunt took place was remote and sparsely populated, it was not feasible to transport large numbers of protesters there. Therefore, instead of a protest, a frontal assault, they would use stealth and deception to get what they wanted.

Glenn's revelation that he had staged the entire demonstration shocked Wainwright. Now he could see what Glenn was all about. He had duped everyone. When he got back to Vancouver, Wainwright had to tell Green Earth everything. They would have to decide what to do.

Chapter 16

News of the Wainwright-led expedition reached Vancouver with the first story Bartlett posted. Within minutes, people started contacting the National Animal Welfare Association (NAWA), wanting to save the baby seals. On Thursday, they received a few dozen calls. By Friday, it had increased to hundreds. Response to Saturday's story overwhelmed NAWA's ability to handle the calls.

After the first calls, NAWA's executive director contacted Green Earth to inquire about the expedition. He asked how they wanted NAWA to handle donations flowing into their office. Although accustomed to handling donations for United States-based animal welfare groups, they had no experience dealing with international groups.

Seeing the opportunity for both organizations to capitalize on the publicity, they agreed that NAWA would open a special bank account in New York. They would deposit all funds received for Green Earth. As cash accumulated, they would withhold a twenty-percent processing fee and forward the balance to Green Earth.

New Yorkers opened their wallets, donating over $100,000 on the first weekend. Besides donations, NAWA received calls from people wanting to participate in the next expedition. They were told to contact Glenn in Halifax. He took their names and promised to get back to them as soon as the next expedition was planned.

The strong response in New York was rendered insignificant by that in California, where television coverage resulted in a veritable gold rush that overwhelmed NAWA's Hollywood office.

In addition to telephone calls and donations by mail, several days after the story ran, a steady stream of chauffeur-driven limousines showed up. Nobody noticed the irony of the ultra-rich and celebrities — who wore fur coats, snakeskin boots, belts, and alligator accessories — being so keen to save the seals.

Besides generating over $1 million in donations, offers came in to adopt a baby seal and to form a rescue party to go to the ice floes and protect them. One group even established the Seal Brigade to travel to Newfoundland in a convoy the following season before realizing it would take a week to drive the distance in winter.

*   *   *

It was hard for Wainwright to believe so much had happened in a week. His departure had been inauspicious. Appelbaum and Montieth had dropped him off at the airport. Uncertain as to how it would go but wanting to lay the groundwork for his return, they sent out a media advisory.

It was low-key, stating that Davis Wainwright from Green Earth would lead a fact-finding mission to the East Coast to learn more about the annual seal hunt. It said he would be accompanied by academics and members of the media. It warranted a few lines on page A7.

The stories in the US media on Friday and Saturday, carried across Canada, left Vancouver news teams scrambling to play catch-up. In contrast to his low-key departure, upon his arrival home, Wainwright faced a media frenzy.

Headline-hungry newshounds scrummed him before he could even pick up his luggage. While he may have been a journalism student, nothing prepared him for the ferocity of the pack of reporters that descended upon him.

He froze like a deer in the headlights, giving "yes" and "no" answers to leading questions, one answer sometimes contradicting the previous one.

"Were you satisfied with your exposé of the annual seal hunt?" one reporter asked.

"Yes. I mean no. Well, I'm not really sure."

"Did you actually see baby seals being clubbed to death?" another reporter asked.

"Yes, but it's not really like that."

"Are the stories in the US media true?"

"Well, yes. I mean, no. There's more to it than that."

Finally, Appelbaum and Montieth intervened. Taking their young colleague by the arms, they led him through the cameras.

"You can see Mr. Wainwright is exhausted from his ordeal and the long flight," Montieth said to the clamouring reporters. "We have a press conference at ten tomorrow morning. He'll provide a full account then, when he's better rested."

The debriefing and board meeting at Green Earth, a fractious event, lasted for hours. The initial bloodletting saw Wainwright criticized sharply for going along with Glenn's charade and not pulling out when he realized what was going on. Then Appelbaum and Montieth were criticized for enlisting Glenn and for sending someone as young and inexperienced as Wainwright to oversee the operation.

Some board members had expressed reservations about having the media along before confirming the facts about the seal hunt. They were overruled by those wanting to raise cash and those who believed all publicity was good publicity. Now they were back with a vengeance. Previously rebuffed, they formed a nucleus that wanted Green Earth to disassociate itself from the seal hunt fiasco.

Others wanted to maintain the course. Bug-eyed at the volume of donations flowing in, they wanted to let the deception continue.

Pragmatists on the board, including Wainwright, Appelbaum, and Montieth, argued there was no way to withdraw without exposing what had happened. That would discredit the group.

However, they also refused to repeat the exercise. They argued that the media would lose interest quickly as long as Green Earth did nothing. They wanted to accept the donations but say nothing.

To rid themselves of Glenn, Montieth proposed that he, Appelbaum, and Wainwright travel to Halifax. They would explain that Green Earth was a reputable organization and did not approve of Glenn's tactics and no longer wanted to be associated with him.

Wainwright agreed they should distance themselves from Glenn, but he counselled them to proceed carefully.

*   *   *

Unknown to Green Earth, Glenn was trying to figure out how to sever his relationship with them. They had succeeded beyond his wildest expectations. He wanted to continue — without them.

At per his request to remain in the background, he appeared nowhere in the media. Now he was kicking himself. Green Earth was positioned to take the lead in the seal hunt protest business. They had no need for him.

Except for the money he had diverted to himself, he had nothing to show for his efforts. Given the news coverage and calls he received from potential volunteers, he knew they had stumbled onto one of the best fundraising rackets in the world.

He concocted a plan to maximize the seal hunt protest revenue. He did not intend to include Green Earth or anyone else. He planned to establish a non-profit corporation in Ontario, which offered more anonymity than Nova Scotia allowed. Operating from Toronto, he would also have easy access to the United States, where he could do public appearances on US university campuses. Using expedition photos and footage, he would inflame opposition to the seal hunt to generate donations.

His advance teams were the people already calling him, wanting to save the seals. They could make the arrangements and advertise his visits. They could also pay his travel and accommodation costs. After all, he was a struggling graduate student with limited means.

The silver lining was an instant and plausible exit strategy from the PhD studies he had virtually ignored. He would explain he needed to suspend his academic plans temporarily to return to Toronto to help Green Earth become established there. It could serve as research for his doctoral thesis. His immediate problem was how to get rid of the granola-crunching tree-huggers who ran Green Earth.

* * *

The hotel room meeting was tense. After greeting Glenn, Montieth took the lead in the discussion. They circled each other in conversation like two prize-fighters, each trying to learn his adversary's weakness while giving away no indication of his own.

Initially, Montieth's comments about Glenn's performance were guarded. He hoped to be rid of their "east coast representative" but did not want to give offense or cause controversy that might be difficult to explain publicly. He explained Green Earth was involved in many global initiatives and did not want to concentrate too heavily in any one area, including the seal hunt protest initiative. He also explained that any hint of impropriety by Green Earth would be used by their opponents and would be damaging to the organization.

Early in the discussion, Glenn realized they wanted to get rid of him. Never missing the opportunity to capitalize on another's weakness, he played along. He said he had jeopardized his academic standing to help them, losing an entire academic year. He explained his funding for the year was nearly gone, and his research work could be jeopardized if they pulled out.

"I'm really sorry if I went too far," he said, appearing contrite. "I must've misunderstood your instructions. I believed you when you said the end justi-fied the means."

Montieth shifted in his seat, even more uncomfortable. "I guess we must share the blame with you. Horace or I should have gone with you instead of Davis."

Glenn poured on the guilt. "You must realize I've just come off years of anti-war protesting. People's lives were at stake. The establishment used misinformation against us. To have any impact, we had to adopt the same tactics. I thought I was helping. I don't know what else I could have done."

His explanation was so convincing, Montieth and Appelbaum were at a loss for words. Finally, seeking a way out, Appelbaum interceded.

"So Glenn, where do you see this going?"

Glenn played his ace. "Well, since Green Earth has no interest in con-tinuing down this road, and since my interest is purely academic, if you can compensate me for my lost year, there's no reason we can't part amicably. Then I can get back to my research, as soon as I find new subject matter."

He paused before continuing. "How are donations going? Your

organization has done okay financially from this little caper, hasn't it?"

Montieth cleared his throat. "How much would it take to fully compensate you?" He had no authority to make an offer, but he hoped to put the matter behind them by paying Glenn off.

Glenn responded in a blasé manner, avoiding the first move in an effort to figure out how much he could hit them for. "I don't know. I haven't given it a thought. The financial setback for me is one thing. The lost year is another. I'm sure you want to be fair."

Montieth glanced at Appelbaum, who nodded slightly. Montieth turned back to Glenn. "Would you mind giving us a few moments to discuss this privately?"

"Sure," Glenn replied affably. "I can go down to the coffee shop to give you some privacy. I'd have breakfast if I had the money, but this place is a bit expensive for a student."

Montieth took the bait. "Never mind the coffee shop. Go down to the dining room instead. Have anything you want. Charge it to our room."

"I really appreciate that," Glenn replied. "My fridge is getting pretty bare. I was beginning to think I misjudged you guys, but this might turn out okay after all."

Minutes later, he sauntered into the immaculately appointed dining room. There, the uniformed maître d' seated him in a cherry wood captain's chair at a table for two near a cheerful fireplace.

Ordinarily, Glenn's scruffy jeans and work shirt would have denied him entry to such a snooty place. Anticipating that, Appelbaum had telephoned down to say their colleague, Dr. Glenn Holmes, would be down for breakfast. They were to serve him whatever he ordered and charge it to their room.

No sooner had Glenn left the room than a debate ensued as to how much it would take to be rid of him.

Wainwright, quiet until then, was bursting to speak. "I can't believe it! I just can't believe it! That asshole is playing both of you. He knew exactly what he was doing and what would happen. I say, just cut him loose. Give him nothing. If he squawks, we can expose him for the phony he is."

"Settle down, Davis," Montieth said. "We can see what he's up to. You've forgotten nothing connects him to this escapade except for his physical presence. He's got that covered by claiming to have been along for academic reasons. We must protect Green Earth. We've got to get rid of him. If it takes a few dollars to do that, so be it."

"He's right," Appelbaum concurred. "We've got to play along with him and pay him off, even if it makes us want to puke. That's the only way we can protect the organization. Everybody's got a price. We've just got to figure out his, pay it, and close this chapter. Besides, Wainwright, we've just raised tons of money. If we've got to give Glenn ten or twenty or even twenty-five thousand dollars to get rid of him, I'm all for it."

"You mean you would go up to twenty-five thousand dollars to get rid of that jerk?" Wainwright exclaimed. "I can't believe it! I simply can't believe it!"

"Now Davis," Montieth said, "you know Horace is right. The three of us created this situation. We must protect Green Earth. How much do you think we should offer him?"

The young prairie horse trader reflected momentarily. "I wouldn't offer him anything. I'd let him make the first move. No matter how much or how little he asks for, I would Jew him down as far as I could."

He realized his faux pas when Montieth raised his eyebrows and Appelbaum grimaced.

"I'm really sorry, Horace," Wainwright said. "It's just what we say where I come from. I didn't mean anything by it."

"Don't worry about it," Appelbaum replied. "After two thousand years, we're accustomed to the way you Gentiles refer to us."

All three shared an uncomfortable laugh.

The telephone rang. It was Glenn. He had wolfed down steak and eggs, coffee, and fresh-squeezed orange juice. Then he moved on to a Belgian waffle with strawberries and whipped cream, but he had eaten only half of it. He wanted to know if it was okay to come back.

Appelbaum met him at the door, wearing a used-car-salesman smile. "Come in, Glenn. Thanks for giving us time to confer. I think you'll be happy."

Glenn entered tentatively. First, he looked at Montieth. Then he glanced at Wainwright. Finally, he focused on Montieth, who began to jabber nervously.

"Well, Glenn, Horace is right. The three of us talked it over. Although we haven't contacted Vancouver yet, because they're four hours behind us, we're pretty sure the board would authorize payment to you of twenty-five thousand."

Having rejected Wainwright's suggestion to force Glenn to make the first move, Montieth also ignored Appelbaum's advice to start at $10,000. Montieth had blown the whole wad with his opening offer.

A genuinely reasonable person, Montieth hated dickering. While, due to his seniority and board position, he had the most authority of the three, he was the least equipped to negotiate over money. Egalitarian, he also found it distasteful.

He could not have made a worse move with Glenn. He loved the game, and he knew he held the upper hand, as long as he did not go too far.

Instead of being excited, Glenn responded with dismay. He appeared crestfallen, akin to a five-year-old being told the family trip to Disneyland had been cancelled or that his pet dog had been run over by a truck. He said nothing, but his look, practiced and refined for over twenty years, said it all.

Montieth could not bear the uncomfortable silence that followed his offer. He made his second mistake by beginning to talk again. "What's wrong?" he asked. "We just offered you twenty-five thousand dollars. That's more than a year's pay."

Glenn still looked dejected. Although thrilled with the offer, he wanted to find out how far he could push them.

"Only twenty-five thousand?" he said at last. "That's it? That's all you want to give me for everything I've done and all the sacrifices that I've made? My academic career may be over. At a minimum, I've lost the year. I'm also in danger of being asked to withdraw. If I don't get my PhD from this university, I won't be accepted at another. How will I explain that I organized a venture that generated worldwide publicity when we've agreed I was just along doing academic research?"

Realizing Montieth was ill equipped to conduct negotiations, Appelbaum injected himself into the discussion, trying to slow the pace. "Well, Glenn we just came up with this amount ourselves after speaking with you. It's too early for us to speak with any board members back in Vancouver for formal authorization to offer anything. We don't really know if they would agree to any amount, but we thought we could get them to go along with the twenty-five thousand Philip suggested."

"Then why are we talking about any amount?" Glenn countered. "You came down here and got me to put on this seal hunt escapade. I got you worldwide exposure. My phone's ringing nonstop with volunteers for the next Green Earth expedition. I'm also hearing from NAWA. They're looking after a flood of donations for you like they've never seen before."

Unperturbed, Appelbaum, the consummate chess player, continued. "I understand your point, Glenn. We thought we could wrap this up this morning, but in our haste, we may have minimized the long-term fallout to you."

He looked at his Swiss watch. "Vancouver is four hours behind us. Let us make a few calls to board members to be sure we're authorized to make an offer and how much. Can we touch base right after lunch? It would help if you said how much you think would be fair."

"How much would be fair?" Glenn asked. "I have no idea how much cash this caper generated and will continue to generate for Green Earth. I'll bet you don't know either. You're trying to get rid of me with a measly twenty-five thousand when this thing could easily generate you a million or more. I would've thought one hundred thousand maybe, not twenty-five thousand."

He paused to let the numbers sink in. "If Green Earth lays one hundred thousand bucks on me, I'm gone with no hard feelings. You'll never hear from me again."

This time, Glenn's voice had a different tone to it, a threatening edge that Wainwright had seen before but the others had not. Wainwright thought that maybe now the others could see this son of a bitch for what he was and what Wainwright had to deal with on the road with him for a week.

Montieth was overwhelmed at the enormity of Glenn's demand, its brazenness, and the threatening tone in which he had delivered it.

Holy shit, he thought, *this guy is serious. What are we going to do?*

Appelbaum flinched as if a dentist had stuck a needle in his gums. He realized Glenn was dangerous. The quicker they put him behind them, the better. He struggled to remain calm as he responded. "That's a lot of money, Glenn. We'll see what we can do, but I'm not optimistic." He looked at his colleagues. "If we can get the board to agree, when and where can we meet?"

Sensing he had them on the run, Glenn became more congenial. "Did you say your flight is at four o'clock?"

"I think so," Montieth murmured, still overwhelmed by the magnitude of the demand.

"It's at four fifteen," Wainwright corrected, his face grim.

"Well, we don't want you folks to miss your flight," Glenn said, completely accommodating now. "There's a doughnut place on Robie Street called Tim Horton's. It's named after a hockey player. A lot of people like their coffee. How about if we meet there at two? From there it's only minutes or so to the airport."

Glenn left the room to let them ponder his proposal.

Unnerved and ashen, Montieth turned to the others. "What do we do now?"

Wainwright was the first to respond. "You can't deal with that prick. He's the devil! I think we should stand him up, not meet him. Just catch our flight back to Vancouver and see what the board wants to do."

Never one for confrontation, Montieth turned to Appelbaum. "What do you think, Horace? It might teach him a lesson. Besides, I don't think the board will pay him a hundred grand."

"They will, or at least the majority of them will, when they realize what's at stake," Appelbaum replied.

"What do you mean? What's at stake?" Montieth asked.

"What we've got here," Appelbaum said, "is a Mexican standoff. Glenn is a dangerous guy. If we don't handle him right, he may go to the media with the whole story. How much do you think he can get for the story of what really went down? Any news agency that missed the big story could do an exposé that the entire story was a fraud perpetrated by Green Earth, *The World Today,* and KWOW. We'd be finished. Washed up. Done."

He wiped his sweaty hands on a paper napkin. "We've got to shut him down. The board must understand the risk of doing nothing."

When they met Glenn that afternoon, they had instructions to pay him the $100,000 and a handwritten confidentiality agreement dictated over the telephone by Green Earth's lawyer.

They would end their relationship immediately, and neither would discuss the issue again.

Chapter 17

On a sunny, spring Monday morning, Glenn Holmes, a man on a mission, strode down Bay Street. With him, barely able to keep up but floating on air, was Virginia Whiteway.

She was absolutely thrilled, having not seen the man she adored since the previous August. Even though they spoke by telephone most Sunday evenings, unless he needed something, he never initiated the call.

Virginia, a dedicated student, was content to remain in the subsidized apartment they shared before his departure. The lease was in his name. For all intents and purposes, he still lived there. Besides paying the rent and utilities from her meagre income, unwittingly, she had also been operating part of the collections side of his loan sharking business.

The loans Glenn made to dozens of desperate students were extortionate. The interest rate was 10 percent per month, plus a penalty of 10 percent of the balance in the case of a late payment. Virginia had no idea of the loans' terms, but she had come close to accepting money from Glenn when her student loan arrived late. But for a streak of prairie independence, which caused her to refuse his seemingly generous offer, she may have become one of his customers. Then she would have learned why she had been warned not to accept his help.

Early on, Glenn needed muscle for collections. The forger Al obliged willingly. He had a nephew in university and a son in high school. Both drug dealers, they agreed to help. If any borrower fell behind with a monthly payment, Al's enforcers paid the person a visit. Payment had to be made within twenty-four hours. It included a 10 percent per day late fee plus a collection fee of $50. The collection fee doubled if the collector had to return.

The system worked superbly. Whenever a borrower — generally a student but occasionally a business owner — fell behind, the collectors would visit. The message was always the same. "Mr. Holmes is very disappointed he had to send me for your payment. This time, you can fix the problem with money. Next time, Mr. Holmes will not be so understanding."

Terrified, the borrowers never needed the second visit. A steady stream of envelopes containing money slipped through the apartment mail slot.

Without question, Virginia collected every one. Then, bundling them unopened into one package, she forwarded them faithfully every month by courier.

Over the years since his unceremonious return from San Francisco, Glenn had parlayed the $2,000 the police had given him into over $100,000, first through drug deals and then by investing his profits into loans.

With no immediate need for the money and unable to spend it without attracting attention, he was fearful of having too much money on hand. He had rented safety deposit boxes in two banks. Each of them held $50,000. He stashed the remainder in the ductwork of his parents' furnace.

The problem of too much illicit cash had been nagging Glenn prior to moving East. The solution came during a discussion with a lawyer in Halifax.

He had received three US$10,000 bank drafts, plus CA$10,000 prior to the Newfoundland trip. Looking for a way to safeguard it, he called a Halifax law firm and, in general terms, explained his problem to a senior partner.

"It sounds like you're asking about an offshore bank account," the lawyer, old Digby Bridgewater, said. "From time to time, we have clients with needs similar to yours."

"What are the legalities?" Glenn asked.

"It's perfectly legal as long as you report your income to the government."

"How do I get around that?"

"That's more of an accounting issue that a legal question," Bridgewater replied.

"Can you recommend an accountant?" Glenn asked impatiently.

"I could, but I prefer not to."

"Why not?"

"Halifax is a small city. Some people can't keep their mouths shut. Transactions like yours, going through a local bank, could generate gossip. You said you're back and forth between here and Toronto. You may be better served by an Ontario solicit—"

"So can you refer me to somebody up there or not?"

Maintaining his composure, thinking this kid had potential but lots to learn, Bridgewater answered mildly. "Absolutely. I stayed here in Nova Scotia after graduation. Couldn't pry myself loose from the Maritimes. But several of my classmates went down the road to Toronto. I can call one of them for you."

"Just give me his number," Glenn blustered. "I'll call him myself."

"Actually, Professor Holmes, I don't think that will work very well for you," Bridgewater replied.

Glenn proceeded cautiously, realizing he was in unfamiliar territory. "And why do you say that?"

The balance of power having shifted back to him, Bridgewater responded diplomatically. "My old classmate is very discreet. He only accepts work of this nature by way of referrals from other lawyers. After all," he continued softly, "people with issues like yours require absolute privacy. He doesn't advertise these services or open his door to clients who haven't been vetted by someone he knows well, someone like me."

Momentarily irked, Glenn was still pleased at the implied exclusivity and confidentiality of the arrangement. True to form, he pressed forward, attempting to learn how the arrangement worked.

"That's just it," Bridgewater said. "I don't know. I merely provide a referral of any potentially qualified client, such as yourself. I never know the details. We both prefer it that way."

That was not true. The other lawyer, Barry Lancaster, established offshore accounts for every lawyer who referred clients to him. He paid a 1 percent finder's fee for the referrals, deposited directly to avoid income tax and sharing with their partners.

*   *   *

Just before 10 a.m., Glenn and Virginia arrived at the Bay Street address of Organ, Mandible, and Lancaster, Barristers and Solicitors. It was an unimpressive, older, six-storey brick building. The first floor had a pharmacy. The second floor had an optometrist and a dentist. The third was occupied by a curious assortment of non-profit agencies and a struggling fitness club.

The only sign of any degree of permanence was an older, engraved brass nameplate that said, "Organ, Mandible, and Lancaster, Barristers and Solicitors, fourth floor."

The elevator stopped, and when the doors opened, the couple found themselves in a small rectangular vestibule. They had to ring a buzzer to gain entry to the reception area.

Small, nondescript, but functional, the reception area was furnished with four old leather chairs, a coffee table, a few fake plants, and an assortment of old prints. The left wall featured a sliding door and a thick glass window like an all-night gas bar. Behind the glass barrier, her silver hair secured in a tight bun, sat an ancient but pleasant receptionist.

Putting the telephone on call forward, she arose and moved to her right, disappearing for a moment. Then she came through the sliding door to the left of the glass barrier to join them.

"Good morning," she said. "I'm Jean, Mr. Lancaster's personal secretary. Our receptionist is away on spring vacation. Rather than hire a temp, you know, someone who doesn't know our clients or how the firm works, the other secretaries and I are covering for her." She continued without waiting for a response. "Mr. Holmes, Mr. Lancaster is expecting you, but who is this lovely young lady?"

"Virginia Whiteway," Glenn replied quickly. "We're just friends."

Virginia was stung by the quick, cavalier, dismissive reply. She said nothing, but the older woman saw the change in her, the hurt look and the blush. No stranger to romantic disappointment, Jean came to her rescue.

"Well then," she said to Virginia, "you can keep me company while the gentlemen discuss their business."

She pointed to the doorway through which she had just come. "They call this the signing room. It's a private place for clients to review and sign documents, but guests of clients often use it to relax while they wait. It has today's *Star*, the *Globe and Mail*, and magazines. Would you like anything to drink?" she asked Virginia. "Coffee, tea, juice, or mineral water?"

The centre of attention for the first time since Glenn came into her life, Virginia appreciated the old lady's perceptiveness and genuine hospitality. "Thank you very much. I'd love an apple juice."

Finally, Jean turned to Glenn. "Mr. Lancaster knows you're here. One of his juniors will see you momentarily." She closed the sliding door behind her, leaving Glenn standing alone in the reception area.

Returning to her position at reception, Jean placed an internal call, speaking in a voice loud enough for the other two to hear. "Hi, Mary, can you bring an apple juice to the nice young lady in the signing room?"

Glenn was furious at the outright snub but had no time to dwell on it before the large, brass-hinged oak door to the right of the glass barrier opened. He was greeted by a thin, sallow-faced man in his early thirties who spoke with the mournful demeanour of an undertaker.

"I'm Bob Holliday. I work for Mr. Lancaster. Please come with me."

Without waiting for a response or even a handshake, he turned and walked through the doorway, leaving Glenn to follow him. The spring-loaded door closed on its own behind Glenn.

Glenn, a cold fish, did not care one way or another whether he shook hands with anybody. He was there for business. He felt all that handshaking and backslapping was simply a charade, a waste of time to be endured but not encouraged. He would have been amused to learn that Bob Holliday, a germophobe, never shook hands and recoiled at being touched by others.

*   *   *

Standing in Lancaster's palatial office, looking past an enormous oak desk, behind which was a high-backed leather armchair, initially, Glenn could not tell if he was alone or not. The question was answered when he heard a man's voice.

"Thank you very much. We'll look after it for you."

The chair swivelled around, and Glenn found himself facing a well-tanned man in his mid-forties. The man stood up immediately.

"Let me apologize for my lack of manners," he said. "I had to take that call. I'm Barry Lancaster. An old friend from Halifax called me about you."

He strode around the desk, shaking hands vigorously with Glenn and inviting him to sit at a marble coffee table.

"Anything I tell you is completely confidential, right?" Glenn asked, unaccustomed to dealing with lawyers.

"Absolutely," Lancaster confirmed. "Anything you tell me or anyone who works for or with me is governed by solicitor-client privilege. That means it can't be repeated unless you consent in writing."

Glenn produced an envelope that contained five bank drafts. One was for $100,000, the others for $10,000 each. "I'd like to start with these. Do you handle cash?"

Lancaster laughed. "Absolutely, but we charge an extra five percent to turn it into paper, so it's to your advantage to convert it before you bring it to us."

"I also understand you can set up a non-profit corporation for me, just like Green Earth. Is that right?"

"You need to speak with my partner, Charlie Organ. He handles the corporate work. Let me see if he's available."

Glenn met with Organ, and by the time he left an hour later, he had provided instructions to incorporate a new company that would be called SOBSI, an acronym for Save Our Baby Seals Incorporated.

PART 2

THE SOLDIER

Chapter 18

The Dictionary of Newfoundland English defines a *spudgel* as a small wooden pail with a handle attached used to bail out a boat. Cheap, simple to make, easy to replace, on shore you rarely think of a spudgel. But if you're at sea in a small open boat struggling to stay afloat, steering into the teeth of a storm, with the bow rising on one wave and crashing down on the next, trying to split each one evenly to avoid capsizing, driving sheets of water left and right, with the spray filling your craft, all you can think of is a spudgel.

Once ashore, the spudgel is not celebrated. It is stored in the shed with the fuel tank, oars, and other equipment. Or, easy to replace and of little value, it may lie in the boat, forgotten until the next emergency.

Billy Wheeler, a soldier, was in most respects a spudgel.

William John Wheeler, the fourth of five children, was born to Brenda and Riley Wheeler on July 1, 1967. Before him came two brothers and a sister, and another sister followed soon after his birth.

Does birth order matter in a person's life?

Maybe.

How about birth date?

Perhaps.

Except for his mother, who carried him for nine months, Billy's birth was nothing special to the people around him. He was not the first child in the family for everyone to make a big fuss over. He was the fourth. He was not the first son to carry on the family name. He was the third. He was not the youngest of the family for everyone to dote on for very long as another quickly succeeded him. He did not even have his own special birthday, because he was born on Canada Day, the day when everyone celebrated the nation's birth, not Billy's.

If birth order and birth date are important, the casual observer might conclude that little good could come from being born in such chronological obscurity. In Billy's case, the opposite was true.

For his first few years, his crib served as a ringside seat, from which he was forced to watch the battles of his four older siblings. He watched as the stronger preyed on the weaker, as the smarter manipulated the others, conniving and conspiring for any advantage. While only a toddler, Billy learned the difference between a lie and the truth, cruelty and compassion, stinginess and generosity.

He also developed a deeply ingrained sense of justice, so when confronted by a sibling being treated unjustly, forced to observe but powerless to intervene, he would become deeply distressed, sometimes physically ill, and throw a tantrum.

If a keen sense of justice evolved from observing the older children compete, Billy Wheeler, a kind little soul by nature, developed a nurturing spirit and helped the youngest child.

His older brothers had followed their father into the fishery. They would take over the family fishing enterprise when he retired, so there was no opportunity there. Billy did not want to spend more time studying than necessary, so in the footsteps of a classmate who had enlisted the previous year, Billy joined the Canadian Armed Forces.

It was a chance for adventure, maybe to learn a trade and to have steady pay while he figured out what to do with his life. Had he given any thought to engaging in combat, he may have chosen something else. But, as far as he knew, Canada had not been in any wars for a long time, so he did not consider combat a possibility.

Although he did not realize it, Billy was an ideal recruit. At age eighteen, he was physically fit, respectful of his superiors, anxious to get ahead, but not too far ahead of his peers so as to incite their jealousy.

Having never left Newfoundland, and his travels within the province limited to a few high school hockey and basketball tournaments, his worldview was limited and naïve. Those attributes were not necessarily seen as shortcoming for someone expected to understand and carry out orders without question.

His wilderness survival skills and familiarity and proficiency with firearms were superb. An intelligent, clean-living, hardworking soldier, after a few years in uniform, Billy decided to make it a career.

Billy was particularly impressed by Josh Short. From Yankee Point, just a two-hour drive north of Spudgels Cove, Josh was the youngest corporal and then the youngest sergeant in his unit. He had been raised by his grandparents, Reuben and Naomi Short, who had done everything in their power to see him continue his education beyond high school — even saving a considerable sum of money for that purpose.

The trouble was Josh was an outdoors guy and did not like school. In his final year of high school, he asked his grandparents to let him to join the Canadian Armed Forces.

"I can go in the Army for four years," he reasoned with his grandmother. "You keep the money invested for me. If, after four years, I decide to go to college or university, the education fund will still be available for me. If I like the Army, I can stay. Whenever I come out, I can use the money to buy a house or start a business."

* * *

By 1992, Billy, now twenty-five and a corporal, had served for nearly seven years. Things were going well for him. For nearly a year, he had been in a relationship with Emma, a young widow with two small children. Her husband, Roger Elms, killed in a training accident, had been a close friend.

While Roger was alive, Billy visited frequently, often bringing gifts to the children and even reading them bedtime stories. They adored him, calling him Uncle Billy.

Before Roger's death, Emma, a chronic matchmaker, had tried several times to set up Billy with one of her girlfriends. While he did not discourage her, each time, he lost interest after a few dates. Emma was beginning to wonder if Billy, so outgoing around her, was even interested in the opposite sex.

She did not realize that while he felt safe around her, around women in general, he was guarded. Shy by nature, in high school he had been rejected by girls he liked. Not wanting to repeat those painful experiences, he rarely showed any more than a casual interest in women.

Roger's sudden death was a shock. Grief-stricken and overwhelmed at the prospect of raising the two children by herself, Emma was in a fog. Then one day she snapped out of it when four-year-old Kayla asked, "Mommy, did Uncle Billy get killed, too?"

"Why would you say that?" Emma asked, stunned.

"Before Daddy got killed and went to heaven, Uncle Billy used to come here all the time. He doesn't come here anymore, so I thought he might've been killed and went up to heaven with Daddy."

"No, honey," Emma replied. "Uncle Billy didn't get killed, but you're right, he hasn't been here for a long time. Maybe he's away. How about if I call him and ask if he would like to come over and have dinner with us just like when Daddy was alive?"

"Do you think he'll read us a story after dinner, just like he did before Daddy died?"

Instead of answering, Emma picked up the telephone and dialled. Luckily, Billy was in his barracks, as she did not want to leave a message that could set off unwanted gossip.

"Hi Billy," she said. "How are you doing?"

"I'm doing fine," he responded flatly, "but I sure miss Roger. I miss you and the kids, too."

"We miss you, too," she said. "You haven't been around, and you haven't called. Is everything okay?"

"I thought of calling you a few times. First your family was here, and I didn't want to be a bother. After that, I just didn't know what to say."

"Never mind all that," Emma said. "When can you come for dinner? We would love to see you, and the kids want you to read to them. Can you manage that?"

"I leave tomorrow morning, but I'll be back in a week."

"What do you mean 'a week'? What about today?"

"Today works fine for me," he replied, "but isn't it short notice for you?"

"Billy, you're like family to us. I'll just order a couple of pizzas from the Hut, a Canadian and a meat lovers', just like when Roger was alive. How does five o'clock work?"

"See you then," he said.

As she hung up, she thought his tone was a little more upbeat than it had been moments earlier.

At precisely five o'clock, Billy was standing on the doorstep of Emma's house. The evening went well. It was just like old times. At eight, with both children sound asleep, Billy gave Emma a hug, promised to call her the following week when he got back to base, and then headed back to his barracks.

A week later, as promised he called and came by for dinner again. This time, he brought the food — Chinese.

For the next few months, whenever possible, he visited, sometimes three or four times a week. Then one evening, as they were standing at the front door saying goodnight, Emma stopped him.

"Billy, one of my girlfriends will be visiting next week. I told her about you, and I think you're perfect for each other."

"Don't bother," he said abruptly.

She paused for a moment. "Did I say something wrong?"

He appeared to relax a bit. "Emma, I appreciate what you're trying to do for me, but I'm just not interested in your friend."

She watched him shift uncomfortably from one foot to the other. "Come on, Billy, you don't even know her. I know both of you, and I think you're perfect for each other." She smiled, "Don't tell me you've met somebody and haven't told me."

Billy blushed slightly. "Actually, I have met somebody."

"Well, tell me about her," Emma said, mystified. "When do I get to meet her?"

"That's just it," he said. "She's a friend. I haven't told her how I feel. I'm afraid if I cross that line, things might not work out, and I might lose the friendship."

Emma put her hands on her hips. "Billy Wheeler, you've got to tell her. You've got to risk it. Otherwise, how can you ever move forward?"

"Good enough then," Billy said, throwing caution to the wind. "It's you!"

Now it was Emma's turn to be lost for words.

"I was afraid this would happen," he mumbled and then turned to leave.

"Wait," she said. "Please don't leave."

He turned back to look at her. In the small, dimly lit porch, he saw tears streaming down her face.

"I'm sorry," he said. "I didn't mean to make you unhappy."

"I'm not unhappy," she said. "I just can't believe you feel that way about me. I know you love the kids, and they love you, but I thought that was because you and Roger were so close. Are you sure you feel that way about me?"

With that, he crossed the short distance between them, took her in his arms, and kissed her — a long, slow, passionate kiss. Her body melted into his.

"Billy Wheeler," she exclaimed when they came up for air. "I can't believe this is you! I can't believe we're doing this!"

Sensing more of an invitation than an objection, he picked her up, carried her through the kitchen, past the living room, past the small bedroom where both children were sleeping, and into the master bedroom, where he placed her gently on the bed.

"Are you sure you're okay with this?" he asked.

"Lock the door," she whispered, "in case the children wake up. I don't know how I'll feel tomorrow, but right now, this is exactly what I want."

An hour later, Billy got up, leaving her in bed. "I'll lock the door on the way out."

"I'll cook dinner tomorrow evening," she replied. "Come over. After the kids go to bed, we've got to discuss what we just did."

They never did discuss the events of that evening. Billy was uncomfortable discussing his feelings, and Emma did not want to jinx it. Instead, their relationship continued in secret with the fierce intensity of people who had stumbled upon a soulmate they had both been seeking their entire lives but never expected to find. They could not get enough of each other.

The only discussion they had was in response to Billy's question about birth control.

"I had an IUD inserted a few years ago," Emma said. "The doctor said it should be fine for five years. I intended to have it removed after we lost Roger, but I didn't get around to it. There's no need to worry; we're safe."

* * *

A few months later, Emma awoke with a familiar, unexpected, and unwanted feeling. Slight nausea and sensitive breasts signalled a possible pregnancy. That might be okay in year or two, if their relationship stood the test of time, but this was too soon. Panicked, she had to find out for sure.

She threw on the children's clothes and then headed to the drugstore to buy a pregnancy test. In her haste, she arrived there a half hour before it opened. Realizing her mistake, she turned to the children.

"Mommy needs to buy something here, but would you like to have breakfast at McDonald's first?"

Her request was greeted with the expected chorus of cheers, followed quickly by, "Can I have ice cream?"

"Breakfast first, and then if you're still hungry, we can talk about ice cream," she replied.

Having no appetite, her mind racing, she sat and sipped a coffee as her children devoured their breakfast. How could this have happened? What would Billy say? How would he feel? They needed more time. Perhaps the test would come back negative.

Grateful the elderly pharmacist was working alone and that she did not have to encounter any of his staff, Emma bought two pregnancy tests. Rushing home, she headed straight to the bathroom and used the first test.

Just as she suspected: positive.

Anxious, she waited two hours and then administered the second test.

Positive.

She called her doctor's office.

"He's completely booked this week and next week," the receptionist said, "but I can get you in to see him next Thursday afternoon."

"That won't work for me," Emma replied sharply. "I've got to see him today."

"But he's really overbooked," the receptionist said. "He's been on call all week, and he's been called out for the past three nights. I know you would prefer to see him, but if it's an emergency, why don't you just go to the hospital?"

"You don't understand," Emma said. "Dr. Maloney inserted an IUD for me a few years ago. He said I wouldn't have to worry for five years, maybe longer. My husband was killed last year, and now I think I'm pregnant. I don't know what I'm going to do. I've got to know for sure before I tell the father. I thought I was safe. He did, too."

"Why don't you go to the drugstore and get a home pregnancy test?" the receptionist suggested. "They're pretty reliable. That's the first thing the doctor will do."

"I did that this morning, and it came back positive," Emma replied, now tearful.

"Okay," the receptionist said, "I'll speak with Dr. Maloney, but just to be sure, why don't you pick up another test, just in case something was wrong with the first one. They're not always one hundred percent accurate, you know."

"I already did that," Emma said. "I've just got to see him."

The receptionist sighed. "Okay, I'll book you for four thirty. He has appointments until five thirty, but sometimes there are cancellations. I'll tell him why you're coming. He may want you to do another test while you're here."

Emma was at the doctor's office by 4:15, and he saw her immediately.

"Calm down, Emma," the white-haired doctor said, fatherly concern in his Irish-accented voice. "First of all, we need to be certain that you're pregnant, and then we can talk. You know Katie, my receptionist. She'll help you if you have any issues administering the test."

The third test came back positive.

It was after 5:30 before she saw Dr. Maloney again. He explained that, while IUDs are highly effective, no birth control method was completely foolproof.

"We can attempt to remove it, but that would probably cause an abortion. If that's what you want to do, it can be justified on medical grounds. But if you do it, you will still need to decide which form of birth control you want to use, assuming you want to continue in your current relationship." He paused, his brow furrowed. "Is it serious?"

"Serious, but complicated," she replied, and then told him about their relationship. "I think he'll propose to me. We haven't been public about our relationship, mostly because of Roger's family."

Dr. Maloney nodded, now having a better idea of her situation. "Sometimes the IUD will work after you become pregnant, resulting in a miscarriage. Sometimes it causes no problems and is expelled when the baby is born. We just don't know how it will go."

Chapter 19

"We're headed to Bosnia in two weeks," was the first inkling Billy had of the life-changing events he was about to face. "You'll get your first briefing at one thousand hours."

Billy's commander went on to say that Billy's unit would be deployed to Bosnia for approximately six months. The announcement took Billy completely off guard, throwing a wrench into the plans he was making for Emma, the kids, and himself — plans he had not yet shared with her, plans he was not sure she would agree with but which he hoped desperately she would.

Billy was planning to propose to Emma and had even bought a ring. He had planned to propose to her over Christmas but lost his nerve. Then he thought he would do so at midnight on New Year's Eve at a party they were attending with friends. But he did not want to do so in front of other people, so he procrastinated.

He was hoping she and the kids would come home with him to Spudgels Cove in July for a big community wedding. Then she could meet his entire family and, after the wedding, spend a few weeks there.

Even though a Newfoundland wedding was his first choice, in truth, he was madly in love with her, adored the kids, and would have done anything she wanted. The last thing he wanted was to be deployed to anywhere for the next six months.

For the rest of the day, he was in emotional turmoil. Should he tell her about the deployment, propose, and then, if she accepted, make marriage plans upon his return?

He had to tell her about the deployment, but was it fair to propose and then be shipped out for the next six months? What if she lost interest in him and found someone else while he was away?

As soon as he finished up at 5 p.m., he started calling her but got no answer. By 6 p.m., still getting no answer, he was completely distressed and decided to drive to her place, arriving at 6:15 and finding nobody at home. Alarmed, his worry changed to anger when Emma showed up with the kids a few minutes later.

"I've been trying to reach you for over an hour," he blurted in a rare display of frustration. "Where have you been?"

He may have gone further, but after taking in her tear-stained and uncharacteristically haggard face, something made him pause.

"I've been to the doctor," she said.

"Are you okay?" he asked. "Are the kids okay?"

"Yes, I'm okay, and the kids are fine. Nobody's sick, but we need to talk. In private."

Apprehensive, but putting up a good front, Billy turned to the kids. "It's six thirty. Is anybody hungry?"

"No, Uncle Billy," they replied in unison. "We had grilled cheese sandwiches and milk over at Aunt Julie's house. Will you play with us?"

By 8 p.m., the kids were asleep, and the Chinese food, delivered earlier, was cold. With both of them seated at the kitchen table, Emma initiated the conversation.

"So, what's the big news you got at work today? Did you get promoted or something?" she asked, a feeble attempt at humour.

Typically, he avoided a direct response. "Ladies first. Why did you need to go to the doctor if nobody is sick?"

She looked down, fidgeting with a fortune cookie. "Do you remember me telling you I wasn't concerned about getting pregnant because I have an IUD?"

"Yes."

"Remember how I told you they work *almost* all the time?"

The colour drained from his face. "You're not," he whispered.

She nodded. "I am."

The fortune cookie crumbled, pieces falling on the table.

"What do you want to do?" he asked.

She looked directly into his eyes. "That depends on what you want to do."

Putting down his chopsticks, he stood up. "Hold that thought."

He left the house and walked to his car, where he unlocked the glove compartment, removing a small, white jewellery-store box.

Returning, he got down on one knee, held up the box to her, and opened the lid to display a diamond engagement ring. "This is what I want to do."

She stared at it, stunned. "How long have you had this?"

"Since before Christmas," he answered. "You didn't answer my question, but before you do, I need to tell you about something that happened today that might make a difference to whether you say *yes* or *no*."

"You mean the fact that I'm pregnant?"

"No. I was hoping to propose as soon as I could find the right moment and get up enough nerve. I was also hoping that you would agree for us to be married in Newfoundland in July, when I'm on leave. You could meet my family, the kids could come, and we would have a nice time."

"That sounds wonderful," she replied, "except now I'll be seven months' pregnant on my wedding day — unless I miscarry, which Dr. Maloney says is a real possibility with the IUD still in place. Besides, I don't even know your family. What will they think?"

"Don't worry about my family," he replied. "They're wonderful people and very understanding. If I love you, they'll love you, too. But what do you mean you might miscarry?"

She explained what Dr. Maloney had told her earlier in the day, giving him one more thing to worry about.

"But what were you going to tell me that happened today that could change any of this?" she asked. "Did something happen to your annual leave that you might not get time off in the summer?"

His face became glum. "Today we were told that my unit is being shipped out in two weeks." He explained it was only a routine peacekeeping mission, but they would be apart for six months.

Slowly adjusting to the sobering realization that she would be alone with the children for most of the pregnancy, Emma fell silent once again.

"You still haven't said if you want the ring!" he said, finally breaking the silence.

"Oh, Billy, I'm sorry for leaving you hanging. Yes! Yes! Yes! With all of my being I want the ring, but more importantly I want what comes with it: You, the man of my dreams. You!" She smiled. "Is that good enough for you?"

"Almost," he said, his face serious.

Her smile faltered. "What do you mean?"

"I can't leave the woman I love, who's carrying my child, to go to a foreign country for six months without getting married. You'd be going around here pregnant and unmarried. That doesn't work for me. Unless you've got a better idea, I want to speak to the chaplain about marrying us before I ship out. That will answer a lot of questions before they're even asked. We can have our big celebration after I return.

It's really the best thing for us to do," he said, seeing her hesitate. "Think of the children. Think of Roger's family. We're going to get married anyway, so let's just do it now, as quickly as possible. Besides," he grinned, "think of how you'll look in the wedding pictures if we get married now compared to seven months from now."

"Asshole!" she said with a laugh. "That's a low blow, even for you." She sighed. "It's really fast, but it feels so right."

He stood up and they held each other in a loving embrace.

"It will be fine Emma; better than fine. You and me will be forever."

Chapter 20

A few days after the wedding, along with the other members of his unit, Billy boarded a military plane and headed across the Atlantic to Canadian Forces Base Baden-Soellingen in Germany.

Upon arrival, they were told they had been selected to be part of a battalion-sized Canadian task force to serve in the soon-to-be-created United Nations Protective Force (UNPROFOR) headed to the former Yugoslavia.

First of all, they were put through four weeks of intense training. The physical training, weapons training, and equipment training were not much different from any training they would have received on any mission. The cultural, historic, and language training was a different story.

The lead trainer told them they needed to be aware of such things. Knowing why people in that small country were killing each other would help them do their job better and could save their lives. He explained the antagonisms and grievances went back a thousand years. The region had been a battlefield for centuries.

The situation came down to three groups: Serbs, Croats, and Muslims. Even though both Serbs and Croats were Christians — one being Roman Catholic and the other Orthodox — they were intent on eliminating as many of the other group as they could, including civilians. The Muslims had also suffered discrimination for centuries. Both Christian groups would be happy to see them eliminated.

Twenty-five million people were jammed into a country smaller than Newfoundland and Labrador that was created artificially at the end of World War Two. They named the country "Yugoslavia", which means "South Slavs".

From the country's creation until his death in 1980, Yugoslavia had been under the control of General Josef Tito and his communist party. After his death, things began to fall apart as different groups tried to form their own countries, breaking up Yugoslavia along ethnic lines.

This had resulted in civil war the previous year, and civilian casualties were high. Each group accused the others of unspeakable atrocities. The United Nations had brokered a ceasefire. As part of UNPROFOR, Billy's unit was there to help oversee it.

They were cautioned that all sides were heavily armed. Some of them were factions of the former Yugoslav army, and some were militias established by the new governments set up by strongmen who had grabbed parts of the country and were intent on holding onto it.

One distasteful feature of the conflict was ethnic cleansing. Over the years, various groups had migrated from one part of the country to another, with minority groups widely distributed. Many leaders were eliminating minority groups from their territory.

Initially, the UN wanted their troops to move in quickly, with trucks for transportation and nothing more than their rifles and sidearms for personal protection, but the Canadian general refused.

"I know these Slavs," he said. "They're a bunch of tough bastards. They fought the Germans to the finish and stood up to the Russians. You might have a ceasefire right now, but if it doesn't last, and they go at it again, this entire region will be a war zone, with my troops caught in the middle. We'll be armed and equipped, or we won't go."

Chapter 21

In the brilliant sunshine, the Canadian unit left Germany by train. As they headed for Yugoslavia, the atmosphere was upbeat. While travelling across the beautiful countryside of Germany, Austria, and Czechoslovakia, the soldiers played cards and smoked. Some talked about things back home while others discussed the peacekeeping mission.

None had seen any combat, but they were not concerned. A ceasefire was in effect. Travelling under the United Nations flag, they believed that by just showing up in their blue helmets, they would have a calming effect on the combatants.

The prior month's training had been intense, leaving little opportunity for personal time; however, the train ride was exactly opposite, leaving them with plenty of free time. On the first evening, Billy and Josh, who was leading Billy's unit, finally had a chance to catch up.

"So, how is all this going for you?" Josh asked.

"I really like this exercise," Billy replied. "It seems like we may finally get a chance to put our training to use. It sounds like the fighting is over."

"Home?" Josh asked.

"I know," Billy said. "I can't wait to go back home to Emma and the kids. She's pregnant, you know."

Josh smiled. "That's great news! I was wondering why the hurry to get hitched before you left base. I would have thought that a man of the world like you would've taken precautionary measures so that didn't happen, accidentally least." He nudged Billy playfully.

"That's just it," Billy answered, blushing slightly, "we thought we were fine, because she had one of those IUD things. I guess they don't work all the time. The doctor said sometimes they work a few months later than they're supposed to and cause a miscarriage, so I'm pretty worried about her being home without me and that happening."

Embarrassed he had made light of Billy's situation, it was Josh's turn to blush. "Let me know if you need any special telephone privileges. I won't mention this to anyone."

Billy nodded his thanks and then changed the subject. "Do you think we really need all this equipment for peacekeeping?" he asked, referring to the M113 armoured personnel carriers they were bringing.

"I hope not," Josh replied, "but the general has already been on the ground ahead of us. These units will protect us from mines and snipers, and none of our senior NCOs are complaining about being over-equipped, so I'm fine with it."

Billy nodded. "I get that, but that doesn't explain why so many of them are equipped with all that firepower. I mean, eight-one millimetre anti-tank missiles. You don't need firepower like that for peacekeeping. You think the general is overreacting, or does he figure a big show of force is a better way to keep the peace?"

"Your guess is as good as mine," Josh replied, "but I'd rather have them than not."

Crossing from Czechoslovakia into Yugoslavia, they went from serene, breathtakingly beautiful landscape to equally breathtaking but conscience-jarring devastation. Deserted towns and villages dotted the area. Where people had lived recently were burned-out homes, businesses, and churches. Crater-pocked roads and shattered bridges impeded travel, the only sign of life being birds and the occasional stray dog.

Apart from gasps of shock and revulsion, silence descended on the rail-cars as the soldiers began to realize what might lie ahead.

"I can't believe it's just eight years since the country hosted the winter Olympics!" one soldier said.

A more sombre group of soldiers than had boarded the train in Germany arrived in Yugoslavia. At their first briefing, their commanding officer warned them to be careful, as another unit had been fired on the previous day. However, they saw no sign of danger on the drive to their camp, which was located in a nearly deserted town.

As they settled in, people who had been in hiding began to appear from what had seemed like deserted buildings. The absence of any military activity and the immediate gratitude of the locals at the arrival of the Canadian soldiers, with their tiny red maple leaf insignia on their uniforms, reinforced the belief of many troops that this peacekeeping mission had already succeeded.

Later that afternoon, two teenage boys came to the camp to warn them they had heard the camp would be attacked that evening. It was passed off as idle gossip, the young fellows trying to ingratiate themselves with the new-comers by pretending to have useful information or possibly even attempting to elicit a response from them.

Later that evening, they heard artillery fire in the distance, but one of the officers said there was nothing to worry about, as the town was well beyond the range of the artillery batteries. He was wrong.

Unknown to him, the artillery had moved. After dark, they opened fire on the town. The unit suffered no casualties, but five members of a family were killed when their home took a direct hit and collapsed on them.

The next day, Billy and Josh's unit went on their first patrol, located the hostile artillery battery, and neutralized it. Word must have gotten back to the militants that the Canadians were equipped and willing to fight, because there were no more attacks.

A few days after their arrival, Billy received the call from home he had dreaded. Emma had been taken to hospital and had miscarried. Although she was okay, there had been complications, and she had to remain in hospital.

For the next few days until he could speak to her, Billy went around in a daze. When he and Emma finally spoke, it was an anguished phone call. The IUD had caused an infection, and Emma had nearly died.

Both of them were wracked with guilt, Emma for the loss of the child and Billy because he was thousands of kilometres away, protecting strangers instead of being home with Emma and the children.

Chapter 22

A few weeks later, some of the NCOs were assembled informally to be briefed on a new mission that barely aligned with their peacekeeping role. The NCOs were told civilians were being terrorized at night by a group known as the Vipers. Their *modus operandi* was to infiltrate defenceless towns after dark, select a family, and the torture them, forcing the men to watch them rape the women and girls and then forcing the women to watch them execute the men before leaving.

The message to others in those towns was simple and effective: Leave now or this will happen to your family! Heeding that message, terrorized villagers left with the few possessions they could carry, vacating homes to be sold to the right ethnic newcomers.

Little evidence of the Vipers existed, except for the stories of traumatized survivors. It was rumoured the plan was devised by a leader, a psychopath trained as a psychiatrist. He knew how to generate maximum terror with minimum effort in a way that also minimized property damage, allowing his supporters to occupy the vacant homes. It was also rumoured that two of his sons had interrupted their university studies to devote time to their father's mission. They were leading some of the squads.

The proposed Canadian mission, unofficial and unauthorized, was being headed up by the camp's second-in-command so the commanding officer could deny liability if things went wrong. The camp was located at a crossroads, so the plan was to load up four M113 armoured personnel carriers with two five-man squads each and send them in four different directions and drop them off before dark, putting eight squads in the field.

After nightfall, they would work their way back toward the camp on foot. If they caught any Vipers, they were to take them prisoner, transport them back to camp, and turn them over to the UN for prosecution as war criminals.

Officially, the mission would never be recorded or reported anywhere

— unless they were successful. Even then, only the squad that apprehended the Vipers would be acknowledged. Any report would be sanitized to show a reconnaissance mission ran later than expected and accidentally stumbled upon the perpetrators.

Cpl. Billy Wheeler was second-in-command of a five-man squad, led by Sgt. Josh Short, which also included three privates. Approximately ten kilometres from the base, after scouting the town, their M113 disappeared behind a burned-out church. There, the soldiers got out, took cover, and waited for nightfall. Then they crept into the darkened town.

As they neared the centre of town, they were surprised to come across a large, two-storey home with lights on inside. Josh motioned for Billy to take one of the privates and check it out while they kept watch from the street.

Entering a rock-walled courtyard through an iron gate, in the dim light coming from inside, Billy could make out that the gate had a lock, which appeared to have been broken recently. The broken lock and the sounds coming from within caused his already elevated adrenaline to rise even more. A sense of dread washed over him.

He heard men laughing inside amid anguished howls and moans, as if somebody was torturing small, defenceless animals. The sound sent chills through his body, causing the hair on the back of his neck to stand up. He stole across the stone walkway and then motioned to the young private to stand watch.

Billy tiptoed through the home's smashed front door and then made his way through a small entranceway into a large kitchen. By the light of a small oil lamp, he saw it was empty. Noticing a crib in a small room off the kitchen, he looked closer — and nearly retched.

Inside were the bodies of two recently murdered children — a two-year-old girl bayoneted through the body as she slept and an infant whose head had been smashed to a pulp, likely by a rifle butt. He steadied himself before going through a narrow hallway to a large room at the back of the home.

Inside, five Vipers were holding the family hostage. Bodies of two men were on the floor. The older, white-haired man's throat had been cut, and he had bled out on the carpet. The other, a dark-haired man in his forties, was riddled with bullets. Four women were huddled against the back wall.

They appeared to be a grandmother, mother, and two girls in their late teens. By their dishevelled look and torn, dirty clothing, all four of them had been raped. Standing unsteadily over them was a jubilant teenage Viper with a half-empty wine bottle in one hand and an AK-47 in the other.

The soul-searing sounds that Billy had heard from outside were coming from the mother and grandmother. The two girls were mute, simply sitting, their bodies leaning up against the wall for support, tears running down their ashen faces.

Three Vipers stood near the back of the room, each drinking from a stolen bottle of wine, cheering loudly. In the middle of the floor, wearing a sergeant's uniform, was a large, bearded Viper on top of a girl no more than ten years old. He was so large and she so small that only her hands and feet were visible. As the others cheered him on, two of them had a foot placed firmly on the backs of two teenage boys, pinning them to the floor, forcing them to watch the tragedy unfold.

Billy lifted his rifle and put a bullet through the big rapist's neck, killing him instantly. The other four froze. The youngest dropped both weapon and wine bottle. He fell to his knees, raising his hands in surrender, his gleeful expression replaced by a mask of fear.

That left all of them unarmed.

The leader, a colonel, was the first to regain his composure as he took in Billy's blue UN helmet.

"I'm afraid you've killed my sergeant," he said in a slurred, plummy, English-accented voice, indicating a private school education. "I can get more sergeants, but how are you going to explain to your superiors that you shot this unarmed man?"

Taken aback at first by the educated, privileged accent, Billy recovered quickly. "I'll worry about that later. Now, up against the wall, all of you. I'm going to take you in and turn you over to the authorities. They can deal with you."

"You're wasting your time," the colonel replied. "We'll soon be released and back at work eliminating these vermin from our country. You can't stop us."

"I can stop you," Billy said. He swung his weapon a few degrees left and shot the colonel between the eyes. The bullet made a small hole in his forehead but exploded out the back of his head. A spray of blood made a round, wet pattern on the wall behind him.

As the two standing with him went for their guns, Billy shot them both, two shots each through the body, driving them back toward the wall. They fell to the floor, dying.

The youngest, who had remained motionless, pleaded for his life. Knowing any witnesses would spell doom for all of them, and that this kid was at least a murderer and rapist in training, Billy shot him through the head. Just then, the private came through the door.

"Get Sarge!" Billy yelled. "I'll stay here with the family until he comes."

*　*　*

Outside, Josh and the others had heard the gunfire. First a single shot and then another single shot, followed by two quick bursts, a brief pause, then another shot. Josh ordered the two privates to take up defensive positions outside of the rock wall while he went inside to investigate.

Before he could enter, he was met by the private who had been with Billy. The private's face was white.

"Sarge, the corporal is fine, but he needs you back there." He nodded toward the inside of the house. "Right now. It's really bad!"

When Josh entered the kitchen, he noticed the crib in the adjoining room. He looked in and saw the dead babies. Then he went through the hall into the large room.

Amid the carnage, Billy was on his hands and knees, his helmet beside him. Clutching his rifle in one hand and supporting his weight with the other, he was vomiting on the floor. In addition to the two dead villagers, Josh saw five dead Vipers. One near the back of the room had pink froth and bubbles coming from his mouth.

On the floor near the left wall, two white-faced boys in their early teens were holding two girls in their late teens. All of them were sobbing uncontrollably.

In the middle of the floor, two women, one of them an older, gray-haired woman, the other middle-aged and black haired, were holding a ten or eleven-year-old bloodstained girl. She appeared to be unconscious.

Much of the blood covering her upper body had come from the Viper who had been raping her when Billy entered the room. However, the brutal rape had caused serious internal injuries, significant blood loss, and a loss of consciousness. Without medical attention, she would die.

Josh's training kicked in. "Soldier. Stand and report," he said in a loud, clear, controlled voice.

Billy stood up, faced his squad leader, and saluted sharply.

Noting the value training brought to situations like this, Josh returned the salute. "At ease, Wheeler. What happened here?"

In a minute or two, Billy explained in detail what had happened, leaving nothing out.

Josh's eyes narrowed, his pupils locked, laser-like, onto Billy's eyes. "That may be what you think happened, but it did not happen. First of all, we're not here tonight. This mission is unauthorized. If that happened, we're looking at being court-martialled. I'm going to give you two stories. If we can put this together right, we may yet get back to base, and nobody will be the wiser. If that doesn't work, and it's found out we were here, you will say we were on a regular patrol. We ran later than expected and were looking to take shelter with these people until the armoured personnel carrier could come and pick us up.

What we didn't know is that these five," he pointed to the five dead Vipers, "were holding the family hostage. When you stumbled in from the dark, you were caught in a Mexican standoff with them. No shots were fired. They took off through the back door. You were the only one of the squad to see them, and we haven't seen any of them since. If they turn up dead, it must have happened afterwards."

He sighed. "I wish somebody here spoke English. I guess we're going to find out how we do with the language training we got in Germany."

The dark-haired woman, who was sitting on the floor and cradling the young girl in her arms while the older one applied pressure to the girl's crotch area to stop the bleeding, looked up. "I speaking English," she said haltingly, tears streaming down her face. She nodded toward Billy. "That man is angel. He save my family from these animals. No court martial for him. My family will say what you want. If you want, we say nothing."

Relieved, Josh nodded his thanks. "We've got to get rid of these bodies. If we had a truck or even a car, we could take them away and bury them."

"We have truck," she said. "Not very good truck, but maybe good for this work."

She turned and spoke sharply to the four teenagers, who were still sobbing. They straightened up, as if they were waiting for her to tell them what to do next. She turned back to Josh.

"I tell one of my sons to take you to my father's workshop behind house where truck is. I tell other one to show where is gasoline for the truck."

Josh turned to Billy. "Corporal, take the two boys out front and team them up with Robitaille and Ducharme. Order them to get the truck gassed up and ready to go ASAP but to stay outside. They haven't been in the house, and they are not to enter under any circumstances. Williams was inside with you, but I don't think he saw much. Order him to keep guard at the iron gate and not let anyone get past him. Then report back immediately for more orders. Understood?"

"Understood, Sergeant," Billy replied crisply.

As Billy left with the two boys in tow, they heard screams from the front room. The two girls, the elder being the mother of the dead children, had discovered the little bodies. Josh's eyes met those of the black-haired woman holding the young girl. He realized she already knew the little ones were dead.

"My husband, my parents, and me were in kitchen when they came," she said, "All others sleeping. We going to leave in truck two, three days from now, if safe. These monsters first killed my grandchildren in front of our eyes. You must take us from here when you go. Tomorrow more will come. Neighbours see you here. We will be killed."

Just then, Billy came back.

"So here's the plan," Josh said to him. "You and me will drag the Vipers' bodies out back and load them into the truck. You, Robitaille, and Ducharme take the big kid with you. Drive back to the church where we took cover. Strip them. If they have any identifying marks, like tattoos, cut them out. Then bury them in the cemetery. Cover the spot with something so they're not discovered too soon. Bring back their clothing. We'll bury it on the other side of town on the way out. I'll let base know we need to evacuate twelve people ASAP, including us. We need a medic, too."

He turned back to the black-haired woman. "We'll take your family. I'm sorry, but we can't take your husband, your father, or the babies. There isn't enough room, and it will only cause more questions."

She nodded in assent. "They will understand. We must help the living."

"Now, I have a more difficult question for you," Josh continued. "We must burn your home on the way out to cover all this." He indicated the bloodstained room. Realizing the implications, he softened somewhat. "They would probably destroy it anyway. Or, since it's a nice home, people like these men might live in it."

Her eyes narrowed. "I burn our home myself before that."

As Josh turned to leave, she reached for his sleeve and stopped him. "You have big secret. Now I need big secret. My husband, my father, and the babies die in fire. Nobody in my family raped. Nobody in my family murdered. House fire killed my husband, my father, my grandchildren. We had no home, so kind soldiers from United Nations took us away. I must help the living."

Good Lord, Josh thought. *She's tough as nails.*

"Your secret is safe with us," he said.

Next, the woman called out to the two teenage girls, who were still in the nursery. Both returned, each carrying a dead child, the mother holding the infant while her younger sister carried the two-year-old. Both were still sobbing. She told them to place one child with each of the dead men, gather personal items, and leave immediately.

Turning to the younger boy, back from the courtyard after fuelling the truck, she told him to bring the remaining gasoline.

Shortly thereafter, at the truck, Josh conferred with Billy. Then he turned to the others. "We'll make two trips to our rendezvous point. Wheeler will drive with the two women and the girl in the front with him. Ducharme and Robitaille will keep lookout from the back. Williams will stay with me for the second trip. Ducharme will stay with the family. Robitaille, ride shotgun on the trip back. Leave the shovels in the truck. We'll need them."

The truck reached the rendezvous point, dropped off Ducharme and the family, and then headed back, stopping halfway. There, Billy and Robitaille cut any identifying information from the uniforms and then buried them in a field.

At the house, as the others waited out front, Josh went inside, soaked the bloodstained rooms in gasoline, trickled some to the front door, dropped a match, and ran to the truck.

With Williams keeping lookout, they drove off. Flames were visible through the windows. In an hour, but for the stone and brick skeleton, fire erased two hundred years of history.

On the way back to base, Josh picked up Billy's rifle, ejected the clip, and replaced the seven spent rounds from a supply he was carrying.

"I was wondering how to explain the missing ammo if no shots were fired," Billy said.

Josh nodded. "Early on, the senior NCOs were briefed on UNPROFOR's strict rules regarding when we can shoot and when we can't. It sounded like rules made up by paper pushers who've never seen combat. They had no clue what we were getting into. Peacekeeping, my ass! There's no peace to keep, and the ceasefire is a farce. Some of us were afraid men would be killed because they didn't shoot first or court-martialled because they did, so we got a stash of ammo for missions like this. The officers don't know."

When they arrived at the rendezvous point, the dark-haired woman approached Josh. "What will become of us?"

"You and your family are now the responsibility of the United Nations," he said. "People like you go to a place for refugees. My commanding officer will need to file a report, so I need some information about you. Can you help me with that?"

She told him she and her husband were both teachers, athletes, and then trainers for the Yugoslavian Olympic team, where she had learned English. Her parents had been grocers but closed the business when the economy crashed after the government fell.

The M113 arrived, cutting their conversation short. The medic took one look at the child and then made his assessment. "It doesn't look good. She needs a surgeon; the quicker the better."

Josh ordered the three privates to help the medic load the family. Then he turned to Billy and motioned toward the truck. "We need to torch it."

Minutes later, as the M113 headed toward the base, the truck's gas tank exploded, lighting up the area.

"Do you think anybody will notice the fire?" Billy asked, his eyes on the explosion in the distance.

"Not around here," Josh replied. "Most places they would, but explosions are common around here."

He was wrong. One person noticed.

Chapter 23

When people think of scavengers, they tend to think of the animal kingdom. They think of gulls, crows, or vultures. They may also think of coyotes, bears, or even hyenas. They don't think of humans — the ultimate scavengers.

In his sixties, born before the Second World War, Sava had spent his life under the communists and was always on the lookout to scrounge anything to add to his stockpile.

Although he lived near the home the Vipers had selected for their attack, he did not hear them come into the town and would not have been aware of their presence, except that he arose to relieve himself in the middle of the night and noticed light coming from the home.

Lights on at night in the small community, which lacked streetlights, were visible immediately to neighbours, resulting in questions. Why were the lights on? Was somebody sick? Did they have visitors? Was there a party? The questions were limited only by the imagination of the nosy neighbour.

Thinking he would investigate it the following day, Sava went back to bed.

Unable to sleep, he arose a little later. The lights were still on. Then, to his surprise, the courtyard gate opened, and the grocer's ancient truck exited and drove past Sava's house. Occupied by three soldiers and one of the grocer's grandsons, it headed out of town. Shortly afterwards, it returned. As the gate opened, the headlights shone on the younger boy, who opened and closed the gate. Perplexed, Sava continued to watch.

Minutes later, the gate opened again, this time by a blue-helmeted soldier, and the truck headed out of town but in the opposite direction. Mystified, Sava wondered who the soldiers were. From the UN? If so, why here, and why at night?

He remained in his darkened home, watching, waiting.

His patience was rewarded when the truck returned again. This time, it stopped in front of his house. The cab light came on as the passenger door opened. A soldier in a UN uniform got out and went into the house. The truck turned around on the narrow street, and the soldier who had gone into the house rushed back out with two others.

Sava did not see them set the fire, but he had no doubt they had set it, because within seconds of the truck's departure, he saw flames inside the home. Disappointment welled up in his throat like acid reflux as he thought of the many nice things consumed by the flames.

Speculating on what had just unfolded before his eyes, he could not believe they had burned all their valuables in the home. The old man and son-in-law were gone, yet the boys were helping the soldiers, and the family seemed willing to go with them. Then it dawned on him. They must have loaded the truck with valuables they took away and hid before leaving in the opposite direction with the family.

Before sunrise, he was on his bicycle, headed in the direction the truck had gone. Riding slowly along the road, he searched for evidence of where they must have stopped to hide the valuables.

Well outside of town, Sava had still seen nothing — no fresh tracks on the shoulder and no grass disturbed by footprints. Experienced at hiding contraband, he concluded they must have used a building. But which building? Then it hit him. The church! The building was too badly damaged to be occupied. Nobody owned it. It had already been looted, so nobody would bother going there again. They must have used the church.

Walking through the door-less entranceway, he looked around. No footprints in the dust. As he looked through the smashed window into the cemetery behind the church, a smile crossed his unshaven face, exposing gaps, separated by the remains of rotten teeth.

His excitement came from seeing a pile of debris that had not been there when he last scouted the place. Going outside, he saw the debris appeared to cover a fresh grave. The soldiers must have killed the two men and buried the bodies before taking the women and boys. Still, Sava had to be sure the freshly dug grave contained no valuables. He went to a stone shed, where he retrieved an ancient, rusty shovel.

After pulling away the debris to expose the grave, he dug feverishly at the rich, black earth. Fifteen centimetres below the surface, he uncovered a man's hand. He dug around the body, uncovering more of it. He discovered more bodies. Then he realized the grave held several men, none of whom he recognized.

Finding no valuables, he stopped digging, covered the bodies, and left the site as he had found it.

Stymied for now, he rode back home, where his wife, asleep when he left, was up and going about her morning chores. Without a word between them, she made him breakfast. Frustrated he had found nothing and tired from being awake most of the night, he went back to bed and slept for an hour.

By mid-morning, Sava arose again and decided to take another bicycle ride. Maybe they had hidden something on their way out of town.

A kilometre or so along the route, he saw where a vehicle had left the road and had driven into a field. Leaving his bicycle, he walked in the direction the truck had taken. Wary of land mines, he stepped precisely in one of the tracks left by the truck, walking like someone doing a sobriety test. When he arrived where the truck had turned around, he found a low mound of freshly dug earth.

He knew that something had been buried there. The site was smaller than the one with the bodies back at the church. It was too small for a grave. He was convinced it had to be where they had hidden the family's valuables. The thought of finding something valuable made his miserly heart skip a beat!

Now he had a different problem. If he could find it, so could somebody else. He did not want to bring attention to the area until he had unearthed whatever was buried there, and he did not want anyone to see him out in the middle of the field digging. Feigning disinterest, he returned home.

Early the next morning, he returned with a shovel and some burlap sacks and started to dig. Just six centimetres below the surface, he found five bloody uniforms, including boots and belts. Two jackets had holes in the front and back.

None of the items bore any identifying insignia, although there were holes in the jackets where epaulets had been. Small pieces of thread hung from areas where something had been sewn onto the jackets. He ignored the tiny, red snakelike emblems on the collars of four of the uniforms.

Expecting to find nothing, he rifled through the pockets of all the jackets and pants and was thrilled to find several Yugoslavian dinars. Their killers had not even robbed them! Reflexively, he looked around to see if anyone was watching before stuffing the money into his pocket.

Realizing he would require several trips by bicycle to carry all of the items home, he worried that if he made too many trips on his bicycle, he might arouse suspicion. Better to stuff the items into the bags, stash them in the nearby woods, and return in his car, a twelve-year-old Yugo.

Soon, he was back in his car, picked up his loot, and was back in his garage. There, he was joined by his wife, his accomplice, who inspected everything.

First, she washed the clothing. Then she repaired the small bullet holes in the front of two jackets. Next, she removed the breast pocket from one of the jackets and cut the material into four equal pieces. She made four neat patches to cover the quarter-sized bullet holes in the backs of two jackets. Finally, she washed the repaired jackets a second time so the repairs would not look new.

The next day, they bypassed the first neighbouring town and headed to the next. There, they visited an old friend, another scavenger, who fenced stolen goods in the local market. Over the years, each of them had acquired goods that could not be sold locally without attracting attention, so for a fifty/fifty split, they sold each other's contraband.

Three days after the five Vipers were killed, their freshly laundered uniforms, polished boots, and belts were put up for sale by the second scavenger, two towns distant. It might have seemed risky to sell the men's uniforms so soon after their demise, but in that war-torn region, the products attracted no more attention than army surplus products in any North American store.

Consumers gobbled up lots of similar items at cheap prices, no questions asked. There was no risk in selling used military clothing. If it could be claimed to be authentic, that only added to the swagger value for some young punk, eager to join a militia to exact revenge for wrongs done to his group, fight off oppressors, or simply get in on the action before it was all over.

No risk, that is, unless a tiny, red snake was embroidered on the collar. Worn by the wrong person, that jacket could spell a death sentence for the wearer and possibly his entire family.

When the Viper squads were created, they needed to be able to secretly identify each other. They knew that all wars and conflicts ended eventually, and anyone accused of war crimes could face prosecution. Anonymity was crucial.

Officially, the squads did not exist. They operated only at night. None of them were permitted to discuss their activities with anyone except other squad members. No written record was prepared. Their activities were never acknowledged.

To self-identify, they decided each Viper would display a tiny red snake embroidered on his jacket collar. It could be worn only on the recommendation of a squad leader and only after the member had participated in a successful operation.

Since their operations took place at night, their absence approved by the commanding officer, their comings and goings attracted no attention. When a unit failed to return, searching for them was difficult, and the search was usually covered up.

However, when a Viper saw a civilian wearing one of the dead soldiers' jackets with a tiny red snake on the collar, the individual was apprehended and beaten. Terrified, he told them where he had purchased it. While detaining him, they sent one of their group to the market vendor to buy more jackets.

Thinking he had landed a new customer, the fence was elated. He produced two more jackets. The repaired bullet holes were obvious. Rather than purchase them on the spot, the Viper paid a deposit. He agreed to return at closing time to pay the balance and bring friends, who would buy additional clothing.

When he returned at the end of the day, he brought three more Vipers. They took the vendor into a back room and beat him until he gave up his supplier. Rather than kill him (in case he was lying), they took him to where they were holding the first civilian they had apprehended.

Later that evening, they went to Sava's home. They beat him until he took them to their comrades' grave, where they forced him to dig up the bodies. To avoid any noise, they strangled Sava and his wife and buried them in the same hole. They also killed the first two captives, and then they reported to their superiors that their five comrades had been killed by blue-helmeted UN soldiers.

The response was quick and savage.

The next night, soldiers closed off roads to the town and went door to door, shooting everyone. Then they burned every building. A handful of survivors escaped by running away in the dark, ending up in the camp of Billy's unit.

Any doubt in Billy's mind about the reason for the massacre vaporized when his commanding officer received a message. It said the town had been destroyed in retaliation for the UN having murdered five soldiers, and anyone who collaborated with foreigners would be killed.

Billy was overcome with guilt. Had he caused the town's destruction? Shooting the first Viper was justified, as Billy was defending the child, but he shot the next one in anger. Then he had to shoot the third and fourth in self-defence.

His remorse was for the fifth one, the teenager, who had pleaded for his life.

After the village incident, Billy had trouble sleeping. He kept seeing the big sergeant raping the small girl and the teenager pleading for his life. Then Emma would appear, covered in blood, having a miscarriage in an emergency room. Kyle and Kayla were standing near her, also covered in blood, screaming. "Don't kill the baby! Don't kill the baby!"

Then he would awake, covered in sweat.

Chapter 24

"Corporal, get the night squad together for a briefing," Josh said to Billy. "We're getting new orders at twenty hundred hours. I don't know anything," he added wryly in response to an unasked question. "It seems our recent efforts working the graveyard shift are about to be rewarded. An all-expenses paid trip to a new destination will be announced."

If he had hoped that his attempt at humour would lighten Billy's mood, it did not. Beginning the day after the night operation, when they had rescued the villagers and, in the process, eliminated five men who deserved a special place in hell, Billy, never a big talker, had become even quieter than usual.

Later, when he learned the town had been destroyed and so many killed, he could not keep it inside himself anymore, and he came to Josh in tears, questioning whether he had caused the massacre. Maybe, if he had followed orders, if he had not killed the men and taken them prisoner instead, the town and its residents would have been spared the Vipers' wrath.

"Soldier, that's water under the bridge now," Josh said without hesitation. "There's nothing you can do, and, if you don't keep yourself together, and if word leaks out, we will all be court-martialled. Your best bet is to do what I'm doing."

"What's that?"

"Whenever I think about those five scumbags, I remind myself that we're here to protect civilians, and that's exactly what we did. If we had brought them in, they would have denied everything. There never would have been a trial. They would never have faced justice. Even worse, they would have been set free immediately. Knowing they were untouchable, they would have kept on terrorizing more families.

Then I remind myself that we will be home in a few months and, if it's still on my mind and I need to I talk to someone, I'll discuss it privately with the chaplain. They have that confidentiality oath going for them, and they hear everything. I'm sure he's heard worse than this before."

"And that works for you?" Billy asked.

"Yup. Up 'til now," Josh replied. "Anyway, never mind all that. We got a new mission. We need you focused. Around here, lose focus for even a few minutes, and it can be game over for you and anyone depending on you."

"You're right," Billy replied, grateful for Josh's advice. "You know what they say back home, a change is as good as a rest. After the rain we've had lately, I'm feeling really dragged out. If anything gets me away for a few days, I'm all for it."

"That's the spirit, soldier," Josh said.

Billy may have been less morose had he known the elimination of the five Vipers had rendered the mission a resounding success. Under torture, Sava said that blue-helmeted soldiers had been at the home that night and had killed the five men. Then they had stripped them and buried their bodies.

Examination of the corpses revealed that the commanding officer and the teenager had been killed by single shots through the head. Another had a single shot through the neck. Two were shot twice through the body. The precision of the shots and powder burns around several wounds indicated they were killed at close range, execution style.

Knife marks on the bodies, due to the removal of tattoos, supported the theory they had been taken prisoner and then executed. Someone had desecrated the bodies first, removed any identifying information from the uniforms, and then buried them at a different location.

While ethnic cleansing continued, the Vipers believed UN troops were operating at night and summarily executing any soldiers they caught. The night raids stopped, nobody wanting to face the same fate.

Among the Vipers and their supporters, this fear, bordering on a phobia, engendered a smouldering hatred toward the blue-helmeted soldiers. Soon, there was talk of rewarding anyone who killed one of those foreigners.

*   *   *

The lieutenant colonel who created the night squads was briefed privately by the sergeants who had led the eight squads. He learned how these previously green men would respond in the field. Thrilled they had developed a unifying esprit de corps, he kept them together for future assignments.

He did not have to wait long. Sarajevo Airport, 350 kilometres away, was under siege. They needed a recon mission before a larger force could be sent to liberate it. They would travel in fast-moving, rubber-tired, amphibious Canadian Cougars, top speed 100 kph on a good road. Operated by a three-man crew — commander, gunner, and driver — the Cougars could carry two additional soldiers.

The Cougar's principal weapon was a 76 mm gun capable of shooting a variety of ordnance, including high-explosive antitank shells with a range of over 2,000 metres. It was backed up by grenade launchers and a 7.62 mm machine gun with 3,000 rounds of ammunition.

Ordinarily, given the Cougar's speed and range, with a ceasefire in effect, it would be a routine overnight mission. However, the ceasefire was not working, and nothing around there was ordinary, so the Cougars would carry backup.

The six-vehicle squadron, supported by ten infantrymen from two night squads, would be led by thirty-year-old, red-haired, freckle-faced Captain Michelle Germain, an Anne of Green Gables replica. Ordinarily, a more experienced major would have led, with the captain as second-in-command, but the major had broken his back days earlier when his Cougar ran over a mine. He was in a German hospital, his military career over.

Perhaps in anticipation of any anti-female bias, they were assured that the captain, a career soldier from a family of career soldiers, had already proven her ability while serving as the major's second-in-command on prior missions. A graduate of Royal Military College, she held degrees in human kinetics and engineering and had a black belt in judo.

"This is a recon mission," the lieutenant colonel said a third time. "As peacekeepers, you will avoid engaging in hostilities. If you encounter potential resistance, go around it. Continue the mission, and find a safer route to Sarajevo. If you can't do that, withdraw to a safe distance and contact base for further orders. Otherwise, only use your weapons in self-defence."

*　*　*

The first day was uneventful; however, they covered only 120 kilometres, due to destroyed bridges and heavy rains. Stopping at 8 p.m., they bivouacked in the ruins of an old monastery.

By late evening of day two, they were in a wooded valley going through deserted villages. Some of the homes were intact, while others had been burnt, leaving only stone walls and chimneys.

At 7 p.m., at the edge of a grassy meadow, under the cover of a stand of enormous trees, Captain Germain called a halt and pointed to a notch in the landscape. "It looks like the valley narrows to a pass," she said. "We don't know what's on the other side. It may open up again, or it may go on for several kilometres. We've got two hours of daylight left. We'll continue through that pass. If it's short, and if there's good cover on the other side, we can bivouac there. If not, we'll turn around and take cover under these trees. We'll tarp up the Cougars like last night and leave at daybreak. We haven't run into any mines, but everyone knows what one of those can do. Does anyone have any questions or, for that matter, any better ideas?"

Nobody did.

With Germain in the lead, the Cougars in pairs, they set out across the meadow. On the opposite side, following a well-worn road not much wider than a cart path, they entered a ravine that widened eventually to a few hundred metres.

Eons ago, someone had cleared the land, attempting to coax a living out of the rocky soil. All that remained were four stone walls, remnants of a thatched roof, and a pile of rotting lumber that was once a barn. The grassy fields were slowly being consumed by a forest that was eager to regain its place in the landscape.

Without warning, an explosion erupted on the right side of the second Cougar, blowing the tires on that side skyward. The force of the explosion flipped the vehicle onto its side, where it rocked back and forth before coming to rest.

Assuming it had run over a land mine, Captain Germain called a halt and turned around to assess the damage and casualties. Unaware, and perhaps unconcerned, that she was in any danger, she opened the hatch and started to get out.

As she rose from her vehicle, gunfire erupted from two positions on the nearby hill. At such close range, she had no chance. A bullet struck her left arm, above the bicep. It missed the artery but smashed the bone. Another nicked an eyelid, rupturing her eyeball.

The impact spun her around. She fell back into the vehicle on top of her now useless arm, still conscious but dazed, bleeding profusely from both wounds.

Amid a hail of gunfire, the driver accelerated toward the other Cougars. A second, crater-producing explosion erupted just behind them, propelling them along. He raced across the clearing, past the second pair of Cougars, and into the trees.

There, he joined the fifth and sixth armoured vehicles. Meanwhile the third and fourth Cougars withdrew a short distance, taking cover among the trees while keeping the disabled Cougar in sight.

Germain's second-in-command, a lieutenant, light on experience but with lots of common sense, realized the seriousness of Germain's injuries. After consulting with his senior NCOs, he decided to divide the squadron, sending three Cougars, including Germain's, back the way they came.

Travelling at night in hostile territory was not ideal, but they had good reconnaissance now. Hopefully, they would be intercepted by a helicopter to medivac the captain.

That left the lieutenant with two Cougars and their six men plus Short's five-man squad, a total of eleven men to complete a mission that began with twenty-eight.

The hostiles were occupying three hillside locations. From the lowest one, they were using a rocket launcher. A few hundred metres higher and to the right was a heavy machine gun. Farther up and to the left, a sniper team had a plain view and a good shot at anyone in the ravine.

Retreating several kilometres and attempting to find a way around the obstacle was out of the question. The disabled Cougar with its five occupants was sitting on the road at the base of the hillside, the fate of its occupants unknown.

Maybe they had all been killed, but that seemed unlikely. The explosion had capsized the Cougar, but the vehicle compartment had not taken a direct hit. Some may have survived, but the blast had knocked out the radio.

The lieutenant turned to Josh. "Sergeant, give me your assessment and tell me what you think we should do."

"Well, it's almost dark," Josh replied. "The first thing we've got to do is take a look inside that Cougar, see if anyone survived, see what kind of shape they're in. We can decide what to do after that."

"I agree, but I can't expose either of these two units to another rocket attack. That would end the mission."

"I wasn't thinking of sending the Cougars," Josh said. "It's almost dark. If you agree, as soon as it's completely dark, I'll send three men on foot."

The lieutenant nodded, satisfied. "You know your men better than I do. What do you need to make this work?"

"A few extra canteens of water, a bunch of painkillers, and some extra bandages. That's about it."

Josh turned to Billy. "Corporal, as soon as it's dark, take two men. Make your way over to the Cougar. Take a look inside for survivors."

A look of relief came over Billy's face. "Thank God!" he replied. "I've been worried about those poor bastards out there. Anyone who survived the blast could be beat up pretty bad, likely deaf, too. I don't know if they'd take a chance on getting out and being shot, but how long can they wait for someone to show up? Which two men do you want me to take?"

"Robitaille and Ducharme," Josh said. "They work well together. Take extra canteens of water. The lieutenant is coming up with some painkillers and bandages."

An hour later, the three soldiers dropped to their hands and knees. To avoid creating a silhouette, they crawled the half kilometre to the disabled Cougar.

A bright moon, rising in the eastern sky, helped them avoid most of the smaller, water-filled potholes. However, they had to crawl through the large ones, which were the full width of the road and a foot deep.

When they arrived at the Cougar, they faced a dilemma. On its side, with the top facing away from the hillside, the vehicle provided perfect cover for them to stand up behind it, open the hatch, and look inside. However, doing so without announcing themselves could result in the occupants mistaking them for the enemy and shooting.

In the calm following the recent rainfall, the air was perfectly still. Sound carried a long distance and would alert the hostiles on the hillside above them.

Billy tapped on the hatch three times. No response. He did it again. Still no response. The third time, instead of using his knuckles, he used a hammer fist and pounded, producing less noise but causing the metal to vibrate. His efforts were rewarded with three taps from inside.

Excited to have found survivors, he opened the hatch — and found himself facing the muzzle of an assault rifle. No shots were fired, and they were able to determine three had survived. Two were badly injured and could not walk, let alone crawl, back to safety.

Billy passed the canteens, painkillers, and bandages through the hatch. Then, motioning toward his watch, he indicated they would be back in a few hours.

He closed the hatch and turned to the two privates. "Both of you go back. Let the Sarge know we have three survivors. Injured. It looks like they'll have to be transported from here by vehicle."

"Are you staying here until someone gets back?" Robitaille asked.

"Nope." Josh pointed to the hillside. "Before we can rescue the guys, we've got to take them out. We'll need better recon, so I'm going up there for a look around."

"Right now? Up there? In the dark?" Ducharme asked, incredulous.

"Yup. I'll follow along this road until I'm well past them and then go up over the hill. I intend to get above them. Get a good look at their positions. Figure out how many hostiles are up there."

"What about our orders?" Ducharme asked.

"We've already carried them out. If Sarge were here, this is what he would order to rescue the guys. When you get back there, be sure you tell him I'll be looking for a good shot of birds at daylight."

"What do you mean by that?" Robitaille asked.

"It's just something we say back home," Billy said. "It'll give him a chuckle when you say it. Just make sure you tell him exactly what I said. Oh, and each of you give me two of your ammo clips, just in case."

Both complied. Then all three dropped to their hands and knees and crawled away from the overturned Cougar — the privates back to their comrades, Billy in the opposite direction toward the small trees and shrubs that lined the narrow, winding road. Once there, he rose to his feet and crept onward.

Now familiar with the way, Robitaille and Ducharme reached the other eight soldiers quickly.

"What's the report, soldier?" Josh asked, seeing there were only two of them. "Keep your voice down. You can start by telling me what happened to the corporal."

Robitaille told him Billy had led them to the disabled Cougar. They discovered three of the five occupants had survived the attack. They were injured, but he could not say how badly.

"Did Corporal Wheeler stay with the injured men and send you back to report?"

"No, sir," Robitaille replied, nervous and excited. "I mean, no Sergeant. Corporal Wheeler went in the other direction. He followed the road. He said he was going to do some recon, because, like he said, we're going to have to take out those hostile positions before we can rescue the men. He said we needed better recon because there might be others up there we don't know about."

"Is that it?" Josh asked.

"Well, I thought he was going take a look around and come back, but then he said something funny, and he asked me and Ducharme to give him extra ammo."

"What exactly did he say?" Josh asked.

"That's just it," the private replied. "It didn't make any sense, like he wasn't even talking about the mission."

"Private," Josh said, "tell me exactly what he said, and don't change anything or leave anything out."

"He said to tell you he was hoping to get a good shot of birds in the morning." Robitaille paused and nodded. "Yup, that's exactly what he said."

The lieutenant had been listening, perplexed by the exchange. "Well, Sergeant, what was he talking about?"

"Sir, it means he's not coming back tonight. He'll be lucky if he gets back at all."

"You don't mean he's gone AWOL, do you?" the lieutenant asked, mystified.

"No, Lieutenant, he's talking in code. He's telling me at daylight, he's going to be up on that hillside, and he's going to start shooting."

"How do you know that? There must be ten or twelve hostiles up there, perhaps more. They were firing from three different positions," the lieutenant replied. "Even if he takes out one of their positions, the others will get him before he gets them. If what you say is true, he's on a suicide mission!"

"Lieutenant," Josh replied, "where Corporal Wheeler and I come from, a lot of boys start hunting and fishing really young. Long before they finish school, they're really handy with a gun and a fly rod, and they've spent lots of time in the bush. If he says he's looking forward to a good shot of birds in the morning, it means he plans to get right up alongside those hostiles in the dark. At daylight, he's going to start shooting."

"There must have been a reason why he wants us to know what he's up to," the lieutenant said. "Is there anything we can do to back him up?"

Encouraged by the lieutenant's response, Josh nodded. "There may be. We should wrap the Cougars in camo tarps. Add some branches to blend in with the landscape. Before daylight, move them into position at the edge of the trees. Turn off the engines and wait for daylight. At daylight, open up on the position where the rockets came from with our seventy-sixes. It's probably sandbagged or fortified, but the seventy-sixes will clean that up. With the rocket position knocked out, we can turn our machine guns on their other positions."

"What about the UN rules?" the lieutenant blurted. "Our vehicles are supposed to be white with UN written on them. We're not supposed to engage unless we're defending ourselves."

"Fuck the UN," Josh said. "And fuck the UN's rules! Those assholes up on that hill knocked out our Cougar, killed two of our men, and wounded three more. Then they ambushed the captain when she tried to rescue them. We are defending ourselves!"

Jarred at the vehemence of the response from the normally even-tempered sergeant, the lieutenant was pleased to have Josh on his side. "But what about the corporal?"

"I expect he'll be in position before daylight. That's about half an hour before sunrise. We should be ready to open fire soon as it's light but wait for the corporal to make the first move."

"What if he doesn't?"

"If the corporal doesn't start shooting by sunrise, he probably didn't make it. But just in case he's late, we should wait another ten minutes and then open fire anyway. Either way, we've got to knock them out before we can rescue our men, and this looks like our best bet."

"Good enough," the lieutenant concurred. "Let's get on with it. The sooner we prep the Cougars, the sooner we can sleep. Tomorrow could be a long day."

Chapter 25

Keeping on the grassy area between water-filled ruts, Billy crawled to the small trees and shrubs looming on both sides of the road. There, he rose cautiously to his feet, unslung his rifle, and crept forward until he reached a T intersection, where a lesser-used, smaller, rocky road went up over the hill.

Halfway up the hill, under a large, leafy tree, he came upon an old, battered Lada, the driver's window halfway down, kept in place by a freshly whittled wooden shim. Using a mini-mag flashlight, with his thumb over the lens to permit only a tiny glow, he checked the ground for tire tracks.

It had rained, but the tracks were clear, so the Lada had been there only a short while. Turning off the light, he went around to the front. Placing his hand on the hood and finding it dry but neither hot nor cold confirmed it had been there for a while.

Stepping back to the driver's door, without thinking, he opened it, activating the interior light. He closed it quickly, cursing to himself for possibly giving away his presence. He walked back down to the larger road and waited five minutes. Then he returned to the car.

This time, he reached through the driver's window and pulled back the hood release. Rewarded by a small click, he went to the front, placed his fingers under the hood, released the latch, and raised the hood. Using his flashlight as before, he lifted the distributor cap and pocketed the rotor button.

Smiling as he left the car, he continued up the hill, wondering if the driver would kill the battery before he discovered why the Lada would not start. He reminded himself to replace the button if he needed the car.

As he walked uphill, on his right, where he knew the three gun positions were located, the moonlight revealed an opening in the trees. He smelled wood smoke. Somebody had a campfire. The familiar scent reminded him of the many nights he spent around campfires in the woods hunting and fishing with his buddies back in Newfoundland. For a moment, he was homesick. He wanted to be home instead of here fighting other people's battles. This was supposed to be a peacekeeping mission. What a crock of shit that turned out to be!

Then he thought of the family he had rescued, Emma and the kids, and the two dead soldiers and their three wounded buddies in the Cougar, hoping to be rescued. They had to be wondering if they would ever see their families again. With a shudder, he shook off the paralyzing feelings and swallowed the bile that had risen up in his throat.

He squatted. Using the small flashlight, he inspected the ground. Seeing a well-worn trail, he smiled, thinking it must be the trail to the gun emplacements. Resisting the temptation to follow it, and deciding that he still had time, he crept uphill, looking around continually for anything unusual.

Three quarters of the way up the hill, his vigilance was rewarded. Using the telescopic sight on his rifle, he spotted a small campsite.

On the hillside, in a level clearing the size of a city lawn, somebody had built a lean-to, similar to a Newfoundland backcamp. The back of the shelter faced the valley, hiding the small campfire from anyone below, while the open side faced the hill, taking full advantage of the level area.

He estimated the size of the structure, by comparing it to the size of the two men by the fire in front, to be seven or eight feet long and five feet high. Satisfied he had identified one enemy position, Billy continued uphill, glancing back frequently, grateful for a clear sky and a bright moon.

Before he reached the crest of the hill, he spied the second clearing. Farther away, larger, and lower on the hillside, it was irregular in shape and more elaborate, with a tent large enough for several men. At the outer edge, overlooking the valley, was a semicircular, sandbagged machine gun nest.

Gaps in the front, left, and right of the sandbags permitted three guns to cover the entire landscape below, but there was only one gun, in the middle. It was covered by a tarp and capable of being moved from one position to another.

Although he did not see anyone, the fire had been fed recently. Whoever was manning the position was in the tent or had stepped into the trees, perhaps to answer the call of nature, a reminder not to walk through any open-air outhouses.

Before reaching the crest of the hill, with only low bushes for cover, Billy dropped to his hands and knees and crawled to the summit. From there, he spied the lights of a distant town.

Heading downhill, he was not overly concerned he had not spotted the third location. He knew it was lower and likely better protected than the others, probably dug into the hillside, perhaps using a cave or an old army bunker, with more room for supplies and a larger group of combatants.

He figured all three locations were connected by trails. If he got past the first two locations undetected, he could get close to the bunker. Then grenades, lobbed from above, would be his best bet. But first, he needed to dispatch the two snipers at the nearest and highest location.

Downhill, he was pleasantly surprised the trail he had discovered earlier provided easy walking. Well before reaching the opening, he saw the campfire and stopped. He wondered if there was a tripwire across the trail. If attached to a grenade, it would kill him. Even if it was attached to a bunch of empty cans, like a bear warning, it would alert the two snipers. He was not concerned about coming out on top in a firefight with them, since he would be shooting from the dark, into the campsite, which was illuminated by the campfire. However, a single shot would wake up everyone on the hillside, eliminating any chance of taking them by surprise.

Checking his watch, he saw it was only midnight. He smiled. He had lots of time. With adrenaline coursing through his veins, he reminded himself that, unchecked, excitement foiled many inexperienced hunters. He stopped and took few deep breaths. Forcing himself to calm down, he surveyed the location again.

Keeping a few metres back from the clearing, he worked his way around the campsite. First, he went to the right, around to the edge of the hill, just a few metres from where two khaki-clad men were sleeping beneath the lean-to, back from the fire.

To have a chance to take out both of them, he needed them separated. Without a sound, he turned around and worked his way over to the other side.

First, he passed the trail he had followed to get to that point. Then he discovered another trail on the opposite side. Presumably, it led to the machine gun nest, to the bunker below, or both.

Then he found what he was seeking. Suspecting the location had been occupied for weeks, or perhaps months, he figured there would be a place designated to throw trash and to use as an outdoor toilet. His nose told him he was at the place.

He calculated that if he could dispatch the two snipers by 0200 hours, he should be able to get to the machine gun nest, if that's where the second trail led, within a half hour to an hour. If he could dispose of the machine gun crew by 0400 hours, he would still have an hour until sunrise to set up for the bunker below.

Hoping one of the snipers would have to answer the call of nature in the middle of the night, he took up a position in the only location where the campfire cast no light — immediately behind the lean-to that sheltered the two sleeping men.

He removed the bayonet from his rifle and took off his helmet and anything else that could slow him down or make a noise. He waited, feeling his pounding heart as it sent shockwaves through his body. He focused his mind firmly on slowing his breathing.

In less than an hour, his patience was rewarded. In a foreign language, one of the men spoke. The other did not reply, so his companion spoke a little louder, this time eliciting a groggy grunt from his companion.

The speaker stood up, stretched his arms skyward, yawned, and walked sleepily toward the outdoor toilet. Standing with his back to the fire, looking into the darkness, he unfastened his pants. They fell halfway to his knees. Billy waited as the man pulled his underwear partially down and pulled out his penis. With both hands in front of him, he began to urinate.

Only then did Billy break from cover, dashing across the short distance between them. In a single motion, he clamped his left hand over the man's mouth and nose, and, with his right hand, drove his bayonet into the middle of the man's back, slightly to the right of his spine, inward and upward, slicing through his aorta and his vital organs. When it brought up solid at the hilt, Billy twisted his bayonet ninety degrees, inflicting a huge internal wound. Then he waited, holding the doomed man tightly.

Blood gushed from the wound, covering Billy's uniform from his midsection to his boots. He continued to hold the quivering man until he was sure he was dead. Then he lowered the warm corpse to the ground.

Next, he turned his attention to other man. Covered in a large blanket, the man was sleeping with his back to the fire. With no time to waste, and afraid the man would awake, Billy hurried toward him.

He drove his bayonet into the side of the man's neck. With full force, he hauled it to the front, taking out both large arteries and his windpipe. Blood sprayed everywhere, and soundless air came from the man's windpipe, the shock of blood loss to the brain bringing about a fast, if brutal, death.

Billy dragged the bodies to the edge of the clearing and threw branches over them, hoping to delay their discovery should their colleagues check on them before daylight.

Worrying that anyone from the other locations might notice the fire had gone out, and come to investigate, Billy took a moment to stoke it. First, he placed small sticks on it. Then he added larger pieces of wood. Finally, he topped it with two large logs. He reasoned it should keep burning for the few hours he needed.

Reattaching his bayonet to his rifle, he grabbed his gear and put on his helmet. Bloodstained and repulsed by what he had just done, he picked up the trail and headed toward the machine gun nest.

From the campsite, the trail meandered slightly downhill, continuing across the hillside. In the moonlight, Billy reached a fork in the trail. One branch headed lower. The other continued across and upward. He opted to continue upward, reasoning the machine gun nest, higher on the hillside, would have fewer defenders than the larger rocket-launching site.

If he could take out the machine gun nest, undetected, before daylight, he would be well positioned at sunrise to start firing on the lower site from higher up and behind. They would have him outnumbered and outgunned, but he would have them outflanked. Eliminating the machine gun nest without firing, he could keep the element of surprise.

To his dismay, a large cloud obscured the moon, eliminating the pale, silvery light it had provided and leaving him in complete darkness.

"Shit," he muttered, disgusted at losing his light. Then he stopped. That was dumb. What if someone had heard him? Then he wondered if he had actually said anything or if he had just thought it so loudly he thought he had said it. Was he losing his marbles up there on the hillside, hunting men and thinking no more of it than if he were back home hunting big game or birds?

Finally, he decided he had better sit down and figure out what to do next. If he used his flashlight, he could be seen. If he went on without light, he would be stumbling around in the woods. They would hear him coming like a big bull moose in rutting season and shoot him before he got close. It was comfortable where he was sitting, and he was so tired he could have drifted off to sleep, which is exactly what he did.

Chapter 26

Panicked and covered in sweat, Billy awoke as if a jolt of electricity had been applied to his neck and passed through his body. Eyes wide open in the dark, he clawed instinctively at his neck with one hand, reaching for his rifle with the other.

Realizing he was alone, he stopped, trying to figure where he was and what had just happened.

As the stinging to his neck continued, it all came back to him. He must have drifted off to sleep and been having a nightmare. He had been reliving killing the two men at the first campsite when an insect, a spider or an ant, had bitten him on the neck. In his nightmare, he had dreamed that someone had driven a bayonet into his neck, just like he had done to the other man a short time ago.

Oh my God! he thought. *How long have I been sleeping?*

His watch showed 0250 hours, so it had only been fifteen or twenty minutes. His panic subsided. He still had enough time.

Just then, the moon emerged serenely from the clouds.

Thank God.

Then he stopped. *Thank God? I wonder if there is a God. If there is, I doubt he would approve of what I'm doing.*

Stop talking to yourself. You're going to make yourself crazy. Then again, maybe I am crazy. In fact, I'm pretty sure I am crazy. Otherwise I wouldn't even be here.

There you go again. Talking to yourself. Why don't you just shut up and go back to work?

Moving as quietly as possible, within half an hour, he reached the campsite. Across a clearing, back from the edge, unseen from the valley below, was a large olive-coloured tent. Its front was open, its flaps tied back to permit air and occupants to circulate.

The back flaps hung loosely, moving back and forth in the gentle draft flowing down the mountainside. Smoke from the freshly fed fire in front but slightly to one side kept most biting insects away.

Behind the tent, no more than fifteen metres away, was the tarp-covered machine gun. Across the clearing, a few feet back from the tree line, Billy waited to be certain only three men were there and that all three were asleep.

He was in his camo uniform with his face blackened and small branches and twigs pushed through the mesh that covered his helmet.

I can't believe I'm acting just like a moose, he thought. After coming to the edge of a bog or a clearing, a moose would wait silently and motionless for several minutes, assessing whether it was safe to leave the protection of the trees before walking out into the open. If not, sensing danger, it would turn quietly and walk back into the forest, unseen.

Billy smiled, thinking of the time he had been hunting late one evening on the Great Northern Peninsula. Across the glade, he had noticed the flick of a moose ear, likely in response to a mosquito. With a shot through its neck, he had brought down the 1,200-pound bull before it could walk back into the heavy timber.

Billy grimaced. *I don't have the big ears of a moose to give me away, but I can't turn around and walk away either.*

A noise from the tent refocused his attention. One man was getting up.

He froze, thinking he might be spotted. Then he smiled. Realizing where he was, as long as he remained silent and motionless, he did not need to worry about being seen. Hopefully, the man was just getting up for a wash-room break and would go back to sleep in a few minutes.

He was wrong!

The guy was the trio's leader and second-in-command of the entire group. An early riser, he went to the far side of the clearing and relieved himself.

When he returned to the fire, he took a long stick and pushed the partly burned wood to the red coals in the centre. Then he picked up a blackened kettle and filled it with water from a barrel. Using a slender branch, he suspended it over the newly invigorated fire.

Reaching into a breast pocket of his khaki jacket, he pulled out a pack of cigarettes. He extracted one and tapped the filter end on the package. Retrieving a Zippo lighter from his pocket, he lit his first cigarette of the day.

Putting the slightly crushed package and lighter back into his pocket, he rolled a log closer to the fire with his foot. Using it as a stool, he sat there and inhaled the cigarette smoke, waiting for the kettle to boil.

Accustomed to arising before daybreak, he was up for the morning, anxious to meet with his leader in the bunker below to discuss what to do about the disabled UN vehicle in the field.

By the sounds from the trees after the ambush, he knew more than one vehicle had departed, returning the way they had come, through the big trees on his left. He knew the first soldier who had attempted to reach the overturned vehicle had been shot and was possibly dead. He also knew, at least during final daylight hours of the evening, none of the occupants of the disabled vehicle had left. He would have seen them. Perhaps all of the soldiers inside had been killed. Maybe they were too badly wounded to be able to leave. Perhaps, under the cover of darkness, their comrades had gone to the vehicle and removed them.

He would propose to his leader that they wait for several hours after the sun came up before doing anything. If the men in the overturned vehicle were still alive, heat would force them out. Then they could decide whether to shoot them or take them prisoner.

Although he was more inclined to get rid of them and to strip their vehicle of anything useful, he suspected his leader, a former officer in the Yugoslav army, who kept referring to the Geneva Convention and war crimes, would want to take them alive.

He was worried the soldiers below would be joined by reinforcements. If so, his group should return home to their civilian lives or risk being killed or taken prisoner. While claiming to be the local militia, they were merely a gang of bandits who had taken up this position, controlling the roadway below.

From this vantage point, against unarmed travellers, their enterprise was lucrative, as they denied safe passage to anyone fleeing hostilities unless they paid, if not money then any valuables the travellers were carrying.

Like most of the combatants in this civil war, they were good at killing unarmed civilians, but few had any military training. This was the first time they had encountered a military force. He thought they should have permitted the white UN vehicles to pass by unharmed.

The previous evening, he had met with the five men in the bunker. Opinions varied. Some wanted to send the Lada to the nearby town for reinforcements to fight the intruders. Others wanted to take their weapons and gear and leave under the cover of darkness, returning when it was safe to set up business again.

Unable to agree, they had decided to meet again after sunrise and make their decision.

Chapter 27

Billy was in a quandary. It was 0325 hours. Sunrise would be at approximately 0500 hours, but it would be daylight a half hour earlier. He planned to attack the tent's three occupants at 0400, a half hour before daylight and the darkest part of the night.

He had hoped all three would be asleep, giving him the best chance to dispatch them quietly. Now, with one awake, apparently up for the day, the others would be up soon. That would eliminate any chance of a quiet kill and force him to use his rifle, alerting everyone in the heavily armed bunker below.

Time was no longer on his side.

Then the moon, now high in the western sky and providing less light than earlier in the evening, was obscured by clouds drifting overhead, leaving him in complete darkness. The silver lining, if it could be called as much, was that, absent any light from the moon, he could not be seen either.

He decided his best and perhaps only chance would be to use a fixed bayonet and get close enough to the early riser to kill him quickly. The man would likely make a noise, possibly even scream, but Billy would be only a few feet from the two sleeping in the tent. If he was fast enough, he could dispose of them before they were fully awake.

Having decided what to do, he knew every second mattered. His plan would not work if the early riser was joined by another. Going around either side of the clearing would not work either. In the darkness, he would make too much noise. He had to get across the opening undetected while in plain view of his target. Risky but possible.

Remembering how, as a boy, he had hunted diving ducks in the small ponds in the bogs around Spudgels Cove, he decided to try it. With ducks, he would wait for them to dive and then run directly toward them, straight across the bog for ten or fifteen seconds, and then drop flat to the ground before the ducks resurfaced. Then he would wait, motionless, for the ducks to dive again and then repeat the process. Generally, by the time the ducks had dived three or four times, he could get to within a few yards and be waiting with his grandfather's old twelve-gauge when the ducks resurfaced for the final time.

The fellow by the fire appeared to be completely relaxed, moving around freely, unconcerned about any danger. And why should he be? Anyone approaching his campsite had to get past the campsite occupied by the two snipers.

Once again, Billy rid himself of all nonessential equipment, including his helmet. Using wet earth from underfoot, he blackened any exposed skin. Satisfied his filthy and bloodstained uniform would not give him away, he removed the scabbard from his bayonet and rubbed dirt all over the bloodstained blade. Then, his senses tingling, he got on his hands and knees and crawled the first few yards toward the fire.

He waited, motionless, until the early riser walked into the tent to pick up something. Billy crawled five or six more steps and then dropped before the man returned.

A few minutes later, the man got up and went to the side of the clearing to fetch more firewood. Billy crawled another ten or twelve steps before dropping to the ground.

Minutes later, the man got up again, took a flashlight, and walked behind the tent, headed toward the machine gun location. Realizing the tent would block the man's view of the campfire area, Billy smiled. He got up and raced across the distance to the tent.

Since the man had gone around the left side, Billy guessed he would return the same way, so Billy went to the right. There, he crouched and waited. He was just in time, because the man spent only a minute or two behind the tent. Coming to the front, he reached inside the tent, where he deposited the flashlight, before turning toward the fire.

He did not make it.

Billy's attack was fast and savage. He lunged at the man from behind, driving his bayonet into his middle back and twisting the blade before hauling it out, causing blood to spray from the wound.

As the man tumbled to the ground, Billy crossed the few steps to the two men sleeping inside the tent. He slammed the 171 millimetre blade so forcefully into the first man it went completely through his body, piercing the blanket beneath him.

Perhaps sensing the commotion, the other man, sleeping facedown, murmured, and started to turn over. Billy's bayonet caught him in the right side. Taking no chances, Billy slammed the bayonet into his torso a second time. Then he bayoneted the other sleeper a second time before going outside and doing the same to the first man. There was no need. His initial thrust had been fatal.

For a moment, Billy was grateful for his bayonet training, his mind flashing back to the merciless drill sergeant who had insisted on perfection. Few modern armies bothered with bayonet training anymore. Most of his unit thought it a waste of time, an excuse for the old-timers to show off. They were wrong.

Breathless, he looked at his watch. Seeing it was 0415 hours, he knew it would be light soon. He needed to get moving. Leaving the bodies where they lay, he ran to the machine gun overlooking the dark valley.

Standing there, breathless, he thought that, after all this rushing, now he had to wait. He chuckled to himself. *Yup, this is the Army. Rush, rush, rush. Then wait, wait, wait.*

As he waited for daylight, he thought maybe for the extra firepower, he should use the machine gun instead of his rifle. Then he thought, *No, this was not the time to try out a new weapon. The C7 would be best.* Besides, if Josh got the message and figured it out, which he probably would because he was from back home, and Billy used the C7, he would know it was him. If he used the machine gun — if he could get it working, that is — his guys might think he did not make it and perhaps take him out by mistake.

As light filled the valley below, he spotted a sentry holding a rifle. The man was leaning against a sand bag wall that provided cover from below. Another man carrying a rifle appeared from the bunker behind him. They spoke. The second one giving the first a cigarette and a light before turning around and walking to the trail that led up the hillside.

Oh boy, Billy thought. He could be coming to check on the guys at the machine gun nest or maybe the two snipers. Sunrise was still a few minutes away. He would find them in minutes.

The sentry was joined by a third man, who was wearing a uniform. He appeared to be in charge. While he was not carrying a rifle, Billy saw a handgun in a holster.

Enough, Billy thought. *I can't wait any longer.*

He aimed at the mid-back of the one who appeared to be in charge and squeezed off two shots. The first struck him in the right shoulder blade, angled downward, and exited through his lower right chest. The force of the shot spun him around. The second shot entered his left side, going through his abdomen, and exited above his right hip, driving him to the ground, screaming.

The other man stood there, seemingly dazed, unable to comprehend where the shots were coming from. That allowed Billy to squeeze off three more quick shots. The first missed, but the next two found their mark. One pierced the soldier's left thigh, smashing the bone. The third went through his right shoulder, exiting through his armpit.

Apparently unaware the attack was coming from above and behind, two men rushed out of the bunker to help their wounded comrades. As they did,

Billy saw twin flashes from the edge of the trees below, followed by two loud bangs. The sandbags blew up, finishing off the two men Billy had shot and killing those attempting to rescue them.

The first two rounds from below were followed by a third, fourth, fifth, and sixth. They scored direct hits on the bunker, destroying it.

Billy still had to stop the fifth man, who had left a few moments before he started shooting. As the early morning sun began to peek over the mountains, Billy ran back down the trail he had crept along earlier in the dark.

In the daylight, it seemed much shorter. He covered the downward leg of the trail to the fork in a few minutes. Then he veered to the right, slightly upward, still going across the hillside. He passed the snipers' camp, where the fire was still smouldering, toward the road that led up over the mountain.

Even before he got there, he heard the sound of someone trying to start the Lada, which was impossible without the rotor button. He slowed to a brisk walk so he could catch his breath and decide what to do with him. Would he take him prisoner, or would he shoot him, eliminating the only witness and a lot of questions?

Coming to the narrow, rocky road, Billy snuck up to the car, pointed his rifle in the window, and shot the fifteen-year-old would-be driver. The bullet entered above and behind the teenager's left ear. At point blank range, it killed him instantly, exiting downward through his right cheek and lodging in the dashboard on the passenger side. The bloody spray contained bits of skin, bone, brain, and hair.

He's only a kid, Billy thought. *The more you kill, the easier it gets.*

He opened the door, grabbed the body slumped over the steering wheel, and hauled it out onto the ground. Then he lifted the hood, replaced the rotor button, and closed the hood. He grabbed his rifle, jumped into the car, and turned the key.

Flooded. It would not start.

Swearing under his breath, he left the ignition turned on, slipped the car into neutral, released the emergency brake, and then stepped out. Putting his shoulder against the doorframe, he pushed as hard as he could.

When the small car began to roll downhill, he jumped back in, shifted into second gear, and popped the clutch. The engine sputtered to life. By then he was almost into the intersection, forcing him to brake and veer sharply to the left to avoid crashing into the trees on the opposite side.

With emergency lights flashing, honking the horn, and hoping he would not be shot, he headed toward the meadow. There, the others were waiting, their guns aimed at the approaching Lada. Avoiding the ruts, he drove up to them, slammed on the brakes, and jumped out, leaving the vehicle running.

He saluted the lieutenant and Josh, who was overseeing the removal of soldiers from the disabled Cougar. Only two were alive, one having died overnight.

Before Billy could speak, Short cut in. "Soldier, the lieutenant and I expect a full report from you as soon as feasible. Right now, can you tell us if all the hostiles have been neutralized?"

"Yes, Sergeant," Billy replied.

"All of them?"

"Yes, Sergeant, all of them."

"How many of them were there?" the lieutenant inquired.

"Ten, sir," Billy replied crisply. "Two snipers, three more in the machine gun nest, and five at the bunker."

"And Corporal, how did you manage to eliminate them without giving away your position?" the lieutenant asked.

"Sir, handheld bayonet for the two snipers. Fixed bayonet for the three machine gunners. Then I opened fire on the ones in the bunker."

Only then, after taking in the bedraggled, vacant-eyed wretch standing in front of him, still saluting, the front of his uniform covered in partially dried blood and mud, his face still blackened, emitting the odour of the human excrement he had crawled through in the dark, did the full impact of what Billy had done register on the young lieutenant's face. Suppressing the urge to hurl, he looked at Josh.

"Get this man cleaned up, and put him in another uniform. He's been through hell. I want him recommended for master corporal when we get back."

"Sir, we don't have any spare uniforms, and we've got no way to clean his," Josh replied.

"Strip one of the dead guys," the lieutenant replied. "Clean the corporal, and give him that man's uniform. Don't tell him it came from a dead soldier. Remove the name and anything that identifies which man it came from. We don't want him having nightmares about taking a dead soldier's uniform."

"What about the body?" the sergeant asked.

"Roll it up in a blanket, and tie it up well. Secure the corporal's uniform in something. Have it cleaned when we get back to base."

At the end of the mission, assisted by Josh, Billy made a full report of his actions. There was discussion about a decoration for valour, but this was a peacekeeping mission. No actual combat was approved, so no recommendation was made.

Instead, a sanitized version of the night's activities was kept on file in case there was an investigation into the deaths on the hillside.

Chapter 28

The doorbell rang at 4 a.m., sending Emma flying from the sofa, where she had spent a fitful night, tossing and turning, unable to sleep yet unable to stay awake. Finally, she had drifted off and was enjoying a nice dream.

In her dream, it was early September. Billy was home, and the children were back at school. It was 8:30 a.m. She had just seen the children off and watched them walk to the bus stop, where they joined several other children.

She had made a fresh pot of coffee, locked the door, unplugged the telephone, and was headed back to join her husband for a rare morning in bed.

Then her dream was interrupted by what sounded like a school bus stopping in front of their house, a tiny, wartime bungalow, rented accommodations for married enlisted men and their families. But that could not be, because the bus stop was at the corner, a few houses away.

She awoke in a panic, thinking she had overslept. The bus had to be coming back for the kids.

Opening her eyes, she saw it was still dark. The clock radio showed 3:58 a.m. She heard the bus drive off. While she was still trying to understand why a bus was on her street at that hour, the doorbell rang.

Then it came back to her. Billy, due home the previous afternoon, had called from Germany to say he did not expect to arrive until midmorning. He said he would call her from the base so she and the children could come and get him.

He sounded subdued. She assumed he was tired.

Disappointed at the delay, she was still excited that he was returning and that they would finally have a chance for a normal life. Excited but apprehensive. They had been married for only two weeks before he left and had not seen each other for over six months.

They had lots to talk about, including one issue she was dreading. The unexpected pregnancy had been a crisis. The hasty marriage, followed by the miscarriage, had thrown both of them for a loop. She had not told Billy that complications arising from the miscarriage had left her unable to have children. She had not told him because he was in a war zone. She did not want to cause him additional stress.

Now she was afraid this bad news would overshadow the good news of his return. She wished she had told him earlier. She decided to wait until he had been home awhile before telling him.

She was apprehensive about what he would be like after so long away. Some of the wives, concerned about how their husbands would readjust to family life, had formed a support group. All of them had read about issues related to other conflicts where returning men came back changed. Some did not fit back into home life. She thought they were overreacting. They were referring to soldiers who had fought in real wars, who had seen action, been shot at. They had seen their buddies wounded or even killed. None of that applied to Billy.

He had been on a UN peacekeeping mission taking care of civilians, helping them obtain clean drinking water, distributing food, and keeping order. If he had been involved in any military action, he would have told her. Her Billy kill someone? Ridiculous!

She expected him to be tired, but who would not be after six months away and a long trip back? Smiling, she walked to the door, remembering the first time they had made love, when he picked her up and carried her into the bedroom.

I hope that he's not too tired, she thought.

Flicking on the outside light before pausing to look through the peephole Billy had installed in the door, she gasped at the slightly stooped figure standing outside. He looked like Billy, but a much older, thinner, gaunter version of the man she expected.

Peephole magnifying glass!

With an expectant smile, she threw open the door. As her eyes took in the full picture of the man standing outside, her husband, she was unable to mask her shock at how much he had changed.

Gone was the fresh-faced, generally upbeat, but sometimes serious twenty-five-year-old, three years her junior. In his place was someone who looked older with deeply etched lines on his stubble-covered face. His previously sparkling, merry eyes had lost their lustre. With weight loss, they had retreated back into his skull.

They embraced but more like old friends than expectant lovers.

"I've been travelling for days, so I really need to shower and put on fresh clothes," were his first words.

Her nose agreed vehemently with his statement. Nevertheless, she smiled. "I've been wearing your bathrobe while you were away. Two days ago, I washed and dried it and hung up in the bathroom, just where you left it. Are you hungry? Can I get you something to drink?"

"They fed us on the flight," he replied, "but I wouldn't mind something to drink."

"I put a half dozen beer in the fridge yesterday."

"Do we have anything stronger?"

"We have some rye left over from our wedding. Would you like some with mix?"

"I don't bother with mix anymore," he said, "and can you make it a triple? It was a really long flight, and I need something to take the edge off."

He headed to the bathroom, she to the kitchen.

Finding a half bottle of Canadian Club, she took a glass from the cupboard and filled it halfway with the amber-coloured whiskey. Walking to the bathroom, where the door was ajar, she opened it wide enough to reach inside and placed the glass on the vanity top.

"Your drink is near the washbasin!" she called out over the sound of the shower. "Can I get you anything else?"

"Thanks, that's fine," he called back. "I'll just be a few minutes."

Grateful for the dimmers Billy had installed nearly a year earlier, she lowered the bedroom lights, disrobed, slipped into bed, and waited eagerly in their partially darkened bedroom, the covers to her chin.

"What did you do with the whiskey?" he called from the kitchen a few minutes later.

"It's in the cupboard. Above the fridge."

Moments later, he came to the bedroom, dropped his bathrobe to the floor, and slipped into bed. There, clean-shaven and smelling of fresh soap, Old Spice, and whiskey, he held her in his arms. Breathing heavily, he fell asleep.

Disappointed and bewildered, she thought it was weird. She knew it was him, but he had changed. It was like having a long-lost pet return. Emaciated, wary, unable to tell you where he had been or what had happened.

She rearranged their naked bodies. Holding him securely in her arms, she gazed lovingly into his face.

"Welcome home, soldier," she whispered in a tone that was more maternal than amorous. Then she drifted off to sleep.

* * *

But for a bathroom break, Billy slept for twelve hours, arising before 5 p.m. to the smell of burgers being barbecued. He stretched, yawned, and got up slowly and put on his bathrobe. Then he joined Emma and the children in the kitchen.

Kyle and Kayla had been asleep when Billy arrived, and he was still sleeping when they awoke. Excited, they wanted to see him so badly that Emma let them stand by his bed for a few minutes and watch him sleeping. Although she feared they would disturb him, she need not have worried. Billy was dead to the world. Still, after breakfast she arranged for them to spend the day at a friend's home while she stayed home to be there when Billy awoke. To her disappointment, he slept through the entire day, so by 4 p.m., she began to prepare supper.

In his bathrobe, unheard over the television in the living room and the lively discussion going on in the kitchen, Billy tiptoed to the kitchen doorway. He paused for a moment and knocked on the door three times.

"Is anyone home?"

The kids flew from their chairs and swarmed him, each one wrapped tightly around a leg.

"Daddy, Daddy, Daddy!" Kyle shrieked.

Kayla, a little less boisterous, but excited, said, "Uncle Billy! Uncle Billy! Uncle Billy!"

Right behind them, Emma closed the distance between the kitchen table and the doorway and wrapped her arms around his upper body. For a few moments, the four of them stood there, a single unit.

When the noise died down, Emma loosened her grip on him. "You're just in time to settle the first debate."

Billy looked at her, mystified and still groggy from having slept so long. "And what would that be?"

"They've been debating what to call you," Emma replied. "Kyle wants to call you 'Daddy', but Kayla isn't so sure. She still misses Roger, and she's been calling you 'Uncle Billy' for such a long time she doesn't want to change."

All three felt silent. Billy realized this was an important issue, perhaps for all three. For a moment, the old Billy, the accommodator, easygoing and good with children, returned. Looking at them, his mind flashed back to the scene in the home where he had shot the five Vipers. He felt lucky to be alive.

"Well now," he said, "let's settle this right now." He paused, "What you think of this solution: If Kyle wants to call me 'Daddy', then Kyle can call me 'Daddy'. That will make me the proudest daddy in the world."

Then he turned to Kayla. "And if Kayla wants to call me 'Uncle Billy', she can call me 'Uncle Billy', and that will make me the proudest uncle in the world. If, one of these days, Kayla wants to call me 'Daddy', then that's her decision. I'm happy either way."

Then he looked into Emma's beaming eyes. "Does anyone have any better ideas?"

He knew it was the answer she wanted when she hugged him tightly. Finally, she released her grip.

"I made burgers and tossed salad for all of us, but this is morning for you. Would you prefer breakfast? How about starting with a fresh coffee?"

"Don't worry about breakfast; the burgers smell great, and I'm really looking forward to some home cooking. I'll have a coffee in a little while. Do we have any beer in the fridge?"

Without waiting for her response, he opened the fridge door, found one, twisted off the cap, lifted the bottle to his lips, and drank half of it before stopping. Then he took a second beer and joined them at the table, finished the first, and uncapped the second.

As they ate, Emma had the feeling Billy's mind was somewhere else. He was more subdued than usual. He did not initiate conversation, responding only when addressed. Sitting with the kids in the living room, still wearing his bathrobe, he read stories to them. However, instead of the usual coffee, he drank beer after beer.

Finally, after eight beers, he and the children fell asleep. Rather than disturb him, Emma put the children to bed. Then she joined him on the sofa and fell asleep.

Chapter 29

Before midnight, Emma awoke to Billy's voice. At first, thinking he was awake and speaking to her, she answered him. When he did not respond but kept talking, she realized he was having a nightmare. She turned on the light and shook him gently.

He awoke wild-eyed, breathing heavily and perspiring profusely.

"Emma!" he said. "What are you doing here?"

"You're home, Billy," she said. "You fell asleep on the sofa. I didn't want to wake you up, so I joined you. You were talking to yourself, like you were having a nightmare, so I woke you up."

"It's a good thing you did, or I would have pissed myself in my sleep," he said. Then he jumped up and raced to the bathroom.

"Do you want to talk about it?" she asked after he had rejoined her.

"Naw, I was just dreaming about some foolishness from over there." He looked at the clock. "It's bedtime, but I'm not even a little bit sleepy."

"No wonder," she replied, "by my calculation, you've slept for sixteen of the last twenty hours. Besides," she continued playfully, "except for the time you've been away, we're still practically on our honeymoon. Maybe we can find something a little more interesting to do than sleep."

Their attempt at lovemaking was a disaster. Initially, he was unmotivated. However, after a while, she was able to arouse him, but it was short lived, leaving him embarrassed and her disappointed and insecure as to how he felt about her.

Any thought of sex caused him to relive the scene he had witnessed in Bosnia. First, the two children killed in their crib, then the huge Viper raping the young girl, followed by him shooting all five of them. Then came the cover-up and the destruction of the town.

As for Emma, the unexpected pregnancy, the rushed marriage, and subsequent miscarriage had left her insecure about how Billy viewed her now.

While she knew he had bought the ring prior to her pregnancy and that he had intended to propose to her in any event, she could not shake the notion, however wrong, that he had been forced into the marriage. She wondered if the miscarriage had left her undesirable to him somehow. Unhappy but outwardly positive, so as not to embarrass him further, Emma drifted off to sleep.

Billy would have been grateful to sleep, but for that night, and for many others to come, sleep eluded him. After listening to Emma's soft, rhythmic breathing for a few minutes, he got up, donned sweatpants, runners, a T-shirt, and a hoodie and went for a long run in the cool midnight air.

Physically fit, even if emotionally damaged, he ran and walked and ran and walked for two hours before turning around and heading home.

He arrived at 4 a.m. and drank six ounces of liqueur left in the cupboard since Christmas. Washing it down with two beers, he fell asleep, fully clothed, on the sofa.

* * *

Over the course of the first week at home, Billy's routine changed little from his first day back, except, as the jet lag wore off, he no longer slept through the day. However, his night-time sleep was interrupted by nightmares, usually ending when Emma woke him. Unable to get back to sleep, he would go for a long run and then drink enough of whatever alcohol was available before drifting off to sleep on the sofa.

Perhaps unable, and certainly unwilling, to discuss what was bothering him, as she felt them drifting further and further apart, Billy's actions drove Emma to wits' end, causing her to turn to Dr. Maloney, the only person with whom she had ever discussed personal issues, for advice.

The appointment had been booked for some time so that, after Billy's return, Dr. Maloney could refer her to a specialist to determine if she could ever become pregnant again and, if so, whether she should be using birth control. She had not told Billy that the early prognosis of her having more children was poor. She hoped that if it remained unchanged, Dr. Maloney could explain it to Billy, perhaps lessening the impact.

Now, sitting forlornly in the physician's waiting room, she thought that family planning required a husband, but hers seemed to be lost in another world. She wondered if Dr. Maloney had any idea of what she could do to get him back.

"It sounds like he's shell-shocked," the old doctor said after listening to Emma explain Billy's behaviour.

"What does that mean?" she asked, wide-eyed, grateful he knew what she was talking about but afraid of the answer.

"Shell-shocked is an old term from World War One," Dr. Maloney replied gravely. "It describes men so traumatized by war that, even without physical wounds, they're unfit for action. You can appreciate their officers, mostly British, were unsympathetic to any soldier who looked physically fit but wouldn't fight."

"What happened to them?" Emma asked, increasingly worried.

"Regrettably, many of them were labelled cowards, court-martialled, and sometimes ... shot."

In the quiet that followed, the kindly doctor watched the colour drain from Emma's face.

"Is there anything we can do?" she asked, dry mouthed and desperate for a solution, a lump in her throat and tears in her eyes as she recalled the old Billy.

"Yes, Emma," Dr. Maloney replied, "there is. The problem is now called post-traumatic stress disorder or PTSD. Patients require counselling, the sooner the better. There seems to be a correlation between the type of military action and the recovery rate."

"What do you mean?" Emma asked, impatient to know how soon Billy would be cured.

"Well, if you compare soldiers returning from World War Two to those returning from Vietnam, it seems Vietnam veterans fared worse. It may be the type of war and how veterans are received upon their return has something to do with it."

"But Dr. Maloney," Emma countered, "Billy wasn't in a war. He was just on a peacekeeping mission. I don't see how he could have changed so much in six months."

Dr. Maloney responded with a knowing smile. "There's a reason they say the first casualty of war is the truth. Those in authority cover things up. You don't know what he's been through, but it's clear it was no picnic."

"So, what can I do to help, to help us get our lives back?"

"First of all, you must be patient with him, even when you don't want to be, even when he doesn't deserve it. A good therapist will help. Give it time, and pray he responds."

"Doesn't the military have counsellors?" Emma asked.

"I'm sure they do. However, I suspect they're overworked and have long waiting lists. Then there's the problem of trust. He may not want to open up to somebody connected to his employment. He may fear it will jeopardize his career."

"I understand," Emma replied. "What can I do?"

"Let me make some inquiries. Maybe I can find somebody to counsel both of you. That tends to produce the best results."

As Emma departed Dr. Maloney's office, she was beginning to realize the problem she was facing. Her immediate challenge was Billy, who was not talking.

Chapter 30

With Emma at the doctor's office, Billy picked up the telephone. He stopped and put it down. He went to the kitchen and poured himself a coffee. He sat at the kitchen table, stewing. He got up, walked back into the living room, picked up the telephone, and dialled the number. He stopped breathing, unsure if he wanted someone to answer or not.

His anxiety was short lived. After one ring, he heard a familiar voice. "Short here."

Billy cleared his throat. "Sergeant Short, I got problems, and I didn't know who else to call except you."

Sensing his anxiety, Josh lowered his voice. "No need to be so formal, Billy. We're off the clock. 'Josh' works for me. How can I help you?"

Silence.

"Is this about what you mentioned over there?" Josh asked, remembering their discussion in Bosnia and wanting to put Billy at ease.

Billy cleared his throat. "Yes, and it's a lot worse now. I'm all fucked up. I don't know what to do. A bullet would solve a lot of problems. I don't know if everyone would be better off with me dead."

Concerned, Josh became more formal. "Soldier, we need to get this under control. I'll be at your place in ten minutes. We'll go for a coffee."

He hung up, grabbed his truck keys, and headed to Billy's. He arrived just as Emma was returning.

"Hi Josh," Emma said. "Billy will be happy to see you. He's been kinda jumpy since he got back."

"Actually, it's work-related. I didn't want to burden you with boring army stuff, so I asked him to meet for coffee," Josh lied. "Since we're not in uniform, we'll likely just drop in at Tim Horton's. I'll have him back to you in half an hour."

Curious but content with the answer, she nodded. "That's okay for now,

131

but if Billy doesn't invite you over for dinner, I will."

Billy joined them, kissing Emma on the forehead. "The Sarge and I are heading out for coffee. We won't be long. Can I bring you one?"

"No, thanks," she replied. "I'm fine. Take all the time you want, and don't talk shop all the time. There's more to life than work, you know."

As they drove away, Josh glanced at Billy. "Wanna check out the new Tim Horton's over near the base that opened while we were away?"

"Sure," Billy replied.

Within minutes, they were seated at the new coffee shop, each holding a fresh brew.

"Man, Emma is really something," Josh said. "By the way she sized me up, she's really protective of you. You're a lucky dog. It's no wonder you didn't want to stay over there any longer than you had to."

"I wonder how she would feel about me if she knew I was a killer," Billy mumbled. "She's got no clue about what we did over there. Nobody back here does.

"Billy, you were just following orders. Every one of them had it coming."

"You can say that now," Billy said, "but we know it's not true. We were supposed to be peacekeeping."

Josh glanced around. "Not here. Too many ears. Let's drive around for a while."

In the truck, they discussed the subject openly for the first time.

"I could've taken the first five prisoner," Billy said, "but I wanted to kill four of them for what they did to that family. Then I killed the kid because he was a witness. That's the truth."

"Okay," Josh said. "Let's say I agree with you on the first five. But you can't feel bad about what you did on that hill. You didn't completely follow orders, but you didn't disobey orders either. If you hadn't done it, we might have suffered more casualties and perhaps not completed the mission."

"No, I don't feel bad about killing them, except for the kid in the car. He was unarmed and running for his life. I should've captured him instead of killing him."

"Billy, we all do things we regret."

"I have nightmares," Billy said, in tears now. "I can still feel my bayonet going into the first one. I feel him stiffen up. I feel him shiver and shake as I'm holding him tight. I feel his warm blood pumping out, past my glove, over my wrist, up my right forearm to my elbow, and I can smell it, the same smell as gutting a moose or a caribou. With big game, I can't stomach the meat for weeks after I kill one. That's nothing compared to having a man bleed to death all over me in the dark. The nightmares are so real I'm afraid to go to sleep."

He paused and wiped his cheeks with his sleeves. "Sarge, I'm really fucked up. As long as I'm alive, it won't be over. What can I do?"

With compassion in his eyes, Josh looked at Billy's drawn face, even more haggard than when he had returned home a few weeks earlier. "Billy, you got to get it together, for everyone's sake, but I don't think you can do it on your own. A good place to start would be a chat with the reverend. I spoke with him once," he added, lying the second time in less than an hour. "He really helped me."

Before Billy could object, Josh continued. "I'll give him a call today and tell him you need to speak with him. I won't tell him anything except you were involved in some heavy stuff over there and need to talk to someone, confidentially, so you can get your head back together. I don't think it's a good idea for you to report it officially. Once it gets in your file, there's no way to get it out. It might be held against you later."

"Are you sure he won't tell anybody?"

"Positive," Josh replied. "He's not allowed to. If he did, he would be finished as a chaplain. He'd be fired by his church, too."

"Are you saying he can't talk about any stuff from over there?"

"That's right."

"What about anything since I came home?"

"None of it," Josh confirmed.

They sat in silence for a while.

"I'm leaving next week," Josh said. "I'll be gone a month, but I've got two things to tell you that might cheer you up."

Billy looked at him. "You're leaving? For a whole month? What if I don't like the chaplain?"

Josh felt guilty he had not waited until after Billy saw the chaplain before telling him he was leaving. "I'm taking all my annual leave in one shot in September and going down home."

Billy's eyes lit up. "September, moose hunting season. Wow, I wish I was going with you."

"You're welcome to join me," Josh said. "I'll be driving, so it won't cost anything for you to ride along. If you want to split the gas, you can, but if money is tighter than you're used to, with you being a new family man and all that, you don't need to pay anything. I'd be happy just to have the company and split the driving."

"That's a great offer, Josh, but I've got to say no. The money's fine. Emma takes care of it, and she's good at it, better than me. Back in the winter when we shipped out, I planned on taking my leave as soon as I got back here so all of us could go down home so everybody could meet Emma and the kids. My folks haven't met them, you know, but right now, I can't handle it. I gotta get my shit together before we visit. They can't see me like this." He paused for a moment. "What are you gonna do while you're down home?"

"Well, I've been away for ten years. Every year when my grandfather applies for a moose license, he puts me down as his hunting partner. I never get to hunt with him though, because I'm never home. Usually, he goes with my uncles, Jacob and Esau, but this year, they're gonna go guiding with one of the big game outfitters from up your way, Portland Creek, I believe. They'll be in the Long Range Mountains in a camp for September and October. Rather than Pop hunting alone, I'm going down to hunt with him."

"You're so lucky your Pop is still alive, never mind being able to go moose hunting with him!" Billy replied, clearly envious. "How old is he?"

"Seventy-five."

"In good shape?"

"I'll say, but we almost lost him last fall."

"What happened?"

"Heart. You know, he's like a lot of the old-timers from around home. They wouldn't go to a doctor for a check-up if their lives depended on it. Pop used to say doctors and hospitals are for sick people. If he ever he wanted to get sick, he'd go to the hospital. Then last fall, while he was lugging a quarter of moose, he got dizzy, took a pain in his chest, and keeled over. It's lucky for him, lucky for all of us, he was hunting with my uncles in Area 1, near St. Anthony, or we would have lost him for sure."

"What did they do?"

"They dropped everything, loaded him in Uncle Jake's truck, and got to St. Anthony Hospital in under an hour. The old doc stabilized him and put him on the air ambulance to the Health Sciences Centre in St. John's. He needed four bypasses. His heart was blocked right up, and yet he was going around like he was fine."

"How is he now?"

"Fit as a fiddle. Nan says he's as good as when he was forty." Then he winked. "But I don't know how she's holding up. She's over seventy herself."

"What did your pop do?" Billy asked.

"Fisherman. He went in the boat with his uncle when he was twelve, after his father, my great-grandfather, drowned. He fished until he was sixty-five. As soon as he started getting the rocking chair money, he turned everything over to my uncles. They were fishing with him anyway, but there wasn't enough in it for three of them to make a living, so they worked away every winter."

"What did they work at?"

"Carpenters. They're carpenters by trade. Good ones, too, but like most of us, they'd rather be fishing. Now with the moratorium, the fishery is finished, so they decided to go guiding this fall."

"Moratorium?" Billy asked, perplexed.

"You haven't heard about it? I only found out about it last week when I called to let them know I was back and coming home in September. A few months ago, the feds shut down the entire cod fishery. Over thirty thousand people back home out of work, walking around with their hands in their pockets. It's only supposed to be temporary. There's supposed to be some money for the fisherman and plant workers, but right now, it's pretty sad."

"You know, I haven't even called Mom and Dad to let them know I'm back," Billy said, suddenly concerned for his family.

"Before you do, let me give you some good news to pass along to them."

Billy looked at him. "Good news?"

"Yes. The lieutenant recommended you for master corporal for what you did up on the hill, but that's not mentioned anywhere. It's for leadership qualities you demonstrated on the recon mission, which is the absolute truth."

"I thought you needed to do a course before you got promoted to master corporal," Billy replied. "And I'm a little short on the time, too."

"You're right," Josh said, "but the course can be waived and the time shortened in some cases. You're the perfect case for both. But for what I'm gonna tell you next, I hope you'll do the course ASAP."

"What's that?" Billy asked, smiling that his efforts were being validated by his superiors. "Master corporal, right on! That means a pay raise, too. Some good news for Emma."

"You know there's a sniper course?" Josh asked.

"Yes. Before we shipped out, I was thinking of it. Now I'm not so sure."

"Billy, one of the issues we faced before our deployment was that none of our guys had any combat experience. Now we do — at least some of us do — and the brass want to make the most of it."

"What do you mean?"

"They want to beef up the sniper course," Josh replied. "Update it and add some instructors with current experience. Add night work and hand-to-hand with fixed and handheld bayonets. I'm supposed to start putting it together in October."

"You want me to apply for it?"

"Apply for it? Hardly. I can pick someone to work with me. You're my first choice. As master corporal, with your experience, you're a shoo-in. But there's another good reason for you to complete the course. It includes leadership training, delegating to subordinates instead of just doing things yourself."

Billy mulled over the possibilities.

"Help me develop the course," Josh said. "Be one of the instructors. You're the only one with one-on-one, night-time, hand-to-hand combat. It'll keep you home awhile. I'm sure Emma and the kids would like that."

Billy snapped back to the present, not the present of the weeks since his return but the present of what life was like before Bosnia. A heavy weight lifted from his shoulders.

"Thanks, Sarge, I really appreciate you looking out for me. What do I need to do?"

"Nothing. Just leave it to me. And when I get to my quarters, I'm gonna call the reverend and ask him to call you," Josh said. "Are you good with that?"

"That would be great," Billy replied, amazed at how much better he felt. He hoped it would last.

When they stopped in front of his home, Billy, grateful for Josh's help, invited him in for supper, all the while hoping he would decline.

"Let me take a rain check," Josh said. "I've got tons to do before I head down home. I'm not on leave like you, so I've still got to work. I'll tell the brass you'll be working on the course with me."

After thanking Josh profusely for helping him, Billy headed briskly for his front door. With a new spring in his step, he was inside before Josh's truck reached the corner.

"I'm back! Is anybody home?" he called out.

Emma appeared from the kitchen. Having pondered the information from Dr. Maloney, and seeing Billy in such good spirits, the look on her face changed from concern to relief, then to disbelief when he picked her up in his arms and smiled.

"I've got some making up to do," he said.

He carried her to the bedroom. Once there, behind a locked door, in a room only slightly darkened by blinds, they made love: the fast, hard, urgent sex of two people who loved each other passionately but who had been apart for too long.

When they finished, he rolled onto his back, breathing heavily. "Give me a few minutes, and maybe we can do it again before the kids show up. Maybe a little slower."

And they did.

A half hour later, they lay next to each other, feeling better than they had in a long time.

"I need to tell you some things about some stuff that happened over there," he said. "I've been really messed up, and I'm sure I've been hard to be around. I talked to Josh. He's going to have the chaplain call me. After I discuss some things with him, it'll be easier for us to talk about it. Then you'll know it's not your fault if I don't seem right sometimes."

"Thank God," she replied. "You've been a completely different person since you got home. I've been going out of my mind. You wouldn't talk, and I didn't know where to turn, so just this morning, I talked to Dr. Maloney. He's familiar with what you're going through. He thought a private counsellor might help."

She knew right away that she had said something wrong. His face went from calm and friendly to shocked and betrayed. Then it darkened into fury.

"You did what? You told that old doctor? I can't believe it! Who else have you told?"

Stung by his response, she wanted to lash back and tell him how she felt abandoned while he went off to war. She wanted to tell him that, since his return, she was the one who had borne the brunt of the change in him and being rejected by him. But then she remembered the doctor's words about being patient, even when she did not want to be, even when he did not deserve it.

"I didn't tell anybody but Dr. Maloney," she said, tears welling in her eyes. "I'm really sorry, Billy, I was only trying to help."

"Then don't help me anymore — unless I ask for it," he said.

Interrupted by the children coming home, Emma jumped up and got dressed. Without a word, she went to the bathroom and washed her tear-stained face before greeting them.

* * *

That afternoon, Josh met with Reverend Harry House.

"Billy Wheeler has seen more hands-on action than most men will ever see, even in a real war," Josh said. "He can't go through regular armed forces counselling. The stuff he did was unofficial, against policy for peacekeepers. There's a risk of discipline."

Reverend House nodded silently as he listened.

"Also, because there's no reported action to support a PTSD claim, some jackass up the line may figure he's just one of the 'People Trying to Screw the Department' and get rid of him. He's got great potential. He's done a lot. I don't want him short-changed."

When Josh left, Reverend House phoned Billy. "I just spoke with Sergeant Short. When would you like to get together?"

"I dunno," Billy replied glumly, feeling guilty for snapping at Emma. "The sooner, the better. How long will it take?"

"The first time we meet, I like to get together for a half hour, just to get acquainted. How about tomorrow morning in my office?"

"That works for me," Billy said.

And so it began. First, they covered Billy's personal background, agreeing to meet three times weekly. After the second meeting, the reverend recommended Emma participate.

Initially, Billy was apprehensive. However, after Reverend House explained how PTSD affects spouses and how informed and understanding spouses can help avoid situations that trigger stress attacks and help cope with the fallout of full-blown panic attacks, Billy agreed to include her.

Counselling went well. Over the next year, after a few relapses, Billy gave up alcohol. His feelings became manageable. Life returned to normal.

While the reverend was concerned that teaching the enhanced sniper course might set Billy back, the opposite was true. As Billy demonstrated hand-to-hand combat, the routine became repetitious, and his service experience merged with the training exercises, allowing him to cope better.

With Kyle starting kindergarten and Kayla beginning grade two, Emma wanted to work. Billy was put off by the idea, considering himself the breadwinner and wary of any change in their routine. But with Reverend House's encouragement, he agreed, and Emma began work as Dr. Maloney's receptionist.

Chapter 31

After wrapping the long, black silk strip around his head, leaving one end to fall in front of his left shoulder, Billy stood in front of the large, old, dusty mirror and took in what he saw. He looked like Osama bin Laden. Beneath the turban covering his black hair, which had not been cut for months, were strong black eyebrows, sun-burnished cheeks and nose, and a full black beard, complete with moustache.

Smiling into the mirror, he shuddered at what the dentist had done to his teeth. Just months ago, they had been nearly perfect and brilliantly white. Now one was missing, and two had been filed down to appear broken. All were stained, adding years to his appearance.

Dressed like an Afghan, with light baggy pants, a long flowing shirt, old sandals, and a well-worn brown vest, in his pockets he carried Afghan Afghanis and Pakistani rupees. His creased and slightly faded identification papers claimed he was Mohammed Khan, a thirty-eight-year-old resident of Karachi, Pakistan.

"You're a long way from Spudgels Cove now, Billy boy," he said to his reflection. "I wonder if you'll ever see home again."

Putting that thought out of his mind, he went downstairs and joined three other men. As the late summer sun set in the western sky, in a sweltering thirty-eight degrees Celsius, they headed to a teahouse. By all appearances, they were simply four Afghan men going out to drink tea, socialize, and catch up on the local news and gossip.

Walking along the dusty street, he thought of the events that had brought him there, to that point in his life, walking down a Kandahar street with another Canadian soldier and two CSIS (Canadian Security Intelligence Service) operatives as if they did not have a care in the world.

His mind went back eight months to Christmas 2000, one of the best times of his life. At age thirty-three, he had completed fifteen years of service and was a sergeant. Thanks to the reverend's counselling, Emma's patience, and joining AA at the tender age of twenty-five, the psychological issues and the need to self-medicate with alcohol were well behind him.

Teaching at the specialized sniper school had kept him and Josh, now a master warrant officer, from a second deployment overseas when, as part of its NATO commitment, more Canadian soldiers were sent to the former Yugoslavia. While a relief to Emma and the children, to Billy, it was a mixed blessing. He felt guilty he was not with his unit.

Guilty or not, if things continued to go well, in five more years he could make warrant officer and retire with a pension. Then he planned to look for a new career or maybe even go back to school.

Emma had started working for Dr. Maloney in 1992. When he retired three years later, the young physician who took over his practice was grateful to have her stay. He also raised her pay.

It had been a nice New Year's evening. Six couples at the Pittmans'. Everyone brought potluck. Everyone but Billy drank, some too much.

After supper, he caressed Emma's forearm softly and gave her "that look". She smiled. "Billy, we can't go home until after midnight."

"Oh, alright," he said in mock disappointment. "But the kids aren't always with your parents, and it's the best way I can think of to start the New Year."

She got up. "I'll help Maisie with the dishes." She smiled slyly. "So we can make a fast getaway."

As they drove home, Emma, slightly tipsy and dozing, Billy was engrossed in his thoughts. Everything was perfect.

BANG!

As he entered the intersection on a green light, he did not realize the vehicle approaching from the right was not stopping. The driver of the large SUV and his passenger, both intoxicated, were arguing. He drove right through the intersection and collided with the front passenger door of Billy's car.

Emma was killed instantly.

When Billy awoke in hospital, his life had changed forever. Mercifully, the children were spending Christmas with Emma's parents, so the news of her death was blunted, somewhat, by them.

Emma's funeral, which took place in her hometown, was a short, sombre affair.

After the funeral, Emma's parents, the Lanes, met privately with Billy.

"Philip and I think the children should remain with us, at least for the time being," said Edna. "How do you feel about that?"

Zombielike he replied, "if that's what you think is best, I'm okay with it."

"Philip also plans to talk to a lawyer about the accident, unless you want to?"

"You just look after everything," he answered. "I'll have payroll contact you so they can send you money every month."

Grief-stricken, Billy returned to the base alone while Josh and Emma's dad packed up the family's belongings and took them away.

Within weeks, completely crushed, Billy moved back into the barracks. While he showed up consistently for work, he had lost his zest for life. Concerned he would resume drinking and relapse into PTSD, Josh sought out Reverend House and asked him to contact Billy.

They met several times. While Billy said he was okay, the preacher was unconvinced. He suggested to Josh that Billy might benefit from a new challenge at work, something to keep him busy and take his mind off his loss.

Chapter 32

When the officer who had organized the Bosnian night squads, by now a colonel, was asked to recruit a few soldiers suitable to be trained for covert missions, he remembered Josh Short, the sergeant who had led the most effective of the night squads. He had been particularly impressed that, in addition to their effectiveness, their activities, while widely rumoured and now legendary in military circles, had remained undetected.

"Can you recommend any men for a special assignment?" he asked Josh, now a warrant officer. "They need to be single, have combat experience, and be able to stay for months at a time."

"There's only one. He was the best one over there for that kind of work," Josh said, referring to Bosnia, "but he's really fucked up right now."

"Why is that?" the colonel asked. "If he's the guy I think you're talking about, after some of the stories I've heard, he might be the kind of guy we're looking for."

"He might've been when he was single, but he's married," Josh replied.

"Oh?"

"Well, he got married just before we shipped out, but he's not married anymore. At New Year's, his wife was killed by a drunk driver. Now he's going around like he's got nothing to live for."

"Really? Kids?"

"Yes and no. Two teenagers, but they're not his kids. They're his wife's kids. They're with her parents. He's got family back in Newfoundland — parents, some brothers and sisters — but that's about it."

Billy received a request to travel to Ottawa to meet some people and do some tests to determine if he was suitable for a new challenge. He met up with Josh to talk about it.

"I've been asked if I would look at doing something else," Billy said. "I'm not sure what it is, but if I get through the testing, it means I won't be around here for a while. How do you feel about that?"

"I'm fine with it," Josh said. "Go and see what it's all about. It's a free trip to Ottawa. If you don't like it, you can turn them down. But you know, something new might be good for you. Help pass the time and get your mind off everything."

Three days later, Billy and fifteen other soldiers arrived at CSIS headquarters in Ottawa. Briefed individually, they were told they needed to commit to being out of touch with family for six months or longer.

Ten declined. Psychological testing eliminated two more.

Then a CSIS representative briefed the final four, including Billy, on the proposed assignment. They were told CSIS operated worldwide. Unlike other spy agencies, perhaps because Canada had not been involved in warlike activities for so long, it was a bloodless spy agency. It employed mostly unarmed operatives. In keeping with Canada's historic role as a peacekeeper, and not being a world superpower, Ottawa had not seen the need for CSIS to engage in the killing arts like other intelligence agencies. Now all of that looked like it was about to change. Through shared, yet reliable, intelligence, it seemed certain that soon, as part of NATO, Canada would deploy troops to one of the world's hotspots: Afghanistan.

CSIS was in a quandary. They could do nothing and rely on American and British intelligence, or, without explicit orders, they could go ahead and put unauthorized, armed operatives in the field.

Both approaches carried risks to the organization. If they did nothing and relied upon intelligence from other friendly nations, and based on this information, Canadian troops were deployed and things went poorly, the hawks on Parliament Hill would demand answers, and heads would roll. If they went ahead, unauthorized, and sent armed Canadian spies into the field, and if they were caught, the doves would accuse CSIS of being a rogue, out-of-control agency. They would demand a public inquiry, exposing Canada's weaknesses to the world. That could force the resignation of senior officials, perhaps even the minister of defence. CSIS would be neutered.

In a typically Canadian compromise, somebody crafted a middle solution. Recruit a small number of soldiers with combat experience. Give them a crash course in espionage. Have them available on short notice should the need arise.

While trained secretly in Ottawa, their documentation would show they were ordinary members of the Canadian armed forces, unconnected to CSIS. With the details kept to a minimum, ministerial authorization could be obtained on short notice. The solution provided protection for the agency and plausible deniability for its political masters.

After all four soldiers received this explanation, in a version sanitized to remove any potential inferences, they were given another opportunity to back out. None did.

Before training began, they were allowed two days to return home to take care of any personal arrangements or commitments. Then they returned to Ottawa and began months of intensive, nonstop training.

That training included immersion in foreign languages, including Urdu, the language of Pakistan; Pashto and Dari, the languages of Afghanistan; and even some Russian — partly because the Soviets had been in Afghanistan during the 1980s and partly because every spy should know Russian.

They would not become linguists, but to master the languages without any hint of an accent, language training started immediately. Eventually, they went for days without speaking or even hearing English. One recruit had little aptitude for foreign languages. He was released from the program. Billy and two others continued.

Chapter 33

By 2001, the Taliban had attracted so many foreign fighters to Afghanistan that Afghan cities were teeming with men from all over the Middle East. Many spoke Urdu but had little background in the local languages, Pashto and Dari.

CSIS trainers exploited this opportunity. The Canadians were taught Urdu by instructors whose first language was Pashto. Simultaneously, they learned both Pashto and Dari from instructors whose first language was Urdu.

This strategy meant that, in Afghanistan, they could pass themselves off as being Pakistani, speaking the local languages with a Pakistani accent. En route through Pakistan, they could say they were from Afghanistan, speaking Urdu with a Pashto or Dari accent. Having a vocabulary in all three languages gave them two alternate language options should they be unable to recall a word they would be expected to understand.

As they became more proficient in the three languages, they were introduced to a condensed course in Islam. All of them read the Koran in its entirety, and an Islamic scholar gave them a few dozen references to recite, should the need arise.

During Islamic studies, a debate arose concerning circumcision. Ultimately, the religious argument against circumcision prevailed, because, based on a strict interpretation of the Koran, not only did it appear not to be mandated, it appeared to be in opposition to the faith, as it was an improper alteration of a person's body. However, since most Muslim men were circumcised, to avoid questions should they be captured, it was deemed expedient to be circumcised. So, at age thirty-three, Billy Wheeler was the first man in his family to be circumcised.

While the language and religious training were difficult, cultural sensitivity was even harder.

"You're leaving one of the most advanced, liberal nations in the world," their trainer explained, "and going to a formerly progressive country, which, as a result of warfare and an extremist governments, is now one of the most backward, poorest places in the world. Human rights don't exist. Even discussing human rights can get you sent to prison, publicly flogged, or executed."

He also explained that men could not touch women who were not members of their immediate family. A man could have up to four wives and could buy and sell children and beat his wives. Fathers and brothers could do the same to their daughters or sisters. People were stoned to death in public on being accused of adultery. Women could be killed if they brought dishonour on the family.

"Because there is a danger you may react instinctively, in a manner showing you're a foreigner, we have designed a program to prevent you from responding normally," the trainer continued. "Even simple things, like speaking to a woman to ask directions, helping a woman climb stairs, or interfering if she's being beaten, can give you away as a foreigner and an infidel. You may be in a public square where someone is being stoned. You can't flinch or show disapproval. You will be expected to know this and be unconcerned about it."

They were shown videos of routine daily activities. Every time they might be inclined to respond instinctively and act out of character for the roles they were assuming, they were administered small electric shocks, a reminder to ignore any impulse to respond with empathy no matter how strongly they felt the urge.

They were told this programming had not been used for spies, but it was used to desensitize sexual deviants, keeping them from becoming sexually aroused. It seemed to work with them most of the time. Their trainer said that, at the end of the mission, CSIS would do its best to undo any long-term psychological effects.

It could not be guaranteed to work.

One of the recruits opted to withdraw. However, since he had been trained extensively, he remained with the spy agency to be deployed in other ways.

Without confirming where they were headed, for training purposes, the CSIS trainers focused on Afghanistan. However, the training and the role-playing was so realistic that the recruits knew exactly where they were going.

Chapter 34

The lead trainer, Major Marcus Quinn, was a huge, insecure man with a nasty streak. He had joined the Canadian armed forces to get a free education twenty years earlier, when there was little possibility of Canadian soldiers being sent into combat.

A paper pusher his entire career, he was acutely aware he was training men, selected, in part, for their combat experience. Feeling inadequate, he preferred to leave the actual training to his subordinates.

"You'll also need weapons training, which I'll take care of personally," he told the two finalists, Billy Wheeler and Angus McIsaac, a young master corporal from Cape Breton.

Billy looked at McIsaac with a wink. "I wonder where he thinks we've been all our lives, Sunday school?"

The comment elicited a smirk from the Nova Scotian, which grated on Quinn. Saying nothing, he opened a box and displayed two pistols and two submachine guns. He held up one of the guns.

"This is a Soviet Makarov nine millimetre semiautomatic. It holds eight rounds. Here, check out how it handles."

He tossed it toward them. Both reacted immediately, as if going after an errant hockey puck or baseball. Billy's fingers closed around the grip as McIsaac caught the barrel.

"Now, girls," Quinn said mockingly, "there's no need to fight over the new toys. We have one for each of you."

He passed the second pistol to McIsaac. Directing their attention to two machine guns and four grenades in the box, he picked up a machine gun. "This is a Soviet PP-19 Bison. It has a sixty-four round magazine. Fortunately for you jokers, it uses the same ammo as the pistols."

He continued with a sneer. "If you non-coms get confused out in the field and don't have an officer to tell you which ammo fits which weapon, they're both the same."

Reaching into the box with both hands, he picked up the grenades. "This is a Soviet RGN," he said, holding out his left hand, "and this," he held up his right hand, "is a Soviet RGO. The RGN has a four-metre kill radius, while the RGO's is six metres."

Still holding both grenades, he inserted his middle finger into the ring hanging from each grenade and pulled the pins. "Both have 3.8-second fuses but will detonate on impact after being armed for just 1.8 seconds."

He tossed both grenades at the men.

While McIsaac froze, standing there open-mouthed and wide-eyed, Billy sprang into action. In one fluid motion, he dropped the Makarov and caught both grenades mid-air. Clutching them to his chest, he fell to the floor to absorb the expected explosions. None came.

As Billy got up from the floor, white-faced, Quinn giggled. "Oh dear, did I forget to mention they aren't live?"

Wild-eyed, Billy launched himself over the table at Quinn. The force of the impact took them to the floor.

Even before they landed, Billy began to beat the much larger man savagely, fracturing his jaw and eye socket and knocking out three of his teeth.

McIsaac tackled Billy, knocking him off Quinn, who was already unconscious. With all three of them lying on the floor, Billy became calm suddenly.

"What's going on?" he asked McIsaac.

"What's going on?" McIsaac asked, aghast.

"Yes, what's going on?"

"You just jumped Quinn. If I hadn't tackled you, you might've killed him," the Cape Bretoner replied.

"Who's Quinn?" Billy asked.

"Who's Quinn?" McIsaac repeated the question, stunned. "Major Quinn is that big son of a bitch who oversees most of the training." Then he gave Billy a curious look. "How come you don't know who Quinn is? Is there something wrong with you?"

By then, Billy was aware of his surroundings. "We'll talk about it later," he said. "Right now, we've got to figure what to do about this situation."

Their discussion was brought to an end by a moan from Quinn, who was regaining consciousness, and by the appearance of Quinn's white-faced subordinate, a captain who had watched the assault from a distance.

"Good Lord," the captain said. "What happened here?"

Leaping to his feet, Billy saluted him. "Training accident, sir. The major needs medical attention. I'm sure he'll file a report."

Relieved the response allowed him a reason not to become involved personally, the captain returned Billy's salute. "Thank you, Sergeant. We'll see to it right away. We're on a short timetable with your training," he added. "I was supposed to handle this part, but this morning, Major Quinn advised me he would do it."

He looked at his watch. "It's nearly twelve hundred hours. Would you men like to take a break, grab some lunch, and see me back here at fourteen hundred? When we get back, I'll introduce you to another one of these Soviet toys, the AS Val. You're booked for three hours on the range from fifteen hundred to eighteen hundred hours."

He went on to volunteer an explanation, something Quinn never would have done. "I understand you may be going into a theatre where Soviet arms are easy to come by and easy to explain, but Western weapons could give you away."

He looked directly at Billy, who was massaging his quickly swelling right hand. "Sergeant, get some ice on that and have it checked out to make sure it isn't broken. If it is, you may not be deployable, and the mission could be over before it even starts."

As he walked away, he rolled his eyes. "A training accident!"

*   *   *

When they resumed two hours later, Billy held an improvised icepack to his hand.

"Do you have anything to report?" the captain asked.

"Yes, sir," Billy replied. "I had it checked out. No break." It was a lie. "The time I spent on the heavy bag built up a callus that protected the bones."

Satisfied, the captain opened a gun case and displayed a rifle neither Billy nor McIsaac had seen before. "This is a Soviet AS Val. Not your typical sniper's rifle. The effective range is not much more than three hundred metres. Instead of high-velocity ammunition to take out a target at a long distance, this one uses low-velocity, subsonic ammo and an integrated suppressor to take out a target quietly at close range."

Intrigued, both men looked at each other and then back at the captain.

"Captain, what kind of trajectory are we talking about for such a slow-moving projectile?" asked Billy, who had sniper school ballistics training.

"We're not sure," the captain admitted. "That's why you and McIsaac will be spending the next three hours on the range. We recently secured this rifle from an arms dealer for special missions. We haven't fired it, and we can't ask the manufacturer for an instruction manual. Wheeler, I understand from your background you're the best person to test fire it and make a full report for future use."

Billy tensed. "What exactly do you know about my background?"

"Perhaps more than you realize," the captain replied, oblivious to the new edge to Billy's tone. "I read your file — actually, I read both of your files."

McIsaac, who had been listening intently interjected. "You mean you read my file, too?"

"Yes, Master Corporal McIsaac, I read your file, too, but I meant the sergeant has two files, and I read both of them."

Billy was stunned to learn there was a second, secret file on him. The captain realized he had gone too far in disclosing it. He began to sweat. McIsaac, after witnessing Billy's unexpected attack on the major, prepared for the worst.

Billy clenched his fists. "Captain, you need to give me that file right now. Otherwise, this exercise is over for me. If I don't like what I read, I might call it off anyway."

The captain looked at McIsaac. "Fine," he said pointedly. "We'll need a little more privacy for that discussion."

"No discussion," Billy replied. "I want the file, and he gets to see it, too."

"You mean you want the master corporal to read it?" the captain asked.

"Yup," Billy replied. "Besides, letting me know what you guys are saying about me, it's a good way for McIsaac to get to know his new best friend. Perhaps, after he finds out about me, he might want to bail while he still can."

The easygoing, young captain realized his unguarded statement may have jeopardized the operation. He became even more accommodating. "Let's delay your visit to the range and go to my office for more privacy."

Up in his office, he unlocked a metal cabinet and gave Billy and McIsaac their files. The information about McIsaac was mostly non-contentious and already contained in his official file. Billy's background, due to the report of Reverend House, was a different story.

The minister had kept extensive notes. Attached to CSIS's request for information was a release signed by Billy. Although reluctant to release the information without confirming it with him first, Billy was already in Ottawa when the reverend had received the request and could not be reached.

At the end of forty-five minutes, during which neither enlisted man spoke, the captain could wait no longer. "So, what you think? Are we still going forward?"

"I'm fine," Billy said, "but McIsaac might want to think it over."

"Not me," the young Cape Bretoner replied. "I'm good to go."

"That's great," the captain said. "I figured as much, but before we move on, do you have any questions?"

"No, sir," Billy replied.

When McIsaac did not respond immediately, the captain nodded at him. "What is it, soldier?"

"Did Major Quinn know all of this stuff about Sergeant Wheeler?"

The captain nodded. "He did. That's why he should never have pushed Sergeant Wheeler as far as he did. The sergeant's psych eval, supported by his actions in the field, predict he will disregard his own safety and act instinctively to protect those around him. It was no surprise to me that he grabbed the grenades and covered them with his body. What's unclear to me is why he attacked the major. Did either the sergeant or the major say anything?"

"Not really," McIsaac lied. "I think the Sarge might've swore, but he didn't say anything. It was fast and confusing. I just wanted it to be over."

The captain seemed satisfied with the answer.

Chapter 35

On July 27, 2001, Billy and Angus received details of their mission. In three weeks, they would be sent to Kandahar, Afghanistan, via Karachi, Pakistan. Once there, they would stop overnight and switch identities.

Their identification papers would show they were Pakistani nationals who had lived in Karachi all their lives. If questioned upon their arrival in Kandahar, they could easily establish that they had originated from that city.

From Karachi, they would fly to Quetta, population 500,000, which boasted Pakistan's fourth-largest airport. From there, a Pakistani business-man, who was also a CIA operative, would drive them 125 kilometres to Chaman, near the Afghanistan border, where two Afghans, Basel and Ramin, former students, would drive them to Kandahar, 115 kilometres away.

Kamin, from the North, was the youngest son of his father's fourth wife. He went by his mother's maiden name. He had gone to Kandahar University to study engineering but dropped out when he saw how the university had regressed under the Taliban. Committed to a free and democratic Afghanistan, instead of leaving the country to study, he risked his life to remain in Kandahar as a spy.

Basel was born in Kandahar, grandson of a prominent Afghan business-man. He was drawn to the Mujahideen as a student in opposition to the corrupt, Soviet-supported government. That changed to silent, vehement opposition of the Taliban when he witnessed the public execution of his younger, gay brother and two of his friends.

He explained that the trio had been arrested and tortured by police under the direction of a mullah. Then they were bound with ropes and placed on a stone wall. A tractor toppled the wall on them, crushing them to death.

"I would've expected a more sympathetic response from Westerners such as you," he hissed, irritated that Billy and Angus did not respond to his graphic description of the execution.

Billy was quick to tell him they had undergone training to quell any instinctive responses to avoid attracting attention and blowing their cover. They assured Basel they were horrified but had been conditioned to offer no response.

Apologetic at having mistaken their silence for indifference, Basel agreed that their approach was the safest. There was no way to know who might be watching. In fact, he admitted he had been forced to watch the execution and forced to agree publicly that the penalty was appropriate.

The official reason for the Canadians' presence in Kandahar was to work for a small nongovernmental agency that made artificial limbs for people who had lost a limb, usually to a landmine. The agency was the brainchild of a devout Islamic businessman from Dubai who wanted to help people in Afghanistan after the war against the Soviets. Affluent and well connected, the businessmen easily convinced the mullah who oversaw Taliban operations in southeast Afghanistan, and who had lost half of his arm in the war, of his venture's benefits.

The businessman did not know his equally devout, Canadian-educated son, Ahmad, who ran the artificial limb enterprise, was horrified at the treatment of women in Afghanistan. A few years earlier, while in Canada visiting friends, he had contacted CSIS and become a CSIS operative.

Although the Canadians had been briefed well by their Canadian trainers, within hours of their arrival in Kandahar, they gained much greater insight into recent Afghan history and culture under the Taliban.

Ahmad explained the Soviets had invaded in 1979 to support an unpopular communist government. In response, the generally divided and warlike tribal Afghans, came together. Mujahideen, or freedom fighters, fought the Soviets and defeated them, as the Afghans had defeated the British in the nineteenth century.

Western governments, happy to have them oppose the Soviets, backed them with humanitarian and military support. In fact, they found such favour in the US that, in the mid-1980s, Ronald Reagan had welcomed their leaders to the White House for a meeting and photo op, publicly comparing them to the founding fathers of the United States.

After the Soviets withdrew from Afghanistan in 1989, the Mujahideen returned to their homes and religious schools. This left a power vacuum, which was filled by drug warlords, who had run parts of the country previously. In response to the ensuing lawlessness, people turned to a religious leader, a mullah, who had been a war hero against the Soviets, to govern them.

His group, the Taliban, Pashtun for student, governed by sharia law, operating in such a backward, intolerant, repressive manner that decades of progress were reversed. Since it was useful to Western nations to have a government in Afghanistan that was hostile to the Soviets, they ignored the plight of ordinary Afghans under Taliban rule.

These nations did not realize the Taliban were as hostile to the West as they were to the Soviets. Soon, Afghanistan became a haven for international terrorists. They established camps and attracted militant jihadists from all over the world. The Taliban trained them to use weapons and explosives and sent them worldwide on terror missions.

Any doubt about the danger posed by these terrorists was erased on April 7, 1998, when they simultaneously bombed US embassies in Nairobi, Kenya, and Dar es Salaam, Tanzania, killing hundreds of people.

Those attacks were followed by more bombings, including the October 12, 2000 attack on the *USS Cole* as the destroyer was refuelling in the Port of Aden. In that attack, a suicide bomber drove an explosives-laden speedboat into the side of the warship. The explosion ripped a huge hole in the vessel, killing seventeen sailors and wounding many more. International terrorist Osama bin Laden took credit for the attack on behalf of Al Qaeda, the group he was reputed to have established and funded.

The only serious opposition to the Taliban came from the Northern Alliance. It was led by a popular, university-educated engineer from the province of Panshir. A brilliant tactician in guerrilla warfare, he had been so effective against the Soviets he was dubbed the Lion of Panshir. However, he was assassinated by a suicide bomber posing as a photographer. Without outside support, and with the Taliban supported by the West, the Northern Alliance was squeezed into a small area in the country's mountainous northeast corner.

Informed commentators had warned that, under the Taliban, Afghanistan could become a safe haven for terrorists, who would indoctrinate, train, and arm others for missions worldwide. Their warnings fell on deaf ears even when US embassies in Nairobi and Dar es Salaam were bombed. Smug Western leaders downplayed the threat as African atrocities. They were confident their technology and heightened security could prevent any further attacks.

The attack on the *USS Cole* changed that, finally confirming the warnings that the threat to Western interests was real and immediate. However, by then, Afghanistan and other Middle Eastern countries had become hotbeds of Islamic terrorists, intent on and capable of exporting their brand of terrorism to the rest of the world.

World leaders began to understand the danger of Afghanistan, controlled by fundamentalist religious leaders, hostile to anyone who refused to adopt their views. Too late, they realized how poorly equipped they were to deal with the threat.

The realization of their vulnerability and the potential electoral backlash if voters blamed them for failing to take their security more seriously sent shockwaves through Western politicians. For the first time since the fall of the Berlin Wall in November 1989, politicians in Washington and London began talking tough, attempting to garner public support against a threat they had ignored previously.

CSIS feared Canadian politicians might follow suit, seeking answers from them. Their desire for self-preservation generated calls to high-ranking members of the Canadian Armed Forces seeking combat-hardened soldiers with the aptitude and skills to become foreign spies.

Billy and McIsaac's mission was simple — but not easy. Go to Kandahar, the headquarters of the Taliban government, and assassinate a few prominent individuals. Then kidnap two and deliver them to an abandoned airstrip outside the city for pick up by helicopters flying under the radar from Pakistan.

The targets were neither Taliban leaders nor the warlords who had ceded control of the country to them. They were too well protected. Instead, the targets were their highly placed subordinates.

While the assassination targets needed to be well known and have high status, their positions could be merely symbolic. However, those kidnapped needed to possess as much strategic information as possible. They were to be turned over to the CIA for interrogation. They needed two so that information provided by one could be compared with that obtained from the other to confirm its accuracy.

Also, as one hard-bitten CSIS handler pointed out, people did not always survive questioning. It would be unfortunate to grab just one Afghan and have him expire before he could share his information. Furthermore, the mysterious disappearances of trusted, highly placed lieutenants from two different groups, immediately after the assassinations of well-known public figures, would cause alarm among those left behind.

They would not know if their colleagues had also been killed and their bodies hidden or, fearing for their lives, had gone into hiding. Even worse, maybe they had switched loyalties to another group planning to overthrow their leader and had staged the assassinations.

The assassinations and kidnappings would be handled exclusively by the CSIS operatives. This would confirm to the Americans and the British that CSIS was a world-class spy agency equipped with the means and the will for serious missions.

The extraction of both the operatives and their captives would be handled by the Americans. Interrogation, likely to include waterboarding, would be carried out by others on foreign soil. That would sever the mission neatly into two parts, allowing politicians from both countries to deny any involvement.

As for Canada, they could deny the mission had even happened. As long as the operatives were not captured by the Taliban, there would be no evidence of any Canadian involvement.

Chapter 36

From his second-storey vantage point, looking through the rear sight of the AS Val, Billy centred the bead of the rifle's front sight on the chest of his target. Based on his practice with the subsonic rifle back in Ottawa, at the estimated distance of less than two hundred metres, he expected the slow-moving bullet to arc like a rainbow and land, dead centre, just below the man's breastbone. Death, while not instantaneous, would come soon enough.

It was 1 p.m. Friday, and his target, a middle-aged, bearded man, had concluded noon prayers and was now administering justice in accordance with numerous Taliban edicts. He was seated on a platform that was seven or eight feet high facing thousands of chanting men. The old arena was packed except for a small, cordoned-off area in front of the portly cleric, whose opponents called the Mad Mullah.

A woman was buried up to her shoulders in desert sand in the middle of the small, open area, awaiting execution. Stones and bits of broken concrete were piled conveniently nearby. A married woman with small children and a severely disabled husband, she had turned to prostitution to survive. Caught and convicted of adultery, now she awaited death by stoning.

It was remarkable she had gone undetected for so long. In Kandahar, a city where women were not even permitted to go outside unless accompanied by a male relative and only if covered in a burqa, she had eked out an existence for nearly two years.

The secret to her survival was she provided free service to a local police officer. A friend of her husband, he turned a blind eye to her work, even introducing new clients.

Sometimes the men paid her, and sometimes they did not. The first time she was denied payment, she complained and was told to say nothing unless she wanted to be arrested and stoned to death. Her husband, without income, would have to send the children out as beggars, where they could be kidnapped and sold.

A young Taliban, one of the morality squad, had caught her the previous evening performing oral sex on a police officer in a darkened doorway. He arrested her but let the policeman go, warning him about allowing women like her to corrupt his morals.

During the night, she was gang raped to teach her the error of her ways. Then she received one hundred lashes with a whip. Finally, after daybreak, she was buried up to her shoulders in sand to await death. She was severely dehydrated, in pain from head to toe, and barely conscious. Her captors were afraid she might die before she could be stoned to death, infuriating the Mad Mullah.

To avoid that embarrassment, a young boy, aspiring to be one of them when he was older, was assigned to keep her alive. Told he would be rewarded if he kept her alive but punished if he let her die, he put a wooden crate over her to protect her from the blazing sun. Occasionally, he removed it. If the doomed woman did not respond to a poke, a prod, or a slap, he dumped dirty water on her head.

It worked, but his water, a precious commodity, ran out quickly. Paranoid she would die, the ten-year-old had men urinate into a pail, giving him an ample supply.

*　*　*

Billy and Angus had been in Kandahar nine days, since Wednesday, August 29. While Ahmad and Kamin kept up appearances at the workshop, Basel, the Kandaharian, discreetly showed the Canadians around the area. Now familiar with streets and landmarks, they had decided on their targets and the best locations.

Basel explained that all but one warlord had been killed or had fled when the Taliban returned. He had entered into an uneasy truce with them. Both sides were pragmatic about the truce. With his opponents gone, the warlord did not intend to leave. Now the only game in town, many of his former opponents' supporters had joined him.

At full strength, the Taliban could have defeated him, but most of their forces were engaged against the Northern Alliance. Pressed up against the border with Tajikistan, the overmatched Northerners were well dug in and putting up quite a fight.

On the first evening, Billy laid out most of the mission to Basel and Kamin, sharing few details with Ahmad. The young Arab was a valuable asset, but having lived a sheltered life, Billy was concerned about giving him too many details. Instead, he proposed Ahmad take a trip back home, or to Canada or elsewhere. Ahmad resisted.

Billy stepped up the pressure. "Let me put it to you this way. Things are going to become more complicated and dangerous around here. If both of us are killed or captured, Basel can easily get to Pakistan. As for Kamin, the

Alliance has many contacts. They smuggle people back and forth under the Taliban's nose all the time. If things go wrong, they will look after Kamin."

He paused to allow what he had said to sink in. Then he looked directly at Ahmad, speaking in a flat, even tone. "You, my young friend, like us, are a foreigner. It will be much more difficult to hide you or to get you out of here. If you're captured, you'll be tortured and executed. That will be bad for your family in Dubai."

Noting the young man's disappointment, he smiled. "Perhaps more important to my superiors, you're a valuable asset for us. It's more for our benefit than yours that we need to protect you. You can help us in the future, but only if we keep you alive and you remain undetected."

Accepting Billy's logic, and pleased he could continue to be helpful, Ahmad left Kandahar, never to return.

Chapter 37

Billy sat on a stool in the sweltering heat. A few feet back from the second-storey window, he rested his rifle on a crutch, waiting to take a single shot. At the same time, one week earlier, the four had gone there to decide the best location to set up and the best route to take without drawing attention to themselves.

On that first visit, Basel had stayed in the minivan while Kamin brought Billy and McIsaac to that place. It offered the best vantage point, and from the back alley, they could access three escape routes.

This time, they were in two vehicles — the minivan and a pickup truck. With Kamin following at a discreet distance in the truck, the others were in the minivan. They were armed with the Makarovs, machine guns, and grenades.

Hopefully, the operation would go smoothly with a single, silent shot taking out their intended target. They hoped to leave the location undetected. However, they were prepared to fight it out, if necessary.

The Afghans would drive. Basel, the local and most familiar with the city, would lead in the pickup, followed by Kamin driving the minivan. McIsaac would crouch in the back of the truck to provide covering machine gun fire, if necessary, and hurl grenades at anyone who got in their way. Billy would be in the minivan passenger seat, ready to kick out the already loosened front windshield and provide supporting machine gun fire at anyone attempting to shoot at the truck. If things went as planned, they would make their way north of the city to a buskashi field for their second attack.

Buskashi is an ancient game played by men on horseback. Generally, the day before the game is to be played, someone slaughters a goat or sheep and removes the head and guts. Soaking it overnight in salted water makes the carcass easier to handle.

The following day, any number of men on horseback meet. In a game, similar to rugby played on horseback, using the animal carcass instead of a ball, contestants try to capture and keep the dead animal.

Played since the time of the Mongols, buskashi, as well as all other forms of entertainment, had been banned by the Taliban. However, instead of lessening the appeal of the macho sport, the ban only heightened the determination of defiant young men to play it.

Among the many children of the warlord and his four wives were three sons. With their father's tacit approval, they defied the ban and played buskashi with friends and cousins every Friday afternoon until dark.

Although they could have been punished for their transgression, senior Taliban officials counselled against doing so. They felt the increased notoriety and risk would increase the popularity of the already dangerous sport and give the warlord another grievance against them.

The preferred location for buskashi was on the outskirts of a small town in Arghandab District, just north of Kandahar. An agricultural area famous for its pomegranates, most of the young men who took part in buskashi came from nearby villages. They were not about to give up an ancient sport for religious leaders, even if they were currently in control of the country. Also, buskashi was such a popular sport that several local farmers earned extra income stabling horses owned by contestants, the most prominent being the warlord's sons.

A week earlier, Basel, Billy, and McIsaac had scouted out the area in the pickup truck, unarmed, to find the best vantage point for Billy and McIsaac. To inflame the warlord, they intended to shoot one or more of his sons as they competed.

It was difficult to distinguish one rider from another in the fast-paced, dusty, chaotic game at a distance of 150 to 200 metres, but it was easy to identify their horses. Astride the three largest and finest mounts on the field, the sons made things easy for the Canadian sniper.

None of the other animals were anywhere near as impressive, most being farm animals that had toiled all week. While some were in good condition, most were broken-down, half-starved nags that some of the younger boys had ridden to town so they could compete. After the game, the horses would be lucky to receive water and grain before being ridden home.

Little wonder that, as long they were not thrown from their horses, one of the brothers usually won the weekly competition.

Billy chose to shoot from the remains of an old stone building, likely a barn or a crop storage shed. At the top of a slight rise, west of the playing field, the area was surrounded by pomegranate trees and accessible by a gravel road a half kilometre distant.

Knowing the sun would set at 1824 hours, he intended to move into position forty-five minutes early to give him time to identify his targets. Then, with the brilliant sun setting behind him, he planned to take down two or three of them before retreating unseen to the awaiting vehicle.

If things went as planned, the competitors on the field, vying ferociously for the carcass, would not realize the downed horsemen had been shot. Anxious to win, perhaps for the first time, they would continue with the game, giving Billy and McIsaac a chance to slip away unseen.

Even if the downed men were only wounded and raised the alarm, the source of the shots would remain a mystery, possibly causing them to suspect each other.

Having visited the site in the pickup the prior Friday, this time the Canadians would take the van. At a leisurely pace, so as not to attract attention, Basel would drive them north to Arghandab District. They would return by a different route, arriving by 1930 hours and killing time until 2100 hours.

Then they would swing into action for the third phase of the operation, which was the most difficult and the most dangerous.

Chapter 38

"Our last play is a double play," Billy said.

His baseball analogy elicited a chuckle from the jocular Cape Bretoner, but it fell flat with the two Afghans until Billy explained what he meant. As soon as they got the joke, they found it hilarious and kept repeating it like a song that had gotten stuck in their heads.

The double play was possible, because a high-ranking member of the Taliban and the warlord's half-brother were cousins. Unknown to their leaders, they were in regular contact with each other. Both were from the same village. Their mothers were sisters. By Afghan standards, they were well educated. Their family bond was strengthened further when they married sisters.

One cousin had joined the Mujahideen against the Soviets. He had become a close confidante of the nearly illiterate, one-armed mullah. His loyalty was rewarded when he was appointed morality minister, making him the third-most-powerful and most dangerous member of the government, right behind the minister of defence.

The other cousin had followed his older brother, the warlord, in his rise to power. Sadistic, eager to please, and completely ruthless, he oversaw security. His *modus operandi* of eliminating opponents had earned him the nickname "the Krait". An Afghan snake from the cobra family with a small but poisonous bite, the krait was primarily nocturnal. Its diet included other snakes. Its bite was so small that a sleeping person might not even awaken if bitten and die in his or her sleep. Or he or she might wake up and, thinking it was merely an insect bite, ignore it, delay medical attention, and die of respiratory failure.

The nickname, originally "the Little Krait" and then simply "the Krait", was given to him when he was still a teenager. At the time, while only on the periphery of the inner circle of his brother's advisors, he had heard discussions regarding the elimination of one his group's opponents who was becoming too powerful.

He took matters into his own hands. Telling the apothecary his older brother's wife wanted to eliminate some household vermin, he obtained a large quantity of poison. Late at night, he slipped into the unsuspecting opponent's residence through an open window and added all of it to the household water supply. Predictably, the entire family died. Without the benefit of autopsies, the cause of death was never established.

When satisfied the opponent was among the dead, he went to his brother, beaming. "I killed him for you."

"What are you talking about?"

"Your enemy. I killed him for you."

"Little one, you shouldn't try to take credit for something like this."

"I did. I did. I did kill him. I killed all of them. Why won't you believe me?"

"Tell me how you did it."

"I used poison."

"Where did you get the poison?"

"From the apothecary. You can ask him."

Still thinking the young fellow was grandstanding, he checked with the apothecary, who confirmed the teenager had purchased poison but had not paid for it. The older brother paid the bill, now convinced his little brother was telling the truth.

Though satisfied at being rid of an opponent, he was unnerved at the cold-blooded ruthlessness of the act. Later, when the warlord explained to the group what had happened, so as not to be upstaged by one so young, he told them the boy had been pestering him, saying he could eliminate their opponent. The warlord said he had told him to go ahead, and to prove himself, he had poisoned the entire family. They could never take credit for it though, because killing the entire family would cause their families to be targeted for revenge killings.

In addition to the bond of kinship, the men were genuinely close. More like brothers than cousins, it was natural that while, publicly, they were opponents, they shared many interests, including Afghan blood sports. While forbidden by the Taliban, both were enthusiastic about dog fighting. The Krait maintained a large kennel outside the city, where he bred fighting dogs.

Every Friday night, the cousins hosted dog fights. Dozens of men would congregate to watch and place bets on the outcome of each fight. The hosts served as bookmakers, taking bets on which dogs would win, how many fights each would survive, and which ones would be alive at the end of the night. Charging 10 percent of each bet, they split the profits equally. Then, at the end of the evening, when all the bettors had gone, they conducted the most profitable part of their business: human trafficking.

Years earlier, the Krait had gotten into trafficking children. It was a natural extension to his loan-sharking business. When his customers, often poor farmers, fell behind, he would let them produce opium and then take it instead of cash. However, not all had enough land for poppy production, and sometimes the crop failed. Desperate to keep their farm and the animals they depended on to survive, sometimes they gave him a child.

If they had girls, they went first, fetching $100–$200 each. Selling them eliminated the need for a dowry if they survived into their mid-teens and the family had to arrange their marriage. After the girls, the youngest boys, too small to work, went next.

Usually, the farmer made up a story to explain the child's absence: A rich family needed a child and this child was fortunate, as he or she would have a much better life. Everyone involved, except for the child, knew this was a lie.

Occasionally, a child might become a servant, ending up with a benevolent family that was looking for cheap, reliable domestic labour. Such a lucky child would have a place to live, not too many beatings, and the possibility of a life of servitude.

However, most were loaded into vehicles and shipped, like livestock, to Pakistan. On arrival, they would be washed, groomed, dressed in new clothing, and fed into the voracious black market for children.

Treated like any other commodity, within hours, their new owners would put them to work at whatever would earn them the most money the fastest, that being the sex trade. Those who survived for more than a few years depreciated rapidly in value, as child sex trade customers were only interested in young, healthy children.

When no longer able to satisfy the demands of a dozen or more customers every day, the children would be sent into the streets as beggars and beaten if they returned without earning a certain amount of money.

With no skills, except for those learned in a brothel, and competition from scores of other experienced beggars, they supplemented their income by becoming pickpockets, shoplifters, and street-level prostitutes. In a culture where amputation of a hand was the penalty for theft and where fornicators and catamites were often executed by stoning, few survived to adulthood.

*   *   *

Squeezing the trigger calmly and confidently, Billy fired. To his dismay, in the half second it took his arcing bullet to reach its target, the cleric moved.

While still seated, perhaps in response to a question or maybe to get someone's attention, he turned to his left. The slug, intended for the centre of his chest, struck him in the right side. It angled upward after deflecting off a rib and lanced through his liver, severing veins and arteries before being stopped by a large rib on his left side.

The heavyset man shuddered and grunted at the impact of the slow-moving, silent projectile. Responding to the stabbing pain in his side, still seated, he reached across his body and raised a bloody left hand. Turning to his right, he looked for his attacker.

Having heard no shot but seeing their leader had been wounded, his body-guards leaped into action, dispatching armed supporters to the arena's exits with orders to prevent anyone from leaving until the attacker was caught.

Billy, thinking he had missed, cursed his bad luck. Meanwhile, McIsaac, standing by Billy, with his binoculars trained on the target, was jubilant.

"No, Sarge, no," McIsaac said. "You got him. Right in the short ribs. I can't tell if he's gut shot or if the bullet angled upwards when he leaned over. Either way, he's out of action. Unless he gets really good medical attention really fast, he's a goner."

The Mad Mullah bled to death in half an hour.

Billy retrieved the shell casing. Within seconds, hiding the folded-up rifle under his clothing with one hand and clutching the crutch in the other, he and McIsaac joined the two waiting Afghans. As planned, McIsaac went with Basel in the pickup while Billy and Kamin followed at a short distance in the minivan.

To their surprise, the streets near the arena were nearly deserted, the men detained in the arena and the women inside their homes.

After a few minutes, as planned, the van stopped so the pickup could increase the distance between them. At the predetermined intersection, the pickup turned off the street, dropped off McIsaac, and drove away. Seconds later, the van arrived, and McIsaac jumped in.

While Kamin headed back to the workshop alone, the other three headed for Arghandab to carry out the second phase of the operation.

Chapter 39

As he had done the previous Friday, but this time over the sights of a rifle, Billy watched the ebb and flow of buskashi players, thinking they reminded him of something. Then it occurred to him.

If the horsemen were divided into two teams, instead of being every man for himself, buskashi was a lot like the pond hockey he had played as a kid back home. In pond hockey, anyone who showed up with a pair of skates and a hockey stick could play. If a player had a stick but no skates, he could be a goalie, especially if, due to extreme cold, only a small group showed up.

Generally, the two best players would captain each team. Using a hockey stick like baseball players used a bat to determine who got first pick, two teams were selected. After the game started, players would come and go, with newcomers added to the team with the fewest members, sometimes without play even stopping.

The puck would be dropped at centre ice. With no referee, no boards, and no rules, players in possession of the puck were pursued by all but one or two defencemen. The poorest skaters were left behind to protect the goalie. Puck carriers would often skate great distances in an attempt to elude their pursuers and skate back to the other team's goal.

For a moment, Billy was a kid again. On a blue, cloudless winter day, intent on winning, he was chasing the puck carrier, his best friend, across a frozen northern Newfoundland lake ...

"Sarge," McIsaac whispered, "why didn't you shoot? You had all three of them lined up on this side of the field."

Billy snapped back to the present, giving no indication he had been day-dreaming. "I know, but with these slow-moving bullets, I think my best bet is to reduce the angle and shoot as they ride away from me like I would with a flock of birds."

The mob of horsemen returned to his side of the field. The two older brothers were wrestling over the goat. The youngest followed behind, waiting to take on the winner. The remaining riders pursued, hoping for the best.

With time running out, the sun setting behind him, and the game about to wind down, Billy made his play. With the Val on semi-automatic, Billy fired. The first two bullets hit the youngest in the middle of his back, driving him forward on his horse. He lurched right, falling to the ground, where he was trampled by other competitors.

Almost before the first two bullets landed, Billy raised the muzzle slightly and triggered two shots at each of the other brothers. The third and fourth shots hit the one on the left, as he tried to pull the goat away from the eldest.

Letting go, he snapped left, falling to the ground. As the remaining brother, still holding the goat, veered right, Billy's fifth shot missed him, striking the goat. The sixth and final shot found its mark, striking the brother in the shoulder. He dropped the carcass.

While the other players fought over the dead animal, the eldest brother realized he had been shot. Suspecting one of the other players, he held firmly to his horse to keep from falling and rode back to check on his downed brothers.

The one he been wrestling with, while still alive, was mortally wounded. Confirming he, too, had been shot, he rode back to the trampled, bloodied heap that was his youngest brother. Seeing he was dead, the wounded rider headed to the sidelines to get help from friends, where, horseless, they had congregated to watch the game.

Using the cover of the setting sun and pomegranate trees, Billy and McIsaac withdrew to the van and entered the vehicle's side door. With Basel at the wheel, they drove off at a leisurely pace.

Back at the workshop, Basel and Kamin were jubilant. Successful covert attacks against both the Taliban and the warlord's family had never happened before. It would certainly raise tensions between the two groups, provoking revenge attacks, especially by the grieving warlord and his supporters.

If the attacks became widespread, to maintain order in Kandahar Province and to wipe out the last warlord, the Taliban would need to recall fighters from the north. That would allow the Northern Alliance to gain a larger foothold and become a more serious threat. To them, no matter what happened now, the mission was already a success.

Their confidence in the Canadians' ability, buoyed by the successes of the past few hours, made the Afghans so eager to get on with the kidnapping they began joking with each other about the group's next move, the "double play".

Concerned their horseplay might jeopardize the mission, Billy brought them back to Earth when he pointed out the next two targets were wily adversaries who had to be taken alive simultaneously. They were protected by bodyguards who would put up a fight and who had to be killed to eliminate witnesses.

Thereafter, they still had to get out of the city, which was on high alert while the authorities searched for whoever had shot the Mad Mullah. There would be checkpoints and roadblocks manned by armed men.

Billy pointed out that while they had experienced some success, if they were caught, that success would turn into failure if they were tortured and talked. Instead of dividing their enemies, the operation could unite them.

His reinforcement of what lay ahead had a sobering effect on the pair.

*   *   *

Once back at the workshop, Billy addressed the team. "We've got to get out of here fast, and we won't be coming back. Make sure we haven't left anything behind. Then fake a break-in."

"Want us to trash the place?" McIsaac asked.

"No, that would be too obvious. Besides, we don't want to draw any unnecessary attention and have someone come looking around too soon."

The Afghans were quizzical at the term "trash the place".

Basel, the Kandaharian, got the meaning almost immediately, while Kamin, the Northerner, required additional explanation. Once he grasped the meaning, his face lit up with a smile as he realized the English language contained considerable slang.

"Yes, double-play," he said. "No trash the place."

They went to work. After searching both the workshop and the living quarters, they tipped over some objects and then broke the ancient front door lock, setting the stage for their departure.

"One last thing," Billy said as they were about to leave. He picked up the large canvas satchel he had brought eight days earlier. Placing the nondescript, dusty flat-bottomed bag on the table, he untied the string that secured the flap and opened it. Reaching inside, he extracted a few personal items: a well-worn pair of sandals, two cotton shirts, and underwear.

When the bag was empty, he reached for his folding knife and opened the smaller blade. Using it as a screwdriver, he removed four screws that secured the bottom. He lifted the false bottom, revealing six tightly compressed dark cotton sacks. Large enough to fit over a man's head, they came complete with drawstrings to secure them.

He gave three sacks to McIsaac and kept three for himself.

"Sarge," McIsaac said softly, "you brought six bags. I thought we were only going to grab two guys."

"That's the plan," Billy replied, "two bags plus a spare."

He looked at the two Afghans. "There's another thing we haven't discussed. Things went well for us today, but tonight could be a different story. If things go bad and we're both killed or, even worse, taken alive, the boys will need to be hooded and their hands tied so they can claim to be our hostages."

Removing the cotton sacks revealed the base had been custom fitted with a one-inch-thick piece of Styrofoam, similar to that used to pack electronic components for shipping. Rectangular slots in the six-inch by sixteen-inch Styrofoam rectangle held a dozen plastic electrical ties. A cellphone fitted snugly in a slot at one end.

Billy picked up the cell phone and pressed the power button. The phone posed no mystery to the Afghans, but they had never seen electrical ties before.

"Sometimes the police use these as handcuffs," Billy explained. "Let me show you how."

He had McIsaac hold his hands behind his back. Without actually using the tie, which would render it useless, he demonstrated how each piece of plastic could be wrapped around a captive's wrists and then pulled tight, serving as a temporary yet effective restraint.

Other slots in the Styrofoam held two hypodermic needles, two small glass bottles, and two small metal flasks. The bottles had pink rubber caps held by aluminum rings so a needle could be inserted through the rubber to extract the clear liquid inside.

Opening a metal flask, Billy passed it under the noses of his Afghan colleagues so they could smell the pungent odour of chloroform. "This is to help our guests cooperate with us, but it wears off quickly, so we'll use this before takeoff," he pointed to the needles, "in case they're afraid of flying in helicopters."

"Helicopters?" both Afghans inquired simultaneously.

"Helicopters. Well, at least one helicopter," Billy confirmed. "After today, it will be too risky to leave by road. By morning, when the two jokers we plan to grab tonight go missing, things could get really crazy."

Then, smiling as if enjoying a private joke, he typed a text message into the telephone. It read, "Horse stinger required, as agreed."

In Ottawa, when they had discussed a simple word for "helicopter", one of his less imaginative handlers had suggested dragonfly. The proposal generated ridicule from another, who pointed out they may as well say "helicopter". Anybody with an ounce of common sense would guess "dragonfly" was code for "helicopter".

Billy came to the stricken handler's rescue. "Why don't you just call 'em what we call 'em back home? Let them figure it out!"

"And what might that be?" the others inquired, amused.

"Horse stinger," Billy replied with a wink, so that's what the code name for the helicopter picking them up became.

Billy's simple text message meant that, as arranged previously, a US Army helicopter would arrive at precisely 0200 hours. It would touch down a few kilometres east of Kandahar airport, where it would pick up six passengers: the two Canadians, their two Afghan colleagues, and two high-value captives.

The helicopter would fly at a low altitude following the highway, a flight lasting less than an hour each way. Speed and stealth were critical to the operation's success. The chopper needed to be out of Afghan airspace before 0257 hours. At that time, a nearly full moon would appear in the east, making the helicopter, silhouetted in the moonlight, an easy target for anyone on the ground.

Chapter 40

They departed the workshop a final time. Kamin and Billy went ahead in the minivan. Basel and McIsaac waited a while and then left in the opposite direction. Both picked up the main highway through Kandahar, at different intersections, before heading east.

They rendezvoused briefly at the city centre, a large roundabout, and then split up again. Basel and McIsaac took the lead in the pickup while Kamin and Billy circled back a second time to ensure they had not been followed. Then both vehicles continued east.

When the pickup truck reached the mosque, Jame Mui Mobarek, it turned off the highway onto the boulevard leading northward to the governor's compound. After parking on the street near the mosque, Basel and McIsaac got out of the truck and strolled northward.

A few minutes later, Kamin and Billy arrived in the minivan, drove past the truck, and then got out and began walking in the same direction, a short distance behind the others, without any indication they were together.

While they may have been headed toward the governor's compound, that was not their true destination. They were actually headed for two buildings on opposite sides of the street, a half kilometre north of the mosque and a few hundred metres south of the compound, the cloth market buildings.

Basel, having spent his entire life in Kandahar, had long heard stories that, on Friday nights, men went to the cloth market buildings for entertainment. With the rise of the Taliban and their crackdown on all forms of entertainment, he had assumed nothing took place there anymore.

However, months earlier, to see for themselves, he and Kamin had gone by, pretending to be looking for excitement. While it was evident from the outside that one building was full of people, they were met by two security guards denying them entrance. They said nothing was happening inside except workmen and merchants preparing their businesses for the next day, and they too would be gone soon. Checking back a few hours later, Basel and Kamin found both buildings locked and deserted.

After discussing it with Ahmad, they returned the following Friday. They were met by the same two security guards, who turned them away once again, offering the same explanation. This time, Basel told them a rich friend of theirs, an Arab, was visiting. To avoid crowds on Saturday, he would like to pay for admission Friday night to make private purchases.

While the new information got the cautious guards' attention, they told them to return the next week. If it was acceptable to their manager, all three would be permitted entry. One guard added they would need to be paid for the extra work required to get the manager to approve their admission.

The following week, the three attended. But for the howling, snarling, and barking dogs, the carnival atmosphere inside rivalled Bourbon Street at Mardi Gras.

While there, Basel and Kamin cased the building. Makeshift electrical lighting revealed a square, two-storey structure enclosed on all four sides with a large, open courtyard. In the middle was a section nearly twenty feet square, the dog-fighting pit. There, dogs of all shapes and sizes fought each other, often to the death.

Some of the dogs were in poor condition, probably strays or dogs that were cheap and disposable. With no chance of survival, they were used in the early rounds to whip up the crowd and to incite the real fighting dogs for the fights to come later in the evening.

While the open courtyard area was jam-packed with spectators, bettors, and some dog owners, the second-floor balcony, the VIP section, which overlooked the courtyard, was less crowded. For an extra fee, men could have a clear view of the savagery below.

One section of the balcony was reserved for the two men in charge — the Krait and his cousin and their bodyguards. The Krait bred, bought, and sold fighting dogs. He also oversaw loan sharking and human trafficking and a large part of the drug business of his half-brother, the warlord. He looked forward to Friday evenings with enthusiasm.

Nothing gave him a greater thrill than watching his fighting dogs destroy other hapless creatures, ripping them to pieces. His favourite dog was a Tosa, a two hundred-pound Japanese fighting dog named Kamikaze. An undefeated winner of over fifty fights, the dog had earned him thousands of dollars in bets and stud fees.

His cousin was indifferent to dog fighting. He looked forward to Friday evenings for a different reason.

Kandahar was the homosexual capital of Asia. As morality minister, his job was to enforce all morality laws. One Taliban edict outlawed homosexuality, yet he was attracted to boys, the younger the better. Even though married with children, he generally ignored his wives, satisfying his insatiable sexual appetite with boys instead.

Some suspected he was intimate with the two young men he employed, but nobody said anything for fear of being arrested on phony charges. As the objects of his affection entered their mid-teens, he was less attracted to them. He yearned for younger companionship but feared recruiting new playmates, the risk of being discovered too high.

That was until he learned of the Krait's human trafficking activities. As part of their deal, he proposed he be permitted to select two children every week. At the end of the week, he could keep them longer or exchange one or both for another.

The exchanges took place in Cloth Market Building No. 2 and were handled by the minister's two young assistants, who arrived after the dogfights were underway across the street. They would meet with the Krait's men in a van or a large tarp-covered truck loaded with children bound for Pakistan.

The vehicle would remain in Cloth Market Building No. 2 long enough for the minister's assistants to select two new children and return those from the previous week, whose vacant, downcast eyes could not hide the horrors of the past seven days.

Then the vehicles would join a heavily armed convoy of vehicles owned by the warlord and carrying his opium. Together, they made a night-long round trip to the Pakistani border, arriving back in Kandahar before daylight.

* * *

While Cloth Market Building No. 1 was the evening's entertainment centre, Cloth Market Building No. 2 also warehoused the cousins' Friday night operation. There, in kennels covered by tarps in the back of a large truck, the Krait maintained an ample supply of fighting dogs. They were muzzled until led or dragged across the street, where spectators watched them fight for their lives and betted on the outcome.

The evening's events would begin around 7 p.m., with preliminary bouts featuring weaker, less aggressive, and often stray dogs. Those bouts would not last very long and did not generate much betting. As the evening progressed, the fights featured stronger, more aggressive animals. Many patrons, having brought their own dogs, would get in on the action by entering their animals and betting heavily on the outcome.

The fights ended at 10 p.m. Like clockwork, evidence of the evening's events was removed and the building restored to its normal state for use as a market. The following morning, market-goers would be hard-pressed to find clues of the prior evening's events.

While Cloth Market Building No. 1 was being restored to its original state, any wealthy patrons who had lost dogs in fights or who wanted to buy a fighting dog were invited to come across the street to Cloth Market Building No. 2, where they could view and purchase new dogs.

Unknown to the buyers, none of the dogs had proven very dominant in training fights back at the Krait's farm. By selling them, he was assuring himself of future wins.

By 11 p.m. or a little later, after the last patron had departed, the minister and the Krait would meet privately in a small room. While their bodyguards waited and their drivers waited in their vehicles on opposite sides of Cloth Market Building No. 2, the two would relax, smoke opium, talk about their families, and split the night's take.

Finally, with bodyguard in tow, one would head for the north exit while the other headed for the south exit for the drive home.

Having staked out the building, Basel and Kamin knew each target left at midnight, exiting through doors on opposite sides of the building. They knew their bodyguards followed a few steps behind. They also knew the men were most vulnerable outside, in the seconds it took to walk to their car.

Earlier in the evening, Billy had laid out his plan to snatch the Krait and the morality minister simultaneously and to transport them to a place a few kilometres east of Kandahar airport. A helicopter would arrive at precisely 0200 hours, touch down briefly, pick them up, and leave.

"Here's what we have to do," he explained. "First of all, and it's last things first, we've got to be there on time. If the chopper crew doesn't see us, they'll figure we didn't make it. They won't even touch down. If we're under attack when they show up, they might not be able to get to us. We'll have to find our own way back. If we miss that flight, our chances of getting out of here alive are slim to none."

He paused for questions. There were none.

"We'll arrive at the dogfights at roughly 2100 hours. That's when you guys tell us the place is going full swing."

"Going full swing?" Kamin interjected. "What it means?"

"Sorry," Billy said. "It means very busy. Lots of people, lots of noise, sometimes lots of confusion."

"Yes, yes, going full swing!" Kamin and Basel answered enthusiastically.

"Instead of being together," Billy continued," we'll be in two pairs. Kamin, you'll be with me. Basel, you'll be with McIsaac. We should avoid each other. If we're drawn into any discussion, you guys will do the talking. You'll also point out the targets to us. We've never seen them. We want to be sure we get the right ones. Is everyone clear so far?"

They all nodded.

"Now," he continued." We're going to grab them around midnight. The cloth market buildings are only a few hundred metres away from the governor's compound, so we've got to be really quiet. We can't fire any shots, and we can't let them fire any either. We're likely to be searched before they let us in, so we'll leave our weapons in the van. I know there's a risk of a break-in and theft, but we're near the mosque, and there will be a fair bit of traffic on the street, at least for the first part of the night, with men coming to the dogfights. It should be okay for a short while."

The others nodded in agreement once again.

"We know the action finishes up by 2200 hours. We should leave when most of the others are leaving and walk back to the van. Then we'll kill time for an hour."

The Afghans seemed puzzled by the expression.

Billy smiled. "'Kill time' means to do nothing and wait for time to pass."

The Afghans looked at each other and grinned.

"At 2300 hours, we'll have taken out both drivers. Like this." He pulled his head back and drew his hand, knifelike, across his throat. "It needs to be fast and quiet. We'll leave 'em in their cars, like they fell asleep. In the dark, in these narrow side streets, nobody will notice they're dead unless they check on them. Just make sure they don't slump over the steering wheel onto the horn.

"You've told us both doors swing outward, so McIsaac and I will take up positions behind each door. We know each target comes through the doorway, followed a few steps behind by his bodyguard, who stops and closes the door.

"Each of you," he motioned to Basel and Kamin, "will hide in front of each car, just metres away. There will be a moment when the target is in front, walking toward you in the dark, and the bodyguard pauses to close the door. At that moment, I want you to step out in front of the target with one of these in your hand." He held up a Makarov. "However you say it in Pashto, in a voice loud enough for them hear you clearly, tell the target he is being robbed."

He paused briefly to confirm they understood. "Are you with me so far?"

Eyes wide open, both nodded in the affirmative.

"With a gun pointed at him from only a few metres away, the target will likely freeze for an instant," Billy continued, "waiting for his bodyguard to move first to protect him. For a few seconds, the bodyguard's hands will be occupied with the door. He won't be any help. Even if his hands are free, he won't be able to shoot at you right away. His boss will be in front of him, directly in the line of fire."

He paused again to ensure they understood exactly what he wanted them to do. "Now, I want both of you to repeat exactly what I just said."

They did so haltingly, first Kamin and then Basel.

Not satisfied, Billy had them do it a second, third, and then a fourth time. He also explained the success of the operation — not to mention their lives — depended on what they did in the two to three seconds when the bodyguard was closing the door.

"We should be role-playing this exercise, but we'd need a mock-up of the location and more time."

"Sarge, you better explain what you mean by a mock-up," McIsaac said, seeing the Afghans' confusion.

Billy did.

"Now, in that brief moment, right after you appear in front of them and each bodyguard wheels around — by 'wheels around' I mean he turns around really fast — McIsaac here," he motioned to the Cape Bretoner, "and I will swing into action with these."

He held up two large kitchen knives. "Ordinarily, we'd use our bayonets. But," he chuckled, "we're travelling fairly light, so these will have to do. When each bodyguard turns toward you, we'll come from behind him and get him really fast with a knife and drop him to the ground. Before the target can get away, we'll jump him from behind. If he hears any noise from the bodyguard and starts to turn around or run, just yell at him. We need both targets alive, so don't shoot unless he pulls a gun and you've got to defend yourself. Remember, a shot fired this close to the governor's compound will alert everyone in the area, which is not what we want."

Realizing neither Afghan had spoken for a while and that both seemed mesmerized, Billy forced a smile. "Relax, boys. Take a breath. Before morning, we'll all be out of here with a couple of high-value targets. When you're old men, you'll have a great story to tell your grandchildren."

A few minutes later, they were aboard their vehicles headed for Old Kandahar.

Chapter 41

As planned, parking near the mosque before 2100 hours, they strolled north to Cloth Market Building No. 1. There, for the next forty-five minutes, amid the noise and chaos of dogfights, drug deals, and ringside betting, the Canadians circulated methodically through the crowd. They got close enough to their intended targets to recognize them later.

Both men were medium height and bore a striking family resemblance to each other. Billy was surprised at how they differed in every other respect. The minister was pudgy, overweight, and pale for an Afghan. The Krait was lean and fit with a dark, tanned face. Both were bearded. The minister's beard was full and flowing and appeared to be regularly shampooed. The Krait's beard was shorter, similar to the beards of many in the building.

The minister was lavishly attired, leaving no doubt he was an important person. The Krait was an average dresser. While nobody would mistake him for a manual labourer, as his high-quality clothing was immaculately clean, it could only be described in Kandahar as nondescript, permitting him to blend in.

Slightly before 2200 hours, the crowd began to leave. So did McIsaac and Basel. At an unhurried pace, they walked the half kilometre to their vehicles. A few minutes later, Billy and Kamin joined them. They waited in the minivan until 2300 hours. While sitting in the van, Billy continued his instructions.

"Okay, so let's assume it's midnight. I'm in the north side alley, or street, if you can call it that. I've got a dead driver and a dead bodyguard. I've captured my target. He's got a bag over his head and," he held up an electrical tie, "his hands are tied with one of these. We need to get back here. We have a flight to catch at 0200 hours."

He paused to let his words sink in. Then he held up a flask of chloroform. "Take a small rag. If you have nothing else, a piece of your shirt will do. Wet it down good with some of this. Hold it in the palm of your hand and clamp it tight over his mouth and nose. Don't worry about the bag over his head; the fumes will go through that. Just make sure you keep his chin up and his mouth isn't open. You don't want the son of a bitch to bite you. Hold it tight for at least two minutes. If he slumps too fast, he might be faking. We want him out."

"How much of this stuff do I need to use?" McIsaac asked.

"Save half in case he comes to and you got to do it again," Billy said, "but I think as long as the rag is only big enough to fit over his mouth and nose and you don't soak up too much of it, perhaps a quarter or a third of the flask might be enough.

"Now, the driver is dead in the front seat, so haul him out and leave him there. Check his pockets for identification. I'm sure dead guys show up in back alleys around here all the time. If they don't know who he is, at least not right away, they might not connect him to the disappearances. Take the dead bodyguard and stick him in the trunk. I get in the backseat with my guy. McIsaac gets in the backseat with his. Then we'll take our time, meet up in front, and drive both vehicles back here to the van. Any questions?"

Hearing none, he continued. "When we get back here, if there's nobody around, we'll transfer our two targets to the van. If that's not possible, we'll have to look for a place nearby. We won't have much time, so we'll have to get it done quickly. It shouldn't take much time; a quick transfer from the back door of the car to the side door of the van. Just make sure the dome light is turned off."

"Sarge, what do we do with their cars?" McIsaac asked.

"The minister's car is fairly distinctive," Billy said, "so there's no point trying to hide it. We'll just park it at the mosque. People may leave it alone for a while, but in the heat, the dead bodyguard in the trunk is gonna get really ripe really fast. Someone will pop the trunk, but by then, we'll be long gone. So both cars aren't found together, we'll take the other one with us and ditch it."

The abductions went smoothly. By 12:45, they were back at the van with unconscious targets in the back seats of each car. With nobody to see them, they transferred the targets into the minivan and were about to leave the minister's car in the mosque parking lot when McIsaac grabbed Billy's arm.

"Wait, Sarge. I got to tell you something."

"Corporal," Billy replied abruptly, "we've got an hour and a quarter to get out of the city and past the airport to meet that chopper, so unless this has something to do with what we're doing right now, tell me later."

"That's just it," McIsaac replied, panic in his voice. "He's not dead. I didn't kill him. I just couldn't; he was too pitiful."

Billy stopped, the wheels in his head spinning, his eyes narrowing. "What are you talking about?"

"I took them both alive," McIsaac responded miserably. "The bodyguard's in the trunk, but he's not dead. He's only a kid. He doesn't even have a real beard. Both surrendered on the spot. He didn't put up a fight. I just didn't have the heart to kill him. Perhaps the Yanks will take him along with the other two."

Suddenly, Billy was back in Bosnia remembering the two teenagers he had executed, one in the family home and the other trying to escape in the disabled Lada. He had less remorse for the first, who was participating in ethnic cleansing, the murder of children, and the raping of women and girls, but he still had nightmares about the second, shot through the head, his blood and brains on the dashboard. Instantly, he knew how the young Cape Bretoner felt. A wave of compassion for the younger man, an emotion he had not felt for a long time, washed over him.

"I understand. I'll tell them we picked him up for insurance. Maybe they'll take him."

"Sarge?" McIsaac asked, fearing the answer as he asked the question, "what if they won't take him?"

"We'll cross that bridge when we get to it. If they won't take him, then I'll get rid of him myself. Either way, you don't have to worry about him."

Within minutes, leaving the minister's car by the mosque, three vehicles headed eastward. Kamin and Billy led the way in the minivan with the three hostages. Basil followed in the truck. McIsaac drove the Krait's car, the dead bodyguard in the trunk.

They came upon a deep roadside ditch and stopped. McIsaac drove the Krait's car to the edge and then got out. With the engine still running, he let the car roll off the road. Then he hopped into the back of the truck, picked up a Soviet submachine gun, and crouched behind the cab, on the lookout for trouble. They did not have to wait long.

A few kilometres farther on, near the edge of the city, they encountered a roadblock. A group of young, well-armed Taliban fighters had a chain across the road.

Kamin, leading the way in the minivan, saw fires in oil drums on both sides of the road from half a kilometre away. However, they were too near the roadblock to turn around without drawing attention.

Getting closer, they made out a canvas-covered hut, probably a cooking and sleeping area. A short distance away was a smaller canvas-covered structure, a privy.

The sentries, previously bored and sleepy, having seen no vehicles for hours, were wide-awake and attentive now. They milled around the minivan, weapons pointed at Kamin and Billy.

Had he been in the lead vehicle, Basel, a Kandaharian, might have been able to talk his way through, offering a bribe to the leader to allow passage, but not Kamin. As soon as the northerner spoke, his accent guaranteed they would at least be detained and searched.

Even worse, a hostage was recovering from the chloroform and making a noise in the back of the van. Basel, who had pulled up twenty-five to thirty metres behind, could see they were in danger. He banged three times on the back window of the truck.

McIsaac, crouching out of sight in the back of the truck, heart pounding and adrenaline rising, eager to redeem himself for failing to kill the young bodyguard, sprang into action. Rising up in the dark like an apparition, he levelled the submachine gun and opened fire.

In a hail of bullets, he dropped the three Kalashnikov-carrying Taliban by the driver's door of the minivan. Then he turned to the two standing by the passenger side, yelling at Billy to open the door, but Billy had already disposed of them.

Certain he and Kamin were doomed, to give McIsaac and Basel a chance to get away, Billy had opened fire. In the dark, he had been holding the Makarov in his left hand across his lap, muzzle against the door, centimetres away from his closest adversary, waiting. When McIsaac opened fire from behind, both Taliban near Billy turned toward him.

The nearest one only made it halfway around before Billy triggered two shots through the door into his midsection. Then he lifted the pistol to the window, firing at the other Taliban as the man raised his gun to shoot McIsaac.

Concerned he might not be accurate with his left hand, Billy fired four shots, saving the last two. Three hit their intended target in the temple, cheekbone, and shoulder, killing him instantly. The fourth ricocheted off his weapon, sending sparks into the night.

"Go! Go! Go!" Billy screamed.

Kamin hammered the gas pedal to the floor, snapping the chain as the van flew down the road. Behind, in the truck, McIsaac grabbed the Soviet grenades and hurled one into the canvas hut and two more at the parked vehicles.

Speeding off as the exploding grenades obliterated the hut and trucks, lighting up the night, McIsaac smiled.

That should take care them, he thought.

He was wrong.

As they drove into the darkness, a fighter who had been relieving himself in the privy when they pulled up and remained hidden when the gunfire started, ran into the road. Furious, he emptied his weapon at the taillights of the fleeing truck.

Unseen by him, his efforts were rewarded. A bullet hit McIsaac in the upper right back and mushroomed when it hit his shoulder blade. It sliced through his body, exploding through his right pectoral muscle in a spray of skin, blood, bone, and muscle, leaving an exit hole the size of a walnut.

The impact drove him forward. He dropped the machine gun and lurched over the cab. Bleeding profusely, he hung on with his left hand.

With his right arm dangling uselessly, he lowered himself to the truck bed. There he sat, his left palm held to the right side of his chest, attempting to slow the bleeding, all colour gone from his face.

Billy was busy in the minivan. The Krait had mostly recovered from the effects of the chloroform and had managed to get his bound hands in front of him, where he was attempting to loosen the drawstring securing the bag over his head.

"Drive another few minutes and then stop for the others!" Billy yelled.

He jumped into the back and delivered a solid blow to the Krait's head with the Makarov, knocking him senseless. Reaching for the chloroform, he soaked a cloth, and administered a dose of the pungent liquid to the mouths and noses of all three captives.

As Kamin slowed the vehicle to a halt, Billy turned on the dome light and took out the glass bottles and a hypodermic needle. Three times he extracted half a syringe of clear liquid. Each time he held the needle upward in the light, pushed the plunger upward until liquid appeared at the tip, and then injected one of the men.

As the truck pulled up behind, he turned to Kamin. "We won't have to worry about them for a while. Stay here and keep the engine running while I check on the boys." He motioned ahead. "The helicopter is supposed to land just a few kilometres away. We've got fifteen minutes to spare. It's best to wait here a while in case we're followed."

Walking past the glare of the pickup's headlights, Billy suspected they were in trouble when he saw Basel. White-faced, he was sitting behind the wheel, staring at the bullet-riddled windshield.

"Are you hit?" Billy yelled.

The young Afghan did not speak, only shook his head.

With his heart in his throat, as Billy came around to the side of the truck, he spotted his buddy. Covered in blood, the young Cape Bretoner was seated with his back against the cab. His head hung forward, and his right arm hung at his side. His left hand, covered in blood, was pressed to his chest.

"Corporal, can you hear me?" Billy said.

McIsaac nodded. "I don't think I'm gonna make it, Sarge."

"Bullshit!" Billy said in a loud voice, probably to cover his fear. "Of course you're gonna make it. Anybody can see that's only a flesh wound. That's why you're bleeding."

Hopping up beside McIsaac, he turned to Basel. "Get Kamin. Right now!"

Using a softer, calmer voice, he turned back to McIsaac. "Let me help you lean forward and take a look at your back."

When McIsaac did so, Billy saw a hole but only a small amount of blood. Most of the bleeding was coming from the large exit wound in front.

"Can you stay like that for a few seconds?" Billy asked.

The young Nova Scotian flashed him a weak smile. "Sure, Sarge, perhaps even a minute."

Billy pulled out his pocketknife and opened the larger blade. Holding McIsaac's clothing away from his skin and using the bullet hole as the centre, he ripped a large X-shaped hole in McIsaac's shirt. Then he cut a small piece of cloth from his own shirt.

"This might hurt a bit, but I need to plug the hole in your back before I can stop the bleeding in the front."

Using the tip of his little finger, he jammed cloth into the hole. By then, Basel and Kamin were back, staring wide-eyed from the sidelines.

Billy glanced at them as he bent over McIsaac plugging the entry wound. "Don't just stand there. Get up here and give me a hand."

They went to the rear of the truck and stepped up.

"We've got to lay him on his back so I can stop the bleeding in front," Billy said. "Help me move him back a few feet. Careful now. Lift. Don't pull. Watch out for his right arm."

They stretched the six-footer the length of the truck bed.

Gingerly moving the young man's left hand aside, Billy ripped open McIsaac's clothing to reveal an ugly chest wound.

"Kamin, place your palm here and apply pressure."

The young Afghan obliged. In seconds, Billy cut a large square from the front of his own shirt and ripped it into strips.

"Move your hand," he told Kamin and then began to push the cotton strips into the wound.

With the wound full of cloth, and using his hand to apply pressure, he turned to the Afghans. "He's lost a lot of blood. We need to raise his legs and place something under them to keep blood to his head and upper body."

"Would the spare tire from the van be sufficient?" Kamin asked.

"Yes, for sure," Billy replied. "Get it right away. Both of you go together and take a look at the passengers. They should be out, but it doesn't hurt to keep an eye on them. Move fast. The chopper is due in five minutes, and we've still got a few clicks to go."

In a minute, they were back with the tire and had it positioned under McIsaac's legs.

"I'm going to stay with McIsaac," Billy said. "I'll keep pressure on his wound and hopefully keep him conscious. Kamin, you lead off in the van, but don't get too far ahead of us. We won't be able to drive fast. Don't worry about the chopper. We won't see it until they're alongside, but they're expecting us. There's no time to lose. Let's get going."

They were off.

Traveling under fifty kilometres an hour, they arrived at their rendezvous point at 02:03, just in time to meet the helicopter, which was also a few minutes late, having been delayed due to ground traffic.

As the chopper touched down, two soldiers jumped out and ran to the truck.

"I'm Specialist Andy Williams," one of the soldiers, a medic, yelled over the noise from the helicopter's rotor. "Who's in charge here?"

"I am!" Billy yelled back. His hands were pressed firmly to McIsaac's chest. "Sergeant Billy Wheeler, Canadian Armed Forces. The corporal here took one through the back nearly an hour ago. I've plugged up the holes, but he's lost a lotta blood. The two guys driving are locals. They're with us. We got three passengers. They're in the van, unconscious, tied up, and hooded, so they won't be any trouble."

Williams reached for his shoulder microphone and yelled into it. "Total for pickup seven! One needs stretcher plus blood. Two friendlies plus three hostiles in restraints."

In less than a minute, the response Billy had been dreading came back. "Orders are for only two hostiles. Get rid of the third."

"Are you sure you can't take the third?" Billy asked.

"Positive," Williams replied. "The major over there," he referred to the unseen officer inside the helicopter, "is a real hard ass. The colonel back at the base is worse. Believe me, those guys would leave their own mother behind if ordered. Pushing back on this one will get you nowhere except maybe written up for failing to follow orders."

Accepting he had to get rid of the bodyguard, Billy asked if Williams had a light.

"Sure," Williams replied, "but don't you think you should wait to get back to base before having a smoke?"

"That's not why I need it," Billy replied. "I gotta get rid of the van. There's too much stuff in it. If you guys can look after my buddy here, I'll get our two Afghan friends to head for the chopper. Then I'll show your guys which two passengers are continuing on and which one terminates here."

Billy yelled at Basel, still in the truck, to head for the helicopter. Then he headed to the van, where Kamin was waiting, and told him to follow Basel to the helicopter.

As Kamin jumped out of the van, Billy motioned for other US soldiers, still in the helicopter, to come for two captives. When they were gone, he picked up the young, unconscious bodyguard. He could not have weighed more than 140 pounds. Billy carried him to the truck and placed him face down in the pool of blood left by McIsaac. He took the Makarov out of his pocket and fired his last two bullets into the bodyguard's back, between the shoulder blades.

With his pocketknife, he cut the plastic ties securing that bodyguard's hands behind his back, turned him over, cut the drawstring, and removed the sack, revealing a young, attractive face covered partially by a juvenile peach fuzz beard.

Billy swore as a wave of remorse swept over him. He thought of those he had shot in Bosnia. He suppressed the urge to vomit, knowing how McIsaac must have felt when, instead of killing the boy with a knife back in Kandahar, two hours earlier, he had taken him prisoner.

The noise from the helicopter brought Billy back to reality. With sack and electrical tie in hand, he headed back to the van. There, using the borrowed lighter, he set fire to the vehicle, destroying all evidence of the abduction.

As he ran to the helicopter, he thought that by morning, if not sooner, the burnt-out van and pickup truck with the dead bodyguard in the back would be discovered. He had not searched the young man's pockets. He likely carried identification. Even without papers, he would likely be identified.

The minister had vanished, his dead bodyguard found in a truck that had exchanged shots at the Taliban roadblock, his car abandoned near a mosque, and his dead driver a short distance away. It would look like the minister had staged his own disappearance.

The simultaneous disappearance of the Krait, right after the warlord's sons were shot, would only increase tension, pointing to a possible power play, at least until a more plausible and less threatening explanation surfaced.

An hour after lift-off, as the rising moon cast a silvery sheen over the landscape, the helicopter landed at a US base, where McIsaac received emergency medical attention. He was stabilized and transported to a US military hospital in Germany.

He remained there until, fully recovered, he returned to Canada. With his medical record left behind, except for a small scar on his back and a larger one on his upper chest, there was no evidence he had been wounded.

The captives were whisked away and transferred to collaborating third parties for interrogation; the fruits shared by US and Canadian intelligence services.

Basel and Kamin were offered the option of travelling to Canada to claim asylum as political refugees. Instead, they travelled north to join the Northern Alliance. In unspoken recognition of their assistance, and to eliminate paperwork, they were given the money the two captives were carrying when they were grabbed off the street in Kandahar.

Billy was given time to clean up, change out of his Afghan attire, and put on fresh clothing. On the ground in Pakistan, before he had even finished shaving off his beard, he was joined by two CSIS representatives. After a cursory review of the events of the past few weeks, they explained they and US and British intelligence would debrief him on the flight home because this was a joint operation.

He was told not to discuss any aspect of the mission with anyone, including commanding officers. Should anyone press him for information, he was to direct them to the Department of National Defence. They gave him a file number for any superiors.

Chapter 42

As usual, nothing went as planned.

Debriefed in the airplane on his way home, he arrived after midnight. He met his CSIS handlers, who took him to his quarters.

"Wheeler, you'll probably want to sleep in," one of his handlers said. "Call when you get up. I expect you'll want to go on leave for a while."

"You got that right. How fast can it be approved?"

"Call when you get up. We'll try to have you on your way in a day or two."

Wide-awake from jet lag, Billy showered and watched TV, *Colombo* re-runs. Finally, before daylight, he dozed off, falling into a deep sleep.

He was awakened by someone pounding on his door, calling his name. Whoever it was would not go away. He threw off his covers.

"What the fuck is going on?"

He stumbled to his door and opened it. Outside was the younger of the CSIS handlers.

"Holy shit, Wheeler. Someone's attacking the US. No details yet, but it looks like thousands are dead in New York and Washington, DC. You got to come with me."

Groggy, none of it registering, Billy pulled on his clothes from the day before and went with the man.

At headquarters, he watched TV as two civilian airliners crashed into the World Trade Centre. He was briefed about one striking the Pentagon and another crashing in Pennsylvania.

They asked his opinion.

He shrugged. "I don't know anything about this stuff."

"National Defence will expect a briefing. Most of our info is second-hand. We want to show we're in the game. We may want to produce you to them as someone who knows the score, privately, of course."

"Fine, but what will I say?"

"Nothing. Everything you know is classified. We just want you available to comment. We'll tell you what to say."

He was never called on and instead spent the next two days at headquarters, watching it unfold time and time again on TV. Despite the tragic circumstances, he smiled, seeing hundreds of planeloads of passengers over the Atlantic denied entry into US airspace and finding a safe haven in Newfoundland. Most were diverted to Gander, doubling the town's population within hours.

After four weeks, his leave was approved. They told him they needed to create records showing he had not left the country, but he suspected he was being kept around while his superiors decided, if and when they might deploy him back to Afghanistan.

His suspicions grew after he asked one of his handlers when he would receive the psychological programming to undo the desensitizing training. He felt empty inside, and sometimes he did not like people anymore.

"We've never deprogrammed anyone before," the handler said, peering over his glasses. "The psychologists are in a debate about whether it can be done and, if so, how long it will take. Meanwhile," he said, taking in Billy's freshly shaven and pale lower face, which contrasted vividly with his sunburnt upper face, "you should grow that beard again. We're putting together a joint task force. You may be part of it, perhaps as an interpreter or as an interrogator. You're more convincing if you look like one of them."

* * *

As the slowly descending Dash 8 made its way northeasterly over Humber Valley toward the Deer Lake airport, Billy peered out the window at the ground below. He was anxious to return home.

Although too high for him to make out details, he could see the Humber River, a dark, meandering line carving through the landscape below. He knew by then, early October, the entire valley would be rich with fall colours.

The bright red maples, nature's inspiration for the Canadian flag, yellow leaves of widespread birches, accentuated by orange-needled larch trees, called junipers by the Newfoundlanders, were arranged against a background of evergreens, as if flung erratically on a gigantic canvas by an abstract artist.

Remembering his last trip home only fifteen months earlier, Billy had mixed emotions. He, Emma, and the kids had driven through the Maritime provinces and had taken the overnight ferry to Port aux Basques before driving the final five hours to his parents' home in Spudgels Cove.

Looking back over the nine months since the accident, everything seemed unreal. When he arrived back in Ottawa from the Afghan mission on September 10, less than four weeks earlier, he had no idea how or where he might be deployed next. The only thing he knew for sure was that, regardless of what the Brass said, he intended to take whatever leave he had coming to him and head for home, back to Newfoundland, which had become known recently as "the Rock".

Smiling as he thought of the dense forests, clean rivers, and lakes that covered his home province, a landmass not unlike Norway, he wondered if they had started calling it the Rock to keep strangers away, preserving an enormous, private playground for the half million locals.

Finally, Billy's plane landed at Deer Lake's tiny, two-gate terminal. He was greeted by his sister, Rhonda, and his new brother-in-law, Josh Short. Now that was a shock! Rhonda, a real bitch on wheels, married to his buddy Josh, the career soldier, nice guy, and confirmed bachelor.

Then the reason for her attraction dawned on him. Josh was a lot like Brad.

Rhonda, three years older than Billy, had spent most of her adult life alternating between having no love interest to having brief, intense relationships. They always ending with her dumping the guy after he failed to live up to her uncommunicated and impossible standard. As each relationship failed, Rhonda became increasingly bitter at how her life was turning out.

Rhonda had not always been that way. As a teenager, she had been madly in love with Brad, the only child of a local business owner. Two years older than Rhonda, they had started dating when she was fourteen. Initially, both sets of parents hoped it was a phase for both of them that would soon be over.

However, it did not end.

It was not even as if they were dating. They simply spent nearly all their waking hours together, interrupted only by time in different classrooms or when Brad had to work at the family business. Even then Rhonda found excuses to drop by and see him.

After graduating from high school, Brad entered Memorial University of Newfoundland (MUN) to study business, intending to return home afterwards. Over the next two years, both remained faithful to each other, keeping in touch with letters and telephone calls and Brad making the 800-kilometre trip to come home at every available opportunity.

By the winter of his second year, to the dismay of Brad's parents, the young couple had decided that Rhonda would also attend MUN to study nursing or social work or something, and without parental interference, they would simply move in together.

Then during spring break, on a sunny day in March, Brad, not yet twenty, went out high marking in the Long Range Mountains. This is a sport where snowmobilers go flying up a mountainside at full speed and then, just before losing control, complete a U-turn and come back down to the bottom of the mountain, challenging others to go higher.

On that day, the group included a half dozen couples and a few younger kids, including Billy and Rhonda, who followed along for the adventure. Stopping at the base of the mountains so the girls could watch the boys compete, the contest began.

Three riders had already gone ahead, each going higher than the one before, when Brad made his run. On his father's powerful snowmobile, he flew up the mountainside, well past the highest mark, three quarters of the way up the hillside, before turning right, intending to make a U-turn and return to the bottom.

However, one of his skis caught the top of a stunted black spruce poking through the deep, powdery snow, and in the momentary loss of control that followed, the snowmobile rolled over with Brad underneath. Then, as rider and machine tumbled toward the bottom, the onlookers watched in disbelief as the disturbance started an avalanche that tore down the mountainside, covering Brad and the snowmobile and nearly engulfing the shocked spectators below.

Dispatching riders on the two fastest snowmobiles back to Spudgels Cove for help, using their bare hands, snowshoes, and anything else they could find, the others dug frantically into the deep snow trying to find Brad. Within an hour, a larger group, including Brad's father, showed up with shovels and lights, but even with their help, it was after dark before they recovered Brad's body.

A few weeks after Brad's funeral, Rhonda woke up feeling nauseated: morning sickness.

Chapter 43

Billy awoke to the sound of tires on the fresh layer of crushed stone on his parents' driveway, and Josh, who was driving with Rhonda sitting between them, saying, "We're here!"

"Wow," Billy said, rubbing his eyes, "I can't believe I slept the whole way."

"Not the whole way," Josh said with a laugh. "You were awake for a good fifteen minutes, but when we passed through Wiltondale, you were dead to the world. Your big sister here," he nudged Rhonda, who was yawning and snuggled up alongside Billy like when they were children, "has only been asleep for the last half hour."

They spotted Brenda in the doorway wearing an apron and holding a tea towel.

"I'll grab your duffel bag," Josh said. "You go see your mom. She's really excited to have everybody home. She's been baking for days."

Mother and son met halfway and hugged for the longest time. Then Brenda stood back from him at arms' length.

"Let me look at you," she said, giggling as she put her hand to his short, three-week-old beard. "I've never seen you with a beard before. You Army boys are always clean-shaven. You didn't join the Navy, did you?"

"No, Mom," he replied. "The only boats I want to be on are fishing boats." Then came a little white lie. "I've got some time off, so I thought I would let it grow, just to see how it looks. I'll shave it off when I go back."

"Hey, what about me?" Rhonda said. "Don't I get a hug, too?"

"Of course you do," Brenda replied, "and Josh, too. You must be hungry," she continued as they headed toward the front door. "After all that city food, I figured you'd want something wild, so I cooked a couple of rabbits your father snared, the first of the season, and a black duck he shot last evening."

"Actually," Rhonda replied, "Josh and I had KFC in Deer Lake while we were waiting for Billy, and I'm working a double starting at midnight."

"Rhonda Wheeler!" Brenda stopped and corrected herself. "I guess it's Rhonda Short now. Why on Earth are you working the Friday night graveyard shift and all day Saturday?" She looked at Josh. "You're married now. How does he feel about this?"

"Oh, Mom," Rhonda replied. "He's fine. The only way I could get Sunday off to be here for dinner with all of you was to swap a shift with one of the young nurses who wanted Friday night off. Besides, Josh is going to spend tomorrow up at Yankee Point, moose hunting with his grandfather. He'll be back in Port Saunders to stay with me tomorrow night, and on Sunday, we'll back here for dinner with you and Dad and Billy and Brad."

"I suppose," Brenda agreed grudgingly. "You young people are always rushing around. I can hardly keep track of where everyone is and what they're doing."

Inside, Brenda heaped food on a large dinner plate, which she set in front of Billy. "Eat. It looks like you could use it. I don't think they feed you enough."

"They feed me enough. It's just not home cooking. Which," he laughed, "I'm going to have to watch out for around you if I want to fit into my uniform when I go back. By the way, where's Dad and young Brad? I can't wait to see them."

"Your nephew got into Deer Lake last evening," she replied. "Henry and Eileen went to pick him up. He stayed with them last night, and they got up early to go moose hunting. He and your father and Henry left before daylight. They should be back any time now."

Billy stared at her, incredulous. "Henry Hurley went moose hunting? I don't know if I've ever seen him pick up a gun!"

"You should have known him when he was young," she replied, "before Eileen got him. Back then, he and your father hunted and fished together all the time. Then Henry went away, and when he came back with Eileen, he was different. Henry told your father that she was petrified of guns. When she was young, her brother was shot by a gun that nobody thought was loaded. She couldn't bear the sight of them, so Henry sold his guns and gave up hunting. When young Brad got old enough to hunt, she couldn't stop him, but she was worried sick every time he went out."

"But that doesn't explain why he doesn't fish," Billy replied.

"I know," she said. "He told your father that Eileen doesn't like any kind of fish, not even salmon or trout. Can you believe that? She's a Newfoundlander, like the rest of us, and she claims she doesn't like fish."

"What about young Brad?" Billy asked. "How old is he now?"

"He'll be twenty in December, the same age as his father when he died," she added quietly. "He's attending Memorial, now in his second year, and he's doing pretty good as far as I can tell."

"What's he studying?"

"I understand in the first year they study a little bit of everything until they figure out what they want to do. Right now, I'm not sure he knows what he wants to do. Too many choices, your father says, but they're all good. Me and your dad, we just want him to graduate."

She paused and checked the oven. "Henry and Eileen — and they've paid for everything, you know — they got plans for him. She wants him to be a doctor, but Henry says that our grandson's got a good head for business and that's what he should study."

Wiping her hands in her apron, she beamed. "Henry says that one of these days he could see our Brad running one of those big companies that you hear about in the news."

*   *   *

Thanksgiving dinner on Sunday afternoon at the Wheeler residence was a festive affair, with Brenda going all out to impress the Hurleys. Eileen, who, in forty years since coming to Spudgels Cove, had never been to their home for dinner, arrived with a large, bakeapple-topped cheesecake.

With a table of eight made up of herself and Riley, the Hurleys, Josh, Rhonda, Billy, and young Brad, Brenda was in her element. "Isn't this great?" she said to her husband. "It's just like when the kids were home. I don't think we've had this many people for dinner since Christmas."

Even though wild game figured prominently in the main courses, uncertain of Eileen's tastes, Brenda also cooked a chicken and a small ham, a precaution that she realized was unnecessary when the stylishly slim Eileen ignored the store-bought food and went for a second helping of wild rabbit.

"Henry," Eileen said, "this is delicious. Why don't we ever have it?"

"The season just opened," Brenda said, ever generous. "Riley always catches a lot. I'll give you a couple of pairs to take home with you."

After dinner, Henry and Riley relaxed in the living room, trying to engage their grandson, who was more interested in watching the football game than discussing his future.

Henry nodded toward the kitchen, where the three women were washing dishes, and then looked at Riley. "Did you ever think you would see that?"

"Per-per-perhaps w-w-when Br-Br-Brad was alive. N-n-not after."

PART 3

THE TRIAL

Chapter 44

Barbara "BeeBee" Beaudoin awoke to the sound of a screaming outboard motor. The clock radio showed 4:55 a.m. Reaching out in the dark, she turned off the alarm, which was set for 5 a.m., so it would not awaken her some-time boyfriend, RCMP Staff Sergeant Brian Buckle. Slipping out of bed, she headed for the bathroom of her small apartment, pausing to turn on the coffee maker she had set up six hours earlier.

She brushed her teeth and inspected her hairline. No tell-tale roots. Good. The week-old dye job, one of her few indulgences since moving to Port Saunders, was holding up. This would be a ponytail day. After a quick shower, she headed into the kitchen.

Pouring coffee into a travel mug, she headed to her tiny living room to dress, where, to avoid waking Brian, she had laid out a grey blazer, pants, white blouse, socks, jewellery, and shoes the night before.

Sipping on the coffee as she slipped on her clothes, her body ached for a cigarette, but she suppressed the urge to light up, as a single whiff of tobacco smoke would likely bring Brian to his feet, setting off an argument. She stood in front of the mirror, fully dressed, and nodded. Not bad. She would do her makeup at the truck stop in Deer Lake.

Returning to the kitchen, she refilled her travel mug with the last of the coffee, rinsed the pot, dumped the hot grounds into the garbage, and set up a fresh brew for Brian to turn on when he got up. Then, tiptoeing to the bedroom door, she looked in. He had not moved in the forty minutes since she got up.

Closing the door carefully behind her, she grabbed her briefcase, ciga-rettes, sunglasses, and coffee. Minutes later, was driving east into the blind-ing sunrise toward the winding, two-lane Viking Trail that would take her nearly 300 kilometres south through several Northern Peninsula villages to Corner Brook, for a bail hearing.

Not exactly what she had planned for July 1, Canada Day. It was a day of national celebration, but it was also a day of conflicting emotions in Newfoundland and Labrador, Britain's oldest colony. It was a day when people wore tiny blue forget-me-nots to commemorate the Battle of the Somme, honouring the sacrifice of the Royal Newfoundland Regiment, because on that day in 1916, more than 90 percent of them had been killed or wounded in a single morning.

Beebee had expected to sleep in until at least 9 a.m., and at 11 a.m., watch the Canada Day parade. Brian would be working the parade in the full ceremonial attire of the Royal Canadian Mounted Police: red serge jacket, blue riding pants with a yellow stripe down each leg, high brown boots, and hat. They had planned a barbecue for later in the evening. Hopefully she would make it back in time for that.

Looking at her watch as she passed the bulbous water tower in Hawke's Bay, she noted it was five minutes before six. She was making good time. If she could get through Gros Morne before the tourists started moving, with a quick stop in Deer Lake, she would be in Corner Brook before 9 a.m.

If they've brought him down from the lockup by the time I arrive, she thought, *I can spend a few minutes with him, then meet with the crown attorney and see what he wants for bail. At least I hope it's one of the men and not the bitch. If it's her, from what I've heard, there's almost no point in talking to her, and I may as well save my arguments for the judge.*

Anyway, she continued, *the hearing is set for nine thirty, and nobody wants to waste Canada Day hanging around the courthouse. Not me, not the staff, and certainly not the judge. We should be out of there by midmorning, lunchtime at the latest.*

The only thing troubling her was that she did not know the charge. According to the accused's sister, he had been arrested in Ottawa on Thursday night and escorted back to Newfoundland on Friday by two RCMP officers.

She knew he had to be brought before a judge within twenty-four hours of being arrested and either released on conditions or, if the Crown opposed his release, entitled to a full bail hearing in front of a judge.

On Friday, three days earlier, the case had not even been on her radar. She knew a helicopter had gone missing back in late winter or early spring. Around then, there had been speculation about it having been shot down, but in the absence of facts, idle gossip was commonplace in small towns.

Then in May, a shrimp dragger's net had entangled something underwater and brought up the helicopter. While sea creatures had devoured parts of the bodies, an autopsy revealed that the pilot had been shot through the chin, and the bullet was still lodged in his helmet.

Forensics determined the calibre, and the police retrieved data from the Department of Fisheries and Oceans and found that only three vessels, sealers, had been operating there that morning. Search warrants permitted raids on the homes of crewmembers, and their firearms were seized. Ballistic tests showed the fatal bullet was fired from a rifle owned by retired Warrant Officer Josh Short.

He, his father-in-law, Riley Wheeler, and nephew, Jeff Wheeler, were brought in for questioning. Josh acknowledged being in the area at the time but denied any knowledge of the shooting. Riley did likewise, but young Jeff had cracked.

Presented with ballistics evidence that Josh's rifle had killed the pilot, under the pressure of being told that Josh would be charged with murder, and that he, his grandfather, and Billy Wheeler would be charged with being accessories, the teenager blurted out, "You can't charge Uncle Josh with murder; he was only steering the boat!"

The skilled interrogator leveraged that information, suggesting that it might simply have been an accident and perhaps if they knew who did it, maybe that person could be guilty of only a minor charge of unsafe use of a firearm and the others might not be charged with any offense. Trusting the interrogator, without the benefit of legal counsel, the gullible teenager told the entire story.

From BeeBee's perspective, it was playing out like a television miniseries. Helicopter crashes in mysterious circumstances. Helicopter hauled from bottom of the ocean by fishing vessel. Autopsy shows pilot killed by rifle shot from boat below. Bullet came from sealing vessel captained by retired soldier.

It seemed like an open-and-shut case. Identify who had fired the shot. Decide whether that person should be charged with first-degree murder or second-degree murder. Offer plea deals on lesser charges to the other occupants of the vessel in exchange for their testimony. If they refused to deal, charge all of them with murder and let a jury decide whom to convict.

There would be a jury trial in the Supreme Court of Newfoundland and Labrador at Corner Brook, preceded by a preliminary inquiry, routine in cases like this.

Since the allegations were against a crew from Spudgels Cove, Port Saunders RCMP, where Staff Sergeant Brian Buckle was the officer in charge, would likely handle the investigation. However, even this detail was still uncertain, as the offense had happened out at sea.

This was a big case that had already attracted lots of international media attention, so it was a high-risk/high-reward assignment for some ambitious police officer. The Mounties would want someone with media training and a good television presence, so every detail mattered.

If they had enough money, the plaintiffs would likely hire a big criminal lawyer from St. John's. If they did not, Legal Aid would represent them. They were lucky Corner Brook had capable Legal Aid lawyers — overworked, but adept. She thought it would be interesting to watch this case play out over the next few years.

Then on Friday, when she was in court in Port au Choix representing a turbot fisherman accused of failing to discard a dead halibut accidentally caught in his turbot nets, during a short smoke break, as she stood outside the ramshackle building that served as a courthouse seven or eight times a year, she was approached by Rhonda Short, still in her nurse's uniform and frantic.

BeeBee knew Rhonda but not well. BeeBee was a few years older, had grown up in a community to the north, and had moved away at seventeen to St. John's to attend MUN. They might have met when Rhonda entered MUN to study nursing, but BeeBee had left after two years to follow her, now ex-husband, Ralph Collins, a petroleum engineer, to Calgary.

BeeBee had completed her undergrad in Calgary and took several years off to have two children. She entered law school when the youngest started kindergarten. Five years later, she was a public defender. Successful at work, her home life was challenging. Finally, it imploded when Ralph, after a series of affairs, moved out.

In the ugly divorce battle that ensued, BeeBee, unable to cope with two unruly teenagers and an antagonistic, estranged husband, turned to the bottle. Within a year, the kids had deserted her for their father and his girlfriend. BeeBee, alone and unable to function, checked into rehab.

Upon her release, unemployed and dispirited, she loaded her personal belongings into her car and drove 6,000 kilometres to Newfoundland. A year later, determined to put her life back together, she passed the Newfoundland and Labrador bar exam. Then she moved to nearby Port Saunders, where she rented a small office and an even smaller apartment and started accepting clients.

She envied Rhonda, who had also gone away but only long enough to complete a nursing degree. Then she returned home, found work at Rufus Guinchard Memorial Hospital, and was now head nurse.

Rhonda had it all together as far as men were concerned. She ran off the losers and the abusers, refusing to settle until she landed her Prince Charming, retired Warrant Officer Josh Short. Local gossip in Port Saunders, population 700, was that Rhonda and Josh, who apparently had money, were planning to build a big home in Spudgels Cove to be near her family.

BeeBee did not know the personal histories or the family connections of townspeople well enough to participate in the local gossip, and being a lawyer, she was wary of doing so. However, she had overheard the assistant manager at the bank say that the hospital administrator was concerned Rhonda might resign as head nurse and work only part-time to spend more time with Josh.

Rhonda's normally cool, take-charge demeanour deserted her as she explained that, the previous evening, police officers had descended on Spudgels Cove looking for her husband, father, brother, and nephew. All but her brother Billy, who was in Ottawa, had been taken into custody.

Without knowing where they were being taken, while Rhonda remained home by the telephone, Brenda took their truck and followed the squad cars to Corner Brook, hoping it was a mistake and that all they would need was a ride home when the police realized they had done nothing wrong.

Rhonda's first call was to Billy's cell phone. Ordinarily, his cryptic message of, "Hi, this is Billy, you know what to do next," would have brought a smile to her face, but not this time.

Afraid to leave the phone in case she missed a call, she paced the floor, smoking cigarettes and drinking coffee until 4 a.m., when her mother called. The three had been released without any charges, but the police still needed to talk to Billy to clear up a few details.

Unknown to them, Billy had been arrested in Ottawa. Based on forensic evidence and Jeff's statement, he had been charged with criminal negligence causing death. He was in a jail cell awaiting transport back to Corner Brook to appear in court.

When Rhonda left home at 7 a.m., her mother and the men had just returned. While they suspected Billy was in police custody, they could not reach him. His whereabouts were unknown and the police were not providing any information.

Rhonda explained to Beebee that Billy had called that morning. He said he had been arrested the evening before, held for questioning, and charged with shooting down the helicopter.

A lawyer from Ontario Legal Aid met with him, and he appeared in court. The Crown opposed his release on bail. Unrepresented, he had consented to remain in custody until he could retain a lawyer.

Over the weekend, he had been transported back to Corner Brook to appear before a WASH court judge on Monday, July 1, his thirty-fifth birthday.

Rhonda was beside herself in disbelief, and like most people, unfamiliar with the criminal justice system. Confused, she asked, "Is there even such a thing as a WASH court?"

"Oh yes," BeeBee responded with a chuckle. "That simply means Weekend and Statutory Holiday Court. We have a couple dozen provincial court judges around the province. People are entitled to be brought before a judge within twenty-four hours of their arrest, so a judge is always on call."

The back door Beebee had left ajar opened fully, and a sheriff's officer appeared. Court was about to resume.

"We break again at twelve thirty for lunch," she told Rhonda. "I only have an hour. You'll find me at the Seagull Café. Try to find out where your brother is being held and when his next court appearance is. Perhaps I can help you."

Chapter 45

At Bellburns, with the morning sun warming her left cheek, BeeBee spied the small lobster boats. Watching them on the calm blue water, their two-man crews hauling up line after line of waterlogged, kelp-laden traps, reminded her that the season was ending, and she needed to call her father and ask him to save her a half dozen lobsters from his last catch.

Her drive through the mountains of Gros Morne was uneventful. She pulled into the Deer Lake truck stop, where she applied her makeup quickly and then called Her Majesty's Penitentiary in Corner Brook.

"Hi, this is Beebee Beaudoin," she said to the guard. "I'm calling for Billy Wheeler. Do have him?"

"Is that the guy who shot down the helicopter?" the guard replied, fishing for information.

She smiled. "I think something like that is being alleged. So, I take it you do have him?"

"Yeah, he's here. Easy to deal with. Doesn't say anything. Follows orders. No attitude like a lot of them. When do you expect to get here?"

"I'm in Deer Lake," she replied. "What's that, a half hour?"

"More like forty minutes. We've got him and several others who were brought in over the weekend, so there's no point you coming to the jail, cuz by then we'll be loading them into the van for transport down to the court-house. You might as well go straight to the courthouse and see him there. None of the others have lawyers, so I'll get the guys to bring him in from the cells first so you won't have to wait so long."

"Thanks. I appreciate it," she replied.

"Did he do it?" the guard asked before she could hang up.

"I don't know," she answered truthfully.

An hour later, sitting alone in a well-worn interview room, before she even met her newest client, she read the sparsely written indictment handed to her by junior prosecutor, Adam Peabody.

"Iris asked me to give you the indictment when you got here," he said. "She's with someone from Legal Aid working out release conditions for a number of others who were picked up on the weekend."

"Did she say anything about my guy?" Beebee asked, hoping to get a hint as to whether the Crown would oppose bail.

"No," Peabody replied. "I looked at the indictment. It's pretty straight-forward. The facts are written up like an accidental shooting, like somebody discharged a firearm carelessly, and even though there was no intent to harm anyone, people got killed, so he's charged with crim neg causing death. He's an active member of the Canadian Armed Forces, so he's really no flight risk, but I'm pretty sure he'll have to agree not to leave the province until this is all over with. That won't be good for his military career."

An experienced criminal lawyer, BeeBee reviewed the single-charge indictment, the most critical clause stating, "On or about the seventh day of April, 2002, the accused, William John Wheeler (DOB July 1, 1967), by care-less use of a firearm, did cause the deaths of Glenn Holmes, Billy Clearwater, Martina Schmidt, and George Villeneuve, and is, therefore, guilty of crimi-nal negligence causing death, contrary to Section 219 of the Criminal Code of Canada."

She looked up when she heard a knock at the door.

"Counsel, are you ready for your client, or do you need more time?" one of the guards asked.

She stood up from her chair. "I'm fine; bring him in."

The door opened, and two guards entered, Billy between them. The guards looked like linebackers — young, clean-cut men with bulging biceps nearly bursting their short-sleeved shirts. Between them, handcuffed and wearing leg irons, all of which were chained together at his waist, in a rumpled tracksuit and runners without laces, looking small and haggard, was her client. His only concession to recent grooming was a freshly shaved face, a trace of soap near his left ear. She thought the date of birth on the indict-ment had to be wrong. It said he was thirty-five, but he could easily pass for fifty.

BeeBee nodded at the restraints. "Do you mind taking these off, at least while he's in here talking to me?"

"All of it?" the first guard asked.

She nodded. "All of it."

"Well, all right," he replied, "but we'll have to put them back on when we take him into court."

"And we'll be right outside if you need us," the younger and slightly smaller guard said.

When the door closed, Billy rubbed his wrists where the handcuffs had cut into his skin. "Thanks for that, ma'am. I'm sorry for my appearance. They picked me up late Thursday night in Ottawa when I was just getting back from a four-hour run. Since then, I managed to get a couple showers, but I haven't been able to get any fresh clothes, so I probably smell pretty ripe."

"Not at all," she said, attempting to set him at ease. "Your sister gave me a small overnight bag with a few of changes of your brother-in-law's clothes. It's in my car. If we get you out of here, we can drop into McDonald's for you to clean up before we head back up the coast."

"Well, that's pretty good service, and I don't even know your name," Billy said, seeking to make light of the situation. He reached out his right hand with a tentative smile. "I'm Billy Wheeler. You must be my lawyer."

"Excuse my manners for not introducing myself immediately," she said hastily. "I'm Beebee Beaudoin, and yes, your sister retained me to come down from Port Saunders and get you out of custody. There may be a bail hearing. If there is, I'll handle it for you, but for now, that's all I'm hired to do. We didn't get any further in our discussion. Your family just wants to get you out of custody and back home."

"Do you always give killers a ride home after you get them out of jail?" Billy asked.

"Alleged killers, Mr. Wheeler," she corrected him, "or should I call you Sergeant Wheeler? Your sister told me your rank."

"Ma'am," he responded politely, "just call me Billy."

"Then, you've got to call me Beebee and not ma'am. It's way too old for me."

"Good enough," he replied.

"Now, let's get down to work," she said, explaining that he had been charged with criminal negligence causing death in the shooting down of the helicopter a few months earlier. "If they don't upgrade the charge, bail shouldn't be a problem."

"What do you mean 'upgrade the charge'?" he asked.

"Well, criminal negligence causing death is a serious charge. It could get you several years in prison, but it isn't murder. The Crown won't want to let you out without a bail hearing. This case has had too much publicity, but your odds of a judge letting you out after a hearing and with conditions are good."

"So, what do I do about bail?" he asked. "I've seen cases on TV where bail is really high, and I've seen ads in the States for bail bondsmen. I don't see any of those around here. How do I get out of here on bail?"

"Bail in Canada isn't like bail in the US," she replied. "Here, the amount is low, sometimes a thousand dollars and sometimes a few thousand. Only occasionally is it higher than that. Here, you have to satisfy the judge there are reasonable grounds for you to be released."

"What do you mean by 'reasonable grounds'?"

"First of all, the judge must believe you'll show up for court and not take off."

"Okay," he replied. "That makes sense. What else?"

"That you're not a danger to the public, and you won't commit any offenses while you're out on bail."

"How do I do that?"

"Well," she responded, "you're a pretty good candidate. You have no criminal record, you're gainfully employed, and you have a place to live. They will require you to report in with the police, perhaps every day, even if it's only by telephone. Standard release conditions will also prohibit you from possessing any firearms or consuming drugs or alcohol."

"Is that it?" he asked, incredulous.

"In most cases, yes, but your case has an extra wrinkle I'm hoping we can avoid."

"What's that?" he asked, now concerned that his release, which seconds earlier appeared imminent, was uncertain.

"Lately," she said, "due to certain high-profile cases, the politicians have been leaning on the prosecutors to start pushing the judges to consider a third condition."

"What's that?"

"Sometimes, when cases have had a lot of publicity, like this one, and the trial is expected to generate even more publicity, prosecutors are being urged by their political masters to argue that, even if the accused satisfies the first two grounds, as set out in the Criminal Code, release could bring the administration of justice into disrepute."

Billy sat back in his chair, perplexed. "Are you saying that even if there's no risk of me taking off, and even if there's no risk of me breaking any laws while I'm waiting for my trial, the government might want to keep me in jail because they might look bad if they let me out?"

"You got it."

"How do they decide when there's been too much publicity to let a person out?"

"Technically, it's a decision that the director of public prosecutions makes. He's a politically appointed bureaucrat in St. John's. He can communicate an off-the-record request to the senior prosecutor for political cover for his boss, the minister of justice."

"Is that even legal?" Billy asked. "I mean, politicians interfering in cases?"

"You have a point. Prosecutors are officers of the court, supposedly immune to outside pressure, whether from the public or politicians. They're also lawyers, professionally bound to act ethically, but that doesn't always happen. The stronger and more ethical prosecutors call their own shots, but by doing so, they antagonize their political masters and limit their own careers and aren't appointed to the bench. The weaker prosecutors aren't much more than mouthpieces, afraid of making mistakes, constantly looking for instructions."

"And the one in charge of my case, is he someone who will call his own shots and do the right thing, or will he simply do whatever his bosses tell him?" Billy asked, suddenly gloomy at learning of imperfections in the justice system.

"Actually, neither," BeeBee replied. "Iris Inkpen has carriage of your case."

"What does that mean?" Billy asked, mystified at the term.

"It means trouble for us. She's impossible."

"Really?" Billy replied, perplexed. "But what did you say about a carriage?"

"Sorry, that's just lawyer talk. The one who is in charge of the file is said to have carriage of it."

"I guess I'm going to learn a lot of new words in the lawyer trade before this is all over," he responded wryly. "Why do you say this other lawyer is impossible?"

"Iris Inkpen is an angry, bitter woman," BeeBee said. "She showed up here over twenty-five years ago, fresh out of law school, with her husband, a local guy, older than her, who was one of her classmates. He followed a common career path for lawyers; starting at the bottom in a local firm. He worked his way up, mostly doing trials and cultivating his political connections in the Tory party. Predictably, after twenty years, he was appointed a federal court judge and moved to Ottawa. That was seven or eight years ago."

"What does that have to do with her?" Billy asked.

"I'm coming to that," BeeBee said. "He dumped her!"

"Okay, so he dumped her. If that was seven or eight years ago, why doesn't she just get on with her life? Lots of people get dumped."

"That's just it," BeeBee said. "I think she feels she is getting on with her life. She's making up for lost years, and God help anyone who gets in her way!"

Billy shrugged. "I still don't get it."

BeeBee leaned forward. "According to local gossip, when they arrived here, the plan was for them to practice law together, make lots of money, and have a big house and the perfect family. However, shortly after they arrived, she got pregnant. They had twins, so she put off her legal career for five or six years until the kids were in school.

Then she went to work in her husband's firm. Being the wife of a junior lawyer, with a chip on her shoulder, things didn't work out. If she hadn't quit, the partners would've gotten rid of her, and perhaps both of them, so she resigned.

She got a job with Legal Aid. That didn't go so well either. She considered most of the clients riffraff, and she was required to travel when the court went on circuit, so she quit that, too. Then she teamed up with another woman who specializes in family law. That's a tough gig around here, too, with only a small population and other lawyers competing for clients, so that didn't work out either."

Billy was anxious for her to get to the point. "So, how did she get to be a prosecutor?"

"Around the time her husband was being considered as a federal court judge, she discovered he was having an affair with one of his staff and was planning to leave her. Realizing the marriage was over and that a huge matrimonial battle would be expensive and public, they worked out a deal. She got the house plus a big settlement. To avoid alimony, he used his political connections to get her hired as a prosecutor."

"So, if that was the deal, what's her problem?" Billy asked.

"She hates the job, she hates the people, and she hates our province. Home prices are low, so if she were to sell out and leave, she would still need to work. I've heard that she wants a judicial appointment, but nothing's open. Even if something opened up, the Liberals are in power. They have too many of their friends drooling over the next judicial appointment, so she's just got to hang in as a prosecutor until housing prices go up or the Tories take over."

"Wow," Billy said, "and I thought I had troubles."

"You do," BeeBee said grimly. "She's your prosecutor, and I'm afraid you'll soon find out why she's called Iris the Inquisitor!"

A knock sounded on the door

"The judge is ready to come in," the friendlier of the two sheriff's officers said. "Ms. Inkpen wants to know if you're ready to go."

"Tell her yes, but give me another thirty seconds with my client."

"Sure, BeeBee. I'll just tell her that we need a minute or two to put the shackles back on him."

"See what I mean?" BeeBee said, rolling her eyes as she turned back to Billy. "Any other crown attorney would want to meet for a few minutes, let the defence know if they were going to consent to bail, and discuss release conditions, but not Iris. Simple civility is beneath her. She won't condescend to reasonableness, one of the reasons she couldn't make it in private practice."

"Does that mean I'm not getting out on bail?" Billy asked.

"Not necessarily. She's so arrogant and on such a power trip that she's going to wait until we're in front of the judge before she tells us anything. It might still be okay. We'll find out soon enough."

Minutes later, they were standing before the judge, and the clerk read the charge in open court for the world to hear.

"Ms. Inkpen," Provincial Court Judge Melody Milloy asked. "What's the Crown's position as to bail?"

"Your Honour, since the accused was arrested a few days ago, the Crown has developed information regarding his mental health. We're opposing his release, and we'll be applying for him to be remanded to the Waterford Mental Hospital in St. John's for a thirty-day psychiatric assessment."

The judge turned to BeeBee. "Ms. Beaudoin, I assume you've discussed this with your client and Ms. Inkpen? What's your client's position?"

"Your Honour," BeeBee replied, "I'm afraid I haven't discussed it with the Crown or my client. There's no indication of a mental health issue in the file, which admittedly is thin, because I haven't yet received the police report, witness statements, or medical records."

Angry that the crown attorney had ambushed the defence, Judge Milloy turned back to Inkpen. "Ms. Inkpen, I'm going stand this matter down right now and give you a chance to discuss it with Ms. Beaudoin. While you're doing that, instead of wasting the court's time, I'll hear the next matter on the docket."

"Your Honour, I have carriage of all matters on the docket," Inkpen said. "Would you prefer that I deal with them first and then meet with Ms. Beaudoin, or should I speak with her first and deal with the other matters on the docket afterwards?"

"Neither," Milloy replied, well acquainted with Inkpen's tactics. "I just saw Mr. Peabody outside. The two of you can work it out. Either you can hand off this file to him, and he can work out something with Ms. Beaudoin, or he can come in here and we'll run through the docket while you're meeting with Ms. Beaudoin, which, quite frankly, you should have done before appearing before me today."

Dumbfounded, Inkpen looked as if she had been slapped. But before she could say anything, Milloy, now on a roll, continued.

"Pick one. You mightn't have anything else to do on Canada Day, but the rest of us do."

Pink-faced, Iris turned around and nodded at BeeBee and Billy to meet her outside. Then she left the courtroom.

Chapter 46

Back in the interview room, Inkpen went on a long tirade about Judge Milloy. "She was nothing but a second-rate loser lawyer with the right political connections. Now she's a puffed-up, politically appointed, third-rate hack judge, dispensing justice in Corner Brook, the asshole of the world."

Searching for sympathy, she glanced at Billy. "This is what we've got to put up with." She turned back to BeeBee. "I'm sorry I wasn't able meet with you and discuss Sergeant Wheeler's case, but I was too busy with all the unrepresented who were picked up over the weekend. If I had a real assistant prosecutor, I wouldn't have to deal with that riffraff, but Peabody doesn't know his ass from a hole in the ground. A real fucking idiot. He wouldn't know which ones to keep in and which ones to let out on bail." She rolled her eyes. "I can only imagine what he's doing back there without me!"

BeeBee listened silently, waiting for Inkpen to cool down, which she did. Then Inkpen forced a phony smile and extended her little, perfectly manicured, white hand.

"You're Beaudoin, right?"

Startled by the abrupt change of pace, BeeBee hesitated and then reached out and shook Inkpen's hand, which felt like a small, warm, dead fish. She forced a weak smile.

"Yes, I'm Barbara Beaudoin."

"I wondered what you'd look like," Inkpen said.

Wary of what was to come next, Beebee frowned. "I'm sorry?"

Inkpen shrugged. "You're the one Brian's fucking now. I wondered what you'd look like."

"The Staff Sergeant and I socialize occasionally," BeeBee managed, red-faced and taken off guard.

As Billy, wearing his best poker face, watched from the sidelines, Inkpen blundered on. "I hate going on circuit. All those hick towns with nothing to do and nothing to see. At least whenever I had to go up on the Northern Peninsula I looked forward to getting it on with Brian. Then on my last trip up there, he didn't have time for me, not even time enough to drop over to my room for a lunchtime quickie. I figured he was getting it somewhere else, so I asked a sheriff's officer. She told me Brian was fucking another lawyer."

Beebee refocused the discussion. "I'm sure my client isn't interested in our personal lives, and the judge will want us to come up with something. What's the mental health issue you're talking about?"

"After your client was arrested," Inkpen replied, "a Major Quinn contacted the Ottawa police, saying that your client is unbalanced. He said we should have him checked out by a psychiatrist."

"That's it?" Beebee asked. It'll take a lot more than that to keep him in. Is there anything else?"

"Lots," Inkpen said. "Quinn claims that your client attacked him for no reason, broke his jaw and other bones in his face, and knocked out a bunch of his teeth. Quinn claims that your client would've killed him but for another soldier coming to his rescue — McAllister or McNamara, or something like that."

"McIsaac," Billy interjected.

"So you admit it's true?" Inkpen asked.

"Stop right now!" Beebee said, raising her hand. "Sergeant Wheeler, do not say another word."

Inkpen smirked. "That sounds like an admission to me. I'll be opposing bail and bringing an application for a thirty-day psychiatric assessment. If we have to, we'll call Quinn and McIsaac as witnesses. By then, we'll have Quinn's medical records. Your client shot a helicopter out of the air, killing four people. I don't think I'll have much trouble convincing the judge to keep him in on public safety grounds, and I don't think I'll have any problem getting the court to order a psychiatric exam."

She raised her eyebrows at both of them. "Your client could save us the time and trouble of the application if he wants to, simply by consenting to the order today."

"Well, Ms. Inkpen," BeeBee replied, "I'll have to discuss this with my client before he agrees to anything."

Inkpen looked at her watch. "How much time do you need, ten or fifteen minutes?"

"Maybe yes, maybe more," BeeBee said.

"Fine," Inkpen said, already standing up. "Just let the officer know when you're ready. I'll go back in there and figure out what kind of a mess Peabody has made for me to clean up."

After Inkpen left, Beebee turned to Billy. "What happened between you and Quinn?"

"Ma'am, I can't remember all of it," Billy replied apologetically, "and that's the truth, but she's right about McIsaac. He was there. He saw the whole thing."

Accustomed to clients claiming not to remember their incriminating acts, she played along. "Just tell me what you can remember. From that, we'll put it together in the best manner we can. First of all, why can't you remember? Were you guys partying or something?"

"No ma'am," Billy replied. "It was during a training exercise, and I understood that it was even written up as a training accident."

"Okay, tell me what happened," she said.

"That's just it, ma'am, I don't know how much I'm supposed to tell you."

Intrigued, she pressed him. "Everything. You need to tell me everything. I'm your lawyer. For me to give you the best representation I can, I need to know all of the facts. It doesn't matter to me what you did, but if you leave things out..."

She could see he did not seem to be paying attention, like his mind was somewhere else. His breathing had increased, and he had begun to rock back and forth ever so slightly in his old, hardwood chair. In the small, poorly ventilated interview room, BeeBee saw that he had begun to perspire profusely, his body odour becoming stronger.

"Billy, do you know how solicitor-client privilege works?"

The question seemed to bring him back to the moment. He stopped the slight rocking motion and responded with a hint of a smile. "You mean like in the movies or on TV? The guy tells the lawyer everything, and he, or I guess in this case, she, goes into court and gets him off?"

"Billy, in a criminal matter, the first discussion I have with my client is about solicitor-client privilege. Because this was supposed to be only a simple bail hearing, and I expected you to be released without getting into the details of your case, I didn't have that discussion with you. In hindsight, I may have sold you short."

After she finished outlining the principles of solicitor-client privilege, he nodded. "Ma'am, I wasn't worried about you being confidential and all that. It's just that I've been doing some work for the government that's classified, and I'm not sure how much I'm allowed to tell you."

Great! Just what I need, she thought, *a guy who claims he's been on secret missions.*

"That's okay," she continued nonchalantly. "Just tell me what you can, and give me the names of anyone I can contact to get the rest of the story."

"Sure," Billy replied. "Where do you want me to start?"

"Since the only issue they've raised so far is Quinn, tell me what happened between you and him."

"Quinn was a training instructor I had up in Ottawa around a year ago. He was instructing us in sidearms and grenades," he began, avoiding the detail about how they were being trained on Soviet weapons.

"When you say 'us'," BeeBee interrupted. "Who else was present?"

"There was a corporal, Angus McIsaac, and there was a captain, I can't remember the captain's name right now, but I'm sure it's available. The captain was watching from the sidelines."

"So," she probed, taking notes, "we have four witnesses, including yourself –Quinn, Corporal Angus McIsaac, and a captain whose name we can get. Was anyone else present?"

"Nope, that's it."

"So, what happened?"

"There's a part of it that I can't remember, but like you said, I'm sure the others will fill you in."

"Right."

"Well, the last thing I remember is two grenades coming toward us. I grabbed both of them midair and hit the deck with one in each hand to smother the explosions. I knew I was gone, but I had to protect the squad."

BeeBee noted his face was completely ashen. "Then what happened?"

"The next thing I remember, I was on the ground — well, I guess it was the floor, because we were in a big training hall with a grey, painted concrete floor. McIsaac was on top of me. Quinn was on the floor, too, moaning, blood coming from his face and mouth. My right hand was numb. The captain was watching from behind a plate glass window. He came out and said, 'We need a medic for the Major,' or something like that."

"So, it sounds like you attacked Major Quinn. Is that what happened?"

"McIsaac said I did, Quinn said I did, and the captain said I did, so I must have." He shook his head. "But I honestly can't remember."

"What kind of discipline did you face?"

"None."

"None?" she repeated, sceptical of the entire story now. "I would have expected you to be court martialled and kicked out for something like that, perhaps after serving time."

"Me, too," he concurred. "But it was just written up as a training accident, with nothing on my record."

She thought the entire story was far-fetched. "Why do you think they gave you such a break after you attacked an officer?"

"There were reasons," he replied. "None of which I can discuss with you, even if you're my lawyer, not until it's cleared by the Department of National Defence."

Whoever defends this guy will have an interesting case, she thought.

"Here's what I recommend," BeeBee said. "First of all, consent to remaining in custody. You don't want someone like Quinn helping the Crown keep you in, which it sounds like he's willing to do. This story has already had way too much press coverage. Helicopter crashes aren't overly newsworthy, usually blamed on pilot error, but when the police announced the pilot had been shot, the story took off. Now with your arrest, and I'm assuming you haven't seen the coverage, because you've been in custody, it's huge — here, down in the States, over in Europe, everywhere. The trial is going be a circus."

"Okay," he said. "Let's say I agree to be kept in jail until my trial. What then?"

"I think you should agree to the psych exam."

He looked at her. "Do you think I'm crazy?"

"No, but there's no harm in proving it," she added diplomatically while thinking that if the Crown proved he was bonkers, that might be his best defence.

"By agreeing to it, you avoid the Crown making an application to keep you in, which they would win. That saves time and expense and avoids details regarding Quinn and anything else they dig up from being discussed in court. At this stage, cooperating with the Crown's request doesn't hurt you. Since you're likely headed for a jury trial, we should start working on your public image."

"Why do you say I'm headed for a jury trial?"

"I'm not retained to represent you at trial," she answered, "just for the bail hearing. That's what your sister, Rhonda, hired me to do, but I don't want to make any poor moves for you at this early stage that could cause a problem for the lawyer who handles your trial."

"Would you represent me for the trial if I wanted you to?"

"I might," she replied, "but that's a much larger discussion for later on. Right now, we need to get you through this part."

"How much would it cost to hire you to defend me?"

"I can't answer that question with any degree of accuracy," she replied. "It's a function of how much time will be required. For that I need to see the Crown's case against you. Besides, with the attention this case will attract, you'll have lots of lawyers interested in representing you."

"Really?"

"Really. Some will want a ton of money. A few are even worth it. Others may offer a cut rate, hoping the publicity will help generate clients for them. You won't be well served by a hasty decision. I suggest you and your family consider who is available and the pros and cons and costs before deciding."

"Fair enough. But you would consider representing me if I wanted you to?"

"I would," she replied, "but right now we need to get back in there." She nodded toward the courtroom. "Are we agreed you'll waive bail and consent to a psych exam?"

He nodded. "We are."

Back in court, Judge Milloy, having finished the docket, addressed the lawyers. "So, counsel, where are we with this matter?"

Inkpen led off. "The accused has consented to a thirty-day psychiatric assessment."

Judge Milloy turned to BeeBee. "Is that correct, Ms. Beaudoin?"

"Yes, your Honour," BeeBee replied, "my client consents."

"And what about bail?"

"No bail until after the assessment," Inkpen said. "Depending on how that goes, the Crown may consent."

"Your Honour," Beebee said, "he will consent to a thirty-day remand as long as he's remanded to hospital and not to the holding cells."

"I don't care where he is," Inkpen said, "as long as he's not on the loose while the psychiatrist is trying to figure out what we're dealing with here."

Judge Milloy turned to Billy. "Mr. Wheeler, I take it you're content to remain in custody for thirty days to be checked out by a doctor?"

"Yes, ma'am," Billy replied.

"Mr. Wheeler," Milloy continued, "we have a choice as to where I send you. The fourth floor at the local hospital here in Corner Brook is a secure psychiatric unit. I can send you there, or I can send you to the Waterford Psychiatric Hospital in St. John's. What's your preference?"

"I don't know, ma'am," Billy replied. "What difference does it make?"

"Mister Wheeler, when I was in practice, the way I would explain it to my clients was that while you're more confined at the local hospital floor, you can still have visitors, including your lawyer. If I send you to St. John's, you will have the benefit of the entire hospital grounds so you can go outside, but it's an eight- to ten-hour drive from here, so you may have fewer visitors. You can think it over for a few minutes while I deal with the lawyers on some other preliminary issues."

She turned back to BeeBee and Inkpen. "Counsel, how are we going to deal with bail when he comes back?"

Inkpen replied first. "After we get the report we can set a date for a bail hear—"

"I don't think so," Milloy interjected. "Summers are short around here. He's already losing July. Here's what I'm going to do. Are both of you available on Friday, August second?"

When they confirmed they were, she continued. "Good. Mr. Wheeler is remanded to that date. I want both of you here at nine thirty in the morning. We'll have the report. If it's non-contentious, I'll expect some agreement regarding bail. If you can't agree, we'll go straight into a bail hearing at one thirty. And Ms. Inkpen," she added, her gaze fixed intently on the crown prosecutor, "if you intend to oppose his release, the Crown will need compelling reasons why I should keep this man in custody any longer than necessary."

Milloy turned back to Billy. "Now, Mr. Wheeler, have you decided whether you would prefer to spend July in Corner Brook or St. John's?"

"Corner Brook, ma'am," Billy answered softly.

"Good," Milloy said. "We're adjourned to August second."

Chapter 47

Gary Philpott slammed on the red Toyota's brakes, swore loudly, and swerved right to avoid colliding with the rear of the Alberta-plated, monster-tired pickup truck that had stopped abruptly to make a left turn onto Mt. Bernard Drive to go up the hill leading to the police station, local jail, regional high school, and college. It wasn't yet 9 a.m., and instead of paying attention to Corner Brook's minimal traffic, Gary had been deep in thought about how he expected, or at least hoped, the day would go.

At age forty-eight, Gary was the senior reporter at the local daily newspaper, the *Humber Chronicle*. Born and raised in Corner Brook, he had studied journalism in Ontario and worked there for two years before packing up and returning home, where he had lived for the past twenty-five years. Initially celebrated by his peers as a professional reporter, someone with a journalism degree as well as big city experience, it was not long before the thrill of being a big fish in a small pond wore off, replaced by the humdrum routine of chasing local stories of little consequence.

Gary missed Billy's first court appearance as he, Jane, and Eric were spending Canada Day weekend at Portland Creek. While Jane slept, father and son went fly fishing on the waters popularized by renowned sports fisherman, Lee Wulff, fifty years earlier.

When Gary's nephew, the younger of the two guards transporting Billy to the courthouse, called to tell his uncle they had the helicopter shooter in custody, he awoke Jane, who, sleeping peacefully in the early morning sun, could only take a message. When the guys returned with their catch, two spectacular grilse, it was too late to make the two-hour drive back before the matter concluded, so he placed calls to both Inkpen and Peabody.

Philpott and Inkpen knew each other well, though neither liked the other. While Philpott's contempt for Inkpen's tactics was concealed, Inkpen's disdain for everything small town, including small-town reporters, was pronounced. However, in a mutually parasitic way, they found each other useful, Inkpen tipping off Gary on confidential details of cases and Gary careful to protect his source so there was no obvious collaboration.

Peabody, new to the prosecutorial role and fresh from law school, this being his first real job, was a fount of information. Still believing in the search for truth and justice and the public's right to know, he shared endless information with Gary, often providing details he ought to have kept to himself.

Keen to keep milking Peabody's naïveté, Philpott never printed anything that could embarrass the young prosecutor, which would cause his source to dry up. Instead, if Peabody provided him with something juicy and confidential, using that information, Philpott would leverage quotes from Inkpen or other prosecutors.

Rarely missing a story, based on a call to his nephew, the guard, and a telephone interview with Inkpen, he met the *Chronicle's* deadline.

His story the next day was the only media coverage of Billy's first appearance. That brief story with the headline, "RCMP Allege Canadian Soldier Downed Helicopter," was picked up by print and electronic media, spawning stories worldwide.

After Gary interviewed court staff, prosecution, and defence lawyers, his second story, the headline screaming, "Soldier Sent for Psych Exam," established Billy's trial as one to watch. Throughout July, Gary, the *Chronicle's* senior reporter, milked every angle, publishing a story every weekend and every Wednesday.

Digging into Billy's background, Gary wrote stories on his upbringing, including Emma's death in a traffic accident. While his military service appeared sketchy, it included his Bosnian service and that he had been a trainer at an elite, little-known school for Canadian snipers.

Gary also covered all four occupants of the helicopter — their hometowns, their backgrounds, and their grieving survivors.

His coverage of Glenn Holmes started with Glenn's first trip to Newfoundland in 1977 with Green Earth. Gary located Davis Wainwright, now an advertising executive in Calgary. Wainwright, still feeling guilty about duping the Newfoundlanders twenty-five years previously, told him the whole story. Gary's front-page exposé that weekend polarized people against the prosecution service. Many said Glenn got what he deserved.

Gary described the pilot, George Villeneuve, in flattering terms as an experienced bush pilot and family man, complete with family photos. A local source even provided a picture of him standing on the float of a Beaver seaplane docked at Portland Creek as he chatted with American hunters boarding for the short flight to a Northern Peninsula hunting camp.

That picture, and the news that George Villeneuve, well known and well liked in northern Newfoundland, was piloting a helicopter chartered by the reviled SOBSI caused consternation among local readers. How could George, who had worked among hunting guides every fall for the past ten years, calling most of them by name, often eating in their homes or taking shelter from bad weather in their bush camps, turn against them and help someone like Glenn Holmes?

Also, if the stories were true, George had flown his helicopter to less than one hundred feet, perhaps to only fifty or sixty feet, directly over the sealing vessel. George would have known aircraft were required to remain at least a thousand feet of altitude and stayed at least a half mile from seals. Some felt George got what he deserved, too.

In the courtroom, while waiting for the accused to be escorted in, Gary studied the assorted faces, new and old. He recognized the accused's sister, Rhonda, from an interview he had done. The clean-cut fortyish guy was her husband, retired Warrant Officer Josh Short. The teenager was Jeff Wheeler, who was also on board the boat during the shooting. An older man, his face deeply tanned and wrinkled, with the pale forehead of a man who wore a ball cap while working in the sun, was Riley Wheeler, the accused's father. The woman with him was his wife, Brenda, deputy mayor of Spudgels Cove. He knew her from municipal stories.

Gary also recognized reporters from NTV and CBC television, shooting footage before the judge entered and called the proceedings to order. Two others were obviously mainland reporters, maybe Halifax or possibly Toronto. The competition had arrived.

Beebee entered and acknowledged Inkpen and Peabody, who were hunched over the prosecutor's table whispering, and then sat at the defence table.

The clerk stood. "Everybody rise."

As everyone stood, Judge Milloy, clutching a single file folder to her chest, entered and assumed her position on the bench.

Milloy turned to the lawyers. "Counsel, are there any preliminary matters before I have the accused brought in?"

"No, your Honour," BeeBee and Inkpen replied simultaneously.

With Billy in the prisoner's dock, the judge addressed him. "Mister Wheeler, the report has been completed. Have you had an opportunity to review it?"

"Yes, your Honour, I have."

"Have you reviewed it with your lawyer?"

"Yes, your Honour."

"Do you take issue with any of its contents?"

"No, your Honour, I don't."

Milloy turned back to the lawyers. "Do you both agree that the report is non-contentious?"

"Yes, Your Honour," BeeBee replied.

"And how about you, Ms. Inkpen? Do you agree that the report is non-contentious?"

"If you mean, the report says he's not suffering from any mental illness and is fit to stand trial, I agree, but in my view, that in itself makes it contentious."

Milloy was accustomed to Inkpen's theatrics and pettiness. "Fine. You can bring that up at the preliminary inquiry, or for that matter, at trial. Right now, all I want is your position on bail. Will you consent to bail, or are we coming back here at one thirty for a hearing? And Ms. Inkpen, given he's only charged with criminal negligence causing death, and there's no evidence of mental illness, he's not a flight risk, and in my view, there's little likelihood of him committing offenses while he's out on bail, I'm inclined to release him. After all, he's not charged with murder."

Inkpen smirked. "I'm about to take care of that right now."

Judge Milloy straightened up in her chair. "Go ahead. Enlighten me."

"Well, your Honour, we've investigated Mr. Wheeler more thoroughly. He's a trained killer, your Honour. His service record is murky, and the Department of National Defence is being less than cooperative, but we know he trains snipers. That means he's very proficient. He's also calm under pressure. That's a job requirement. He suffers from no mental defect. From a moving vessel, this man, a trained killer, shot a helicopter pilot through the head with a single shot."

She paused, placing her forefinger to her temple like a pistol, eliciting a glare from the bench.

"We intend to upgrade the charge to first-degree murder," Inkpen continued. "In fact, I have the new indictment with me. If you agree, he can be arraigned on the fresh charge now and save us some time. Or we can come back at one thirty, and instead of wasting time on a bail hearing, it will be for arraignment on the murder charge."

"Well, Ms. Inkpen," Judge Milloy said with biting sarcasm, "you seem to have outdone yourself this time, and it is so considerate of you not to want to waste anyone's time. I don't suppose you happened to mention to Ms. Beaudoin that you intended to upgrade the charge to first-degree murder, did you?"

"I would've, but she was late for court," Inkpen shot back.

"What's the date on the new indictment?" Milloy inquired.

As Inkpen attempted to stall, Peabody whispered to her loud enough for everybody in the court to hear.

"July second."

His unwelcomed assistance netted him an icy stare from Inkpen.

"So, Ms. Inkpen," Judge Milloy said before Inkpen could respond, "you've been sitting on this murder indictment for a month, and yet you didn't advise defence counsel. You waited until today to ambush her client. Is that right?"

"Well, your Honour," Inkpen replied glibly, "we didn't know how the psych exam would turn out. If it had gone the other way, we might not have laid the murder charge."

"So, let me get this right," Milloy replied, unwilling to let her off the hook. "If the psychiatrist says he has a mental illness, the Crown wants to put him on trial, but only for criminal negligence causing death. However, if he has no mental illness, you want to put him on trial for first-degree murder. Have I got it right?"

"I guess so, your Honour," Inkpen replied.

"When did you receive the psychiatric assessment?" Milloy asked.

"A week ago," Inkpen said.

"I thought so, because three copies came to my office. I asked that one each be sent to the Crown and defence. So you had the murder indictment prepared a month ago, and you received the psychiatric assessment a week ago, yet you kept your colleague, defence counsel, in the dark about upgrading the charge to murder. Now to save us all this time, you want me to permit you to do the arraignment this morning, because it will be more convenient? I don't think so."

Silence.

"Here's what I'm going to do," Milloy said. "We're all coming back here at one thirty. Mr. Wheeler will be arraigned then. Regrettably, given the gravity of the new charge, I won't be able to grant bail. However, to save everybody another trip back, I'm going to allow Mr. Wheeler to elect whether he wants to stand trial by judge and jury and whether he wants a preliminary inquiry. I presume he does, given the seriousness of the charges. Am I clear?"

"Yes, your Honour," both lawyers replied.

"Furthermore, Ms. Inkpen," Milloy continued, "when you come back at one thirty, you're going to tell me how much time you need for the preliminary inquiry and how soon you can do it. I don't mean months from now. I mean in September, and I'll tell you right now, I think three to five days should be adequate. I'll expect both of you to have your appointment books, and we will set the date."

"But, your Honour," Inkpen said, "I'm fully booked for trials and circuit court for all of September and October. I can't possibly do it before November."

"I'd be concerned if Ms. Beaudoin had an issue but not the Crown. I believe she practices alone. You have backup. If you're busy, get another prosecutor."

Judge Milloy turned to BeeBee. "What are your thoughts, Counsel?"

Seeing how badly Inkpen had antagonized the judge, Beebee wanted Milloy to handle the preliminary. "Your Honour, I have matters set for September, but none as serious as this one," she said sweetly. "Since it's only early August, I can apply to postpone them, so my client can benefit from the early dates you're offering."

Chapter 48

Andrew Bartlett picked up the telephone in his office. Looking at a number scribbled on a piece of paper, he dialled. On the second ring, a woman with a pleasant voice and a distinctly Newfoundland accent answered.

"This is the *Humber Chronicle*. How may I direct your call?"

"I'd like to speak with Gary Philpott," he said.

"Gary," Andrew said after he had been put through. "This is Andy Bartlett from the *World Today* in New York. I've been following the story you're covering about the helicopter that was shot down and the guy who's charged with the shooting."

"Yes, Mr. Bartlett," Gary replied, smiling into the telephone, flattered yet intrigued that a reporter from a large New York newspaper was reading his stories. "What can I do for you?"

"No need to be so formal, Gary. Just call me Andy. After all, we're practically colleagues, doing the same work but in different places. I've pitched my paper on covering your story and got their approval. The only problem is the expense of sending me — you know, airfares, hotels, and all that. If your courts are anything like ours, with postponements and delays, I might have to go back and forth a dozen times just for two or three stories. That's not practical."

"I understand," Gary replied, his curiosity piqued. "How can I help you?"

Pleased to find the local reporter so receptive, Bartlett continued. "I was thinking of having you give me the rundown by phone. Over the next month, we can carry short items, adding new details each week."

"Mr. Bartlett—"

"Andy."

"Okay, Andy. What about the byline?"

"The byline will say me but give full credit to you. It'll say 'with files from Gary Philpott, on location'."

"What about when the trial starts?"

"That's the best part," Bartlett said. "I'll come down there, and we can collaborate. Our bosses will need to work that out, but my guys don't see a problem."

"It sounds good to me," Gary said. "Where do we go from here?"

"I'll speak to my guys, and you can speak to yours. It's the same story, but we're not in the same market, so there's no downside for either paper. I'm sure they have some intellectual property lawyers they'll want to run it past. But I think we should push them to avoid delay and keep the story going."

"What sort of timeline are we talking about?" Gary asked.

"No more than two or three days, I would say. My guys have done this before, so it's nothing new to them. If your guys are serious, they should be able to do it in two or three days. Anything else?"

"Two things," Gary said, excited at the possibilities.

"What's that?" the hard-driving, competitive New York City reporter asked.

"How do I get hold of you?"

Bartlett chuckled, reminded by a question he was rarely asked by other reporters anymore that this guy was in another country, 2,000 miles away. Some people had not heard of Andrew Bartlett—yet.

"Right," he said, giving him his work number and his cell number. "Sorry about that. You said there were two things. What's the other one?"

"Well, Mr. Bartlett," Gary responded, almost apologetically.

"Andy," Bartlett corrected him.

"Okay then, Andy," Gary continued, almost sheepishly. "When you mentioned intellectual property and lawyers and all that, you got me thinking. I've been following this story, and I've got lots of material. There's more to come, and I've been thinking about writing a book about it when the trial is over. I think there will be a demand down here. If I give you my material, you might write the book. Where would that leave me?"

"Good point," Bartlett replied. "I hadn't thought of that," he continued, with a new appreciation for the small-town reporter. "I've published a half dozen books, and yes, this may have potential. We won't know until it plays out. How about if my lawyer writes up an agreement that will protect you for all publishing rights in Canada, but if my New York publisher picks it up, we split everything fifty-fifty?"

"That seems fair to me," Gary replied, thrilled at the possibility of being published in the United States.

Chapter 49

Jenny Colson-Villeneuve was jostled awake by the aircraft's wheels touching the runway, her momentary unawareness of place erased by the nauseatingly nice voice over the PA system.

"Welcome to Deer Lake. That's not fog outside, folks, that's just a little early morning mist from the lake that will soon be gone in the early morning sun. Current temperature outside is a pleasant eighteen degrees Celsius. Today will be another scorcher in Deer Lake, with forecast temps to hit thirty-five degrees. If we have any guests with us from the United States, you will recognize that as sixty-four going right up to ninety-five on the Fahrenheit scale. We hope you enjoy your stay in Deer Lake or wherever your final destination is. Thank you for flying with Air Canada Jazz. We hope to see you again."

The chirpy voice did nothing to improve the foul mood that had gripped Jenny since 4 a.m. Dreading the coming days, she was drawn to this place like a moth drawn to a light bulb to batter its wings incessantly until, exhausted and broken, it fell to the ground.

Jenny's light bulb was to find out what her husband, George Villeneuve, had been doing to be shot from the sky by some crazed sealer, apparently a soldier on leave, leaving her at thirty as a widow to raise two small children.

Fixed-wing, propeller-driven aircraft she did not mind, perhaps because she was also a trained pilot, but she had never liked helicopters, and now she hated them. Early in their marriage, just eight years earlier, George had sold his Cub aircraft. Taking the cash from the sale plus all he had saved, together with an older, investor partner, an aircraft mechanic, he had acquired an airline — if you could call two Cessnas and a Beaver, all on floats, an airline.

Hardworking, well liked, and willing to take risks, they made so much money that, after three years, and over Jenny's concerns, they bought a helicopter.

George was excited by the acquisition, which permitted them to take on work their fixed-wing aircraft could not perform. But the higher rewards of firefighting, flying in reduced visibility, at lower altitudes, and in tight mountainous terrain also brought higher risks.

Jenny's worries of an accident grew. She knew that, although easygoing and stable on the ground, in the air, perhaps because he had piloted aircraft since he was a teenager, George was prone to push the limits.

The inherent danger of his work, both breathtaking and appealing when they first met, had been replaced by worry for his safety as she fell in love with him. Then it became near paranoia as the children, Jimmy and Gillian, now six and seven, came along.

Not wanting to hold him back, she kept most of her fears to herself, even when he was away for weeks flying in northern Newfoundland and Labrador. The planes stopped for only brief intervals in spring and fall to change from floats to skis and then back again. Then even that brief respite was taken away by that damned helicopter. It flew year round.

"I know you would never intentionally do anything so that our children grow up without a father," Jenny told George one day. "I know you can glide a fixed wing back to the ground if things go wrong, but the helicopter has no wings. If the engine dies, it just falls like a stone, or if you're over water..."

"Honey," George replied, "helicopters are a lot safer than you think. They can fly at very low speeds, and they can set down anywhere. Engine failure is a remote possibility, and even if it happens, I can auto rotate — reverse the prop as the aircraft is descending to break the fall. At worst, it would be a hard landing, maybe with some equipment damage."

"George," she replied quietly, looking into his eyes, "you forget you're married to a pilot. What about if you experience engine failure at low altitude and have no time to auto rotate?"

"Honey," he replied gently, "there's a risk to everything we do, even driving a car. You know I'll hear any sound of engine trouble. If I'm at a low altitude, I'll set the chopper down immediately and not run that risk. You'll be stuck with me for a long, long time. Now, don't we have something important to do?" he asked, grinning as he picked her up and carried her to the bedroom.

From a business point of view, the helicopter was an outstanding acquisition. After three years, the dizzyingly high revenues permitted them to retire the entire debt incurred for its purchase. If George could have kept on operating the bush planes and helicopter without bank payments, they would have been set for life in a few years.

However, his success in aviation, instead of satisfying his needs, barely whetted his appetite to grow the business. He did that by selling the first helicopter and using the proceeds to acquire a larger one with more capabilities than the first. The sale proceeds, coupled with a new bank loan, would not have caused an excessive burden, but George's partner wanted to retire and pressed George to buy out his 50 percent. Faced with the dilemma of buying out his partner and curtailing his growth long enough to rebuild equity, George, a risk taker in the air, elected to gamble in business as well and borrowed every penny he could.

No longer able to count on his partner to match his excessive airtime with long hours of unpaid mechanical overtime, George had to hire two mechanics. The new guys had to be paid for every minute they worked, were not as capable as George's departed partner, and refused to cut corners, doing everything by the book.

Predictably, the increased bank loan and payroll expense, coupled with lost flying time as the new mechanics refused to send aircraft in the sky with even minor deficiencies, resulted in substantial operating losses, forcing George to work even harder to avoid defaulting on loans, some of which he had concealed from Jenny to avoid worrying her.

She remembered the moment she knew he was dead. He had left two days earlier, picking up his passengers in Halifax, then going on to Deer Lake to refuel. It was early April. He had told her he was flying a film crew doing a documentary and would be gone three, maybe four, days, depending on how the shoot went.

By then, she was accustomed to him flying helicopters and had more confidence in the newer model. Unaware of their precarious finances, she was grateful for the new guys and the fact that someone was looking after his safety.

She arose early, having been awake much of the night, which was not uncommon when he was away, and woke, dressed, and fed the children. By 8:30, they had left for the bus stop down the street. Tired, she went back to bed for a while, falling asleep quickly in their darkened bedroom.

The nightmare made her lurch upright, perspiring profusely and gasping for air. She had dreamt she was on a roller coaster, strapped into the seat and wearing a full-coverage helmet. Unable to move a muscle, someone had just shoved a hot barbecue skewer through her head. The point entered from below, under her chin, skewering her tongue and penetrating the roof of her mouth before exploding through the top of her head, jolting her body upwards.

Stunned, she could not move as her helmet filled with blood — her blood — suffocating her, blinding her, drowning her. She heard people screaming, a woman with a foreign accent and two men, then a solid thud, the feel of her seat hitting the ground, jarring her body, causing her to bite her tongue, but without any pain. Then she heard rushing water, and it was cold, so cold, then nothing.

Sitting in her bed, she realized she was screaming.

"No! No! No!"

Screams, which in her dream were silent, reverberated throughout the empty house. In that instant, she knew George was dead, and she simply sat there in bed, sobbing and sobbing and sobbing.

Steadying herself, she reached for the cordless phone and dialled the number of the Moncton Flying Club. She was greeted by the familiar and friendly voice of the former chief instructor.

"Hi, Karl. I'm worried about George. Have you heard anything?"

"I'm sure he's fine," he said, "but if it makes you feel any better, I'll make a few calls. How are the two of you doing anyway? George is putting in a lot of time with the new chopper. He's not neglecting you and the kids, is he?"

Jenny forced a weak smile. "Oh no. Everything's fine. I wish he worked less and spent more time with us, but I suppose every wife feels that way. How long will it take you to find out if he's okay?"

"I'll get back to you in less than an hour," Karl pledged.

Hanging up, Jenny looked at the clock. It was nearly 10 a.m., and she was still in bed. Time to get moving.

An hour later, Karl called. "They last had contact with the chopper around nine thirty this morning, Newfoundland time. That's a half hour earlier here. They made one run north of Pointe Riche, but the straits were blocked with ice, so no sealing vessels were operating. They had turned around and were working their way southward. It was snowing, so they were operating below one thousand feet due to poor visibility."

"What do you mean?" Jenny asked, growing alarmed. "George told me he was taking a group for a photo shoot!"

"He did?" Karl said. "I see. Let me do more checking and get back to you. Maybe they're overdue, because it's snowing too heavily to fly fast, or maybe they set down to wait for the weather to clear. Sometimes pilots don't realize how much unnecessary stress they cause by not checking in as often as they should. How about if we meet for lunch, just to kill time and give George a chance to check in?"

"The kids will be home by twelve fifteen," Jenny said. "You can join us. They haven't seen you in ages, and I'm sure it would break the monotony of lunch with me."

"Let's do that," Karl replied.

Chapter 50

Within hours of the helicopter being reported overdue, perhaps due to international news of the passengers' identity, search and rescue shifted into high gear, but without success. The helicopter was gone without a trace.

Initially, Jenny avoided telling their children, but as their home took on a wake-like aura, she told them their dad's helicopter was overdue, explaining that, due to poor weather, he may have been forced to put down in a place without cell phone service.

By day three, with both sets of grandparents present, white faced and with dark circles under her sunken eyes, she told them the worst; the helicopter had likely crashed.

Later that day, Karl called. "Maybe I should have already told you, but I was hoping he would show up. Before George left, he gave me an envelope for you in case anything went wrong. He's done it before, but every time he's returned, and I returned it to him. This time we're not so lucky. I can drop by the house with it."

Jenny thought for a moment. Her mother was at the house, having arrived only hours after George went missing. She did not want to open the envelope in front of her. She did not want to go to the flying club either, the place where she and George had met a dozen years earlier. She might run into other pilots and friends. She was not ready for that yet. She felt numb, dazed, as if this was happening to somebody else.

"Thanks, Karl. Can we meet at Tim's, midtown? I need to get out of the house."

Karl was there when she arrived, sombrely sipping coffee and reading the *Moncton Inquirer's* coverage of the missing helicopter, now only a small story on the bottom of the front page. The remaining coverage, mostly background about the passengers and shortcomings in search and rescue services, was buried inside the paper.

Seeing her approach, Karl stood up and folded the paper, putting it face-down on the table. "Let me get you a coffee. How do you take it?"

"Thanks, Karl," she replied, "but I'm already coffee'd out." She smiled weakly. "I can't believe this is happening to me, to the children, to George." She nodded at the envelope Karl had retrieved from inside his bomber jacket, tears in her eyes. "I just want to find a place to read it alone."

Moments later, using a rattail comb from the glove box, she slit the envelope open and extracted the contents: two white, folded sheets, one blank with a safety deposit box key taped to the center, the other a letter to her. Also inside was a $10,000 bank draft with the payee name blank. It could be cashed by anyone. She went straight to the letter.

My darling Jenny,

If you're reading this, something awful and unexpected has happened, and we won't be seeing each other again, at least not in this life. First of all, don't feel sorry for me. Flying has always been my life. To feel fully alive. I must fly. Any other work, work that would bring me home every night, would leave me miserable, only half alive, slowly dying day by day until I was no longer the man you married.

I am truly sorry for leaving you and the children like this.

This is the fifth time I have written this letter and left it with Karl, starting when we bought the first helicopter and I recognized how worried you were.

Buying the second helicopter so soon was a mistake. I should have waited and paid down our debt and perhaps even found another mechanical partner, but I didn't, and now I have no choice except to work as much as I can over the next few years until the company is in a better financial position. Hopefully, then I can work less, and we can spend more time together.

I'm on a charter with an organization known as SOBSI, like I've done the past four years. They oppose the seal hunt. I have no opinion one way or the other, but since so much of our regular flying is in northern Newfoundland and Labrador, being associated with this group would be bad for business, so I always pick them up in Halifax and stop in Deer Lake for fuel, coming and going without them even getting off.

They pay top dollar to the company plus a $10,000

bonus to me personally to get really close to the sealers working so they can shoot film for their ads. The key opens a safety deposit box at the credit union where I have banked since before we met. It has $40,000 in it. None of it shows up anywhere.

You are authorized to open it, so you can go and open the box and take the cash. Large amounts of cash should not show up anywhere, as that will attract attention.

Your dad will know what to do, or, if you don't want to involve him, you can open your own safety deposit box, preferably at another bank, and leave most of the cash there. Then buy a small fireproof safe for our home and keep $5000–$10,000 in it in for emergencies. That will reduce the number of times you need to go back to your own safety deposit box. Less attention that way.

You know I'm not good at talking about feelings, but I fell in love with you when we met. First, I believed you were out of reach for me. I was astounded when you changed your plans twelve years ago to be with me. Four years later, I could barely believe we were married. You have made me the happiest man alive. Most people envy what we have.

I hope you never have to read this letter.

George

Jenny held the letter, shaking. Tears fell from her face onto the paper, blotting some of the meticulously formed letters until a concerned elderly lady tapped on her window.

*   *   *

Deep in thought while driving from Deer Lake to Corner Brook, the honking of a tractor trailer, into whose lane she had strayed absentmindedly, brought Jenny back to reality. Arriving minutes later, she found the ten-storey Sir Richard Squires Building, described by Iris Inkpen as Western Newfoundland's only skyscraper.

Upon arrival, Jenny made her way to the crown attorney's seventh-floor office to meet with Inkpen, the prosecutor handling the case.

Chapter 51

Driving westward through the picturesque Humber Valley on that same sunny September afternoon, Helen Holmes made her way toward a Corner Brook hotel. Eight months pregnant and widowed at age thirty-three, it had been a tumultuous year for her.

The year had started well, no different from those she and Glenn had enjoyed for several years. Christmas at their Muskoka chalet, cross-country skiing, and socializing with her family, and a lavish New Year's party, followed by six weeks basking in the Caribbean sun on their yacht, their needs attended to by a six-person crew, including an executive chef.

It passed too quickly, and soon they were back in Toronto, facing February's biting cold, planning the new season. March flew by as they put together the details of Glenn's annual expedition to the Gulf and the Front, two words she wished she had never heard.

"The Gulf" was the Gulf of St. Lawrence on the western side of Newfoundland, where Glenn's helicopter had gone down, treacherous in winter but nothing like "the Front", the North Atlantic. Had they gone missing in the Front, where sealers operated their small vessels up to 200 miles offshore, the helicopter may have never been recovered, its disappearance another maritime mystery.

Helen neither expected nor wanted children, so, while in her early twenties and unmarried, she had gone to a private clinic in United States for a tubal ligation. Sterilization, the most effective method of birth control, had failed her, or had it?

For a few days before Glenn left Toronto, she had felt tired, a little bloated, and nauseous. Busy, and thinking that it was a cold or a minor stomach flu, she said nothing to him. After leaving him at the airport, on the way back downtown, she dropped into a walk-in clinic to ask the doctor on call for a prescription.

"Are you pregnant?" the doctor asked after examining her.

The question stunned her, the slight gasp and the colour draining from her face confirming that she had not expected the question.

"That's not possible!" she said. "I've had my tubes tied. What else could it be?"

The doctor scratched his head, his eyebrows furrowed. "Some conditions mimic pregnancy, some serious, others less so, but I'm not comfortable prescribing anything until we rule out pregnancy. It could harm the baby."

He glanced at her wedding ring. "I assume you and your husband don't want children?"

She looked up at him. "What do you suggest I do?"

"Leave a urine specimen, and we'll perform a pregnancy test."

"How long will that take?"

"A few days. If it's negative and the symptoms persist, we can send you for further testing. If it's positive, at least we'll know there's nothing wrong with you, medically, that is."

"And all of this will be in my medical chart?"

He nodded, the inference obvious. "Alternatively, you can pick up a pregnancy test at the pharmacy. They're simple to perform and generally reliable. Then decide what you want to do. I'll write that you came in with cold symptoms and that I suggested an over-the-counter remedy."

She went and got the test.

Positive!

Since Glenn would be away for a week, she decided to keep the test results to herself until his return so they could decide the best way to get rid of it.

Then the helicopter vanished, and he was gone forever. As his sole beneficiary, while she stood to inherit everything, she faced a dilemma. What would she do with the baby? If it had been anyone else's, she would have gotten rid of it, but this was Glenn's child. Having an abortion would be like killing part of him.

She could not do it, but she had no interest is child rearing either. Maybe she would look around for a childless couple, a couple too old to adopt, and arrange for them to raise it. That way she could remain involved in the child's life, at least from a distance.

Chapter 52

Helen grew up in Grimsby, just south of Hamilton, Ontario, the third child and the only girl of a middle-class Hamilton couple, who, shortly after their marriage, moved from the industrial, steel-producing city to the picturesque fruit belt town to raise their family.

Her adoptive parents — her father a mid-level manager at the steel mill, her mother a legal secretary who withdrew from the labour force to raise the children — explained to Helen when she was old enough to understand that she was special. They were very fortunate to have her as a daughter. Because her other mommy was unable to take care of her, she had allowed the Hardings to be her parents. Nobody mentioned the absent father.

Common at the time, Helen's teenage mother did not see her baby, whose birth records, but for her June 1969 birth certificate, were sealed immediately.

Initially satisfied with the explanation, as Helen grew older, she became less satisfied but asked no questions so as to avoid offending her adoptive parents, who she adored. However, she made a pact with herself that one day she would track down and confront the two people who had rejected her.

Exceptionally bright, when she entered kindergarten, due to tutoring by her mother, who was anxious that Helen perform at least as well as their two sons, Helen was advanced immediately by a grade. Then, two years later, to keep her challenged, she was advanced another grade, placing her ahead of her peers. Graduating from high school two years early, by age twenty, she had completed an undergraduate degree and was accepted into law school, graduating at age twenty-three.

In her final year as a commerce undergrad, determined to find her biological parents, Helen convinced a professor to permit her to complete a research paper comparing economic outcomes of adopted children raised by two parents to that raised by single biological parents. To complete the study, it was necessary for her to obtain large amounts of confidential birth data.

Intrigued that she wanted to take on such an ambitious research project while only an undergrad, and perhaps because it allowed the professor to access raw data for any future endeavours, he signed confidentiality agreements with local hospitals. He identified Helen as his research assistant, obtaining permission for her to access hospital records.

Helen could not remove any records, but she could inspect them and note dates of birth and identities of birth parents. She obtained the data she wanted and then returned to her professor. Saying the assignment was beyond her abilities and resources, she asked for a less challenging assignment.

Then she tracked down her birth mother, the only teenager to give birth in the Toronto area on her birth date. She was now a thirty-nine-year-old nurse who was married and the mother of three children.

Unaware her birth mother worked nights, Helen skipped classes for a week, hoping to see her. Then one morning when she arrived early, their paths crossed. Not yet ready to introduce herself, Helen drove on, but the chance encounter gave her goosebumps.

The next morning, after the woman's youngest child left for school, unable to contain herself, Helen rang her mother's doorbell and waited. She was greeted by an exhausted woman who took one look at her Helen and froze.

"It's you!" she said, regaining her composure. "I wondered when you'd show up. You look just like him. Please come in."

Turning around, she stepped over children's shoes, schoolbooks, and clothing, leaving Helen to follow her. She walked wearily into the living room and slumped into an overstuffed chair.

"What do you want to know?" she asked sadly.

Inwardly Helen raged. For fifteen years, since her adoptive parents had explained she had another mother, she had fantasized about meeting her. It was not supposed to be like this. She felt rejected all over again. Rejected again by the woman who had rejected her at birth. The old wound inside her reopened with a vengeance. Her face masked her fury as she sat down.

Without realizing it, Helen's mother had missed the only opportunity she would have to explain the decision the eighteen-year-old version of herself had made. There would be no more chances.

"Can I get you a coffee or something?" she asked nervously.

"That's okay. I don't want anything," Helen replied.

"What do you want to know?" the woman asked again.

"Nothing really."

"Oh."

Silence.

"It must have been difficult for you when I was born," Helen ventured. "All alone. Having to give me up. When I was little and found out about you,

I couldn't understand how you could have given me away."

"I'm so sorry."

"Then, when I got older, I understood how hard it must've been for you. I've been worried about you. I wanted you to know you did the right thing, letting strangers raise me. They have given me a great life."

Missing the mildly sarcastic tone, and wanting to put Helen at ease, the woman denied being haunted by having given her up for adoption. "Oh no," she said, "It wasn't that bad. I always think about you on your birthday, but I figured you were fine. They gave you a better life than I could have."

During their brief time together, most of it filled with awkward silences, Helen learned the name of her biological father. Finally, she looked at her watch.

"Well, I have to go, I don't want to be late for class."

Her mother, warming up to the idea of having Helen in her life, was thinking of how to tell her husband and three younger children about Helen. "Oh my, you're leaving so soon? We've only just met. Can we could meet again sometime?"

"Oh, I'm sure we'll meet again," Helen replied. "Now that we know each other. Next time I'll call first."

At the doorway, her mother attempted to hug her.

Helen stiffened at her touch.

Chapter 53

"Save Our Baby Seals Incorporated, how may I direct your call?"

Helen smiled into the receiver as the receptionist answered her call, feigning helplessness. "I'm in my fourth year, studying commerce. I'm planning to apply to law school or maybe do an MBA. My professors suggested some volunteer work. I'm concerned about animal welfare. You guys do a great job, so I was wondering if I could help."

"Glenn looks after that," the receptionist replied. "He's away this week, but he'll be here on Monday morning. Why don't you drop in then?"

"Oh," Helen said, telegraphing her disappointment. "I was hoping I wouldn't have to wait that long."

The receptionist, a university student herself, softened. "Well, you can drop in and have a look around, but we're pretty busy, and like I said, Glenn looks after that."

"That's great," Helen replied. "Is right now okay?"

"Sure." The receptionist's tone indicated she was rolling her eyes at this newbie's enthusiasm.

To avoid traffic and to save money on downtown parking, Helen took the subway from North Toronto to downtown. She walked the final few blocks to a ramshackle six-storey building in the garment district. She took a slow, ancient elevator to the sixth floor. When the doors opened, Helen walked into the world of professional fundraising.

The young receptionist was keen to demonstrate her authority by providing an impromptu tour. The entire floor was constructed of drywall on studs, some taped and painted, some parts bare. Acoustic tiles covered the ceiling. The floor, a patchwork of pre-existing flooring, indicated demolished walls.

With naked florescent lights, electrical outlets, and phone jacks in place, the entire floor appeared under construction, barely meeting the needs of a shoestring operation scrounging money to stay afloat.

"How long has it been like this?" Helen asked.

"I'm not sure," her host replied. "I've been volunteering for three years, and it was like this when I got here. If anyone mentions making it look nicer, Glenn tells them any money we spend on upgrades is money we won't have to protect the baby seals. He says he can't justify diverting money from the cause for his personal comfort."

"Really," Helen replied. "This guy sounds totally committed. I can't wait to meet him. Where is he anyway?"

"I thought you knew. He's down in the US doing SOBSI's fall tour."

Helen looked at her, mystified. "I'm new to all this, so you'll have clue me in. Fall tour?"

"For years, Glenn has gone to as many US university campuses as he can reach in two months," the receptionist said, eager to impress, "speaking out against the seal hunt. NAWA and other animal welfare groups set up rallies. I think they cover his costs, and I believe they split the donations."

As they walked past one of a half-dozen telephone boiler rooms surrounding a large central area, through the open door, Helen saw a group of people. They were speaking earnestly in a foreign language, staffing a telephone bank.

"What's that all about?" she asked.

"It's six hours later in Germany. They've been here since four in the morning. After the Americans, we raise more money from the Germans than anyone else."

Helen nodded, intrigued. "Where do you find people who speak German?"

"Exchange students. Always looking to make money. The time difference means they can spend time on the phone before classes."

They passed other equipped yet empty rooms.

"Who uses all of these?" Helen asked.

"We use them sometimes, but mostly Glenn rents them to fundraising groups. Or, for a percentage of the take, we do custom fundraising for them."

"Is fall your busy time?" Helen asked.

"Oh no," the receptionist said. "You should be here in the spring when the east coast seal hunt is underway and Glenn goes down to Newfoundland." She lowered her voice. "I've never gone down there with him, but one of the girls, who's good with the media, has gone. She said it was exciting. She told me Glenn picks a big name US celebrity, and there's a line-up waiting to go with him. He gets someone from the European media to make sure we get lots of coverage over there. He rents a helicopter, and they buzz sealers killing seals. Then they come back to Halifax for a big press conference. We buy ads from the media outlets who work with us."

"But how does that make you busy here in Toronto?" Helen asked.

The receptionist beamed. "Glenn is brilliant. We run ads in different media markets with different toll-free numbers for each country. We staff our phone banks with students from those countries. When we have everyone's attention, we hit them with the news stories and the new footage — well, we mostly use older footage of sealers clubbing the little white seals, with blood everywhere. We add new footage, so it looks current, and the phone banks explode!"

She stopped herself suddenly. "Look, I'm not sure how much of that I should've told you, but if you come back and meet Glenn, please don't tell him I said anything. He's a bit of a control freak. Just let him tell you himself. That is, if you still want to come back and volunteer."

"No problem," Helen reassured her, "this is just between us girls. Speaking of which, this guy, Glenn, is he, you know, is he involved with anyone?"

The receptionist looked around before responding. "Involved with anyone?" she asked under her breath, "I think he's been involved with almost everyone who's ever come through here. Certainly everyone who's ever gone on the road with him."

Noticing a slight wistfulness come over the other woman, Helen probed. "What about you? Have you ever gone on the road with him?"

"No, not really."

"Oh my, I'm sorry," Helen said tactfully but without sincerity. "I didn't realize..." Her voice trailed off, implying she believed the receptionist was sleeping with the boss.

"It was just once," the receptionist said, red faced. "After the Christmas party last year. I had too much to drink. It was late. He offered me a ride home. I really liked him, so I invited him up to my apartment. Well, you can pretty much guess the rest."

"That was it? Just the once?" Helen asked, oblivious to the other woman's embarrassment. "What was he like? I mean, he's older than us, right?"

Then, with fake modesty, she withdrew the question. "Oh my God, I can't believe I asked you that. Sometimes I'm such a dummy. I blurt out whatever I'm thinking. I haven't had much experience — well, none with older men — and I feel almost like we're already friends, you having been here for years and me, well, I hope he'll let me volunteer here, and that would practically make us coworkers. I'm sorry, I shouldn't have..."

Her voice trailed off, leaving the receptionist little choice but to say something.

"It's no big deal, really," she said. "If I had to use one word, it would be 'disappointment'. He wasn't very good, only interested in himself, if you know what I mean. It was my own fault, really. I should have known better. I guess I was curious. I wanted to know if the stories were true."

"Stories?" Helen asked.

"Yeah. He has this big reputation for supporting causes. We raise tons of money, and we've practically shut down the seal hunt, but when it comes to women, he's just like any other rock star, a real pig. But what can you do? Everybody's got their faults."

"I see," Helen concurred, nodding in implied agreement.

Chapter 54

FIVE YEARS LATER

Helen sat near the window of a Tim Horton's coffee shop near the Oakville exit, just off the well-travelled Queen Elizabeth Way, waiting for her guest, who, probably because of the heavy rain, was running late for their 8:30 a.m. meeting.

Finally, she saw her biological mother's small, low-budget, four-cylinder car. It was the same one she had been driving when they had first met at the woman's home.

Since then, things had gone well for Helen. Her plan was falling nicely into place. Now this. The prior evening's call to her office at SOBSI from the woman who had spawned her twenty-five years before and then abandoned her threatened to jeopardize everything.

The call was taken by the receptionist, who had confided in Helen five years earlier. Helen had convinced Glenn to hire the receptionist full time. She explained it helped project the image of permanency to stakeholders. It was cheaper than renovating the building, which might make donors question how their money was being spent. Helen's real motivation was that the receptionist, having naïvely opened up during their first meeting, believing they were friends, was a useful tool to keep around.

"Do you have a Helen Harding working there?" the caller asked.

"Ms. Harding is our corporate counsel," the receptionist said. "Let me see if she's available. Whom shall I say is calling?"

"She wouldn't recognize my name. Just tell her I'm a friend of her mother."

Alarmed at a call from someone claiming to be a friend of her mother, and unsure of which mother, Helen agreed to take the call. She recognized the timid, self-effacing voice immediately. It grated on her, but she forced a smile.

"Well, isn't this a pleasant surprise. After I showed up on your doorstep, unannounced, I wasn't sure what to do next. I hoped you would reach out to me, and we could get to know each other."

"You did?"

"Yes," Helen lied. "When I didn't hear from you, I discussed it with my therapist. She said to put it behind me. She said you might contact me in time, and now you have."

Her mother began to apologize for not calling sooner.

"Never mind all that," Helen interrupted. "The important thing is you're calling now. Is everything okay? I mean, are you okay? Is your family okay?"

"Everything is just fine, but I'm concerned about you. You know he's your father, right?"

"Yes," Helen replied, "and I'm really grateful to you for helping me find him."

"That's a relief," her mother said. "I've followed his career for years. He's got a big reputation, but unless he's changed since high school, he's a really rotten person."

She paused and then continued. "After you contacted me, I've followed you, too. I read that you joined his organization. I assumed you contacted him like you contacted me. I assumed he accepted you and you were working together."

"All true," Helen replied. "And I have you to thank."

"Then, the other day, I nearly died when I read that you and him were an item. I was certain I had told you who he was. I just had to call to be sure."

Helen forced a hollow laugh. "Me and him? Oh no, it's nothing like that. But I see why you'd be concerned, with us in the papers and all. Now, since you called, can we meet for coffee?"

"I'd love to. When?"

"How about tomorrow morning? We have a lot of catching up to do. We shouldn't let any more time pass."

"I'd love to," her mother replied, reassured. "I work until eight. How about eight thirty?"

* * *

Sitting in the near empty coffee shop, their voices drowned out by the torrential rain falling outside, they were a study in opposites. Helen, the young, up-and-coming lawyer and business executive in a business suit; her mother, a nurse at the end of a nightshift, her uniform covered by an overcoat. Having no umbrella, she was soaked from head to toe. But for their DNA, they had nothing in common.

Parting company after only fifteen minutes, in addition to promises to call each other soon, Helen had learned what she wanted. Her mother had not disclosed Helen's existence to anyone. She still worked the midnight shift at the nursing home. She took the same route as she had five years earlier. She even drove the same car.

At ten that night, Helen left her car in the SOBSI parking lot, took a large, nondescript, older truck they used to carry supplies for rallies and demonstrations, and drove off.

Waiting with the lights turned off a half kilometre from the railway crossing, she watched as her biological mother's small car drove past. In the distance, with the window slightly down, she heard the approaching train.

On the first occasion she had followed her mother, five years earlier, she had panicked when the small car stopped to let the train pass, forcing her to pull up behind her and wait. This time, she was hoping the situation would repeat itself, which it did.

As she had hoped, well before the train reached the crossing, the arm came down. Her mother made no attempt to get across quickly. She pulled up and waited, giving Helen time to start the truck and lumber toward her. She attracted no attention; there was nobody around to see.

Approaching the small car without slowing down, the heavy bumper of the truck slammed into the rear of the car, driving it forward, breaking the wooden arm, and propelling the car into the path of the locomotive. By the time the train came to a full stop, a half kilometre away, the car had been sheared in half, Helen's mother killed on impact.

Helen reversed the truck and drove off. A hundred kilometres away in a well-lit but deserted parking lot, she got out and checked the front bumper. Satisfied the minimal new damage to the front bumper blended with the old damage, but for a little paint that she scoured away with a wire brush, she returned the truck to the SOBSI parking lot.

Then, taking her car back to the upscale address she shared with Glenn, she entered the apartment, undressed, showered, and with her hair still damp, walked into the darkened bedroom. Sliding into the king-sized bed, she snuggled into him in the spoon position, her cool hands sliding under the waistband of his pyjamas and fondling him.

Within seconds, though not yet fully awake, he was fully erect. She manoeuvred him onto his back, unbuttoned his top, slid his pants down, and then mounted him, riding him like she was competing at the Calgary Stampede, before she collapsed on top of him, spent.

As Glenn drifted back to sleep, Helen, energized, got up and got his housecoat from behind the bedroom door. Before she put it on, she pressed it to her face, inhaling deeply.

Him.

She just could not get enough of him, and now their secret was safe.

Forever.

Walking to the kitchen, she poured a glass of wine, lit a cigarette, and went to the living room, where she turned on a light and picked up one of several bridal magazines on the coffee table.

Which wedding dress would she select for their big day?

Chapter 55

Realizing SOBSI was a profitable outfit during her first visit, Helen had decided to seduce her father. She had intended to compromise him without letting him know who she was. Then she would extract money from SOBSI, threatening to go public with their relationship unless he cooperated.

Then she met him.

Forewarned of his proclivities toward women, while volunteering at SOBSI, she drew him into a prolonged cat and mouse game. Then she allowed him to seduce her.

Things did not go as she planned. For reasons known only to him, he opened up to her. As she got to know him better, she realized he was the male version of her.

For Glenn's part, he could not believe he had found someone so perfect. Helen seemed to know, even anticipate, his every thought.

They bonded.

He fell in love with her and she with him.

She was in a quandary. This was not supposed to happen!

Should she end the relationship? Claim he was too old for her? Tell him they wanted different things in life? Move on without revealing her true identity? Or should she confess who she was and force him to end it?

Unable to confront the issue, she waited for the best time. She procrastinated.

Then one Sunday morning as they lay in bed, he uncharacteristically attempted to engage her in pillow talk. Generally the instigator of such intimate chats, Helen was remote. She was pondering how to end their relationship.

"Do you think you might move in with me?" he blurted.

Realizing she had placed him in an impossible situation, Helen, whose usual emotional range was that of an alabaster statue, began to cry.

"I can't!"

Glenn, unaccustomed to rejection, was surprised at her refusal and dumbfounded at her tears. Immune to women's tears, having caused so many of them over the years, he was generally contemptuous of them, but this was different. This was Helen. He had never seen her shed a tear. He admired that about her — that and the fact she was so much like him. They had a kinship he could not explain. They had similar attitudes, and she always seemed to know what he was thinking, sometimes before he did.

Concerned that something larger was at play, something that might threaten their relationship, for the first time in his life, Glenn backtracked. "That's okay. We're spending so much time together I thought you might like to move in, but I'm okay to leave things as they are."

She shook her head and sobbed. "There's something I've been trying to tell you."

"Is there someone else?"

"No," she replied forlornly. "I love you like I've never loved anyone. This is too big. I should have told you. It's something we can't get past."

He looked at her, concerned. "You're not sick or anything, are you? Because if you are, I can help. I've got money. I can pay for anything you need, anywhere in the world. Just let me help."

"No," Helen replied sadly, "you can't help me. In fact, you're the one person in the world who can't."

"Tell me what it is," he croaked, mystified.

"I'm your daughter!" she said in a low voice, her face downcast.

He was stunned momentarily into silence. "That's not possible," he said finally. "You're twenty-two, well, nearly twenty-three. I'm forty-two. I would've only been nineteen when you were..." He looked at her. "Who's your mother?"

She raised her eyes to meet his, "Ruth—"

"Winters," he said.

Helen nodded. "She has another name now."

"How long have you known this?" he asked gently.

"Since before we met."

"And you still feel this way about me?"

She nodded silently. She was about to speak, but he placed his finger on her lips.

"Shhh..." This time, with him as the instigator, they made love again. He was even more aroused at having discovered the illicit nature of their relationship.

"I know it's not supposed to be like this," he said afterwards, "but I just can't get enough of you. Who else besides your mother knows?"

"Nobody. Just her."

"Good," Glenn replied. "We need to be discreet until we figure out how to deal with her."

Helen's eyebrows knitted in disbelief. "You don't want to end it?"

"Never," Glenn responded vehemently. "You're part of me. That's why we're so much alike. I'll do whatever it takes to keep us together!"

Two years later, three months after Helen had killed her mother, before a group of friends on the SOBSI yacht in the Caribbean, father and daughter exchanged wedding vows.

Chapter 56

Court convened at 9:30 a.m. on Monday, September 9, 2002, before Provincial Court Judge Melody Milloy for the preliminary inquiry to determine if there was enough evidence to send William John Wheeler to trial before a judge and jury of the Supreme Court of Newfoundland and Labrador.

"Good morning counsel," Judge Milloy said. "I trust you had a nice summer. I see we've booked the entire week for this preliminary hearing. That seems like a lot of time to me. Hopefully, it won't take that long."

She shuffled some papers on her desk. "Madam Clerk, have them bring in the prisoner," she said in a tone that left no doubt of who was in charge.

Moments later, two young, burly guards escorted Billy into the courtroom. His hands shackled and chained in front of him, his leg irons forced him to shuffle as he walked.

As soon as they reached the prisoner's box, Judge Milloy gave the trio a sour look. "Take those things off."

She turned to the lawyers. "Do you want me to make any preliminary orders?"

As Inkpen stood there, thinking of the publicity the trial would bring to her, BeeBee dashed her hopes.

"Your Honour, if my client is committed to stand trial, it will be before a jury. This case has already generated lots of publicity. Everyone will have heard of it, so it will be hard enough to select an unbiased jury. More coverage may make that impossible and force a change of venue, perhaps to St. John's. Your Honour, my client is seeking a publication ban."

"That seems reasonable enough to me," Judge Milloy replied. "Ms. Inkpen, what's your position?"

Grudgingly, she had to agree.

"Anything else?" Judge Milloy asked.

"Your Honour," Inkpen replied, "I assume you'll make the usual order to exclude witnesses. When you do, I ask that Staff Sergeant Brian Buckle be permitted to remain with me, seated at the counsel table."

She smirked slightly as she glanced at BeeBee and Billy, who was rubbing his wrists, the red marks from the tight handcuffs clearly evident.

"The Staff Sergeant is the investigating officer and also the police officer who is assisting in the prosecution," Inkpen continued. "His testimony is expected to be short, dealing with the continuity of the evidence from the time the RCMP took possession of the helicopter and the bodies."

"It seems routine me," Judge Milloy replied. "Ms. Beaudoin, do you have any objection?"

"No, your Honour. The crown attorney can use Staff Sergeant Buckle any way she sees fit."

Judge Milloy nodded. "Fine. Staff Sergeant Brian Buckle may sit at the prosecution table." Making a note in her ever-present black notebook, she continued without looking up. "Ms. Inkpen, how many witnesses do you expect to call?"

"Your Honour, at least seven or eight," Inkpen said, "and depending on their evidence, perhaps ten or maybe as many as twelve."

Judge Milloy rolled her eyes. "That seems like a lot of witnesses to me. It's only a preliminary inquiry, but don't let me tell you how to run your case."

She turned to BeeBee. "Ms. Beaudoin, I don't imagine you'll call any witnesses."

"Probably not," BeeBee replied, "but I don't want to make that commitment until after I've seen the Crown's case."

"Smart," Milloy replied. "Now, Ms. Inkpen, I've got to step over into courtroom number two to deliver a decision in a family law case. It shouldn't take me more than a half hour. We will resume back here at eleven after the usual morning break, and you can begin calling witnesses."

Accustomed to the more leisurely pace of some other judges, Inkpen was caught off guard. "Your Honour," she said, "I wasn't expecting to call any witnesses until this afternoon, so I didn't arrange for any to attend this morning."

Milloy nodded toward Brian, sitting in the front row in his Mountie's uniform, with a smile that hinted she was aware of their relationship. "What about the Staff Sergeant? I presume, as the investigating officer, he'll be giving evidence. Rather than waste time, why don't we hear from him?"

"Your Honour, let me confer with Staff Sergeant Buckle and see if he can be ready by eleven," Inkpen replied.

"Fine," Milloy said, "but if he's the investigating officer and also assisting you in the prosecution, I can't imagine there are many secrets between the two of you — related to the case that is."

The obvious innuendo brought blushes to the faces of both the prosecutor and the policeman.

Inkpen stepped over to Brian and bent over to whisper in his ear. "I'm going to tell that fucking bitch you've left your case files in your hotel room. You've got to go back there, pack them up, and return here and organize your exhibits before you can testify. There's no way we can start at eleven. Back me up on that if she challenges you."

Aware that every eye in the courtroom was trained on them, Buckle nodded.

Inkpen returned to the prosecution table. "Your Honour, Staff Sergeant Buckle was not expecting to testify this morning, so he left his case files back in the hotel. There's no way he can get there and back by eleven."

Undeterred, Milloy pressed on. "Well, do the best you can. We'll reconvene at eleven. If you're ready to get started, we will. If the Staff Sergeant is a few minutes late, you and Ms. Beaudoin can use that time to come to an agreement as to which exhibits and reports you want to introduce. I assume that everything has been fully disclosed to defence counsel, but I don't imagine you'll use every exhibit at the preliminary. If you tell her which exhibits you plan to use, that will save us time as the next few days unfold."

The real reason Inkpen did not want to start until the afternoon was that she wanted to use what remained of the morning for media so she could preen in front of the cameras before any evidence was called and discuss the case without risking running afoul of the publication ban she expected.

She wanted to be featured on the midday news, with the same clips being re-run as the trial progressed. If challenged, media outlets could claim that the ban did not cover interviews or stories carried prior to any witnesses being called.

After Judge Milloy exited and Billy was led back to the cells, Inkpen turned and looked as the two groups of onlookers departed through the double doors. A throng of reporters had exited ahead of them to get the first shots of them leaving court. News coverage would be relentless now.

On the first morning, most of the pew-like benches were empty, with roughly thirty people sitting quietly in Courtroom No. 1, the capacity of which was over one hundred. As was typical in criminal cases, the victims' families were on one side, the accused's on the other. A few courtroom regulars sat here and there, and a half dozen reporters, triple the usual number, sat in the front row taking in every word.

As the Wheeler clan hung back, respectfully permitting the three strangers to leave first, Inkpen nudged Brian with her elbow and nodded at the two groups. Helen Holmes, eight months pregnant, wore the finest business maternity wear Toronto offered. Fashionably yet conservatively attired, Jenny Villeneuve followed her, accompanied by her father, Henry Colson, in a tailored business suit.

The shock of his daughter's early widowhood weighed heavily on Henry and his wife, who also wanted to attend the trial. However, they decided she should remain behind in New Brunswick to care for the children, who were back in school after their first summer without their father.

The court proceedings in Corner Brook also weighed heavily on the Wheelers, who were simple, rural, fishing people, whose lives in outport Newfoundland, but for a few modern conveniences unknown a generation earlier, had changed little over the past century.

Riley, still erect after a lifetime of sometimes punishing labour, led them. Dressed in his Wal-Mart best, the new jeans not yet broken in, and holding his Toronto Maple Leafs ball cap in his right hand, he walked with his eyes downcast. The shocking white of his forehead contrasted with his dark, leathery, lined face and hands. His gnarled left hand absentmindedly clutched his wife's right.

Behind his grandparents was Jeff, dressed similarly but wearing runners. Right behind him, looking apprehensive and bewildered, were his parents.

Bringing up the rear were Josh and Rhonda. In appearance, they fit in better than the rest of their group. Josh, accustomed to leading in combat, was dressed in a grey suit. Rhonda, experienced in medical emergencies, wore contemporary Sears mail-order fashion. It would take a lot for either of them to unwittingly display any emotion before this crowd.

Most lawyers who did trial work were content to leave partisan commentary behind when they were no longer on the record, and then there were lawyers like Iris Inkpen, who took every trial, every motion, deposition, or application personally and could not resist taking shots at the other party's lawyer whenever the opportunity arose.

She looked at Billy's out-of-place, uncomfortable-looking relatives. "Beaudoin, I hope you've got a good retainer. When he goes to jail, you could be a long time collecting from them."

"How considerate of you to be concerned about whether I'm paid for my efforts or not," Beebee replied sweetly. "I'm not at all concerned, but if it becomes a problem, I'll be sure to ask your advice. I hear you have quite a bit of experience in that area."

Her response was a stinging rebuke to Inkpen, whose foray into private practice had been a complete flop. Inkpen had a reputation as a punitive biller, charging for every service performed, whether real or imagined, whether required or not. It had resulted in legendary billing disputes with clients, who refused to pay and who refused to hire her again, making it impossible for her to stay afloat.

Beebee wrestled regularly with billing clients, struggling with whether she might be overcharging a client, feeling it even more keenly when things went poorly. However, this time, she was going forward with the rare assurance for a private, small-town lawyer that no matter how long the case took or how much it cost, she would be paid for her work.

Her good fortune resulted from her being contacted by Josh shortly after her Canada Day court appearance. He advised her that she need not worry about Billy's ability to pay. Unknown even to Billy, Short gave her a $10,000 retainer, saying it would be replenished as many times as necessary.

Thinking Billy was fortunate to have such a generous brother-in-law, BeeBee did not know that, while Short was, indeed, generous in general, and even more so to Rhonda's family, he was merely a front for the payments, not the source. When news of the arrest broke, he had been contacted by one of Billy's CSIS handlers.

"We've got a lot invested in Sergeant Wheeler, so we want to make sure he has a good defence," he told Josh. "We can't discuss any operational details, but we'll cover his legal bill. We're asking if you will be the conduit for those funds. He needs a good lawyer but not too flashy. We don't want to draw any more attention to this case by having some big-name lawyer who shoots off his mouth every chance he gets. Can you look after that for us?"

"No problem," Josh replied. "We hired a local lawyer for the bail hearing that didn't go ahead. She seems capable. He asked if she could represent him. We haven't got her bill yet, but I don't think she's too expensive."

"Okay," the handler replied. "We'll leave that part up to you, and when her bill arrives, you can pay it from the money we send you."

"Want me to send you copies of the bill?" Josh asked.

"No," the handler replied. "This call didn't happen, and you have no way to contact us. We will make untraceable electronic transfers into your personal bank account, as required. If you talk to Wheeler, tell him his legal fees are being looked after. Otherwise, tell nobody. Tell the lawyer you're covering your brother-in-law's legal fees and that you and he will work it out after the trial. Any questions?"

"None," Josh replied.

Chapter 57

Court resumed at precisely 11 a.m. After noting the now half-full courtroom, and seeing Buckle seated at the counsel table with the prosecutor, Judge Milloy turned to Inkpen.

"Ms. Inkpen, are you ready to call your first witness, or would you like a little more time?"

Her attempt at delay having failed, Inkpen ignored the exhibits and jumped right into the middle of Buckle's oral evidence.

Within fifteen minutes of taking the stand, the staff sergeant, a veteran of dozens of preliminary inquiries and hundreds of trials, and a skilled witness, generally able to assist prosecutors secure convictions, began to have serious misgivings about Inkpen's competence to conduct a complicated trial. Maybe the stories of her flubbing relatively routine cases in circuit court in Port au Choix were true.

He had never appeared as a witness in one of her cases. Being the officer in charge of the detachment, Buckle's juniors handled most of the policing. He oversaw their investigations, prepared them for trials, and did office administration.

While his policing skills, including giving evidence, had grown rusty, when the trial came, he recognized his girlfriend would need help with it. He was not concerned about the outcome of the preliminary inquiry because the evidentiary threshold was so low the accused was routinely committed to stand trial.

All Inkpen had to prove to win a committal for trial was sufficient evidence for a jury to find Billy guilty of the charge. Buckle had no doubt the preliminary inquiry would go her way. Convincing a twelve-member jury might be a different story.

After three hours, split evenly before and after lunch, Inkpen completed her meandering examination of the staff sergeant. She sat down and sneered at BeeBee, tossing her head in a challenge to ask him whatever she wanted.

"Ms. Beaudoin, do you have any questions for the witness?" Milloy asked.

BeeBee, who had been listening quietly and taking notes from time to time, shook her head. "No, your Honour."

"I didn't think so," Milloy replied. "Ms. Inkpen, are you ready to call your next witness?"

Inkpen, certain BeeBee would cross-examine Buckle, if for no other reason than to embarrass her former lover, had not counted on that answer. She intended to call her experts next but had not arranged for any of them to attend court until the following day.

If Milloy had permitted her to begin at 1:30 p.m., Buckle's testimony would have taken the entire afternoon, but because Milloy had forced Inkpen to start his evidence at 11 a.m., she had run out of questions, and it was only 3 p.m. With an hour and a half remaining in the court day, Milloy was breathing down her neck to call her second witness.

"We'll take our ten-minute afternoon break while you're deciding who to call next," Milloy said and then stood up and left court.

As soon as Milloy left the room, Inkpen leaned over to Buckle. "I wasn't going to call any more witnesses today. I figured she," she glanced toward BeeBee, "would use up the rest of the afternoon with you."

"Why don't you call one of the Wheelers or Short?"

"I wanted to have the expert witnesses testify first, you know, the ballistics guy, so we can tie the rifle to Short. Then get the old man and the kid to testify that Short couldn't have been the shooter, because he was in the wheelhouse steering the boat. Then I want to get the DFO guy to explain how the vessel-tracking devices work. Then show only Short's vessel was in the area when the chopper went down. If I eliminate Short, the old man, and the kid, that means the only other person onboard, Wheeler, must have been the shooter."

Brian nodded. "That simplifies it for you. You've got all three of them here waiting outside, so why not call one of them as your next witness?"

"Which one would you call?" Inkpen asked.

Brian grinned. "You can pick up the most brownie points with the judge by calling the kid."

"How so?"

"Just tell her the kid is losing time from school. Tell her you're happy to call him on the first day, so he'll only miss one day. If you finish up with him before four thirty, Beaudoin won't have much time to cross-examine him today. She'll have to shorten her cross-examination or make the kid come back tomorrow."

Inkpen smiled at the obvious solution. "Oh, Sergeant, there's so much more to you than meets the eye!"

"That's Staff Sergeant to you," he said, chuckling. Then his face turned serious. "Be careful though. Go easy on the kid, even if he's a bit reluctant with his answers."

She looked at him, mystified. She rarely gave any witness a break. "Why would I do that?"

"Now, Iris," Brian responded, "you can't be concerned about him missing school one minute and then kick the shit out of him the next. She'll be expecting that. So will Beaudoin. If you rough him up, it'll undo any headway you've made by pretending you're concerned about him missing school. Just put him in the witness box and let him say his piece. The old man and Short won't know what he said. They're outside. Go after them. The judge will be less sympathetic to them than the kid."

When court resumed, as Buckle had recommended, Inkpen called Jeff Wheeler to the stand. The anxious youngster explained that he, his grandfather, and his two uncles were sealing aboard the *Reuben and Naomi* several miles off Spudgels Cove.

It was morning when a helicopter came over the vessel. He could not say how low it was, but it was low enough it scared the seals, and they dove into the water. Right after that, the helicopter went into the water between two pans of ice near the vessel.

Perhaps because she had been cautioned to go easy on the youngster, or maybe because she had yet to examine either Josh Short or Riley Wheeler and expected to elicit all the evidence she needed about the shooting from them, after no more than twenty minutes of questioning, without ever asking Jeff if he had seen Billy shoot down the helicopter, she advised the judge she had no more questions for the teenager.

"Really?" Milloy replied. "Cross-examination, Ms. Beaudoin?"

"No questions, your Honour."

"I didn't think so," Milloy said. She looked at her watch and then at the prosecutor. "It's only three forty-five. We're making good time. Ms. Inkpen, would you like to call your next witness?"

"Your Honour, there's only forty-five minutes left in the day, and I expect my next witness to be considerably longer. If the court has no objection, rather than start that witness now and have to split his evidence over two days, I would prefer to resume in the morning."

"That's fine with me," Milloy said. "However, before we break for the day, for scheduling purposes, can you give me some idea of which witnesses you plan to call over the next two days?"

"Yes, your Honour," Inkpen said, examining her notes. "Tomorrow morning, I plan to call a ballistics expert. In the afternoon, I plan to call someone from the Department of Fisheries and Oceans who works with the vessel-monitoring systems. I expect they'll use up the entire day. Then, on Wednesday, I plan to call Riley Wheeler and Joshua Short, the other crew-members from the vessel. Depending on how long they take, I expect to finish the Crown's case sometime on Wednesday."

"So, if I tell Mr. Wheeler and Mr. Short they don't have to come back until Wednesday, that won't interfere with your case in any way, will it?" Milloy asked. "I'm sure they have better things to do than sit outside the courtroom all day tomorrow."

"No problem, your Honour," Inkpen replied.

* * *

"How do you feel after the first day?" BeeBee asked Billy once they were back at the cells.

"Okay, I guess," Billy said, his eyes searching for answers. "I'm not sure how I'm supposed to feel, but shouldn't you be asking some questions or something?"

"I understand how you feel," she replied, "but real trials aren't like you see on TV. They are nowhere near as exciting, and from a defence point of view, preliminary inquiries are even tamer. This is where the Crown lays out a case to prove to the judge that there should be a trial. If I cross-examine witnesses and point out shortcomings, the prosecutor will only re-examine the witness. Based on my questions, they can fix any problems they have.

"Also, they have to prove so little at this stage, and because my questioning could help them, I prefer to sit back at preliminaries and take notes. Since you can pretty much assume a preliminary inquiry will result in a committal to stand trial, I prefer to use prelims as an opportunity to better understand the case against my client, to size up witnesses who will be called at the trial, and of course, to obtain a copy of the transcript so I can pin down any witnesses on what they say at trial."

"I see," Billy replied, still unsure his lawyer knew what she was doing. However, for now, he was willing to trust the first woman to interest him since Emma's death.

Chapter 58

Tuesday went pretty much as Inkpen had predicted. The ballistics expert, who had considerable trial experience, completed his evidence in two hours. The vessel-monitoring system expert took longer. It was his first trial, and Inkpen had not prepared herself on the technical aspects of vessel-monitoring systems — devices the fishermen, who were legally required to have them onboard so that the DFO could track their every move, contemptuously called "black boxes".

On Wednesday morning, Inkpen called Josh to the stand. After establishing his relationship with the accused, first as the non-commissioned officer responsible for Billy's unit and then as his brother-in-law, she concluded by placing Josh in the wheelhouse of the *Reuben and Naomi* on the morning the helicopter went down.

However, since Josh had not provided a statement to the police, Jeff being the only one of the group to have done so, she had no way of knowing what Josh would say under oath. It was a dangerous situation for a trial lawyer, made worse by Inkpen having let the youngster get away without asking him several critical questions.

Josh's answers were straightforward but less helpful than Inkpen hoped. The trouble was, he had neither seen nor heard anything until after the helicopter crashed.

He could tell her what the weather was like. (It was snowing.) He could also tell her where he was (in the wheelhouse). He could tell her what he was doing (operating the vessel at a low speed, picking his way among pieces of ice, some of them tiny, the size of a beach ball, others as large as a front lawn, all of them surrounding a large pan that was bigger than a football field with dozens of seals on it — singles, twos, threes, and fours on the smaller pans).

Frustrated the retired warrant officer was not intimidated by her and calmly providing accurate answers that were not advancing her case, she began to cross-examine him harshly. In the midst of the tirade, for the first time in three days, BeeBee stood up to voice an objection.

Rather than sit down and wait for the judge to rule, Inkpen glared at her. "It talks!"

Milloy, entertained by the reserved, retired soldier as he answered every question carefully and politely without hesitation, who would have ruled the last question out of order even if BeeBee had not intervened and then chastised Inkpen about her lack of courtroom decorum, ruled in BeeBee's favour. Then she called the morning break, permitting Inkpen, who was nearly apoplectic, to compose herself.

When they resumed, outwardly composed, but inwardly seething, Inkpen resumed her cross-examination. "So, Mr Short, on the morning in question, did you hear a helicopter?"

"No, ma'am, I didn't."

"And why was that?"

"Well, ma'am, I was in the wheelhouse, which is really just part of the cabin. It was freezing outside. I had the door closed to let heat from the engine keep it—"

"Are you telling me you couldn't hear a helicopter hovering above you because you had the door closed?"

"Yes, ma'am, but only partly because the door was closed. It was mostly because of the noise from the engine. I had the engine room hatch open so heat would rise. With the noise from the engine and the doors closed, I couldn't hear anything outside."

"Did you see the helicopter go into the water?"

"No, ma'am I didn't," he answered truthfully. "I was looking straight ahead, because I didn't want to run into a pan of ice. If you run into one of those, even at a slow speed, you can put a hole in the side and sink in no time."

Disgusted at having made such little headway with the vessel's skipper, but still expecting to get the full story from her last witness, within an hour of Josh having taken the stand, Inkpen advised Judge Malloy that she had no more questions for him.

Predictably, BeeBee had no questions either.

The Crown's final witness was Riley Wheeler. Only as he was being sworn in did Inkpen realize he stuttered, even worse when he was stressed. A normally routine examination-in-chief proved to be long and burdensome for both witness and lawyer.

Inkpen, nevertheless, established that Riley was the accused's father and also the father-in-law of Josh Short and grandfather of Jeff Wheeler.

Stammering and stumbling in response to her questions, Riley explained he and Jeff were on the deck behind the wheelhouse. Their job was to haul seals over the side, confirm each animal had been shot dead, and sever arteries so the animals would bleed out quickly. If time permitted, and if the ocean was calm enough, they removed the pelts and dumped the heads and guts overboard before storing the pelts and carcasses below deck.

"What were you were doing when you heard the helicopter?" Inkpen asked.

"I d-d-d-didn't hear the helicopter," Riley replied.

"What do you mean?" she asked sarcastically. "Do you have a hearing problem?"

"Y-y-y-yes ma'am, I d-d-d-do," was his polite, if embarrassed, response.

A more capable and more insightful prosecutor would have noted and adjusted for the witness's discomfort, perhaps altering course somewhat to secure the best outcome for her side, but not Inkpen.

"Are you able to hear everything going on in court today?"

"I-I-I don't k-k-know about everything," he replied, "b-but I can h-hear you j-j-just fine. The p-p-problem with n-n-not hearing s-s-something is that y-y-you don't know w-w-w-what it was that you d-d-didn't hear, unless someone t-tells you."

"Did someone else hear the helicopter and tell you?"

BeeBee rose to her feet to object to use of hearsay evidence, but Riley answered before the judge could recognize her.

"Y-y-young J-J-Jeff ta-ta-tapped m-m-me."

Ignoring both BeeBee and Judge Milloy, who was attempting to rule on the objection, and hoping to elicit more evidence before the ruling could be made, Inkpen pressed on. "And what did he tell you?"

The older man, seeing BeeBee rise to her feet and hearing the judge say Inkpen's name in a raised voice, stopped speaking.

"Ms. Inkpen, you know better than to attempt to use hearsay in this court," Milloy said. "You'll have to rephrase your question."

"Yes, your Honour, thank you," she replied. She turned back to Riley. "Mr. Wheeler, on the day in question, did you see a helicopter?"

"Y-y-yes," he replied.

"What was the helicopter doing when you first saw it?"

"F-f-falling into the w-w-water."

"And where in relation to the boat did the helicopter fall into the water?"

"O-o-off to the st-st-starboard, a l-l-little bit b-b-behind us."

"Could you see anything wrong with the helicopter that would make it fall?"

"N-n-no."

Frustrated at how poorly the examination was going, Inkpen closed her notebook and tossed it on the table in front of her in disgust. "That's it for me, your Honour. I have no more questions."

Milloy looked up from her notepad. "Ms. Beaudoin?"

"No questions, your Honour," BeeBee replied.

Judge Milloy surveyed the courtroom, which had started out nearly empty on Monday morning but was now full to its legal capacity, with sheriff's officers, like doormen at a popular bar, refusing entry to people milling around outside unless to replace someone who was leaving.

"It's nearly lunchtime, Ms. Inkpen," she said finally. "Would you like to begin your next witness now or break and come back a little early?"

"Your Honour, that was my last witness."

Milloy turned to BeeBee. "Ms. Beaudoin, I don't imagine you want to call any witnesses, do you?"

BeeBee shook her head. "No, your Honour."

"So, Ms. Inkpen, do I understand that's the end of the evidence?" Milloy inquired.

"Yes, your Honour."

"Okay, counsel, I'm ready for your final submissions whenever you are. I don't suppose you want to make your final arguments this afternoon?"

"Your Honour, with all the evidence we've heard over the past three days, I'll need the afternoon and evening to prepare," Inkpen replied.

"Ms. Beaudoin?" the judge asked.

"Tomorrow morning is fine with me," Beebee replied.

"Tomorrow morning we will reconvene at ten, as I have a few short matters at nine thirty," Milloy advised.

Chapter 59

Oftentimes, inexperienced lawyers, even when presenting strong cases, conducted long, slow, laborious, and sometimes irrelevant arguments, hoping that the presiding judge would find in their favour based on volume rather than weight of evidence.

Sometimes, experienced lawyers, realizing they have a weak case, would demonstrate their exquisite knowledge of the law. They filled their argument with a wide-ranging review of the facts and then urged the judge that they had satisfied the required elements to gain a conviction. In preliminary inquiries, the tactic worked sometimes, because a favourable ruling only meant that the accused was ordered to stand trial.

Inkpen fell into the first category. She went on and on and on for more than three hours, nearly putting everyone in the courtroom, including Judge Milloy, to sleep.

First, taking nearly an hour, almost as if instructing a first-year law class in criminal law, in excruciating detail, she covered the potential charges on which Billy could be committed to stand trial: first-degree murder, second-degree murder, or manslaughter.

When she ended that part of her evidence, Judge Milloy noticed some people in the courtroom beginning to nod off while others squirmed uncomfortably. She announced the morning break.

Upon resuming, Inkpen launched into an hour-long review of the expert evidence, including ballistics and vessel-monitoring systems, that was so dry it left everyone longing for her previous discussion of the law, which was a little more interesting and where she at least appeared to have a grasp of the fundamentals.

Oblivious to the world around her, and mistakenly believing she was making headway with her arguments, at 12:15 p.m., Inkpen wrapped up. "Well, your Honour, unless you have any questions about expert evidence, particularly ballistics and vessel-monitoring systems, I'm ready to go into a review of the evidence presented by Staff Sergeant Buckle and the three civilians who were onboard when the helicopter went down. I expect to take perhaps as much as an hour. I see there's only fifteen minutes left until our lunch break. If it would please the court, I can break early and present the final hour of my closing argument beginning at one thirty."

By then, everyone was desperate to escape the monotony of the past few hours.

"I can't imagine anyone will object to such a sensible proposal," Judge Milloy said.

Mistaking the mild sarcasm as an endorsement of her position, Inkpen beamed at the judge. "Thank you, your Honour," adding a collegial, "see you at one thirty."

When court resumed, Inkpen spent an hour rehashing the evidence presented by Staff Sergeant Buckle, Jeff, Josh, and Riley.

"So you see, your Honour," she concluded, "the Crown having more than met the burden of proving that William John Wheeler should be committed to stand trial, I will take my seat, unless I can be of any further assistance to the court."

"Thank you, Ms. Inkpen. Now would be a good time for us to take the afternoon break." She looked at BeeBee. "We'll hear from you, Ms. Beaudoin, when we return."

The afternoon break was longer than usual, lasting until 3:15 p.m. When court resumed, everyone was waiting to hear from defence counsel.

"I took a little extra time over the afternoon break," Judge Milloy said. "Based on my review of the evidence, Ms. Beaudoin, I don't need to hear from you. Unless either of you have any questions, I will render my decision at nine thirty tomorrow morning."

As both lawyers sat in stunned silence, the judge stood and exited, leaving behind a courtroom full of mystified spectators. Quietly optimistic, Beebee motioned to Billy that she would see him back in the cells.

Thinking she had won, Inkpen was jubilant, boasting that she had put on such a strong case that the judge would not even listen to Wheeler's defence lawyer. However, her mood darkened quickly after she spoke with Peabody.

"Mrs. Inkpen, I don't think that's what it means."

"What do you mean?" she snarled at her junior prosecutor. "What else could it mean? And stop calling me 'Mrs. Inkpen'. I'm not that much older than you!"

"I think it means she's going to dismiss the charges," he said reluctantly.

"Don't be foolish," she hissed. "She's going to commit him to stand trial. It's only a matter of whether it's first-degree or second-degree murder. My only worry is that Beaudoin might appeal, because Milloy wouldn't let her present her arguments. If that happens, I might have to do the prelim all over again."

Back at the cells, Beebee met with Billy. "I don't want to get your hopes up. I've only seen this happen a few times before. When the judge tells one side she doesn't need to hear from them, it generally means she's going to rule in their favour. If she's going to rule against them, they always get a chance to have their say. Otherwise, the losing party appeals, and as a matter of fairness, the court of appeal sends it back for another hearing."

Billy shook his head, unable to fathom what he was hearing. He looked at BeeBee through the iron bars. "What do you mean?"

"Like I said, I don't want to get your hopes up, but it looks like the judge is getting ready to dismiss the case against you. She probably wants the evening to review some precedents. She may even speak with an older judge, who will likely tell her to do whatever she thinks is right but to say little in open court and provide written reasons in case of a Crown appeal."

* * *

The next morning, Judge Milloy read her decision to the full but hushed courtroom. The lawyers knew what to expect. Beebee had told Billy the decision was likely in his favour. Inkpen had said nothing all night, not even alerting her superiors of the likely outcome. Cowed, Peabody clammed up. Notepad in hand, he was ready.

Nobody in the media had an inkling of what was coming.

"In the case of Regina versus William John Wheeler," Milloy said, reading her statement, "I have reviewed the evidence, and I cannot find a single shred of that evidence that would cause me to conclude a jury would find the accused, William John Wheeler, guilty of the charges against him, causing the deaths of George Villeneuve, Billy Clearwater, Glenn Holmes, or Martina Schmidt.

"I am satisfied that the helicopter crashed and that all four of the named individuals died tragically. I'm also satisfied with the ballistics evidence that proves conclusively that the pilot, George Villeneuve, was killed by a single shot from below that entered under his chin, travelled through his brain, and lodged in his flight helmet. However, there is no evidence whatsoever that the shot was fired by William John Wheeler.

"It may have been; however, as is common in preliminary inquiries, the accused did not testify. All three of the other individuals who were on that vessel did testify, all were credible, and I have no reason to doubt their evidence. However, they were never asked if they saw a shot fired or even if they, themselves, had fired the shot.

"Even if they had been asked, and if they had denied firing the shot, by process of elimination, there may have been circumstantial evidence against the accused, but this did not happen.

"Therefore, in the circumstances before me, I have no choice but to dismiss the charges against the accused, William John Wheeler."

The hush was replaced by a ripple across the room. Beebee looked at Billy, the slight nod of her head cautioning him to remain silent. Then the room erupted, lasting a few minutes before Judge Milloy could restore order.

"Mr. Wheeler," she said once the courtroom had quieted down, "the charges against you have been dismissed, and you are free to go. If you have personal effects up at the penitentiary, you may pick them up in person. If you prefer, you may have them forwarded to whatever address you wish. Or I understand the superintendent will give them to somebody who has your signed authorization to pick them up."

White faced, Inkpen sat in silence, furious that what had started out as a routine preliminary inquiry had blown up in her face and fearful at how her superiors would view such a high-profile public defeat and what it would mean to her career as a crown prosecutor. Visibly angered, her lip quivering, she was barely able to remain composed.

Moments earlier, she had looked forward to going outside and basking in the limelight of the largest media scrum Corner Brook had ever seen. There, she would deliver her well-rehearsed lines. "I can't comment on the merits of the case due to the publication ban, but my office is pleased the judge saw fit to rule in our favour. We hope the jury will do likewise."

Now, with such a ridiculous decision dismissing the charges, she would be forced to run a media gauntlet, with every reporter's question tearing at her. She knew she would face TV cameras from at least three news services, perhaps more, and that the questions hurled at her in the full glare of their lights, and her response, whatever it was, would be broadcast and rebroadcast, time and again.

She would be labelled not only as the prosecutor who had lost the biggest case ever to come this way, but as the prosecutor who had been shut out, skunked, and beaten even before she got to the trial. Dazed, she did not even want to think about what questions would be put to her, let alone how she might answer them.

Then there were her superiors. Maybe she should have accepted the offer to permit a more experienced crown attorney to be her co-counsel, but she had been unwilling to share the limelight with anyone, and the very suggestion that she could not handle the case on her own had sent her into a rage, with her accusing anyone who made the suggestion, right up to the director of public prosecutions, of gender discrimination. Besides, as she pointed out to them, it was only a routine preliminary inquiry, and the judge was a woman. So was the defence lawyer, so there was more to be gained for the government politically if the prosecutor was a woman as well.

She had pushed hard to be the prosecutor in this case because when she won, as she was certain she would, it would establish her as a high-profile, winning lawyer, bringing her the satisfaction she had never realized in her private practice. Now that stupid judge had ruled against her, and she had to figure out who to blame — even better, how to put it back together and erase this humiliating defeat.

Across the courtroom, having packed up her briefcase, BeeBee was speaking to Billy in a low tone. He was amazed that the case had ended so quickly. BeeBee was wary as to how Inkpen would react to such a public spanking.

"When we go outside, there will be reporters," she said. "Do you want to speak to them?"

He shook his head. "Not really. I don't know what I would say."

"Do you want me to say anything to them for you?"

"I don't know," he replied, "what usually happens?"

"Well, that depends on whether the client wants a message put out there, although sometimes it depends more on whether the lawyer is a media hound or not."

He looked at her, perplexed. "This is all new to me. I just can't believe it's over. What do you think we should do?"

"I think we should just get you out of here as quickly as possible and say nothing. I'll just offer the standard 'no comment'. My car is parked on the other side of the parking lot. It's slightly farther to walk, but I left it there so we wouldn't be blocked in. I know you've got family here. They'll be anxious to see you and talk to you, but it's best to get you away from the zoo outside. I'll get to the highway, or perhaps the mall parking lot. They can take you home from there."

He smiled slightly. "So, I guess you're not giving me that free ride home after all!"

Thinking they had never had a normal conversation without him being in custody every time they spoke and wondering what he would be like under normal circumstances, she smiled. "You haven't seen your family for a while, so I thought you'd want to drive back up the coast with them."

Feeling awkward that she may have begun to clue in to his feelings for her, he blushed but persisted, making a joke of it. "I expect to be spending most of the fall at home with them. I don't know when I'll see you again. It seemed like a chance for me to get to know you other than as a jailbird or mental patient!"

His awkwardness made her tingle. Suddenly, they were co-conspirators, bent on finding private time together. She blushed. "I'll take care of the media. You deal with your family."

Both stifling a laugh, they headed outside, slipping around the media throng that was laying siege to Inkpen and Peabody. The reporters were so intent on covering the abrupt and unexpected end of the case that the pair made an easy getaway, the only record of their speedy departure being a photo shot hastily by one of the photographers, who was more focused on getting the best picture of the beleaguered Iris Inkpen to go with a screaming headline, "Inquisitor Irate at Unexpected Loss!"

Once they reached her car, BeeBee called Rhonda, who had taken the week off from work and had spent every minute in the courtroom, to ask if she and Josh could drop by the jail to pick up Billy's items.

"When you first hired me to get your brother out of custody, I rashly offered to drive him home," BeeBee added. "He didn't forget, and now he wants to take me up on the offer."

"No problem," Rhonda replied, wondering where things would lead. "Just take good care of my little brother."

Chapter 60

When they stopped at Marble Mountain Service Centre, before BeeBee could even unfasten her seatbelt, Billy hopped out and began to refuel the car. BeeBee got out, walked around to where he was, and gazed up at the towering alpine meadows. In winter, they would be under snow, a favourite playground for local skiers.

It was nice to have a man around, even for the little things. Looking at Billy's sinewy forearms, now exposed by his rolled-up sleeves, she thought he did not eat enough. Her eyes moved upward. Only then did she realize he was looking at her. Instinctively, both looked away, as if to hide guilty thoughts.

"It's nearly lunchtime," she said once they were back in the car. "Deer Lake is a half hour away. Would you like to stop for something to eat? My treat," she added, realizing he had no money.

"Sure," he replied, "this time, but next time, it'll have to be on me."

After a moment's silence, he asked if she would mind if they picked up something and found a place outside to eat. "I don't do so well cooped up inside, and I haven't been getting outdoors much lately!"

"As you wish." She smiled, prompted partly by his humour and partly at the thought of private time together away from jail cell cameras. "I haven't been on a picnic in years."

"Oh my God," he blurted a few minutes later. "We haven't even discussed how much I owe you. I imagine I've got a pretty big bill by now. You don't have to worry about it though; I've got money."

"You don't owe me anything," she replied. "Your family, or least your brother-in-law, Josh, covered it. Whatever it comes to, that's between you and him. I didn't mention it, because I assumed you knew."

He looked at her in surprise. "Josh? Josh did that for me?"

She nodded.

A few minutes later, they were approaching Deer Lake and its array of roadside restaurants. "Okay, soldier, what would·you like to eat on our first picnic?"

"Why don't we stick with the military theme and go with the Colonel? Chicken, fries, and a big container of coleslaw?"

She laughed. "The Colonel it is!"

Back in the car and headed north on the Viking Trail, she glanced over at Billy. "Is there a special place you'd like to stop?"

"Any place you choose is fine with me," he replied.

"There's a spot I drive by regularly. I always think it's a great place for a picnic, but I never have the time. It's at the top of the mountains, a few kilometres into the park."

"Sounds good to me."

"The only problem," she warned, "is that it's a half an hour away. The food will be cool by the time we get there."

"I'm fine with that as long as you are. I haven't had anything hot to eat since I was arrested in June. I may even need to be retrained on how to eat hot food."

But for the New Hampshire-plated Volkswagen minivan leaving the parking lot as they arrived, the mountaintop lookout and picnic area was deserted. As they ate and chatted, their discussion, which had started out with general topics, became more personal.

Before long, they were sitting on top of the picnic table facing westward, his body wrapped around hers. Through her back, he felt her rapid heartbeat, and she felt his slower heartbeat vibrate through his chest. As they sat there in the afternoon sun, feeling each other's warmth, her heartbeat slowed a little as his increased slightly.

They were interrupted by four teenagers looking for a place to pitch a tent. The spell broken, they hit the road again.

An hour later, as they cleared the town of Parson's Pond, she glanced over at him. "Have you ever seen the Arches?"

"Lots of times. We used to go there when I was a kid. I haven't been there in years."

"It's a provincial park now," she said. "A paved road takes you almost to it. I drove out once but only had time for a quick look; I was on my way to court. Do you mind if we stop so I can take a closer look?"

"Mind? Of course I don't mind," he said. "I think it's a great idea!"

Within minutes, they had arrived at the small parking area, descended the wooden stairs to the seashore below, and were walking across stones toward the geological formations. Littered along the Northern Peninsula shoreline, as if placed there by a forgetful giant when he built the Long Range Mountains, were a handful of natural rock formations. Among them, the most striking was the Arches, a formation the length of a football field, perhaps sixty feet wide and rising an equal distance into the air. Over the eons, the ocean had carved natural arches in the stone. When filled with seawater at high tide, to the delight of children, and some adults, they were completely dry when the tide fell.

BeeBee looked up at the jagged rock face. "I wonder what's up there."

"Would you like to see?" Billy asked.

"Sure, but what I don't see is a way to get up there."

"Watch me."

He went to a spot that looked no different than any other and quickly scaled the bottom few feet. From there, he was able to go right to the top.

"What are you waiting for?" he called down to her.

Accepting the challenge, she attempted to follow him, but halfway up, she stopped. Seeing she could go no farther, he removed his belt, descended to a few feet above her, and dangled it to permit her to finish the steep climb.

To her surprise, the top was covered by short mountain grass, small irises, shrubs, and lichens. Together, they walked from one end to the other. As she explored the elevated subarctic terrain, he inhaled deeply, savouring the ocean air.

Midway on the ocean side was a slight hollow, where they sat side by side looking out to sea. Hungry for each other, for the first time, they kissed.

"Sergeant, if you're thinking what I'm thinking, we should find ourselves a more private spot."

"Stand up and look around you," he replied.

Standing, she could see for miles in every direction. Seated or lying down, they had complete privacy on three sides, the fourth side being toward the ocean.

"You won't find many places like this," he said.

Turning back to him, she laughed. "You don't have the nerve!"

Within seconds, they were back on the ground, making love for the first time.

*   *   *

"Now that all this legal stuff is over, do you think we can find a way to see each other?" Billy asked as they drove the remaining fifteen minutes to Spudgels Cove.

"I don't see how we could possibly see any more of each other than we just did!" BeeBee replied with a saucy smirk.

Mistaking her meaning, his face turned downcast. "I just thought we could spend some time together, but I guess you and the cop will be getting back together."

"Brian and me? Never. It only went on for a little while, more a matter of convenience than anything else. It wouldn't have lasted much longer. He's too controlling and way too judgmental."

"I see."

They drove in silence, her letting him make the next move, he not knowing what to say, the imagined rebuff paralyzing him. As they neared Spudgels Cove, feeling compelled to act or miss the opportunity, he popped the question.

"Do you have any plans for the weekend?"

"My parents have a cabin in back of Hawke's Bay," she said, proceeding carefully. "They spend a lot of time there. My dad likes to fish for salmon and trout. My mother gardens and picks berries. In the winter, it's ice fishing and snowmobiling. I was planning to spend the weekend there."

"Oh," he replied.

She slowed her car to permit them a few more moments before they arrived. "I thought of inviting you, but I didn't, partly because, well, I didn't know if you'd be interested. If you were, I didn't want you to get the wrong impression. Then I thought you'd want to enjoy your first free weekend with your family, so I left it alone."

Billy warmed inside, smiling. "And now?"

"After the last hour, I don't think I have to worry about the first two. But what about your family? They've been going out of their minds over the past few months. I'm sure they'll want you to spend the weekend with them."

"Yes," he agreed. "Maybe by tomorrow afternoon they'll have had enough of me and I can borrow something to drive and drop down for a visit."

At the edge of town, BeeBee nudged Billy, pointing out a yellow ribbon someone had stapled to a stake, fluttering in the wind. Any question of how the rest of the town felt was settled as they approached the sign that said, "Welcome to Spudgels Cove, population 350." It was covered in yellow ribbons.

Pleased Billy was so well received upon his return home, she glanced to her right and saw his tears.

As they pulled into the Wheeler driveway, the warm welcome was repeated as they were greeted by a huge crowd of well-wishers.

Chapter 61

At the crown attorney's office in Corner Brook, the mood was anything but celebratory. Having run a media gauntlet when she exited the courtroom, rather than wait for the slow-moving elevator to her seventh-floor office, Inkpen passed her briefcase to Peabody and took the stairs at a run.

Red-faced and gasping for air, when she reached her floor, she was met by the same cameramen she had just left behind. They had hopped on the elevator with Peabody and arrived ahead of her and filmed her standing outside her office, frantically ringing the buzzer to be let in.

Once inside, the receptionist stopped her. "Mr. Griffiths wants to see you in his office right away," she said, her voice fearful. "He's been on the phone with Raymond for the past twenty minutes, and I don't think it's going very well."

Inkpen exploded at the cowering woman. "Not going very well? Not going very well? Well, I'm the one who just spent the morning being shit on by that stupid judge. I'm the one who had to go through that mob of reporters. Not going very well for them? What about me?"

Even if the receptionist had wanted to respond, she could not as Inkpen raged on. "Right now, all I want to do is go to the washroom and pee. Then I'm gonna drag a brush through my hair, which must be a mess by now. Then I'm gonna look in the mirror, if you could even call that piece of crap hanging on the wall a mirror, and see what's left of my makeup. When I'm bloody good and ready, I'll talk to both of those assholes!"

"But what will I tell Mr. Griffiths?" the receptionist asked timidly.

"Tell him whatever you want."

Several minutes later, immaculately groomed, Inkpen emerged from her office. While she may have appeared fully composed, as she headed straight to her boss's office, she seethed like a volcano preparing for its next eruption.

Her boss, Gerry Griffiths, was sixty years old. He had been with the crown attorney's office since he was forty after a dozen unspectacular years in private practice. A competent advocate, he had no interest in the non-stop flow of paperwork required to keep a solo practice afloat, so when there was an opening for a new prosecutor, he applied for the job.

An ideal choice as small-town prosecutor, he was well known on the provincial court circuit. He had also handled jury trials in Corner Brook. The starting salary, a step down for most of his peers, was a step up for him. He was not good at keeping track of time spent on files or billing and collecting money from clients.

The prosecutor's job also came with a pension. Having started at age 40, he would not be able to get out early, but by age 65, he could still retire with 50 percent of his pay.

Initially, things had gone well for him. He enjoyed being a prosecutor. There was only minimal paperwork, he had a chance to see files from the police side of the crime blotter, and his former defence colleagues came to him now with their clients' woes.

With a dozen years of defence work behind him, he knew which cases to plead out and which ones to take to trial. Against younger or less competent adversaries he usually won, but he often lost against more seasoned lawyers in complicated cases.

Then, five years earlier, he made what he realized now was a career blunder. After spending half of his time on circuit for the past fifteen years, living in motels and carting files from town to town, at his wife's urging, when the opening came up, he applied for the position of senior regional crown attorney. The position meant he would rarely have to go on circuit and be away from home again. The nice bump in pay would also result in a better pension and a somewhat lighter caseload, even if he was now expected to handle primarily complicated cases.

Only weeks into the new position did he realize how much of the dreaded paperwork came with the job, and the office politics were far worse than he, having spent much of his time on circuit, had realized were possible.

Easygoing by nature, Griffiths, who generally avoided conflict, was now required to mediate disputes among other prosecutors and staff, ranging from who was assigned to which cases, prioritizing of time-off requests, and even who cleaned up the tiny kitchen. Then there was Nigel Raymond, the director of public prosecutions in St. John's.

A hard-driving career public employee — himself a lawyer but with little trial experience and determined to become the deputy minister of justice, his eyes fixed on the media — Raymond drove his prosecutors mercilessly, always demanding detailed explanations whenever a high-profile case went off the rails.

In Raymond's mind, since every accused was guilty, any time there was an acquittal, the case must have gone off the rails, and someone was to blame, so he always demanded an explanation that his boss, the deputy minister could use to satisfy the big boss, the minister of justice. This dismissal, without even a trial and a jury on which to blame it, was a disaster.

Truthfully, over the summer, Griffiths had not paid any more attention to the case than a weatherman would pay to a distant tropical storm that might never increase in intensity and, even when it did, might stay out to sea. As the case had the potential for media fallout that would affect his political masters, just before the preliminary inquiry, Griffiths had briefed them thoroughly on the file. He had reassured them that the case would be a slam-dunk when it went to trial, and preliminary inquiries were routine, always resulting in the accused being committed to stand trial.

Politically, Raymond liked the notion of using Inkpen, as it would demonstrate his office's commitment to gender equity. Finally, Griffiths reassured him, since there was a publication ban place, any news coverage of the preliminary inquiry would focus on generalities, and the accused would be sent to trial on the charges.

The real story was still months into the future, when the jury would find Wheeler guilty of murder. With the trial over and the publication ban no longer in effect, Raymond could bask in the glory of having overseen the prosecution, personally taking the public through all the steps of the difficult, high-profile case.

"And what about if the jury lets him off?" Raymond asked.

"No problem," Griffiths countered. "You outline the case and say the jury must have had their reasons. Then point out we will never know those reasons, because in Canada, it's a criminal offense for jurors to disclose their deliberations."

"I see," Raymond replied, giving up one of his small, closely rationed smiles.

Chapter 62

Preoccupied with other matters in his St. John's office on the opposite side of the island, 600 kilometres away, with little information regarding the preliminary inquiry being published in the provincial capital due to the publication ban, Raymond was not concerned. However, just minutes after the decision, everything changed.

Griffiths, in his seventh-floor office, received a panicked call from Peabody. He was still on the ground floor, besieged by reporters and abandoned by Inkpen who had taken the stairs.

"She dismissed the case!"

White faced and dry mouthed, before the story hit the news, Griffiths called Raymond with four words the director of public prosecutions least expected to hear. "She tossed the case."

"What are you talking about? Who tossed what case?" Raymond responded irritably, unable to comprehend what he was hearing, having been called out of a meeting with the deputy minister of justice.

"The preliminary in the helicopter shooting, Judge Milloy dismissed the case."

Raymond was alarmed now. "What the fuck are you talking about? This isn't even the trial. This is only the preliminary. You said he would be committed to stand trial. Can she even do this? Dismiss the charges at the preliminary?"

"She can," Griffiths confirmed, "but it hardly ever happens."

"But it just did," Raymond countered. "How do you explain that?"

"Well," Griffiths said, searching for an explanation, "the decision only came in a few minutes ago. Inkpen is still down there, I presume facing the media, but Peabody thinks she dropped the ball."

"Who the fuck is Peabody? What you mean by 'dropped the ball'? And why would she be facing the media with a publication ban in place?"

265

"Peabody is the new kid we just hired. No experience, but he's smart and works hard. The judge reserved her decision yesterday and delivered it today, in writing, probably because she knew it would be controversial and likely to be app—"

"Never mind all that," Raymond said. "What about the media and the publication ban?"

"It's over," Griffiths answered morosely.

"What do you mean it's over?" Raymond screamed, nearly hysterical. "It can't be over!"

"You see, sir," Griffith explained, hoping to convey the necessary information as simply as possible to his superior, "the only reason for the publication ban was so that the case would not be discussed publicly to avoid influencing potential jurors, who would hear the case at trial. The case has been dismissed, so there will be no trial, so the publication ban is no longer required. If we had expected this outcome, we could have been ready with a notice of appeal and an interim application to keep the publication ban in place until after the appeal could be heard."

"Appeal?" Raymond said, sounding like somebody drowning, grabbing onto anything to stay afloat. "That's it, we can appeal. How long will it take?"

"Even if we work all weekend and file an appeal on Monday, with an emergency interim application on Monday morning for a publication ban, by then, the story will have run its course, so it will be of no benefit."

By then, Raymond was certain he would be blamed, and his hope of ever becoming deputy minister of justice was fading before his eyes. "Is there any way around this?" he asked, practically crying into the phone.

"Perhaps," Griffiths replied, "but it's potentially messy, and because it's regarded by some people as an extreme measure, it requires the minister's approval."

"Well, stop beating around the bush and tell me what you're talking about!"

"It's called a direct indictment," Griffiths said. "The criminal code provides for a direct indictment to be used in rare and unusual circumstances. I'm not sure it was intended for cases like this, but if we massage the facts enough, we may be able to put this back together."

With a solution in sight, Raymond regained his composure. "Why didn't you tell me this in the first place?" he asked in a snarky voice. "What do you need to pull this off?"

"If we're going to get it done by Monday, I need Inkpen and Peabody to work all weekend, I need the court transcripts typed by no later than tomorrow, and since I've never put one of these together myself, I need you to send out the Fixer. If anyone can make this fly, he can."

"Done," Raymond said, sounding noticeably relieved. "Anything else?"

"Just one thing," Griffiths replied. "Some people believe direct indictments are a denial of fundamental justice, a sleazy way to get around double jeopardy. The minister has to sign off. He'll need to be fully briefed and available on Sunday evening so we can file everything and re-arrest Wheeler before anyone figures out what we've done."

"What about the media?"

"I'm afraid there's nothing we can do about that until we get in front of a judge. For now, this case is over, and you can be certain that the dismissal will be big news. What I suggest is we give no interviews. You keep the minister away from the media until Monday, after we file the indictment. I'll get another judge to issue a new publication ban and get the RCMP to pick up Wheeler. The last thing we want is him at large when all this comes down. The guy is a loose cannon.

"If you think news coverage has been a problem so far, just imagine if he gets wind of what we're doing and takes off. He's at home on the Northern Peninsula. He's a bit of a local hero. They would help him. With his training, and with bush camps everywhere, he could disappear for months. If he decides to put up a fight, you don't even want to think about that."

Chapter 63

Beebee carefully navigated along Bateaux Road, a newer logging road that headed southeast, away from the seacoast and toward the Long Range Mountains. Halfway to the mountains, she turned onto Bowater Road, an older, poorly maintained logging road that headed northeast toward her parents' cabin.

The large potholes and basketball-sized boulders poking through the roadbed were only part of the reason for her snail's pace. The more important reason was her passenger, who had dozed off nearly an hour earlier, just a few minutes after they had left a party thrown in his honour at the local bar in Spudgels Cove.

After dropping Billy off to a hero's welcome in his hometown, BeeBee had intended to head north to her apartment in Port Saunders. She would pick up a few items and, unnoticed by the police officers, who she was certain would communicate her whereabouts to Brian, she would backtrack twenty kilometres to Hawke's Bay and take the north entrance of Bowater Road.

Using the more-travelled and better-maintained northern part of the gravel road, she would head to her parents' cabin for the weekend, hoping that, after spending Friday night with his family, Billy would join her on Saturday.

Her plans changed when the ever-hospitable Brenda, thrilled to have Billy home and out of harm's way, had put on a spread that would impress even the prodigal son's father. In typical Newfoundland fashion, she insisted Beebee join them, shutting down any discussion about Billy's lawyer leaving before she had joined them for supper.

"Show her to the bathroom, Rhonda, and let her use your room so she can freshen up," Brenda said. "We owe everything to her for bringing Billy back to us. The girl's been on the road for a week. She mightn't even have anything clean to wear, so let her have some of your clothes; you look around the same size."

Then she focused on her son, smothering him in hugs, kisses, and tears.

Billy, who had only seen his mother cry once before — when Brad was killed — wept with her.

Shortly afterwards, the entire family shared their celebratory evening meal. They sat around a dining room table that Brenda had extended by the kitchen table. She had used mismatched tablecloths, cutlery, and dishes to accommodate everyone.

Brenda, in her element, made an announcement. "Later this evening, the community is having a get-together for Billy up at the bar. The band is starting around nine thirty or ten. There's no cover charge, and there's a potluck for the early birds at eight."

She turned to Beebee. "I know you'd like to get home to your place, but I would really like for you to stay, at least for the potluck. You're a hero around here. People would love to meet you. A lot of the older folks have only ever seen a lawyer on TV. They won't stay late, so you can still leave fairly early."

Happy to have an excuse to spend more time with Billy and his family, BeeBee agreed.

Arriving at the bar a little after 8 p.m., after greeting everyone present, sitting like a guest of honour at a table with Billy, Brenda, Riley, Rhonda, and Josh, BeeBee required little encouragement from Rhonda that she stay until after the band started playing and drag her little brother, a reluctant and infrequent dancer, out onto the dance floor.

The slow dances gave them their first opportunity to speak privately since they had pulled into the Wheeler's driveway several hours earlier, and before long, they agreed to spend the entire weekend together.

"We're going to take off now and spend the weekend at BeeBee's parents' cabin," Billy whispered to his mother a while later. "They're away, so we got the place to ourselves."

"Okay," Brenda said, completely in favour of Billy's lawyer and wanting to encourage her. "But I'm planning dinner for Sunday at two, and everybody will expect you. Perhaps she'll join us."

Since they were already running late, and because BeeBee wanted to delay the inevitable gossip that would result from her being seen with him in Port Saunders, instead of going home, she had taken the southern, less-travelled Bateaux Road to the cabin.

Now, as she glanced at the sleeping soldier beside her, she smiled at the prospect of them spending the weekend, and hopefully much more time, together.

Chapter 64

At first, the widows, Jenny Villeneuve and Helen Holmes, evaded the madness of the media scrum that engulfed Inkpen and Peabody immediately after Milloy's decision.

Initially, Jenny, unfamiliar with the courts, could not comprehend that the case had come to an end. As everyone else was exiting the courtroom, she approached the clerk, who was packing up her files in preparation to leave.

"Excuse me. I'm Jenny Villeneuve. The pilot was my husband. What happens next?"

The clerk, experienced in dealing with victims and their families, gave her a sympathetic, if uncomfortable look. "I'm really sorry for your loss, Mrs. Villeneuve, but the case is over."

"Over? Over? How can it be over? We still don't know how it happened or even who killed my husband."

"I'm sorry, Mrs. Villeneuve, but I'm not permitted to discuss the case with you. I suggest you speak with the prosecutor, Ms. Inkpen. I'm sure she'll discuss the details with you."

Helen, sitting nearby and taking in the exchange, knew exactly what had just transpired. The wheels in her head were spinning as she played out her next move. Glenn was dead, and she wanted anyone who was responsible for his death to suffer.

In addition to making someone responsible for Glenn's death pay, she intended to leverage the outrageous dismissal of the charges to her maximum benefit. While civil toward Jenny since they first met, she had remained distant from her, blaming George for having gotten her husband killed.

The court clerk scurried away, leaving Jenny standing open mouthed.

"I wonder if you could help me," Helen, eight months pregnant, pleaded in a tiny, practiced voice. "I really don't want to go out there alone. I don't know what I would say if they ask me any questions."

Like the turtle carrying the scorpion across the river, Jenny took Helen by the hand and headed toward the exit. "Come with me," she said with false bravado. "We'll get through this together."

Before they left, Helen pulled a floppy hat from her purse, donned it and a pair of sunglasses, and together, they bypassed the mob of reporters surrounding the prosecutors. However, just as they were entering the parking lot, one of the television reporters, whose cameraman had been unable to fit into the elevator, saw them. He gave chase, catching the two women before they reached their cars.

"How do you feel about the judge's decision to set your husbands' killer free?" he asked, the camera rolling.

Her back to the camera, Helen fed Jenny to the wolves. "I don't know anything, but my friend's husband was the pilot. I'm sure she can help you."

Then she walked straight to her car, leaving Jenny to fend for herself. Inexperienced in dealing with the media, Jenny stood in the parking lot peppered with questions regarding her late husband and his passengers.

Upstairs, a reporter, unable to get at Inkpen, looked down from the seventh floor. He spied a single reporter and cameraman covering a young woman in the parking lot while another woman, obviously pregnant, got into her car and left.

Within a few minutes, the entire mob encircled Jenny, giving up only when the hapless young woman began to sob uncontrollably — a picture flashed repeatedly worldwide for days to come. Finally, the mob departed, some to meet deadlines, others in search of more prey.

Jenny returned to her hotel room, caught the next flight, still giving Helen the benefit of the doubt for having panicked, leaving her alone to face the media onslaught. Only later, when Jenny learned of the role Glenn Holmes had played in her husband's death, would she understand Helen's parking lot duplicity, and swear to eventually even the score.

As for Helen, as soon as she entered her car, she was on the telephone to SOBSI in Toronto, shouting instructions.

"This whole thing down here just went to shit," she told the receptionist, "but we may still be able to salvage something. I need you to find two reporters. Glenn told me about them. Hopefully, they're still around. One is a guy named Bartlett — Andy or Arthur or something like that. He's in New York. The other one, a woman, was with a Los Angeles TV station. Dee Aucoin, I think."

"But how will I find them?"

"Use your brain, but move fast. We need to be in the next news cycle, before this story dies."

Within the hour, Helen was on the phone with Bartlett. "Mr. Bartlett, I'm Helen Holmes. I think you knew my husband, Glenn Holmes?"

Gary had already advised Bartlett that the case had been dismissed. "Yes,

Ms. Holmes, it's terrible what happened to your husband and those other people. I'm working on the story with a local guy in Corner Brook. We're planning to cover it tomorrow, but I guess there's not much of a story anymore, with the case being dismissed."

"Not much of a story?" Helen asked. "Is that what he's telling you?"

Bartlett jolted upright in his chair. "You take issue with that assessment?"

"Mr. Bartlett," Helen replied, "your small-town reporter down here might see it that way, but I'm a lawyer myself. As far as I'm concerned, the whole preliminary inquiry was simply for show. The case was fixed before it even started."

"Wow," Bartlett replied, "that's quite an accusation. What proof do you have?"

Usually, that challenge went unmet, but not this time. Helen recounted that on the first day, the judge had pressured the crown attorney to call her first witness, the investigating officer, when he clearly was not ready to testify.

"But, Ms. Holmes, judges usually want to avoid delays," Bartlett said.

"I know that," Helen hissed. "But then the crown attorney called a series of witnesses, and she avoided asking them critical questions related to the shooting."

"What did the defence do?" Bartlett asked.

"Nothing. She asked no questions. She made a few lame objections, just for show."

"But at the end, the judge concluded there wasn't enough evidence to have a trial," Bartlett countered.

"Bullshit!" Helen stormed. "Mr. Bartlett, the threshold of evidence in a preliminary inquiry is very low: whether a jury could find the accused guilty; that the helicopter went into the water; and that the pilot had a bullet through his head from Short's gun. She had them all in court, and there's not even going to be a trial."

"Did Gary Philpott ask you to comment?" Bartlett asked, now completely attentive.

"No. Even if he did, I wouldn't say anything to any of these locals. I think they're all in it together."

"So you don't want to discuss your theory of the case being fixed with Philpott and have him funnel it to me?" Bartlett asked.

"You got it. I don't want anyone down here to benefit from my husband's death, and that includes local media."

Bartlett's mind raced as he wondered how to sidestep his agreement with Philpott. "The story takes a different angle than the local media are presenting. Can you give me twenty to thirty minutes to run it past my editor and get back to you?"

"Sure," Helen replied, "but that's it. The story needs to go now. I came to you first, but I if don't hear from you within half an hour, I'll pitch it to another paper."

"No problem, Ms. Holmes. Anything else?

"Well, yes. The bullet came from a gun registered to someone on that boat, so why was only one person charged instead of all of them? One was the shooter, but the others covered it up."

Hanging up on Bartlett, Helen called Deanna, a.k.a. Dee Aucoin. Now in the twilight of her career, she had proposed doing the story in conjunction with a younger, popular male newscaster. Her producer suggested they use twenty-five-year-old footage of the first story, when Aucoin was in her heyday, for background. As a teaser clip, it would pump up the audience for the story to follow.

"I have only one request," Helen said.

"What's that?" Aucoin asked, worried her final shot at TV fame was in jeopardy.

"You've got to get your network to book time for my company to run ads in conjunction with the story."

Aucoin laughed. "Not a problem. This is LA. We'll always find a way to spend your money."

After confirming with Bartlett that the *World Today* would run their own story without any reference to Gary, she called back to Toronto with instructions to activate the boiler room with enough student operators to process the tsunami of donations that she knew would wash over them after the TV coverage originating from Los Angeles was picked up by other news outlets and rerun all weekend.

Finally, feeling hungry after what had turned into a productive day, a day that would have had Glenn beaming if he were alive, she telephoned room service and ordered a filet mignon with all the trimmings. Then she took a nap while she waited for her food to arrive.

Chapter 65

At precisely 5 a.m. on Monday, September 16, the calm of the predawn Port Saunders morning was shattered by breaking glass, followed by a loud bang. A flash of bright light emanated from the broken window of the apartment rented by local lawyer BeeBee Beaudoin.

Moments later, with his hands shackled behind his back and his feet chained together, hogtied and wrapped in only a light blue bedsheet to cover his nakedness, Billy was carried to the waiting paddy wagon, deposited on the vehicle's floor, and transported to Her Majesty's Penitentiary in Corner Brook, a three-hour drive to the south.

Unable to protect himself on the high-speed, siren-activated, three-hour drive, Billy rolled from side to side and slid full speed into the front divider each time the van came to a screeching halt.

Upon arrival in Corner Brook, the van entered the prison through a large door and then disappeared from view. Inside, still chained, Billy was hauled out of the vehicle and dropped, naked, dazed, and bloodied, onto the cold concrete floor. Landing with a soft thud, the defenceless man stiffened and let out a grunt.

"That's enough," the superintendent barked.

His late summer golfer's tan vanished when he saw the wretched creature who had just been delivered into his custody. The superintendent rarely left his office, avoiding contact with inmates whenever possible. However, before joining the corrections service decades earlier, he had done a four-year hitch in the Canadian Navy.

Aware that Billy was a soldier, when he first arrived before Canada Day, the superintendent had let it be known that Billy was to receive every courtesy possible as well as special treatment in the form of extra food and greater access to the showers.

When the superintendent's assistant relayed that information to Billy, he graciously declined any special treatment. "I don't mean to seem ungrateful, sir, but over the years I've served with a lot of men. When it looks like somebody is getting special treatment, it's bad for morale, and sometimes it backfires. I imagine it's pretty much the same in here, only worse, because none of these guys want to be here. I'll be fine with whatever everyone else gets."

At 7 a.m., Deputy Minister of Justice Paul Sinclair had telephoned the superintendent at home to say that William John Wheeler, the alleged helicopter shooter, had just been arrested by an RCMP tactical team in Port Saunders. He was being transported to Corner Brook to be arraigned on new charges. Besides being a flight risk, his case had attracted international media attention, so special care needed to be taken that he did not escape.

"Escape? Billy Wheeler? Are you sure we're talking about the same guy," the superintendent asked. "If it's the same guy we've had here off and on the past few months, you've got nothing to worry about. He's a model prisoner."

Sinclair was surprised, as the description did not fit with the information with which he had been provided. "Just make sure there's no screw ups involving this guy," he said. "It could be bad for your career and mine."

Now, looking at Billy — battered, bloodied, and bruised — the shocked superintendent turned to his equally dismayed assistant. "I'm not taking the blame for the shape he's in. Call the doctor. Tell him we have a prisoner in distress, and we need him here right away."

He turned to the two police tactical team officers. "I need your names and contact information for my report," he said curtly.

"It's against policy for us to provide any personal information to anyone outside our unit," the larger one pushed back. "Anything you need to know about us you can find out from Staff Sergeant Brian Buckle of the Port Saunders RCMP."

They both got aboard their vehicle, motioned for the door to be opened, and drove off. The entire exchange lasted no more than five or six minutes.

*   *   *

Beebee awoke just before 5 a.m. in response to Billy touching her lightly on the shoulder.

"Shhh," he whispered. "I think we've got company."

As they lay in total darkness, Billy quietly put one leg over the bed. Before he got any farther, a stun grenade came through the window and exploded, temporarily blinding and deafening both of them. In the next few seconds, tactical team members beat down the door and hauled Billy off the bed and onto the floor. Then, with the apartment lights on, they subdued and hogtied him.

As they carried him through the door, still naked and bleary eyed, Beebee threw the blue bedsheet she had wrapped around herself at one of the officers, ignoring her own nakedness. "Cover him with this," she said, her ears still ringing.

Then she reached for the housecoat she had dropped to the floor six hours earlier and grabbed her telephone. She dialled the local RCMP.

"Fucking Brian! Fucking Inkpen! I should have known they'd pull a stunt like this."

Only then did she realize she was deaf.

She dressed, washed her face, and threw a few items into an overnight bag. Before 5:30 a.m., she was in her car and heading to the police station. When she arrived, she saw no sign of activity.

"Corner Brook," she muttered. "They took him to Corner Brook."

As she headed out of Port Saunders, she looked at the gas gauge. Only a quarter tank, and no gas stations were open that early. She wondered if she could make it to St. Paul's. She was pretty sure they opened at seven. Then, thinking she should slow down a little to save fuel, she throttled back to 80 kph, which was agonizingly slow, and continued on.

The deep red eastern sky of daybreak found her crossing the Bellburns barrens. At ten minutes before seven, she pulled into the service station at St. Paul's just as the attendant showed up for work. After refuelling, she hit the road again, covering the second half of the drive much quicker.

When she arrived in Corner Brook at 8:30 a.m., apart from a slight ringing in her ears, her hearing had returned, and her vision was normal, the light sensitivity caused by the bright flash of the stun grenade having worn off. However, now, due to caffeine withdrawal, she had a throbbing headache.

Suppressing a slight twinge of guilt that wherever Billy was he would probably appreciate a coffee, too, she purchased a coffee at the drive through and headed across town to the penitentiary.

Chapter 66

In his fourth-floor office in the Confederation Building in St. John's, Minister of Justice Dean Jamison huddled with Deputy Minister Paul Sinclair, Director of Public Prosecutions Nigel Raymond, and his chief of communications, Hillary Ringrose.

In a province that had not bothered to establish a law school, content to rely on lawyers educated elsewhere, it was not uncommon to have a minister of justice who was not a lawyer. That was the case with Jamison, a teacher by profession who was truly a square peg in a round hole. Although he possessed the intellect for the position, without the benefit of having practiced or even studied law, he had spent most of his life in the classroom talking to captive audiences, so the term "rule of law" meant little to him who was accustomed to ruling the roost.

Two decades of "I'm right, because I'm the teacher," had been replaced by years of, "We're right, because we're the government," an attitude that brought him into regular, unnecessary confrontations. If those confrontations resulted in court challenges, usually the government lost.

Jamison's experience as minister of justice left him with the profound belief that the courts always sided with citizens who had a beef with government. While that did not change his long-ingrained autocratic style, it did cause him to confer regularly with the three underlings with him that morning.

Sinclair, with a brilliant legal mind and no stomach for confrontation, had joined the department twenty-five years earlier straight out of law school. While risk averse, he could always be counted on to tell Minister Jamison how far he could push in any given situation as well as the probable outcome if the minister went too far.

Raymond was drawn to criminal law and had dreamed of becoming a prosecutor since high school. However, when he graduated from law school and passed the bar exam, the prosecutor's office in St. John's was not hiring, so a lawyer friend a few years his senior suggested he apply to work with Legal Aid in Goose Bay, Labrador.

"Are you out of your mind?" Raymond replied. "Me, work for Legal Aid, defending scumbags for free, and in Goose Bay, of all places? I've heard the court up there is a zoo, with a steady stream of natives, construction workers, and the occasional drunken passenger taken off an international flight!"

"Exactly," his friend replied. "Imagine how you can use that to your advantage."

"How so?" Raymond asked, still sceptical.

"Last night, I had a few drinks with a buddy from law school who's now a judge. To get the appointment, he agreed to spend a few years in Goose Bay until something opened up back on the island. Now he's back here on the bench, years ahead of older, smarter, more experienced lawyers, all because he agreed to go to Goose Bay."

"Yeah, but I don't want to be a judge, and even if I did, you've got to be a lawyer for ten years before they'll even consider appointing you," Raymond replied.

"But you want to be a prosecutor, right? A crown attorney right here in St. John's?"

Raymond rolled his eyes. "Well, duh, what do you think we've been talking about?"

His friend chuckled. "Settle down, and let me lay it out for you. Legal Aid is always crying for lawyers in Labrador. The pay is shitty, and apartments are scarce and cost a fortune. As for the workload, that's a whole different nightmare."

Raymond held up a hand to stop him. "So, why the fuck would anyone want to work there?"

"Let me finish," his friend persisted. "It's almost as bad for the prosecutors, but most of them look at it as paying their dues."

"Okay. What does this have to do with me becoming a crown attorney?"

"That's easy. You get yourself hired by Legal Aid in Goose Bay, and believe me, if you have law degree and a pulse, they'll take you. You spend six months up there, maximum a year, doing mostly plea bargains. They're all pretty much guilty of something anyway. Guaranteed with the turnover in the crown attorney's office, they'll be hiring, and you'll be there, Johnny on the spot, resume in hand, criminal law experience and ready to start work in two weeks."

Raymond shook his head. "Even if I could pull it off, I just can't see myself spending my career as a prosecutor up in Labrador."

"Not your whole career, dummy. I'd say no more than a year at Legal Aid, followed by three or four more at the Crown's office. By then you'll be senior crown attorney, something that could take you fifteen or twenty years back here. Then you start pushing for a transfer back, which, rather than lose you, they'll do." He nodded, agreeing with himself. "That's your best bet for your career path, my young friend, your best bet."

Finally, the light went on in Raymond's head. He grinned. "So, how do I get hired by Legal Aid?"

"Just go to the office here in St. John's, give them some bullshit story about being very privileged to be in the legal profession, and tell them that while you're still young and without too many obligations, you'd like to work for the underprivileged who come in contact with the law — not locally but in a remote posting where people really need your services. I guarantee that before you can say 'Bob's your uncle,' you'll be doing plea bargains in Labrador."

Leaving family and friends, and even a long-term girlfriend, behind in pursuit of his ambition to become a noteworthy prosecutor, Raymond spent the second half of his twenties in Labrador, applying presumption of guilt to anyone who had the misfortune of being arrested by the police.

Finally, at age thirty-two, after four years as senior prosecutor — in his mind, two years behind schedule — he accepted what he considered a demotion to ordinary prosecutor and transferred back to St. John's.

On his return, anxious to make up for his lost years in Labrador, he attacked files with a prosecutorial zeal unmatched by his colleagues. Within three years, he was senior prosecutor, but this time he was running the show not in remote, under-resourced Goose Bay but in St. John's, the province's largest city.

During that time, the office was responsible for three wrongful murder convictions and a judicial inquiry that recommended compensation for the three men wrongfully imprisoned. However, his unwavering career trajectory continued with him being appointed the director of public prosecutions before his fortieth birthday.

The third person counselling the justice minister as to how he should deal with the Billy Wheeler matter was Hillary Ringrose. At fifty-eight, she was the oldest of the group, had handled communications for numerous government departments as well as two former premiers, and had retired at age fifty-five but was coaxed back to work two years earlier to help Jamison deal with the media.

One of the best spin doctors in the business, her nickname was "Ringtrue", given to her by a former premier who said, "If you want your message to ring true, get Ringrose to put it together for you."

Long accustomed to crisis management, she had been with Jamison on Friday morning crafting a ministerial response to a fish and wildlife officer's having shot an unarmed salmon poacher the day before. A few years earlier, someone had decided that fish and wildlife officers should be armed, the division transferred into the justice department, and given new militaristic uniforms to replace the green ones worn by conservation officers, who fell under the Department of Natural Resources. The decision had been criticized, and now a fatal and likely unnecessary shooting had to be justified.

When the Billy Wheeler dismissal hit the minister's desk late Friday morning, Ringrose's well-crafted message, a combination of condolences for the victims' families, full investigation to follow, etc., etc., was replaced by a simple statement. It said the matter was under investigation, and the minister would provide a full report.

Then they devoted their undivided attention to the Wheeler case.

* * *

Ringrose concurred with the request to send Bob Courage, a.k.a., the Fixer, to Corner Brook to review the file and make a recommendation. Close in age, she had worked with Courage on several occasions over the years, and together, they had manufactured solutions to delicate problems, which she had packaged for presentation by ministers to members of the local media who willingly communicated the message, with little scrutiny, to the public.

A lawyer by profession, Courage's business card said he was assistant deputy minister of justice, and so he was. However, his job description, if one were ever written, would include a litany of government problems that, over the past two decades, he had fixed or had minimized to such a degree that he was simply called "the Fixer".

Initially, Ringrose and Courage thought they were dealing with a problem that could be downplayed as a low-level regional issue. Someone screwed up. Find out who it was, throw the person under the bus, and move on with no repercussions for government.

The only real complication was whether they would blame Inkpen or the judge. The problem was, both of them were women, appointed by the current government, and their self-congratulatory message of gender equity could suffer, which was especially bad considering it was an election year.

Ideally, they could downplay it as a minor technicality, something that happened in the courts from time to time, something the Criminal Code allowed by permitting the minister to authorize a direct indictment. They could re-arrest Wheeler on the same charges, and by Monday morning, Jamison could do a press conference with a solution instead of a problem.

That was before KWOW television in Los Angeles did its story on the six o'clock news, and everything went sideways.

The story opened with twenty-five-year-old footage of white-coated seals being clubbed to death and then skinned, steam rising from their still-warm bodies as their blood stained the white snow. It was followed by what was called the "St. Anthony riot", the story that had launched SOBSI into being.

Then a tearful, eight-month pregnant Helen Holmes, having hired a local cameraman in Corner Brook, appeared on Los Angeles television with a simple plea for justice for her murdered husband as well as for the pilot, George Villeneuve, and his young wife and children. It was followed by a clip of well-known, if somewhat over-the-hill, Hollywood entertainer, Billy Clearwater, and finally, in German with English subtitles, a glowing tribute to the young magazine reporter, Martina Schmidt.

Helen's accusations of the whole process being fixed in order to protect the local killer were broadcast back across North America, hitting Newfoundland at 10:30 p.m., local time, and Germany in the wee hours of the morning, only to be re-broadcast across the EU as Europeans were waking up. The outrage from viewers calling their politicians threatened to turn the dismissal of the charges into an international incident.

Before midnight, in a panic, Minister Jamison convened his first meeting with the four who were now in the room, as well as with Courage and Griffiths by telephone from Corner Brook, to deal with the crisis.

Chapter 67

The trial in the case of Her Majesty vs. William John Wheeler began with jury selection in the Supreme Court of Newfoundland and Labrador at Corner Brook on March 10, 2003, just under six months after Billy's second arrest the previous September. Two factors brought about this remarkably early trial date, which involved charges that routinely required a year or two or even longer before they went to trial.

First of all, a direct indictment dispensed with the need for a preliminary inquiry. While shortening the time required for a trial to begin, the heavy-handed approach was criticized frequently for denying the accused any real indication of the facts and evidence the prosecutors would bring against them at trial.

Conveniently, since a preliminary inquiry had already occurred, transcripts from it were available to contradict any witnesses who might tell a different story to the jury. Minister Jamison pointed this out eager to support his decision to use a direct indictment to override Judge Milloy's dismissal of the charges.

Second, as was the norm in murder cases, the Crown had opposed bail, so within forty-eight hours of his arrest, Billy was transported to the province's main prison, Her Majesty's Penitentiary in St. John's, to await trial.

Completed primarily with inmate labour in 1859, the same year as Alcatraz was completed, Her Majesty's Penitentiary was a relic of a bygone era. Overcrowded, understaffed, and with few modern conveniences, it sat on the shore of historic Quidi Vidi Lake, location of the Royal St. John's Regatta, which had begun two centuries earlier and was North America's oldest regatta.

Given the nature of his charges, prison authorities deemed Billy unsuitable to be in the general prison population. Instead of being held on one of the temperature-controlled prison ranges or even in the relatively humane unit for inmates serving weekends, Billy was confined to an ancient, concrete block and iron-barred unit populated with five high-risk sex offenders and two other inmates awaiting trial for murder.

In a case where the government would have preferred the trial delayed until at least after the next election, Billy had become a political liability. Over the course of the fall and the winter, he had become a folk hero, proving that while publication bans may prevent electronic or printed coverage, in a province with just half a million people, word-of-mouth communication and good old-fashioned gossip travelled quickly, even more embellished than some news stories.

As the trial approached, Jamison realized he was in a no-win situation. If Billy, a local hero, were convicted, the tide of local public opinion would go against the government. If he were acquitted, there would be even more bad press internationally, possibly resulting in tourism and seafood boycotts that would further impoverish Canada's newest and poorest province. The Department of Justice had to find a way to force Billy to take a plea bargain. A guilty plea to even second-degree murder would take the shine off Newfoundland's new Robin Hood while placating international opponents of the seal hunt.

However, they had little leverage available to force him to plead out. It was too late to go back and charge the other members of the crew — his father, his nephew, and his brother-in-law — and then make a deal to withdraw their charges if Billy pled guilty. Even a child would recognize that as a desperate, bad faith ploy, causing the public to heap scorn on the prosecution, driving an unpopular government even lower in the polls.

As they huddled in the minister's office, Sinclair blurted out a question more to himself than for serious consideration. "I wonder if we could knock his lawyer off the case?"

For a moment, there was silence.

"What do you mean?" Jamison asked.

"Well, that would buy us some time," Raymond said. "By the time he found another lawyer, in say, two or three months, there's no way a new lawyer would be ready for the trial before fall, at the earliest, and the court has three weeks set aside for this one, so if we could push it into late fall, that would put us past the October general election."

He turned to Deputy Minister Sinclair. "I don't think we've got any grounds to support an application to disqualify Beaudoin, and even if we did, we're so close to trial, the judge will go out of his mind if we pull a stunt like this."

"Fuck the judge," Jamison said. "If there is any possibility of delaying this trial until after the election, and if we can do that by having his lawyer kicked off the case, then let's do it. By grounds, do you mean dirt? Surely we must be able to find dirt on her. Everybody has a few skeletons in their closet."

"Actually, Minister," Sinclair said, "it doesn't mean dirt, although if it was bad enough, it might work. *Grounds* means something about the other lawyer that might make it look like the trial was unfair, like maybe there was a conflict of interest, like, say the lawyer worked for one side and then attempted to represent the other side. The court also looks at whether there's anything that might bring the administration of justice into disrepute."

Quick to sniff out anything scandalous, the old hen, Ringrose clucked. "Disrepute? How about if the lawyer is sleeping with the client? Would that disqualify her?"

"Well, the law society has rules about that," Sinclair replied, "but that's more to protect the clients, so if the client complained to the law society, the lawyer could be disciplined, but that would likely be after the trial and no help to us. Besides that, I understand that Wheeler has been in jail and denied bail since he was arrested, so I don't see how we can pitch that unless they were getting it on in the interview room at the jail, and I don't see how we could ever prove that."

"But what about when he was out?" Raymond asked, seeing a possible angle. "Could that work?"

"If we had anything like that, we could use it," Sinclair said. "It would dirty both of them up a little bit and make for some juicy media stories, but as for getting her disqualified, I doubt it." He shrugged. "Like I said, we've got nothing on her."

"What do you mean we have nothing on them?" Jamison said, agitated at the back and forth. "Haven't you read the file?"

Cowed by the outburst, made even worse by smirks from both Raymond and Ringrose, Sinclair apologized. "Yes, Minister, of course I read the file, but there's no mention of the lawyer in it. It just says that Wheeler was arrested without incident at the residence of a female friend."

The resulting laughter from the other three caused Sinclair to turn beet red, realizing he was the last one in the room to make the connection.

"Don't worry about it," Raymond said. "I vetted the entire file and took out all the details surrounding the arrest. We let Buckle pick him up without realizing the staff sergeant had his own axe to grind with both of them. Instead of a routine, low-key arrest, he blew it out of proportion and ordered a tactical team to do the job. Can you imagine? The only good news was that they pulled it off at 5 a.m., so even the locals don't know what happened. They roughed up Wheeler a little bit, too, so I sanitized the file and deleted her name before we gave it to his lawyer."

Minister of Justice Jamison, always needing to be the centre of attention, could not resist getting in on the story. "What was she supposed to say? That you left out the part where you caught me in bed with my client?"

The group broke into gales of laughter.

Chapter 68

Court convened at precisely 10 a.m. on Tuesday, March 11. Billy stood in the prisoner's dock. The judge, Mr. Justice Colin Drinkwater, asked the lawyers to identify themselves for the record.

Inkpen responded first. "Good morning, my Lord. I'm Crown Attorney Iris Inkpen. With me is my co-counsel, Senior Crown Attorney Gerald Griffiths, QC. We will be representing the prosecution in this matter."

"Thank you, Ms. Inkpen." Drinkwater nodded at Griffiths, his long-time golf and curling partner. "Mr. Griffiths, I believe this is the first time you've appeared before me."

Griffiths nodded back with a knowing smile. Both men were the same vintage. However, Griffiths had spent his career before the courts, arguing cases, while Drinkwater had worked virtually chained to a desk, doing small-town real estate and business deals in and around Corner Brook. Only once in his career had he ever appeared in court. On that occasion, as an inexperienced junior associate, he had lost badly and had taken the loss so personally that he never ventured back to the rough-and-tumble arena over which he now presided in his regal judicial gown.

One of the shortcomings of the Canadian judicial system was that any lawyer with the right political connections and ten years' experience could be appointed a judge. Whether that experience was closing real estate deals, drafting wills, incorporating companies, or appearing in court every day, once a lawyer had put in ten years, he or she could become a judge.

The newly minted judge was then set for life with a handsome salary, full benefits, and a pension. But for having decisions overturned by the court of appeal, something that rarely happened, as few aggrieved parties could afford to pursue a successful appeal, the newly appointed real estate lawyer, attired like a peacock, wielded enormous power over everyone appearing before him.

Human nature being what it is, most judges meant well but lived in fear of making mistakes, delaying cases continually in the hope of getting it right or that the parties would give up, never really considering the maxim, "Justice delayed is justice denied!"

Others avoided delays by relying on arguments made by the more senior of the lawyers appearing before them, presumably reasoning that the older lawyer was more likely than the younger one to be correct, without considering that more recent legal graduates could be more current in their legal knowledge and, therefore, more likely to be correct.

Seeing that one of the lawyers on the case was his old friend, Griffiths, a competent lawyer with a reputation for being a straight shooter and unlikely to mislead him, Drinkwater's anxiety lessened just a little before he turned to BeeBee, a lawyer he had never laid eyes on before.

"And you are?"

"My Lord, I'm Barbara Beaudoin. I represent the accused, William John Wheeler."

Drinkwater nodded and then addressed both lawyers. "Are there any preliminary matters or any orders that counsel are requesting before we bring in the jury?"

To his dismay, Inkpen arose from her seat, holding three bound documents. "Yes, my Lord. The Crown is applying to disqualify defence counsel."

Stunned that in his first jury trial he was being called upon to make a decision that could result in a mistrial, Drinkwater's mind raced. All eyes in the packed and suddenly hushed courtroom watched to see his next move.

Remembering advice he had received from an older colleague about what to do when he did not know what to do, Drinkwater adopted a solemn expression. "Well, Ms. Inkpen, this is a bit of a surprise. I'll take a brief recess and review your materials."

Then he stood up, and as quickly as possible, clutching his large, black judicial notebook like a security blanket, exited through the rear door. His seasoned clerk was left to obtain the prosecution's brief containing the written arguments, asking him to disqualify Beaudoin, soon to be made to him orally.

Drinkwater's eyes opened wide as he read the part about the tactical team finding Beaudoin and Wheeler in bed together and subduing the stark naked Wheeler, while Beaudoin, also naked, stood by, handing them a bedsheet to cover him for the ride to Corner Brook before casually retrieving her housecoat from the floor.

Had Drinkwater ever practiced criminal law before being appointed to the bench, he would have experienced the ribald nature of the criminal courts. Criminal lawyers, judges, and others who continually witnessed the depravity of human nature often became desensitized to information that would shock most people. Had this been his experience, Drinkwater likely would have glossed over the arrest, perhaps snickering at the situation before moving on to ask whether the Crown had any legal basis to disqualify BeeBee. However, without exposure to the realities of criminal law, and prudish by nature, Drinkwater could not get beyond the images in his head to assess the strength of the legal argument being made.

Then he remembered advice he had received for dealing with complicated issues: Let the lawyers make their best pitch. Take good notes. Reserve your decision. Have the clerk type up a transcript. Then take all the time you need and render a decision. Don't be in any hurry. Everyone knows that the important work of the court takes time.

Satisfied he was on the right track, he rang the court clerk in her office to say he was ready to return. She buzzed the sheriff's officers to tell them the judge was coming back in. One of them unlocked the main door, which had been secured while the judge deliberated, and advised the spectators that they could return. Two others went to the cells to retrieve Billy.

In his most regal manner, Drinkwater resumed his position on the bench and addressed Inkpen, as she had filed the application. "Well, Ms. Inkpen, you've raised some interesting legal arguments. I take it you're ready to make your oral submission?"

His statement was akin to a tentative question by someone trying to feel his way, blindfolded, across a minefield, looking for direction and praying he would not make a misstep.

Inkpen gloated, knowing that whether Drinkwater granted the application or not, she could denigrate the other woman. "Yes, my Lord. I'm ready any time the court is."

Drinkwater turned to BeeBee, who had received the three-volume application to disqualify her at the same time he had. She had reviewed it feverishly, highlighting and writing comments in her notepad.

"Ms. Beaudoin," Drinkwater said, "Ms. Inkpen can proceed, but it appears you aren't ready."

In the twenty minutes that Drinkwater had recessed, BeeBee had consumed the contents of the two thinner volumes and was blazing through the third. The thinnest volume was a factum, a ten-page, double-spaced brief of the oral arguments the Crown intended to make. Each legal argument was cross-referenced to a second volume containing a dozen cases. The final volume contained the evidence. Also included were affidavits swearing that when her client was apprehended, he was in bed with her, both of them naked.

Looking up from her counsel table as she scrambled to assess the strength of the arguments, Beebee put down her pen. She replaced the cap of her fading yellow highlighter and adjusted her barrister's string tie. Then she stood up to face the judge.

"That's correct, my Lord," she answered evenly. "I had no notice of this application until the prosecution raised it in court today. As you can see, I haven't yet finished reviewing it."

Drinkwater was relieved at another opportunity to delay, to look at the materials more closely, and perhaps to confer by telephone with another judge. "It's still early," he said, "but let's take the morning break now. And let's take more time than usual, say an extra half hour. Do you think that will give you sufficient time, Ms. Beaudoin?"

"Well, your Honour — I mean, my Lord — BeeBee replied, fighting for time, "I may be through the cases by then, but I don't see how I'll be ready to respond. I should've received this application weeks ago. There's another issue, too. Since I'm the one they're trying to disqualify, shouldn't another lawyer make these arguments on my behalf? I need to call the law society and confirm that I'm not ethically prohibited from appearing on this application."

Panicked, Drinkwater turned to a potential ally. "Mr. Griffiths, you're the Queen's Counsel. We have yet to hear from you. What do you have to say?"

Uncomfortable, the older lawyer rose slowly from his chair. What Drinkwater did not know, and what Griffiths was not about to say, was that he disagreed completely with the Crown's application. He had only learned of it the prior evening.

The application had been cooked up in Raymond's office in St. John's, with the affidavits forwarded to the police officers for signature. Case law that looked more or less relevant had been thrown together and the whole package sent to Griffiths' office the prior day while he was in court selecting the jury.

Unimpressed, he had spent the late afternoon and evening tearing it apart. He was convinced it could not succeed. Even if it did, it would likely be overturned on appeal.

"Do it anyway," he was told after he pointed out the shortcomings. When he balked, Inkpen, eager to prove herself, jumped in.

Now he was caught in the middle. He agreed with Beaudoin's arguments. In her position, he would have made them himself. Her forthrightness to call the law society to review her conduct impressed him.

"My Lord," he answered, "there is merit to counsel's argument. I agree she should have received more notice. However, for reasons that I'm unable to discuss, Ms. Inkpen and I did the best we could. Ordinarily, I would consent to a week or two delay to allow her time to research and prepare. As for the law society and whether she should be defending herself, ethical canons are nice on paper, but sometimes they need to be relaxed when reality takes over. We've already selected a jury, and we need to get on with the case. Then again, sometimes if we hurry in cases like this, we're merely creating grounds for appeal."

Judge Drinkwater, hanging on Griffith's every word, thought he saw a solution, until Griffiths said the word "appeal". The mere mention of being appealed on his first jury trial in his hometown and on such a high-profile case caused his heart to race and his palms to sweat.

On wobbly judicial feet, like a kid who had just lost his training wheels, Drinkwater turned to Beebee. "Now that you've heard from the other lawyers, what request would you like to make of the court?"

"My Lord," she replied, "as to whether it's appropriate for me to appear, I will commit to having an answer after the lunch break. If the answer is *yes*, then I would like the evening to prepare my response."

"What if the law society says it is not appropriate for you to argue the case?" Drinkwater asked.

"I'll ask another lawyer to take my written arguments and appear on the application. If someone can do so within a few days, then the trial can proceed. If not, then it will have to be postponed until the fall."

Relieved the lawyers had shown him a way out of the predicament, Drinkwater said, "Court is adjourned until after lunch." He arose, and clutching his moleskin memo book, hurried crablike to the calm of his chambers.

Chapter 69

Over the extended lunch break, unable to eat, Drinkwater calmed his nerves with a few glasses of vodka and orange juice and then phoned numerous judicial colleagues and listened to opinions that ranged from the heavy-handed, "I would simply dismiss the application immediately and tell those assholes from the Crown that they should've filed it ages ago," to the timid, "Well, you don't want to make a mistake on a big case like this. I would give the defence lawyer all the time she needs. I know it might mean a postponement until fall, but we're all doing very important work, and we must be careful not to make any mistakes."

The most practical advice came from a seasoned, if cynical, colleague, who had been appointed to the bench ten years previously after twenty years as a trial lawyer. "Most of these pre-trial applications are bullshit, with one side or the other trying to gain a tactical advantage. They can generally be dismissed without any consequences to the outcome, particularly when a jury is going to decide guilt or innocence anyway.

"Being a trial judge in a jury trial falls somewhere between a referee in a boxing ring and one of those old time traffic cops standing in the middle of a busy street trying to direct traffic without being run over. Your job is to keep everything moving forward. The main thing is to look like you know what you're doing. Sometimes you got to slap the lawyers around. Whether you're right or wrong is less important than letting them know you're in charge and you know what you're doing."

When court resumed at 2 p.m., well lubricated, his face flushed, a different Colin Drinkwater than the one who had presided in the morning assumed the bench.

First, careful to avoid criticizing Griffiths, he berated Inkpen for filing such a late application. He criticized her even more so for not giving Beaudoin adequate notice to respond. Then he turned his attention to Beebee.

"Ms. Beaudoin, while Ms. Inkpen may not have provided you with as much notice as would be ideal, I'm going to allow her to make her pitch at 10 a.m. tomorrow."

Then, addressing the packed courtroom, he explained that judges were routinely required to make important rulings in the course of a trial and that nothing out of the ordinary was going on.

"And counsel, I don't want any long, drawn-out arguments tomorrow. I'm going to allow the prosecution no more than twenty minutes and the defence no more than twenty minutes. If defence raises an issue that requires a response from the prosecution, I'll give you five minutes to do so and no more. One way or the other, we're going to get this show on the road."

*   *   *

An hour before court resumed the following morning, Beebée delivered a four-page brief to the crown attorney's office and then delivered a copy to the court.

Afterwards, on foot, she navigated across snow-covered Mt. Bernard Avenue to the local coffee shop, partly to grab a muffin and freshly brewed coffee but mostly to kill a little time, hoping to avoid seeing Inkpen in the lady barristers' change room, which was located just outside the courtroom. She need not have worried, as the prosecutors, whose offices were only two floors above the courtroom, always arrived at court fully gowned.

At five minutes after ten, Inkpen began her oral argument, Drinkwater letting her go for twenty minutes uninterrupted before stopping her.

"Ms. Inkpen, before you conclude I'd like to ask you a few questions."

"Yes, my Lord."

Inkpen beamed with confidence, remembering her law school mooting coach's words: "If the judge is asking questions, at least you know he listened to the arguments and may only want clarification, often before ruling in your favour, so never be concerned about a judge asking you questions. It's almost always a good thing."

"I take it you read the brief submitted by defence counsel?" he inquired.

"Yes, my Lord," she replied. "Not exactly a long read," she added sarcastically. "Four pages, double spaced, including the cover and signature page."

"And you read the part where the defence, at least for the purpose of this application, agrees with the facts, as put forth in the Crown's application, as true?"

"Yes, my Lord."

"And I take it from your written materials that at the time the accused was arrested on the charges that are before this court, he wasn't charged with anything?"

She began to feel a little flustered at being questioned in open court by the judge on facts that were not in dispute. "Well, he was charged. It's just that the provincial court judge dismissed the charges and set him free. We could have appealed that, but the minister decided to go with a direct indictment instead."

"So, as I understand it, any charges against him, charges where Ms. Beaudoin represented him, had been dismissed. No appeal had been filed, and he hadn't been charged under the direct indictment that's now before this court. Is that correct?"

"Yes, my Lord."

"I understand that Mr. Wheeler has been in custody since his arrest," Drinkwater said, proceeding cautiously. "Is that correct?"

"Yes, my Lord."

"And he was also in custody from the time he was first arrested in late June until he was released from custody when the charges against him were dismissed in September, is that right?"

"Yes, my Lord."

"So, at most, the only personal time he could have spent together with Ms. Beaudoin was one weekend when he was not charged with anything. Is that correct?"

"Yes, your Honour."

"Thank you, Ms. Inkpen. I have no further questions for you."

Inkpen slumped into her chair, worried now. Soon, her worst fears were realized.

Before Beebee could even rise to begin her oral argument, Drinkwater held up his hand. "I don't need to hear from you. Thank you for the short, well-reasoned legal brief you filed this morning."

Then he turned to address the court. "I'm dismissing the application to disqualify the accused's lawyer, brought by the prosecution. I'll file written reasons before the end of trial. In summary, today I will say the following. First, the prosecution has brought an application to disqualify the accused's lawyer, setting out facts that support a finding that there was a personal and intimate relationship between the lawyer and client. These facts have not been contested and, therefore, can be considered, at least for the purposes of this application, to be true.

"Second, the only time available for the lawyer, Barbara Beaudoin, and the accused, William John Wheeler, to have been together was a weekend after the original charges were dismissed and before the current charges were laid, so there was no time when they were together while he was charged with anything.

"Third, the court will not lightly interfere with the accused's choice of counsel. That being said, while titillating to some, this application doesn't even approach sufficient grounds to disqualify Ms. Beaudoin from representing Mister Wheeler.

"Now that the application has been dismissed, and since it's still early in the day, I'd like to make up for lost time. We'll take our midday break now. Instead of returning at two, we will return at one thirty, and Ms. Inkpen, you can call your first witness."

Relieved that he had overcome what he felt to be the first major hurdle in his first jury trial, and mildly surprised that it had not been as difficult as he expected, Drinkwater still felt like a fish out of water in his new role.

After rendering his decision, he returned to his chambers, where, for the next two hours, he buried himself in a book titled, *Evidence: What's Relevant and What's Not — A Practitioners Guide*, which he scoured line by line like a college student cramming for a final exam, pausing only briefly to nibble at the sandwiches his wife, still glowing at being a judge's wife, had prepared for him before sending him off to work that morning.

*   *   *

When he ventured out of his chambers at 1:30 and returned to the bench, Drinkwater may have been the only person in the courtroom unaware that his decision just two hours earlier, had catapulted his case to the top of the news on two continents.

In Canada, headlines ranged from, "Sensible Judge Dismisses Sex-based Application to Disqualify" to the more humorous "Nookie No Legal Loophole — Lady Barrister to Stay On Lover's Case." Stateside, spurred on by quotes from Helen Holmes, who was seated prominently in the front row alongside a sheriff's officer and taking in every word, the headlines were more riveting and the commentary vitriolic.

The *World Today*, having burnt their bridges with local reporters by blindsiding Gary and the *Humber Chronicle* with their own inflammatory, and much more widely distributed, coverage of the preliminary inquiry dismissal six months earlier, had been forced to send a reporter from New York. Realizing by now that the story might have legs among its readers, they had sent Andrew Bartlett, himself.

Keen to get the most out of the anticipated two- or three-week trial, Bartlett had contacted every person who could conceivably provide him with any information, whether it be simply a few quotes or some background on any of the witnesses. In the case of Helen and Jenny, he had done extensive personal and business interviews, and by day one of the trial, he was well equipped to show the locals how a murder trial should be covered.

For him, having covered scores of high-profile trials earlier in his career, he saw the application to disqualify Beaudoin as simply a prosecution tactic to shake up the accused and his lawyer right from the outset, so the dismissal of the application was no surprise to him.

However, the grounds for the application advanced by the prosecution, initially unknown but now in full public view, were newsworthy. *Wow*, he thought as he listened to Inkpen speak, taking down every word in shorthand, which he had learned years ago, *I wonder if there's anything to this.*

Then, as Drinkwater made his ruling, first of all confirming that both the defence lawyer and her client acknowledged that the facts were true but still dismissing the application to prevent her from representing her lover, the accused murderer, he thought, *Holy Shit! This is the story. The lawyer's sleeping with the client. Everybody around here knows it, and nobody cares. Even if they find him guilty of murder, the verdict won't be as big a story as this!*

As soon as Drinkwater delivered his ruling, before court recessed, after acknowledging both widows, Bartlett raced out the door to be the first to file the story in the US.

His first headline read, "Licentious Lady Lawyer Leaves Court in Shock."

The story explained how accused killer, William John Wheeler, had been holed up in the small, remote town of Port Saunders, in bed with his lawyer, the pair acting like a modern day Bonnie and Clyde, when he was arrested in the early morning hours by a Royal Canadian Mounted Police SWAT team.

The story of the trial had appeared in the paper on two previous days but as part of the section devoted to international news. Except for regular Andrew Bartlett fans, and an even smaller number of readers interested in international legal stories, it had attracted so little attention that management was beginning to wonder if it had been worthwhile to send a reporter.

Finally, his editor, recognizing this story as a huge break, convinced the publisher to give them space on the front page with much more coverage and photos on page A3, and the story took off, selling out every day. Readers were anxious to find out what would happen next to the killer and his lawyer lover.

In Los Angeles, KWOW television, with an exclusive interview with Helen Holmes, held off running the story until its midday news show. However, every thirty minutes, beginning with its 8 a.m. news and public affairs program, it began to run teaser clips with the headline: "To Come — The Sordid Sexual Escapades of Canadian Lawyers and Their Clients."

By the time it ran at noon, 4:30 p.m. Newfoundland time, it had an enormous and diverse audience. Regular viewers, animal rights activists, fans of court shows, and even members of the religious right sent KWOW`s ratings into the stratosphere.

The Germans, tight-fisted but nevertheless committed to following the story that involved the trial of the accused killer of their reporter, Martina Schmidt, arranged for an English-speaking correspondent, fluent in German, to travel from Toronto to Corner Brook. Committed for the first few days of the trial, and possibly to return for the verdict, or depending on if the verdict was guilty, for the sentencing, they got their money's worth.

Being a weekly and unable to run the story immediately, they syndicated it to another German news service and also to a British tabloid, earning a handsome profit and increasing their circulation overnight when they, themselves, carried the story a few days later.

The British tabloid, one of Fleet Street's most widely circulated slap-and-tickle rags, accustomed to covering shenanigans of a sexual nature, both at home and around the world, even by their standards, had a field day. Their headline, "British Barristers Could Learn From Colonial Counterparts," introduced a story that began, "In a titillating story from the Canadian courts, it seems that British barristers have a considerable lot to learn from their colonial counterparts, at least those in Canada, that is!"

Chapter 70

At 1:30 p.m., surveying his courtroom and surprised at the level of chatter, Drinkwater surmised that, like himself, everyone else had become more relaxed. He called the court to order and then asked the sheriff's officers to bring in the jury.

As they filed in, some looked straight ahead. Others could not help looking at BeeBee and Billy with knowing grins. Drinkwater assumed the jurors must have gotten to know each other very well already.

Unknown to him, since they had not yet heard any evidence and were not sequestered, they had just returned from their taxpayer-funded lunch at a local hotel dining room. There, everyone was talking about the murder trial in the case of the helicopter shot down by the local sealer, a soldier, who was having an affair with his defence lawyer. Realizing it was their trial, most could not wait to get back to court.

When the jurors were seated and had answered the roll call, Drinkwater demonstrated his inexperience yet again.

"Okay, Ms. Inkpen, we're ready for your first witness."

Inkpen stood but said nothing.

The judge repeated his order, louder this time. Uncomfortable, Inkpen realized Drinkwater had no clue what he was doing. Nevertheless, she remained diplomatic.

"My Lord, if it pleases the court, would I be permitted to give an opening statement first?"

Realizing his error, Drinkwater nodded. "Oh yes. Oh yes, with all the goings on of the application to disqualify and all that, I had forgotten you had not opened to the jury yet. Thanks for reminding me. Please proceed."

In response, Inkpen launched into an hour-long diatribe of how the Crown would proceed, referring to every witness that she would call, a summary of what they would tell the jury, and why that evidence would prove beyond any reasonable doubt that William John Wheeler was guilty of murder in the first degree of four individuals. Then she thanked the jury for willingly participating in her quest for justice, apparently forgetting that jurors were subpoenaed to attend, jury duty being something that most people preferred to avoid.

The more she talked, the more Griffiths cringed as he watched BeeBee take page after page of notes. An experienced trial lawyer, he knew that the more Inkpen told the jury what she intended to prove, the more difficult she was making their case, and the more opportunities she created for Beaudoin to use later. He also knew that an experienced defence lawyer would note everything she said she would prove and, later on, remind the jury that the Crown had fallen far short of what it had claimed at the beginning of the trial, thereby making it easier for her to raise doubts about other key elements of the case against her client.

Although he did not know how experienced BeeBee was, from the efficient manner with which she had gutted Inkpen on the application, admitting the facts and condensing the evidence and the law into a simple brief for the judge to use, he could tell she was no amateur.

When Inkpen finished, Drinkwater turned to Beebee. "Ms. Beaudoin, we're nearly on time for our afternoon break. Now that you've heard the crown attorney's opening statement, would you like to wait until after the break to deliver yours?"

Beebee rose to her feet. "Thank you, my Lord. I won't be making an opening statement."

Drinkwater frown, perplexed. "No opening statement? Well, it's up to you."

"My Lord," BeeBee replied, "I would, however, like an opportunity to confer privately with my client during the break."

"As you wish. Ms. Inkpen, we will be ready to hear your first witness after the break."

He waited for the jury to file out before recessing court.

As soon as he returned to his chambers, Drinkwater received an urgent message to call his wife.

"Oh my God, Colin," she said, panic in her voice, "your case is all over the news. I tried to call you around one thirty, but they said you were in court."

"That's because we resumed early to make up for time lost by that application," he replied, unconcerned. "As for the case being in the news, you knew to expect that cases I handle will be in the news from time to time."

"But Colin," she said, near tears, "there's a big story about how the lawyer is sleeping with the guy who shot down the helicopter and that the other lawyer tried to get her thrown off the case, but you said it was okay for her to defend him. It was on the news at twelve thirty and again at one thirty, and people are saying all kinds of things!"

"What?" he exclaimed. "Good Lord, I forgot to sequester the jury. I'm sorry, but I've got to hang up and look after that right away."

He called his clerk, relayed the information to her, and was even more shocked to find out that he was the only person unaware of the news coverage and that, assuming he was aware of it, she had said nothing to him.

"What do you think I should do?" he asked, pleading with her.

"Justice," she replied, having clerked dozens of jury trials but only occasionally having a judge ask her opinion. "You've got to sequester the jury immediately. There's no real harm done yet, because they haven't heard any of the evidence, but it might be a little dicey later on if there is an appeal and someone can prove that the jury was tainted by a decision that you made about the defence lawyer that influenced them in their deliberations."

"Oh, thank God," he said. "Now, if you'll indulge me with just one more dumb question, what's the fastest way for me to sequester the jury?"

"I'll take care of that for you, sir, by calling the officers right now. You simply make the order that the jury be sequestered when we return back to court in a few minutes. That means keeping them isolated, without access to the news, for the duration of the trial."

"I see," Drinkwater replied, pondering the implications of keeping a dozen adults away from anyone or anything that could influence their decision. "You've been through several of these, what have other judges done?"

Happy to be validated by the new appointee, the clerk explained that a block of rooms could be booked at one of the three local hotels, that jurors could take their meals together, but they could have no communication, even with family members, unless such communication went through one of the sheriff's officers, beginning immediately with requests that a family member pack a suitcase for each juror, all of which could either be delivered to the courthouse or picked up by a taxi.

She also explained that since jurors would be overseen for twenty-four hours of every day, it would be necessary to bring in additional officers from St. John's or one of the other regional judicial centres and provide their accommodation as well — or pay substantial amounts of overtime or likely a combination of both.

"Oh my," Drinkwater replied, "this is certainly a larger undertaking than I initially realized. Who arranges all of this?"

"You do, my Lord."

"I do," he said, appearing overwhelmed by this new information.

"Oh, my Lord, you just make the order," the clerk said, hurrying to correct any misunderstanding. "You tell me, I tell the senior sheriff's officer, and like clockwork, they do the rest. Judges just make orders or render verdicts, and then somebody else does all the work."

* * *

Back in court, still apprehensive about how the media were communicating his order to permit Beaudoin to stay on the case but now confident in his ability to sequester the jury and fortified by the last two inches of vodka in the bottle, Drinkwater turned to Inkpen and asked her to call her first witness.

"Thank you, my Lord," she replied. "Mr. Griffiths and I will be sharing this part of the trial, with him handling most of the technical witnesses, so I'll defer to him."

Griffiths rose, and with a smooth proficiency that validated him having been appointed Queen's Counsel a decade earlier, called the skipper of the fishing boat that had snagged the helicopter in its shrimp trawl and brought it to surface. In an organized manner, he conducted a wide-ranging examination-in-chief, akin to an informal discussion between friends, which left no questions for defence counsel to ask. He finished his evidence in thirty minutes.

Then he called the pathologist who had conducted autopsies on the four bodies. Clearly adept at medical terminology, Griffiths moved back and forth easily, using the appropriate medical term to which the pathologist responded, and then, before moving on to the next question, without a hint of condescension or superiority in his voice, rephrased the question in lay terms to make it easy for the jury to follow along.

Throughout the detached pathologist's evidence, Griffiths painted a gruesome picture of how the four died — by drowning, as proven by the pathologist's examination of their lungs. Even the pilot, with a bullet through his head, had died of drowning, although his lungs were full of blood, whereas the others were full of seawater.

At 4:25, Drinkwater interrupted him. "Mr. Griffiths we're approaching four thirty, the end of the court day. If you're nearly finished with this witness, I can give you an extra few minutes. If not, I would like to conclude now, as I need to communicate some information to the jury regarding their arrangements for the night and for the rest of the trial."

Griffiths, who, out of the corner of his eye had been watching the jury's reaction to the pathologist's evidence, knew he had most, if not all of them, in the palm of his hand, graciously gave way to the judge, leaving the jurors with the mental image that he wanted them to sleep on, the same image he would resume with and elaborate upon the next morning.

The following day, Griffiths continued to question the pathologist about how the four occupants of the helicopter had died. Yes, they all had fractures, likely sustained on impact. The three passengers had broken fingernails. One, the woman, had managed to unfasten her safety harness, but she died with the straps still around her shoulders. By the time Griffiths concluded his examination of the pathologist, the morning was over, and most of the jurors looked like they had seen a horror movie.

When Drinkwater turned to BeeBee to ask if she had any questions, some of the jurors shot her venomous looks while others could not even look at her or Billy.

Beebee, having concluded that asking this witness any questions would not make things any better for her client and, in fact, might make things worse, thanked the pathologist for his attendance but said she had no questions.

When court resumed in the afternoon, Griffiths called the area director of the Department of Fisheries and Oceans (DFO). His pleasant, professional, if condescending demeanour toward fisherman, belied the considerable power that he wielded by federal legislation.

Constitutionally, in Canada, fisheries and oceans was an area of federal responsibility, and the *Fisheries Act* was administered from Ottawa, thousands of kilometres away from the three oceans on the west, north, and east coasts, by an entrenched bureaucracy and a revolving cast of ministers, whose haphazard and inconsistent approach to fishery regulation regularly brought DFO into conflict with citizens in small coastal communities who were attempting to earn a living from the sea.

The area director explained how all fishing vessels, except for the tiniest open boats, which fished close to the shore, were required to have onboard vessel-monitoring systems, contemptuously called "black boxes" by skippers, who were required to purchase them and have them operational whenever they were at sea or else be subject to fines for noncompliance.

East coast Canadian waters, including those in the Gulf of St. Lawrence, had been divided into an array of fishing zones. If a vessel strayed over an unseen line on the map while setting gear or pursuing fish, the DFO laid a charge under the *Fisheries Act*, and the operator was dragged into court and fined.

All of this information was stored electronically, so from DFO records, the area director was easily able to trace the course of the vessel, *Reuben and Naomi*, showing that it was operating in the same area as the helicopter was found.

By the end of the day, Griffiths had completed his examination of the area director. Once again, Beebee had no questions.

Next came the RCMP ballistics expert, Henry Smitherman, a man who liked to talk, particularly when it came to his knowledge of firearms. Through him, by the middle of Friday afternoon, Griffiths was able to prove to the jury that a bullet, fired from a rifle registered to Joshua Short, was found lodged in the helmet of George Villeneuve.

At the conclusion of the ballistics evidence, Drinkwater turned to Beebee. "Ms. Beaudoin, do you have any questions for this witness, or should I release him and have the Crown call their next witness after the break?"

She had declined to ask any questions of the three earlier witnesses, so when she began her cross-examination after the break, it was before an attentive audience.

"You've certainly given us a very thorough understanding of how ballistics work and your conclusions in this case," she began in a neutral, low-key manner. "I'm sure when the jury deliberates, they will be grateful for your evidence. Tell me, does your knowledge of firearms also include those used by the military?"

"Of course," he replied, eager to demonstrate his knowledge, "as long as you're referring to small arms used by most of the NATO countries, but I wouldn't go out on a limb when it comes to large-calibre firearms, artillery, or foreign firearms."

"So tell me," BeeBee asked, "the gun — and I know you guys, I mean experts like yourself, you call them by all kinds of names, rifles and shotguns and pistols and revolvers and other names, but to me they're all guns."

She paused to let him interrupt and reassure her that he did not mind if she simply referred to all of them as "guns", which he was happy to do.

"So tell me," she continued, "this gun, the one that shot the bullet that I guess might've killed the pilot, I don't imagine they use a gun anything like this one in the armed forces, do they?"

"Of course they do," he said. "The firearm in question is the civilian version of the C7, the most commonly used rifle of the Canadian infantry."

BeeBee shook her head, apparently unable to grasp the answer. "I'm sorry, but I think you'll need to explain it to me a little better. My father has an old Lee Enfield. He said it's the same as they used in the Army a long time ago, but when I saw the pictures of the ones from the war, they looked completely different. Perhaps I'm the only one who's not getting it, but could you explain the difference between the one in our case and the one you just called, what I thought I heard was a C7, something like that?"

Thinking he really had to dumb things down for her, Smitherman went on for several minutes explaining that the C7 used the same ammunition, had the same firing mechanism, handled in the same way, and for all intents and purposes, was the same firearm as the one that killed the helicopter pilot.

"Thank you for simplifying this for me. Now, if you would allow me one more dumb question, say as a hypothetical, if someone familiar with using this gun was using the one that we're talking about, but in this case without looking at it, would the person automatically know which gun he was using?"

"No. That's the point I've been trying to make. They're practically identical in every respect, except they look a little different."

"So, Mr. Smitherman, just to put this all into context, I'd like to ask you a hypothetical question. Let's say someone who was very experienced in using a C7 was handed the civilian version, let's say, in an emergency, would that person have to do anything to familiarize himself with the weapon, or could he respond immediately as if he had been handed the military version?"

"That's easy. It would be like using the same firearm, and I would go even further. One of the purposes of training is that, by repetitive action, a well-trained person can simply react instead of having to figure out what to do."

Griffiths, while wary of what use BeeBee would make of Smitherman's testimony, elected not to re-examine his witness.

Drinkwater glanced at the clock "I see there's less than an hour left today. Mr. Griffiths, would you like to bring your next witness, or would you prefer to end a little early and call your next witness on Monday morning?"

"My Lord," he answered, "when we resume on Monday morning, Ms. Inkpen will begin conducting the remainder of the Crown's case."

Chapter 71

When court resumed on Monday morning, energized and on a mission, Inkpen resumed the lead for the Crown. Having had the application that she brought to disqualify Beaudoin dismissed, with her continually referred to in the extensive news coverage that followed as the "losing lawyer", the one who had lost at the preliminary inquiry and who had lost again on a routine application, was bad enough.

Even more galling was being forced to sit by and watch Griffiths smoothly examine witness after witness that she had secured for the prosecution. These were her witnesses, whose evidence she wanted to place before the court so she could redeem herself and leave no doubt that she, Iris Inkpen, was a force to be reckoned with. The thought that Griffiths was reaping the credit burned her up inside.

She intended to return to centre stage in the trial, and in a week or two, when the jury convicted Wheeler of murder, she intended to be the winning lawyer, and what better way was there to show who was in charge of the case than to grill the four occupants of that cursed fishing boat?

She called Josh to the stand first. In an examination that lasted the entire day, perhaps attempting to emulate Griffiths' style but ill-equipped to do so, limited by both her temperament and her inexperience, she used the entire morning before even asking about the shooting.

She began with Josh's family background, including the names of his grandparents, Reuben and Naomi, for whom the vessel had been named — not by him but by his uncles, Jacob and Esau, who had owned it previously. Then, from a photo, she had him identify the short, wide fishing vessel. Its design sacrificed speed but allowed it to drag large nets across the ocean floor or, in the case of a scallop dragger, to haul huge iron buckets behind it that carved long-lasting trenches across the sandy bottom, destroying habitat for years to come.

Then she produced, for his interpretation, a cross-sectional view of the vessel prepared by a naval architect, having him explain where each crew member was positioned at the time of the shooting. She also had him describe the small forward deck, raised to accommodate a four-berth cabin and tiny galley below, and the small wheelhouse, where he was steering the vessel. It was built with thick glass windows that limited visibility but also permitted his sturdy craft to resist the severest of weather.

Perhaps, as he described the layout of the vessel's deck, she realized that, by design, the wheelhouse partially obscured the forward view of the two crew members who were working on the low, flat rear deck, because when they reached that part of the description, she paused briefly and then moved on quickly to ask him about his military experience.

She questioned him at length about where he had served, when he had first met the accused, how much time they had spent together, and how he had come to marry the accused's sister, Rhonda.

Preening and prattling and strutting back and forth behind the prosecution table, asking question after question that elicited largely irrelevant and only mildly interesting information, a collective sigh of relief rippled across the court when she wound things down.

"My Lord, I see that we are approaching the time for lunch break. Now that I've laid the foundation for the part of my examination that deals with what actually took place, may I suggest that we stop here and resume at two o'clock?"

Ordinarily, an insecure judge, like Drinkwater, would have been at least mildly irritated that a lawyer was telling him when his court should break and when it should return and, if for no other reason than to let her know who was in charge, might have forced her to continue just a little longer to teach her some manners. However, on this occasion, Drinkwater was just grateful that she was stopping, so he went along with her suggestion.

While Griffiths was mildly amused at Inkpen's ineptness, Beebee scribbled notes throughout Inkpen's meandering examination, noting all of the areas she covered so that when it was her turn to ask questions — on which she would expect to be challenged to show relevancy; questions that, if answered in the way she hoped, would make her client more sympathetic to the jury — she could simply point to the issues as having been raised by Crown counsel in her examination-in-chief of the witness.

Instead of demonstrating her own competence, Inkpen's overly broad examination-in-chief of the soft-spoken, composed, retired warrant officer, or at least the first half of it, opened numerous unnecessary avenues for questions that a capable defence lawyer, like BeeBee, could exploit later.

At 2 p.m., Inkpen gave up her overtly mellow, if forced, performance of the morning and reverted to the familiar, harpy-like style that had earned her the nickname "Iris the Inquisitor", going after Josh with only slightly veiled aggression. The change in her manner was no surprise to Josh. Having faced her during the preliminary inquiry six months earlier, he was on guard.

"So, Mr. Short, when did you first become aware that the helicopter had been shot down?"

"Like I told you before, last fall, I was in the wheelhouse steering through pans of ice. Billy was up front shooting seals. Young Jeff and Rhonda's dad, Reuben, were on deck hauling them in over the side. Then Jeff was at the door yelling to me to come quick. We were only doing three or four knots. I cut the power, slipped her into reverse, and went on deck to see what was up."

"What did you see?"

"Billy was just coming back from up on the bow. He had a strange look on his face. He asked me about signing up again and why I brought his father and Jeff. He sat on a crate with my rifle across his knees. He had a blank look on his face."

"What were the others doing?"

"Rhonda's dad, Riley, was just standing there. He wasn't saying anything. He looked shocked, you know, kinda pale. And young Jeff, well, young Jeff, he was just blubbering on. He looked like he was going to burst into tears."

"What did you do?"

"I took the rifle out of Billy's hands, and we all went into the wheelhouse, where it was warm, so I could figure out what happened."

"Did you figure out what happened?"

"Not completely."

"Whaddya mean 'not completely'? You were there weren't you?"

"Yes, ma'am, I was there, but I didn't see it happen," he answered evenly.

"Well, what do you think happened?"

Beebee stood up. "My Lord, I object to the question. Crown counsel can ask the witness what he saw, what he did, and what he saw others do, but she cannot ask his opinion of what happened. That's a question for the jury to determine based on the facts."

Inkpen started to respond, but before she was able to do so, Drinkwater, even with his limited experience, combined with the look on Griffiths' face, knew that Beaudoin was correct.

"Defence counsel is right. Ms. Inkpen, please withdraw the question."

Steamed that she had been picked off with such a simple objection, and taking the judge's ruling personally, Inkpen's tone became even more sarcastic. "Well, if you're going to pretend you don't know what happened, tell me what your brother-in-law said."

"Ms. Inkpen," Drinkwater said, "you may refer to someone by his or her name. If you're referring to Mr. Wheeler, you may refer to him as 'the accused'. Your question, as posed, is improper. I'll also ask you to pay a little more attention to your tone when you're appearing in my court. Now, if you have a proper question for this witness, ask it. Otherwise, move on."

Inkpen was stung at being chastised. "My Lord, may I have a brief recess to confer with my co-counsel?"

"That would appear to be a good idea," Drinkwater replied sourly.

When court resumed ten minutes later, Inkpen resumed her examination, a little more contrite. "So, Mr. Short, did you have any discussion with the accused after you removed the rifle from his hands?"

"Yes, I did."

"And can you tell us who initiated the conversation?"

"I did."

"And what was the nature of the discussion?"

"Well, I needed to get to the bottom of whatever just happened. Mr. Wheeler — Billy's father — was pretty shook up, like he had just seen a ghost or something. The young fellow, Jeff, was hysterical, and Billy, well, Billy looked shocked."

"Had you ever seen the accused look like that before?"

"Just once," Josh replied. "But that was a long time ago, in Bosnia."

"Before I interrupted you, you said you needed to get to the bottom of what just happened. Did you?"

"Well, more or less. You see, the first thing I needed to do to make a sense of it was to bring Billy around, so I just chatted with him, asked him how things were going. After Bosnia, he had a bad time with nightmares — a lot of us did. We saw a lot of stuff there, stuff you can never be prepared for, and, you know, if you don't get it under control, you're finished. A lot of people drink."

"Mr. Short, I wasn't asking you about what a lot of you guys claim you saw. I'm sure you've all got your war stories. I'm interested in what happened on your boat the day the helicopter went down. If you don't start giving me some straight answers, I'm going to ask to have you declared a hostile witness so I can cross-examine you."

Beebee stood up. "My Lord, maybe if crown counsel would stop interrupting the witness—"

"Defence counsel has a point," Drinkwater said, motioning BeeBee to sit down. "Ms. Inkpen, continue with your questions."

"Please continue, Mr. Short," Inkpen said, seething.

"So I asked Billy how things were going. He said things were fine except that he had dreamt the night before that we were out sealing, and he shot down a helicopter."

"And what as your response?"

"I told him that wasn't a dream; it had just happened."

"And what was his response?"

"He went white. He looked like he was going to vomit, and he asked me to give him back the rifle so he could go up on deck."

"And why do you think he asked for the rifle?"

"I was pretty sure at that point he was going to kill himself."

Having gotten the information she wanted from Josh, Inkpen finished the day, leaving the jury to ponder his evidence overnight.

Chapter 72

The next morning, BeeBee elected not to cross-examine Josh, so Inkpen called Riley to the stand. After a few questions to establish his relationship to the accused and to the other two crewmembers, Inkpen had only a few short questions for him.

"On the day in question, were you a crew member on the *Reuben and Naomi*?"

"Y-y-yes."

"Did you see a helicopter?"

"N-n-no."

"Did you shoot at a helicopter?"

"N-no."

"Did you see anyone else shoot at helicopter?"

"N-n-no."

Even though the questions posed to Riley were few and brief, due to his speech impediment, his evidence required nearly an hour.

There was no cross-examination.

The next witness the prosecution called was Jeff, now seventeen years old. He trembled as he took the oath to tell the truth.

Cutting through routine questions, Inkpen went straight to the heart of the matter. "Mr. Wheeler, how many people made up the crew of the *Reuben and Naomi* on the day in question?"

"Well, ma'am, if you include the skipper, Uncle Josh, there wuz four of us."

"By 'Uncle Josh', do you mean Joshua Short?"

"Yes, ma'am."

"And who were the others?"

"Pop and Uncle Billy."

"When you say 'Pop', to whom are you referring?"

"My grandfather, Riley Wheeler, we always call him 'Pop'."

"When you say 'Uncle Billy', first of all, do you see him in court here today?"

"Well, yes," Jeff said, surprised at the question. "He's right there." He pointed at Billy.

"My Lord," Inkpen said, "I ask the jury to note this witness has identified the accused."

Jeff shifted from one foot to the other and cast an uncomfortable glance toward Billy.

"Where were you when this happened?" Inkpen asked.

"I was on the back deck," Jeff replied softly.

"And was anyone else there with you?"

"Pop."

"Where was Joshua Short?"

"In the wheelhouse."

"And where was the accused?"

He hesitated briefly, casting a guilty glance at Billy.

"It's no use looking at him," Inkpen said. "He can't help you. Just answer the question."

Red-faced, Jeff looked back at her. "Uncle Billy was up on the front deck."

"And what was he doing up there?"

"Shooting seals."

"And could you see him shooting seals?"

"Sometimes I could, and sometimes I couldn't, but most the time, I couldn't."

"And why was that?"

"Well, you see, the wheelhouse is between the front deck and the back deck. The back deck, where I was, is a little bit lower, so if I was on the same side as he was, I could see him. But if he was shooting a seal that was dead ahead or on the other side, then I wouldn't see him make the shot."

"You said 'the shot'. Did you mean *shot* or *shots*? Was there more than one shot?"

"Shot," he replied. "When Uncle Billy is the gunner, there's only one shot." A fleeting smile relaxed his peach fuzz-covered face.

Inkpen detected an opportunity. "Are you saying the accused never misses when he shoots?"

The teenager thought for a second. "I suppose everyone misses sometimes, but not Uncle Billy," he said with undisguised pride. "At least not that day. If we heard a shot, we knew there was seal for me and Pop to pick up."

"Now, Mr. Wheeler," Inkpen continued, "do you recall seeing the helicopter crash?"

"Yes, ma'am," he whispered, his voice barely audible.

"Can you describe what happened? And remember, you're still under oath."

"Well, we were going about our business hunting seals. Like I said, Uncle Josh was in the wheelhouse steering, Uncle Billy was on the front deck — he was the gunner. Me and Pop were on the back deck hauling in the seals after they got shot. Pop would make sure they were completely dead, bleed them. If there was enough time between shots, he would skin them while I watched. If we got into a small patch of them and Uncle Billy shot five or six, there wouldn't be enough time to—"

"Okay, okay, we're not here about seals. We're here about the helicopter. Tell the jury about the helicopter."

"Well, like I was trying to tell you, we were working, and the helicopter came out of nowhere."

"What do you mean by 'came out of nowhere'? How far away was it when you first saw it?"

"When I first saw it, it was little ways away, not a long way, perhaps no more than a football field, not very high, but I heard it before I saw it."

"So you heard it, and you looked in that direction and saw it?"

"Well, not really like that," he answered. "I heard it coming toward us, but I couldn't see it. It sounded like a boat gaining on us, but I knew it couldn't be a boat."

"Why not?"

"Because a boat couldn't go through the ice that fast. It was snowing really heavy, and there it was, a helicopter, out of nowhere, right behind us, really low. We were in a patch of seals, and the helicopter drove them into the water. Then it stopped in the air, a little behind us."

"How close was it?"

"Real close and real low," he answered.

"How close?"

"So close the wind from the propeller blew the snow off the boat. That's close."

"Could you see the people in the helicopter?"

"The pilot. I could see the pilot. I could see other people aboard, too."

"What did you see next?"

He stalled and glanced at Billy.

"Mr. Wheeler," Inkpen said. "We're waiting for your answer."

He continued to stall.

Inkpen turned to Drinkwater. "My Lord, I ask you direct the witness to answer the question."

"I saw a puff of white on the Plexiglas," Jeff said tearfully, "and I saw the pilot's head snap back. It was like the helicopter tried to rise, and then it went into the water, kind of sideways and head on. Then it sank."

"What did you see next?"

"I turned around fast. I saw Uncle Billy."

"What was he doing?"

"Nothing."

"Nothing?"

"He was just standing there, his hands by his sides. He was holding his rifle — I mean, Uncle Josh's rifle — in one hand."

"And what, if anything, did he say?"

"Well, I wouldn't be able to say for sure," Jeff replied. "He was twenty-five or thirty feet away, and it was snowing, but when he came back around the wheelhouse to where me and Pop was, he kinda had a blank look on his face, almost like he didn't know what was going on."

"What did he say?"

"Well, that's just it, what he said didn't make any sense."

"Just tell us what he said. The jury will decide if it makes any sense or not," Inkpen countered.

"He said something about teaching a lesson to some ragheads, and then he swore."

"What exactly did he say?"

Jeff glanced at Drinkwater. "I'm not sure if I'm supposed to say it. I mean here, in court."

Sensing that Jeff was seeking confirmation to use profanity in court, Drinkwater nodded. "Go ahead, young man. Courts are accustomed to hearing everything. To the best of your ability, repeat what you heard."

Jeff cast another embarrassed glance at Billy. "I'm pretty sure he said, 'Those ragheads won't fuck with us again.'"

"Was there any doubt in your mind that he had fired the shot that brought down the helicopter?"

"Not really," Jeff said. "No. I just couldn't believe it." He looked at Inkpen. "I just couldn't believe it." Then he began to sob. "I'm really sorry, Uncle Billy. What could I say?"

Inkpen smirked. "I have no more questions for this witness, my Lord."

"Cross-examination Ms. Beaudoin?" Drinkwater asked.

"No cross-examination, my Lord," BeeBee replied.

Distraught, Jeff, with the assistance of a sheriff's deputy, left the stand.

Drinkwater turned to Inkpen. "Counsel, we will resume after lunch with your next witness."

Convinced she had won, Inkpen smiled smugly. "No more witnesses, my Lord. That's the case for the Crown."

"Ms. Beaudoin, how many witnesses do you intend to call?" Drinkwater asked.

"Just one, my Lord, the accused. However, I reserve the right to call additional witnesses after Mr. Wheeler gives evidence, if it seems appropriate to do so."

"Are you in a position to begin the defence right after lunch?"

"No, my Lord. We've heard quite a bit of evidence. I would like the afternoon and evening to review it."

"Granted," he replied. He turned to the jury. "Ladies and gentlemen of the jury, you've just heard the evidence for the prosecution in this matter. I think you'll agree there's been a substantial amount of evidence. Defence counsel has asked for time to review that evidence. It's a reasonable request, which I have granted.

"Please remember you are still sequestered. It's important you are not influenced by anything except the evidence you hear in this court. Sheriff's officers will attend to your needs, including any communication with family members or others that you require. Again, thank you for your service. We will resume at ten o'clock tomorrow morning. Adjourned."

As soon as Drinkwater had departed, Beebee rushed over to Billy, who looked dejected. "I'm gonna grab a quick bite. That'll only take me a half hour. By then, they'll have you transported back up the hill. I'll come up. We'll go over everything we've heard and plan your response."

"Is there really any point?" he asked gloomily.

"Shhh..." she said with the feigned confidence of a trial lawyer reassuring a losing client. "They've given us more to work with than you may think. Don't say anything to anyone."

Chapter 73

Concerned that Billy seemed to be giving up, Beebee headed up O'Connell Drive to the Tim Horton's. She picked up a coffee and a chicken wrap and then headed straight back to the penitentiary parking lot. Arriving fifteen minutes before the van carrying Billy showed up, she sat in her car eating and reviewing her notes.

They met in a small, painted cinder block interview room. It was approximately six feet square with a heavy steel door fitted with a four by twelve-inch vertical plate-glass window to allow guards to look in. The room was furnished with a small, graffiti-covered hardwood table and two decrepit stacking chairs that even the Salvation Army would send to the dump.

When Billy was shown in, BeeBee was already there, her briefcase open on the floor and exhibits and notepad on the table. Barely looking at Billy, she acknowledged the guard, the congenial one to whom she had spoken when he was taken into custody.

"I hope you're taking good care of my client."

"Always the best," he replied. "He's not much trouble for someone so famous," talking about Billy as if he wasn't in the room. "Do you want me to leave the door open?"

"No, we'll be fine," BeeBee answered.

As soon as the door closed, BeeBee stood up. Pushing Billy into the corner, behind the door, out of view of anyone looking through the tiny window, she embraced him tightly, and they shared a long, warm kiss.

Billy's demeanour brightened. For a few moments, it seemed as if the weight of the world had lifted from his shoulders.

Then she sat down. "Quick. Sit down in case anyone looks through the window."

As he sat, he nodded at the file spread out in front of them. "Before we get into all of this, let's talk."

"Okay," she replied, sitting back. While encouraged that he might take a more active part in his own defence, she sensed she would not like what she would hear.

"We both know I'm guilty. I'm not gonna get up there and lie. I might be a killer, but I'm not a liar. I'm really sorry for killing those people. Is it too late to plead guilty? Wouldn't that get this over with?"

Alarmed he might insist on pleading out, she wanted to scream, "No, no, no! You can't do that!" Instead, she responded in a measured, detached manner. "There are degrees of guilt, Billy. I'm willing to concede that you're guilty of something, but what is it, and then to what degree?"

He stared at her, uncertain as to whether she was agreeing with him or not. "You'll have to explain that to me."

Relieved he was willing to discuss the issue, she pointed to the indictment. "You're charged with four counts of first-degree murder. If you're found guilty, there's an automatic life sentence, without parole for twenty-five years. You're thirty-five. You'll be sixty by then, so a guilty plea means your life is over."

"Is that it?"

"No, but that's what the Crown wants."

She paused briefly to let him consider what he had just heard and then continued. "Two other verdicts are available to the jury."

"Which ones?"

"Second-degree murder and manslaughter."

"Okay."

"This is where what I call the 'degree of guilt' is important," she continued. Then she explained that with second-degree murder, parole eligibility began after ten years in prison. She could see by his expression that it had dawned on him that he could be found guilty of murder and possibly get out of prison at forty-five instead of sixty.

"When you say a minimum of ten years, that means it could be higher, right?"

"Yes it could," she confirmed. "That's what I'm worried about. This is a highly publicized case. I don't think the Crown will agree with the minimum of ten. They'll likely push for a minimum of fifteen or twenty."

"You said manslaughter, too. How does that work?"

"Manslaughter is still culpable homicide," she said. "There is no minimum sentence. The range is two to twelve years. I've read cases where the person was convicted but didn't even go to jail, but that was in cases like a battered wife, for example. None of that applies here," she added hastily.

By then, she could see he was becoming overwhelmed by the information, so she stopped speaking, waiting for him to catch up.

"What do you think I should do?" he asked.

"I think we should review the evidence against you. Then we should take a break. This evening I'll return, and we'll prep you for tomorrow."

"I know what you're saying," he replied, "but you still didn't say which one of the three we should go for."

"It's a little more complicated than that," she answered. "If you're wondering if I have an objective and a strategy to get there, the answer is *yes*. We need to be well prepared. We need you relaxed but not cocky or arrogant or whiny, which I know you're not."

Chapter 74

Tired and hungry, BeeBee dropped into a fast-food place for a burger, fries, and a diet cola. While standing in the two-person lineup, she knew she had been recognized.

Ordinarily, she would have engaged the locals in harmless chitchat, but not today. She had too much on her mind, so she took her tray and headed to the farthest corner. Along the way, she picked up the local newspaper.

Preoccupied by the case, she had not paid any attention to the news. The trial was being covered by the media. No publication ban was in place, as the jury was sequestered. Unfolding the previously read and now disorganized pages of the little daily, she could not believe how much coverage there was.

But for a small section on the lower right corner, the entire front page featured the trial. With one main story complete with photos of the victims, a smaller story and the photo of Billy, and another similarly sized story matching up the two lady lawyers like prizefighters, readers could follow every witness's testimony blow by blow. Corner Brook had never hosted such an event.

Ordinarily, with the morbid curiosity of most readers, she would have read every word, but not that day. Instead, she looked at the headlines and scanned the stories. Aware that other patrons were talking about her, she wolfed down her food. Leaving the paper on the table, she took her drink, cleared off her tray, and headed back to her room.

Once inside, she cranked up the thermostat a few notches. Mentally fatigued, with the food increasing her drowsiness, she crawled into bed and was asleep by 6:30 p.m.

*   *   *

Across town, their laborious review of the trial had the opposite effect on Billy. Ironically, he ate an identical evening meal. The jail had a contract with a few local restaurants to feed inmates. With limited choices, instead of pizza, Billy had selected a burger and fries with a diet cola.

Instead of bringing on drowsiness, the meal energized him. With his mind racing as to possible verdicts and nowhere to go, he simply walked back and forth in his eight by eight-foot cell. Every two or three laps, he dropped to the floor and did push-ups and sit-ups, killing time, waiting for Beebee to return.

* * *

A noise in the hall awoke Beebee from her deep slumber. She panicked, thinking she had slept too long. Then she saw the red numbers on the clock radio. It was only 7:03 p.m. Good. She had slept for only a half hour, but it had refreshed her. She was ready to go.

She brushed her teeth, pulled on an old pair of jeans, T-shirt, sweatshirt, and winter parka, grabbed her briefcase, and headed for her car.

It was minus fifteen outside. Cold and clear. She heard the snow crunch under her feet and felt the frost in her nostrils. But for the streetlights, it would be clear overhead.

Up north on the peninsula, it would be colder and clearer. The northern lights were in full bloom. Galaxies of stars were visible, including the Big Dipper, its two end stars pointing toward her favourite, the North Star. The one that was always constant, never changing its position, the one she could look to for direction.

For an instant, she thought it would be a great night to be back home snowmobiling, taking Billy to the cabin. Even if they had to shovel out the doorway, the thought of the reward — a hot drink and sliding into a double sleeping bag with him — made her tingle.

A car horn brought her back to reality. Although driving below the speed limit, the reduced traction of the snow-packed street caused her to slide through a stop sign. She would have been T-boned but for the other driver swerving around her.

She swore, chastising herself. "Refocus. Refocus girl. You've got to get this right, or he'll be going away for long time."

With her law school ethics professor's words ringing in her ears about all the reasons a lawyer should never become personally involved with her client, she felt a twinge of guilt. Had she done anything to compromise his rights or the outcome? She stopped short of the answer.

* * *

Finally, just after 7:30 p.m., the intercom buzzed.

"We're coming for you Wheeler," the guard said. "Your lawyer's here again."

Moments later, Billy was shown into the room they had occupied previously.

"Buzz me if you need anything," he said and then closed the door and left.

This time, Beebee, who had already laid out her documents, did not rise to greet him. Billy remained standing, a smile on his face.

"This is it? This is my greeting?"

She stood up and pushed him into the same corner. "We've got to be really careful," she whispered. "If they think we're up to anything, they could make me leave. We really need this prep time."

"Oh, all right," he replied in mock disappointment.

Then they got down to business, with BeeBee explaining that for many, and perhaps most, of the jurors, it could come down to whether they liked him or not.

"Billy," she said, "up 'til now, we've been dealing with the facts of the case, or at least the facts that the Crown wants the jury to believe. Now we're going to add more facts. In addition to supplementing the facts, which should help you, at least a little bit, we're going to work on the emotional side of the case to balance out the equities and give the jury more to work with."

"What do you mean?" he asked. "It seems pretty simple to me. I shot down the helicopter and killed four people; that's obvious. It seems to me that, based on everything we've talked about, the jury will find me guilty of murder. The only issue up for debate seems to be whether it's first-degree or second-degree."

"We'll get to that in a little while," she said. "Right now, I want to discuss two factors that criminal lawyers use to their clients' advantage."

He leaned in, suddenly more attentive. "Okay."

"First of all, it's a well-known fact that assholes go to jail and nice guys go free."

"Seriously?"

"Very serious. That's why we need them to like you. It isn't always the case, but generally speaking, juries want to give the benefit of the doubt to someone they like rather than someone they dislike. That's just human nature. We're all like that."

"Okay, but you said there were two factors. What's the other one?"

"Juries have a mind of their own."

Mystified, he shook his head. "You'll really have to explain that one."

She explained that, unlike US jurors on TV, jurors in Canada were prohibited by law from discussing anything that took place within the jury room. However, it was clear from their verdicts that, from time to time, compromises had been made. It seemed that many juries first decided what verdict was fair instead of which one was simply legal.

"First, we need them to like you. Inkpen will tell the jury that you're a cold, professional killer who callously shot down a civilian helicopter, killing the four people inside. She'll argue that you're one of the worst offenders, a menace to society, and to protect the public, you should be found guilty of first-degree murder."

Billy nodded in silence, staring at the documents on the table, and then looked up at her. "What will you be saying?"

"That depends on your evidence," she replied. "What you say is important, but how you say it is even more important."

He nodded. "Okay, now you've got my attention."

She explained she wanted to show him as an ordinary person who had served his country well. Based on his training and experience, he had acted spontaneously and made a terrible mistake that cost four lives. He was extremely remorseful for what he had done.

"Well, that's all true," he agreed, "but it seemed like I was having a dream. I just don't see how we can get that across to them. Even if we do, I'm still guilty."

"Most importantly," she continued, "you have to tell the truth. If they think you're lying about anything, no matter how small, they won't trust you. They won't like you, and your whole defence will fail. Don't dwell on the shooting. Admit it and move on."

"If this part goes well, what do you think the jury will find me guilty of?"

"That's difficult to predict, Billy," she responded thoughtfully, "because there's such a range of possibilities. There's the possibility of a first-degree conviction, but I think second-degree is more likely. Because it's the judge who passes sentence, it's important to perform well. If you're convicted of second-degree murder, your performance could determine whether you're paroled in ten years instead of twelve or fifteen or even longer."

"And what about you?" he asked with a wry grin. "What'll you be shooting for?"

Shaking her head, glad to see his sense of humour was still working, she chuckled. "I won't be using those words, but if things go well for you, I hope to pitch them for manslaughter."

"You mentioned that before. How does that work?"

"Manslaughter is tricky to prove. It involves doing something unlawful that results in someone being killed, but you didn't intend to kill that person."

"But how can anyone know there was no intent to kill?"

"You've got it," she answered. "That's exactly what we need to prove to the jury. You shot at the helicopter, which was an unlawful act, but you never intended to kill anyone. If they believe that, they could find you guilty of manslaughter. Now do you see why you must be absolutely truthful and why we need them to like you?"

"If it's manslaughter, how much time am I looking at?"

"If the jury brings in a manslaughter verdict, I'll be pitching the judge for four or five years. That's the low end. You can expect Inkpen to ask for ten to twelve. I'd say that's your range. Hopefully the judge will come down somewhere in the middle."

"So, if they go for manslaughter, and if the judge gives me ten years, will I get any time off for good behaviour, or will I have to serve all of it?"

"If it goes our way and you get ten years, you could be out in three."

"Really? How does that work?"

"If you get ten years, and the judge gives you credit for time served, that will bring it down to nine years."

"Nine years? I thought you just said three."

"It could be three. You're eligible for parole after a third of your time.

She let him process the information.

"But I'm still guilty. I killed them."

Chapter 75

Billy's evidence began at 10 a.m. the next morning and lasted the entire day. Before getting into the details of the case, Beebee devoted the morning to letting the jury get to know her client. Starting with his family, she took them methodically through the highs and lows of his nearly thirty-six years on Earth.

In less than a half an hour, she covered his first eighteen years, working in his happy, normal family life and carefully, so as not to make it appear he was looking for their sympathy, took him through the shock of Brad's death in the snowmobile accident. She showed him to be an average student from a small-town fishing family who enlisted in the armed forces, initially to find out if he would like military life. When he realized that he did, he decided to make it his career.

Then, slowing the tempo to a crawl, more in the manner of a sensitive psychologist than a trial lawyer, she took him through his friendship with Roger Elms, their time together at work, and Billy's frequent visits to the Elms' residence, where he got to know Emma and the kids. She ended that line of questioning with the shock he felt at seeing Roger killed in a training accident and the loss he felt afterwards.

Pausing slightly, appearing to look at her notes, she gave the seven women and five men of the jury a few moments to reflect. As they did, Inkpen rolled her eyes, and the judge refilled his crystal water glass from an oversized crystal pitcher that his wife had given him to replace the cheap plastic ones court services provided.

Next, Beebee explored Billy's relationship with Emma, beginning with her telephone call to him and how she explained that the children were missing him. Leaving out nothing, she took him through Emma's unexpected pregnancy, Billy's deployment to Bosnia, his insistence that they marry before his departure, and how he learned of Emma's miscarriage and how he felt at being away from her.

She skipped over most of the details of his Bosnian experiences but left a few baits for Inkpen. One question dealt with his reaction to ethnic cleansing. Another was whether, as peacekeepers under the protection of the United Nations, they were ever in any real danger.

Continuing before what was becoming a sympathetic jury, she asked him about his return home, his nightmares, how he had turned to alcohol, and the effect it had on Emma and the children. She delved into Emma's patience and how her love for him and her commitment to him had saved not only their marriage but also his life.

Then she covered the next several years of his career and his promotion to sergeant, dwelling only briefly on his work training snipers and the evolution of his relationship with Josh Short, intentionally creating opportunities where she hoped Inkpen would cross-examine him. Eventually, she brought him to Christmas 2000, where, once again, she slowed the tempo, asking him detailed questions about Christmas gifts, Christmas day dinner, and how he felt at the time.

By then, Inkpen, concerned that Billy was being cast in too favourable a light, attempted to shatter the mood. "My Lord," she objected, "I feel compelled to ask how any of this is relevant to the case before the court. I don't think the jury cares if the accused had a Norman Rockwell Christmas or not. We're here, because four people died in a helicopter that this man is charged with shooting down."

Without asking Beebee to speak to the objection, Drinkwater overruled Inkpen but gently, perhaps because, like many of the jurors, he, too, had been reflecting on Christmases past. "I understand your objection, Ms. Inkpen. Perhaps in less serious cases, I would sustain it. However, given this man is on trial for murder, I'm willing to allow his lawyer more latitude in examining him than I would if it were a less serious case."

He turned to BeeBee. "I see that we've almost reached the time for our midday break. I assume that, given where we are so far, your examination-in-chief will continue for the rest of the day, perhaps even until tomorrow. Would you like to stop here, or would you like to take a few more minutes and find a natural break in your client's evidence and continue with a different area after lunch?"

"Thank you, My Lord," BeeBee responded. "I'll finish this area before the break."

Then, with just a few more questions, she "killed" Emma.

"Now, Mr. Wheeler, things seemed to be going really well for you at that point in your life, but I understand something happened to change all of that at New Year's. Can you tell the jury what happened on New Year's Eve?"

The jury watched as his upbeat mood became sombre when he explained that they had been at a friend's house to celebrate the New Year. It had been a nice evening. Everyone brought a dish. Emma had a few glasses of wine, while he, an abstainer for several years, drank black coffee. Not long after midnight, as he was driving home, Emma, asleep in the passenger seat, was killed by a drunk driver who ran a red light while arguing with his passenger, broadsiding them.

While Inkpen fidgeted and the jury, dismayed, watched Billy stand there, tears streaming down his face, Beebee turned to the judge

"My Lord," she said in not much more than a whisper, a lump in her throat, "this may be a good time for us to break for lunch."

Visibly relieved to get away from the emotionally charged but hushed courtroom, Drinkwater was only too happy to oblige.

Chapter 76

More composed, but still white faced, Billy took the stand after the lunch break, seemingly unaware that every eye in the courtroom was riveted on him.

"Mr. Wheeler, before the lunch break you told the court about the events that led up to the accident that caused your wife's death," BeeBee said. "What do you remember about the accident?"

"Nothing," he replied. "One minute we were driving home. The next minute, I woke up in hospital, and people were telling me Emma was dead. I couldn't believe it. I just couldn't believe it. They took me to the morgue, and there she was, all beat up on the right side of her face, head, and shoulder. That's the side where we were struck."

The rapt courtroom, completely silent, waited for the next question. Reporters who had filed their midday stories with headlines that included, "Wheeler's Wife Killed by Drunk Driver," scribbled furiously as Beebee continued.

"What's the next thing you remember?"

"I could see it was her, but I just couldn't believe it. Except for being beat up on one side, it was almost like she was asleep, so I touched her. She was cold, so cold."

"And then what did you do?"

"I got sick and threw up in a wastepaper basket."

"And after that?"

"I guess I must've passed out, because the next thing I remember was waking up in the hospital bed all over again."

"And what's the first thing you remember when you woke up?"

"The kids. Where are the kids? Who's looking after them? Then someone told me they were with their grandparents, and it all came back to me. The kids were away at the time of the accident. I guess, being in the accident, I must've forgotten that..."

His voice drifted off as he remembered the events.

"And what did you do next?"

"I remember I was lying on my back, nobody else in the room, and I rolled over on my side, put my face into the pillow, and cried."

"You cried?"

He nodded. "Like a baby."

"Why?"

"Because she was everything to me. I just couldn't see going on without her." BeeBee waited. Eventually, he continued.

"And then I thought of the kids, and I felt ashamed."

"What do you mean by that?"

"Well, their father was killed when they were little. Now they had lost their mother. Except for their grandparents, I was the only one they had. Here I was, a grown man, feeling sorry for myself, when I should have been worried about the kids."

"How long were you in hospital?"

"Not long. I think only about thirty-six hours."

"And after you got out of the hospital, what did you do?"

"I think I must've been in a bit of a daze for a good while after I got out, because there's a lot that I don't remember."

"That's okay," she said. "Just tell us what you do remember."

"I can remember the funeral, but I'm not sure how I got there or how I got back. It was a cold day, grey, overcast. I think Josh, my warrant officer, might have driven me, but I don't remember the drive or even what vehicle we went in."

"And after the funeral?"

"After the funeral...after the funeral..." he frowned, struggling to remember. "I'm not sure if it was a few days after or perhaps even a few weeks after. I was sitting in the house alone with just my stuff. Emma was dead. The kids were gone to live with her parents. All their stuff and their mother's stuff was gone, and I was alone."

He seemed to drift off.

"What happened next?" BeeBee prompted.

"The phone rang. It was Josh, I mean, Warrant Officer Short, well, actually Master Warrant Officer Short. He had just got another promotion, but that's not why he was calling. He didn't even mention the promotion. I found out when I saw him that he had called because another NCO needed my quarters for his family. He said that, under the circumstances, nobody would ask me to move back into the barracks, but if I did, it would help another guy."

"What happened next?"

"The house was empty for months. I didn't know, because I was gone. Only later Josh told me he lied to get me to move. He said I shouldn't be living alone, stewing in my own juices. He figured I would give up the place if someone else needed it."

"You said you were gone?"

Billy nodded. "Yes. A month, or perhaps a little more than that. The DND put out a call for a few NCOs who had actually been in the field who could rotate among different units and share their experiences. I took them up on their offer, figuring that a change of scenery might be okay, might help me get past her death."

"And the kids?" BeeBee asked. "Were they still with their grandparents?"

"Yes."

"Did you see them?"

"For a while after their mother's death, no. I'm not sure why, just avoiding the memories, I suppose. Then I was talking to their grandparents. They thanked me for the money but said the kids really missed me, so I went to see them. Then I saw them more often until this happened."

"Tell us about the money," she said. "What money?"

"Well, you know, Emma used to handle all the money. After she died, I didn't know what to do or how much it would cost for the kids, you know, so I had payroll split my cheque down the middle and send half of it to her parents to look after the kids. I told them I would try to do a little better if they needed more, but they said it was enough. Then all of this happened."

"When you said, 'all of this happened,' what did you mean?"

"I mean the helicopter, the shooting, all of it."

Beebee turned to the judge. "My Lord, I intend to examine Mr. Wheeler next on the events aboard the vessel. I expect to conclude the evidence for the defence today. Now may be a good time for the afternoon break."

* * *

Fifteen minutes later, Beebee picked up where she had left off. "Mr. Wheeler, before the break, you referred to the events of the morning that brought us all here. Can you tell the jury what happened?"

"Yes. Well, it was just like the others said. We were out in the boat. Sealing. Me, Dad, young Jeff, and Josh. I'm not sure how far out, probably thirty or thirty-five miles. We could see as we approached the ice flow that it wasn't really big, perhaps five or six miles long and a couple miles wide, a few big sheets of ice, almost a mile long, with smaller sheets and pans between them and lots of little pans everywhere. The ice was running to the south, perhaps four or five knots. The morning started out clear, calm, no wind, but you could see by the grey sky that it would likely snow fairly soon.

We left around daylight. About an hour later, we got into the seals. Then it started snowing, you know, just a few big flakes coming straight down, then more, and before long, you could only see fifty or sixty yards ahead of you. That didn't really matter, because we were already into a good-sized patch of seals. Josh was taking his time, slowly approaching each one, careful not to strike any ice too hard. Like the others told you, I was the gunner. We had almost sixty seals aboard when the chopper showed up."

"How did the helicopter first come to your attention?"

"Well, it was the seals," he said. "It was the way the seals hit the water before I even fired a shot."

"Can you explain what you mean?"

"We were in the middle of a dozen or perhaps fifteen seals. They wouldn't dive until we got close. I would wait until some of them were only twenty or twenty-five yards away before firing. That way sometimes I would get two or three instead of just one.

"It was almost like we were on patrol. You know, you get pretty keyed up when you're on patrol, because anything could happen. You could hit a land-mine or you could be ambushed or something might come at you from the air. Everything is a threat when you're on patrol."

"But you weren't on patrol," she countered.

"Yes ma'am," he answered, "I know that. Like I said, it was the seals. All of a sudden, without warning, they started going into the water like they were trying get away from something. Behind me, I heard rotors, and the wind came up from behind, picking up the fresh snow. I wheeled around, and there was a helicopter right on us. All of a sudden, it was like I was in a dream. It wasn't real. I fired a single shot and brought her down. Even after the helicopter went down, I was pretty sure it was only a dream."

"Why do you say that?" BeeBee asked.

"Because I only fired one shot. It had to be a dream. Otherwise I would've emptied the magazine. If I were on patrol, under attack from that close, I wouldn't have stopped shooting. The chances of bringing down a chopper with only one shot are really slim, so I would've emptied the magazine."

"And what happened after that?"

"Well, this is where it got really confusing. With the helicopter gone, I walked back to speak with the rest of the squad. Then I realized it must've been a dream. I was actually out sealing. There was no helicopter, except Jeff was going nuts. Dad wasn't saying anything, but he looked really shook up. Then Josh told me I had just shot down a helicopter. I couldn't believe it. I just couldn't believe it. I was numb all over."

"Do you accept now that you shot down that helicopter?"

"Yes, ma'am, I do," he said, nodding sadly.

"And how does that make you feel?"

"Awful, ma'am. Just awful." Tears streamed down his cheeks. "Even though I know I did it, I can hardly believe it's true."

Beebee said softly "My Lord, I have no more questions for Mr. Wheeler."

Drinkwater turned to the prosecution table. "We have less than an hour remaining today. Do you want to begin your cross-examination today, or would you prefer to begin in the morning?"

Afraid Griffiths might answer, Inkpen leaped to her feet. "My Lord, I'll be conducting the cross-examination. I would prefer to start in the morning."

Chapter 77

With the jury gone, Inkpen turned to Griffiths and, for the first time since the trial began, sought his assistance. "Can we get together upstairs and go over what we heard today?"

Griffiths, who had been watching from the sidelines for days, welcomed the opportunity to assist. While Inkpen's examinations of Josh, Jeff, and Riley, had been somewhat amateurish and rough at times, he was satisfied that his overreaching junior, had nevertheless delivered the goods and had convinced the jury that Wheeler was guilty of murder.

That was until Beaudoin examined Wheeler. Griffiths had watched the effect that his evidence had on the jury and even the judge. Now he was not sure which way it would go and was anxious to share his views with Inkpen. However, given her mercurial temperament and sensitivity to any criticism, real or imagined, he knew he would have to proceed carefully.

One thing he knew for certain was that he could not give Inkpen even an inkling of how much BeeBee had impressed him with her level of preparation and the way she examined her client. He was certain that the accused had, for now, won the hearts of most of the jurors, and it would take a skilful but not too heavy-handed cross-examination to undo the damage to the Crown's case. Nothing he had seen from Inkpen made him confident that she was up to the job.

"So, what do you think, Gerry, how am I doing so far?" Inkpen asked as they sat at the small, round side table in Inkpen's seventh-floor office, which overlooked downtown. "Are we going to get him on first-degree, or do you think, with all that foolishness his lawyer got into today, some members of the jury might have softened up and want to give him a break with only second-degree?"

Oh brother, Griffiths thought. *How can she be so far off base?*

"Yes Iris," he said carefully. "I think you've done a fabulous job. There's no doubt in my mind the jury will find him guilty, but guilty of what?" he asked, as if posing a question to himself.

Inkpen looked alarmed at his question. "Well, murder, of course, but will it be first degree or will we have to settle for second degree?"

"Let's look at the dynamics of a jury," Griffiths replied in a manner that he would use explain to a five-year-old that there was no Santa Claus.

"Okay," Inkpen replied, and for the first time since she had been hired as a prosecutor, she actually listened to what another, more senior, lawyer had to say.

Griffiths began by explaining something that should have required no explanation: that jury verdicts in criminal trials had to be unanimous. "So you see, Iris," he concluded, "in spite of you having done an outstanding job, the odds of these twelve jurors finding Wheeler guilty of first-degree murder are against us."

"Why do you say that?

"First-degree murder is only applicable if you can prove that there was planning, premeditation, or that the murder happened when the accused was carrying out another serious offense, like kidnapping."

"So, are you saying drop first and just go with second?"

"No, not right now. That would only reduce the pressure on the defence."

"But you agree we've got him on second, right?"

Griffiths nodded. "Probably, yes, but I'm concerned that they might go to manslaughter."

"Manslaughter? Manslaughter? Why the fuck would they go to manslaughter?"

"Think about what's going to happen in the jury room," he continued. "Twelve ordinary people, probably nice people, certainly civic-minded people — otherwise they would've found a way to avoid jury duty — are going to sit around a big table and go over the evidence. After they agree on the facts, they'll have to agree on a verdict, all twelve of them. If they can't agree, then we've got a hung jury, the judge declares a mistrial, and we get to do this all over again six months or a year from now. Nobody wants that."

"Go on," Inkpen said, sensing she could benefit from his experience.

"Okay, so let's say they reject first-degree murder out of hand, and now they're discussing second degree, but a few of them, based on what we heard today, a few of them are starting to feel sorry for him, sorry for his dead wife, sorry for the kids, and they want to give him a break."

Inkpen grew increasingly alarmed. "What are they going to do?"

"I don't know."

"What do you think they'll do?"

"The judge will have instructed them on manslaughter, so they'll know that's available."

She stared at him, aghast. "Do you seriously believe we might only get a manslaughter conviction?"

Griffiths shrugged. "With a jury, anything is possible."

"But you agree," she insisted, looking to him for reassurance, "they will find him guilty. Probably second degree, right? But even if this thing goes sideways on us, no worse than manslaughter, right?"

"Maybe, but have you considered that they may be setting us up for an NCR verdict?"

"NCR? NCR, as in 'not criminally responsible'? Temporarily insane? Bullshit! Whose side are you on anyway?"

Griffiths held up his hands. "Relax, Iris, we're on the same side. They're in a real jam. There's no doubt he shot down the helicopter, but I think they're up to something. They've got to pull a rabbit out of a hat, or he's likely going down on second-degree murder. You were probably watching him while he was giving evidence, but I was watching the judge and the jury. There might be nothing to it, but that bit about him thinking he was on patrol and when he said he went back to check on the squad got me wondering if they're accepted that he's done and they're setting an escape route for him."

"But he didn't claim any mental issues, and even when we had the psych assessment done, he came up clean," she said. "If you think that's where they're headed, what's the best way to close it off?"

"Well you're dealing with two distinctly different issues, and either one could hurt our case. Manslaughter is a fine line. He claims he had no intention to kill anyone and that he's remorseful. If the jury buys that line, manslaughter might be their verdict. To defeat the manslaughter argument, you need to show malice. You need to show he was angry they were buzzing his vessel and scaring away the seals. Show they weren't in any danger. Show he intended to bring down that chopper, and he did."

"What do I do if Beaudoin tries to get the jury to go for not criminally responsible?"

"Well properly speaking, we should have gotten the defence to agree to file the psych report back when we were presenting our case against him. If they refused, we could have called the psychiatrist to testify that he doesn't suffer from any mental defect, but it's too late for that now, so I think the best thing to do is to get it in as evidence during your cross-examination."

"And just how do you propose we do that?"

"Simple," he replied. "Trap him into either admitting or denying the existence of the report. If he admits it, you can ask the judge to let you file it for the jury's benefit. His lawyer will have to go along with it or else they'll appear to be hiding something from the jury."

"And if he denies it?"

"Even better," said he, "because that means you'll catch him in a lie, and that Boy Scout performance the jury just spent the whole day buying will go out the window along with any sympathy they may feel for him."

"Perfect." Inkpen smiled, delighted at the prospect of trapping Billy in front of the jury.

Chapter 78

With the jury over her left shoulder, Inkpen trembled with excitement as she turned forty-five degrees to her right. Across the courtroom, she faced her quarry. Finally, she had him exactly him where she wanted him.

Then she froze.

Performers call the unexpected and paralyzing jitters that come out of nowhere "stage fright". Big game hunters call the rapid heartbeat, the shallow breathing and trembling body just moments before pulling the trigger or releasing the bowstring that causes easy shots to be missed "buck fever". No matter what anyone called it, Inkpen had a bad case.

Griffiths' well-intentioned advice, aimed at helping his associate, had only made matters worse. Staying up until well past midnight, going over her notes, reviewing copies of the exhibits, and preparing lines of questioning would have given her a short night's rest, if she had been able to sleep. But she could not. After a few hours of tossing and turning, by 4 a.m. she was up, drinking coffee, and attacking the file all over again.

Two hours later, finally satisfied she was ready, that there was no way the accused could escape from her punishing cross-examination, she dozed off on the sofa and overslept, awaking to the professional voice of the CBC world newscaster.

"This is the CBC World News at eight o'clock, eight thirty if you're in Newfoundland. And speaking of Newfoundland, we'll be checking in with our reporter in Corner Brook, where the prosecution will finally get to cross-examine the accused in that tragedy, where a helicopter carrying a number of prominent personalities crashed into the ocean, allegedly having been shot down by a Newfoundland sealer. Yesterday, the accused, William John Wheeler, a sergeant in the Canadian Armed Forces, admitted to firing the shot that brought down the chopper."

Flying off the sofa, Inkpen ran to the bathroom, skipped the shower, washed her face, brushed her hair, and put on makeup.

Thank God for court gowns, she thought. *At least I don't have to worry what to wear.*

She headed for her bedroom closet, pulled on a pair of black trousers and a fresh, white barrister's shirt, and slipped her gold cufflinks into her pocket, to be put on as she drove across town. Then she headed back to her dining room table, where she re-filled the two bankers boxes and her briefcase with the materials. She strapped them to her upright, wheeled, aluminum carrier and secured them with bungee cords. Briefcase in hand, she hurried out the door.

An hour later, she was in her office frantically organizing documents that she wanted for her cross-examination, which was set for 10 a.m.

Now, before the packed courtroom, squaring off against the source of her anxiety, she found herself stuck for words.

"Excuse me, my Lord," she said after a few moments. "I just need a few seconds to confer with my co-counsel."

"No problem, Ms. Inkpen," Drinkwater replied. "Will a few seconds do, or would you like a little more time? Because if you need a little more time, perhaps the jury could be permitted to go back to their room?"

His inquiry, asked in good faith, only added to her anxiety.

"Just a few seconds will do, my Lord," she said. Then she turned to Griffiths. "Gerry, I'm drawing a blank," she whispered. "I don't know what to do. Where should I start?"

"Relax, Iris," the veteran litigator responded softly. "Just start with a few warm-up questions, and then take your time before you move into the areas we discussed yesterday. You'll be fine."

She ignored his advice and dove right in. "Mr. Wheeler, what is your current employment status?"

"Ma'am, I'm a member of the Canadian armed forces."

"I think we know that much by now," she said a tone that was already beginning to irritate everyone. "What I'm asking is, and you'll have to fill in the correct military term for me, is if somewhere, up along, likely Ottawa, or maybe some forces base somewhere, there's a file with your name on it, correct?"

"Yes ma'am."

"I'm pretty sure it doesn't say 'posted to Corner Brook to be tried for murder,' does it?"

"Probably not, ma'am," he replied, "but they know I'm here."

"So someone, somewhere, knows you're here, and they have a file on you. Can you tell the jury your current status according to that file?"

"Well, ma'am, I've never actually seen my files," he replied, "but I understand that I'm currently on leave."

"And what happens when the trial is over?"

"I don't know ma'am."

"What are your plans when the trial is over?" she asked, floundering.

"Ma'am, I don't think someone in my situation should be making any plans," he responded truthfully and respectfully.

"I see," she replied. "So, what should someone in your situation be doing?"

"Simply concentrate on the task at hand, ma'am. We're trained to concentrate on the task at hand. Complete the task at hand. Then wait for further orders."

"Would you agree the task at hand, for you, right now, is to say whatever it takes to get the charges against you dismissed?"

"No, ma'am."

Expecting a different answer, she pressed on. "Well, what would you say is your current task at hand?"

"To tell the truth," he said. "That's the only way these people," he nodded at the jury, "will be able to make the right decision."

Finally, Beebee, initially curious as to how Inkpen would conduct herself, rose to her feet. "My Lord, I object to this line of questioning. First of all, I don't see the relevance. Even if the crown attorney is able to establish some minor relevancy, I think the questions, as put to the witness, are improper."

"Ms. Inkpen," Drinkwater said, "I agree with defence counsel. Unless you can convince me this is an appropriate line of questioning, I'm going to ask you to move on."

Inkpen smiled weakly, asked a few more questions, and then addressed the judge. "My Lord, it may be a little early for our morning break. However, my next line of questioning will go on for a while. I will need to refer to several of the exhibits, and to do so, I will require the assistance of Madam Clerk. If we break now, after lunch we can resume uninterrupted."

An audible sigh of relief permeated the courtroom when Drinkwater agreed.

After the jury left, Griffiths turned to Inkpen. "Iris, what's got into you?" he whispered. "I've seen you do a better job prosecuting a speeding ticket. There's no way you'll get a murder conviction unless you take him down with your cross-examination. The better the jury gets to know him, the more they may like him. His lawyer went for their heartstrings yesterday. This is your only chance to undo that."

"I know, I know," Inkpen said. "I was a little scattered this morning, but I've got it together now. I'll be fine after the break."

Her comments reassured neither of them.

Just then, the clerk, who was still at her table where all the exhibits were laid out in order, spoke up. "Ms. Inkpen, the exhibits are all here. I just need to step out for a few minutes, but I'll be right back, and if there's anything else that you require, I'll be happy to help you."

"Thank you," Inkpen replied.

"Why do you need to see the exhibits?" Griffiths asked the moment they were alone. "Am I missing something?"

"I don't need to see the fucking exhibits," Inkpen growled. "I needed to put my own in order. Besides," she added with a sly grin, "by taking the break early, the second half will be longer than the first, giving me more time to corner him before lunch."

Griffiths smiled. "Atta girl. I'm glad to see that the inquisitor is back and in fine form, too."

*   *   *

After the break, Inkpen lost no time, using rapid-fire questions, to everyone's surprise, except for the other lawyers and Billy. He was prepared for her assault.

Inkpen quickly established the time and place the helicopter had gone down. Then she had Billy confirm, all over again, that he had been the shooter. She also probed deeply into his military experience.

"Now, Mr. Wheeler, or is it Sergeant Wheeler?"

She waited for him to answer. When he paused, expecting her to ask him a different question, she continued.

"I asked you a question, are you gonna answer it?"

"Yes, ma'am," he replied. "Generally, it's just Billy. When it's work-related, my rank is sergeant. I guess here in court it would be Mr."

"So, Mr. Wheeler, I understand you've been in combat. Is that correct?"

"Yes, ma'am, I have."

"Have you killed people?"

He took a deep breath before answering. "Yes, ma'am, I've killed people."

"How many people have you killed?" she asked before the hushed courtroom.

This time he was slower to answer. She waited, watching him fidget and bite his lip.

"I couldn't say for sure," he said finally in a lower voice.

"Why is that?" she pressed.

"When you're exchanging fire, sometimes during daylight, sometimes after dark, you won't always know who fired which shots that took out which opponents," he replied.

"So can you confirm for this court that you have actually killed people, other than the ones that you killed in the helicopter?"

"Yes, ma'am," he replied, perspiring visibly.

"But you don't know how many you've killed?"

His breathing picked up as he shook his head. "No, ma'am."

Realizing she had hit upon a subject he wanted to avoid, she continued. "Okay, let me put it to you this way. Have you killed more than ten people or fewer than ten people?"

334 | Jim Bennett

Breathing heavily and perspiring profusely, he reached for the plastic water glass and drank half its contents before answering. "More than ten people, ma'am."

He looked at the floor to avoid making eye contact with the eyes in the courtroom he knew were fixed on him.

Enjoying his discomfort, and thinking she had hit pay dirt, Inkpen continued. "Have you killed more than twenty people?"

"I don't think so, ma'am."

She nodded, satisfied. "Okay, let's talk about the four people that you killed in helicopter. What do you know about them?"

"I've heard of the pilot. A lot of people around home knew him, because he used to fly hunters for local outfitters. Except for what I've heard in court and read in a few newspaper stories, I don't know anything about the others."

"Okay. Let's focus on the pilot. Did you know he had a family?"

"Yes, ma'am, I heard that he did."

"Did you know that he was breaking the law by flying so close to your vessel?"

"I never gave it any thought at the time, but I've heard if he had lived he could have been fined for coming too close."

"Do you agree that he was disrupting the hunt by flying so close?"

"Yes, he was."

"Some people might say he deserved what he got. Do you feel that way?"

"No, ma'am," he answered softly. "Nobody deserves that."

"You know what I think, Mr. Wheeler? I think you were really angry that the helicopter was scaring the seals away and that, in a fit of anger, and based on your training and experience, as someone who has already killed lots of people, perhaps as many as twenty, it was easy for you to lift a rifle and put a shot through the pilot's head just to teach them all a lesson. That's what I think, so I ask you, why shouldn't the jury think that's what you did?"

By then, Billy had tears running down his face. "I don't know. I can't answer that. I can only tell you what happened. They have to decide for themselves what to believe."

I've almost got him, Inkpen thought.

"Madam Clerk," she said, "can you show Mr. Wheeler the autopsy photo of the pilot, George Villeneuve?"

For the longest time, Billy stood looking at what remained of the pilot's face. Most of the flesh gone. Empty eye sockets remained where George's eyes had been eaten by tiny sea scavengers that had crawled up his neck and into his helmet, leaving the larger lobsters and crabs to feast on the exposed parts.

Suddenly, the silence was broken by a crash. Ice water, bits of ice, and shards of glass sprayed over several people, including four jurors near the front. Drinkwater, reaching for the crystal, condensation-covered water

jug while still studying the expression on the accused's face, had accidentally pushed it over the edge. Three quarters full, it plummeted to the floor,
exploding into a thousand pieces. Eyes that had been fixed on Billy darted to
the front of the room.

Although initially it was the loud crash that attracted everyone's attention, it was Billy's response that shocked them. One second he was standing
there studying the photo of the dead pilot, tears streaming down his face.
The next second, his expression changed, and he looked skyward.

"Incoming! Incoming! Take cover! Take cover!"

Then, as everyone watched, he dove to the floor of the witness box, out
of sight.

"Officers, take charge of the prisoner!" Drinkwater ordered.

His command was unnecessary, as two sheriff's officers had already
jumped into the witness box, grabbed Billy, and put him in restraints.

With reporters running out the door to report on the shocking event they
had just witnessed, unable to restore order, Drinkwater closed court until
after the midday break.

Chapter 79

Before court resumed at 2 p.m., the clerk located the lawyers. "Come with me," she said. "The judge wants to speak with you."

She led them back to Drinkwater's chambers.

"Given what happened before the break," Drinkwater said, addressing all three of them, "I'd like to have your perspective on whether we can continue the trial. Ms. Inkpen, we're in the middle of your cross-examination, so I'll let you go first."

"Continue the trial? Of course we can continue the trial," she said. "Wheeler might have a few issues, but most people on trial for murder have issues. Besides, we had a psych assessment done on him, and he came up clean. For all we know, he staged that outburst after I brought him face-to-face with one of the people he killed. Continue the trial? Hell yes!"

"And how about you, Ms. Beaudoin?" Drinkwater asked. "Have you spoken with your client?"

"No, my Lord. As you pointed out, he's under cross-examination. It would be improper for me to speak with him until the cross-examination is finished."

"Ah yes, good point," he replied, his lack of trial experience on display once again. "Mr. Griffiths," he said, turning to the most experienced of the trio. "What are your thoughts?"

"Well, my Lord," Griffiths replied, "I think we have to continue. Outbursts by people on trial are nothing new, and I agree with Ms. Beaudoin that it would be improper for her to have any discussion with him, as it might appear that she was attempting to influence his testimony midway through his cross-examination. However, as you know, appeals are common in cases like this, so I think you should offer Mr. Wheeler the opportunity to confer with another lawyer, that is, if he wants to, before we continue."

Drinkwater turned back to BeeBee. "Ms. Beaudoin, he's your client. How do you feel about Mr. Griffiths' recommendation?"

"I agree with it, but on two conditions."

"And they are?"

"The offer to speak with another lawyer needs to be done in open court in front of the jury, and I think you will need to explain to them the reason you are offering him the opportunity to speak to another lawyer is because it's improper for me, his own lawyer, to speak with him while he's being cross examined to eliminate any possibility that I could influence his answers."

Drinkwater glanced at Griffiths who nodded in agreement, and then turned to Inkpen. "I don't imagine you have any disagreement with the recommendation of your senior co-counsel, do you?"

"No, my Lord," she replied.

While miffed that Drinkwater seemed too willing to defer to Griffiths, Inkpen was relieved that the judge was no longer considering declaring a mistrial. She was looking forward to going after Billy again so the jury could see he was a menace.

* * *

When court resumed at 2:30 p.m., half an hour later than usual, Drinkwater began by addressing Billy. "Mr. Wheeler, when we broke before the lunch hour, you seemed to be in some distress. Are you okay now?"

"Yes, sir." Billy replied.

"Now, I understand that you haven't spoken with your lawyer over the break. Is that true?"

"Yes, sir, but I didn't expect to, because she told me I had to go through the cross-examination without any help from her."

Drinkwater nodded. "Now, Mr. Wheeler, I don't want to interrupt or unduly delay your trial, but the lawyers and I had a discussion, and we agreed that it would be okay for you to consult with another lawyer if you have any concerns about being able to continue with the trial."

"Thank you, sir," Billy responded, "but I'm fine to continue."

Drinkwater turned to the prosecution table. "Ms. Inkpen, are you ready to continue your cross-examination?"

"Yes, my Lord." She stood up. "Mr. Wheeler, before the break and the little bit of excitement that you caused, you were looking at a photograph of George Villeneuve, the dead pilot. Do you recall that?"

"Yes, ma'am, I do."

"And what was going through your mind as you looked at the photograph?"

"I was thinking of some of the bodies that I've seen," he replied.

"How many bodies would you say you've seen?"

"Hundreds," he answered, his voice flattening and losing much of its energy. "I've seen hundreds of bodies up close like that."

"In your experience, did Mr. Villeneuve's body resemble any you have seen?"

"In some ways, yes, and in some ways, no."

"Can you explain that?"

"Well, most of them are blood covered, whereas he was clean, I guess from the water, but other than that, pretty much the same. The eyes were gone. The birds go after them first. Then, within a day or two, the maggots take over. Then animals go to work. I was thinking of the bodies I've seen, and then I heard a boom and felt a shower of something, for a second, I thought we were under attack. I'm sorry. I just reacted."

"But you knew we weren't under attack, didn't you?"

"Yes ma'am."

"Just like you knew you weren't under attack when you shot down the helicopter, right?"

"Yes ma'am."

"And you agree that you don't suffer from any mental illness, correct?"

"Yes, ma'am, I agree."

"Have you ever had a psychiatric evaluation?"

"Well, ma'am, you know I have, because last summer, I agreed for you to send me to the Waterford for one."

"And how did that turn out?"

"Well, ma'am, you know how it turned out. We've all read the report. It says I don't suffer from a mental illness. Sometimes I almost wish they had found something wrong with me."

"And why is that?"

"Because that would explain why I shot down the helicopter. I think that would make it easier to accept what I did."

Inkpen turned to the judge. "My Lord, I have no further questions."

"Any re-examination, Ms. Beaudoin?" Drinkwater asked.

"I'll confer with my client during the break, my Lord," she replied, "but I think not."

As predicted, after the break Beebee had no questions, advising the court that she had no more witnesses. Drinkwater set Friday morning for summations, with the defence going first, and advised that he intended to give his instructions to the jury either later in the morning, if the lawyers had concluded, or at 2 p.m. on Friday.

Chapter 80

The following morning, Beebee stood before the jury. "My name is Barbara Beaudoin. On behalf of my client and myself, I want to thank you for taking the last two weeks out of your lives to serve as jurors. Without your time and attention, the criminal justice system, particularly in very serious cases such as the one before you, couldn't work. I don't intend to review the evidence with you. You've heard the evidence. I don't think any elaboration is necessary. Instead, I will discuss two legal principles that Justice Drinkwater will likely elaborate upon later."

She paused and took a sip of water. The courtroom was dead silent. She let the jurors look into her eyes.

"First of all is the presumption of innocence. The presumption of innocence means the accused person must be presumed innocent until being found guilty, beyond reasonable doubt. It means he does not have to prove he is innocent. Instead, it means the prosecution has to prove he is guilty."

She paused to let her words sink in.

"Beyond a reasonable doubt doesn't mean the accused may have committed the offense or likely committed the offense. It means a high degree of certainty that he committed the offense. Does it mean one hundred percent certainty? Of course not. Rarely, can we be one hundred percent certain of anything. However, you must not be left with any lingering doubt or concern of his guilt.

"This case is highly unusual. There is no doubt my client fired the shot that killed George Villeneuve and took down the helicopter, killing the other three occupants. If you are to convict him, there are three potential guilty verdicts."

She paused and turned a page in the three-ringed binder in front of her. Then she continued in a conversational tone. "He could be found guilty of first-degree murder. That would require you to find the killings were planned and premeditated. There is no evidence of that."

She looked at the jurors. A few nodded slightly in agreement.

"He could be found guilty of second-degree murder," she continued. "That means he intended to shoot down the helicopter and kill the occupants but didn't plan it in advance. There was no pre-planning. No premeditation. The killing was done on the spur of the moment. I suggest to you there's no evidence that my client intended to kill those people."

She paused. Some jurors were still with her. Others looked perplexed.

"Or you could find he intended to shoot at the helicopter. Perhaps he intended to fire a warning shot. That would be an unlawful act. It caused four deaths. If you find he didn't intend to kill anyone, but his unlawful act caused their deaths, you could find him guilty of manslaughter. I'm going to ask you reject all three of those verdicts and find him not guilty."

She paused and moved closer to them, leaving her notes behind.

"If there was any evidence my client was suffering from any mental disorder, you could find him not criminally responsible. Some people refer to that as temporary insanity. However, there is no evidence he suffers from a mental defect. You heard him say he had a psychiatric examination. He suffers from no mental defect. How then, could he be not guilty?"

She let the question hang in the charged courtroom before continuing.

"Automatism." She paused to let the word sink in. "In all the circumstances, I submit to you that when he fired that shot, William John Wheeler — Billy, to people who know him — was in an automatistic state."

She paused and looked at Billy. Most jurors followed her gaze.

"There are two types of automatism: insane and non-insane automatism. My client suffers from no mental defect or disorder. The appropriate verdict, therefore, in my submission to you, is non-insane automatism. To arrive at this verdict, you must believe it possible that what my client was referring to as a dream was actually an automatistic state.

"For a brief moment, likely the most important and tragic moment in his life, he believed he was under attack. Under attack by a helicopter. It appeared out of nowhere. Without warning. He reacted with tragic consequences.

"You can see he is deeply remorseful, but he is unable to correct what he did. Therefore, I ask you to find him not guilty."

*   *   *

As Beebee addressed the jury, Inkpen rolled her eyes, fidgeted, and shuffled paper to demonstrate her disagreement with defence's submissions.

Finally, when she had her chance, instead of focusing on her own submission, Inkpen tore into the defence's theory of automatism. She labelled it as a ridiculous fairy tale, a desperate move by a desperate killer and his equally desperate lawyer to avoid responsibility for killing four people who even he acknowledged he had killed.

Then she described the evidence before the jury, evidence she said needed no describing, evidence even the defence did not refute. After a wide-ranging and generally unfocused closing argument, she labelled Billy as a professional killer. She said he knew exactly what he was doing. He was able to kill, without remorse, on a moment's notice. She claimed that while his training may have turned him into a killer, his experiences should not be used to excuse his actions.

When Inkpen concluded at noon, Drinkwater elected to break for lunch half an hour early and return at 1:30 to instruct the jury.

His instructions to the jury were short. He explained that the identity of the shooter was not in question. All they had to do was decide whether he was not guilty, as argued by defence counsel, or guilty, as urged by the prosecution. If he was guilty, was he guilty of first-degree murder, second-degree murder, or manslaughter, all of which were available.

The twelve jurors filed to the jury room to deliberate. Everyone else waited. They did not have to wait long.

Within forty-five minutes, the jurors returned. Spectators and journalists piled back into the courtroom. Expecting a verdict, they were disappointed to learn the jury wanted to rehear one part of the accused's testimony.

With bated breath, everyone waited while the court clerk located the section. Then everyone heard Billy state clearly that after he shot down the helicopter, he went back to check on the squad.

The twelve retired again to the jury room. An hour later, they advised the judge they had a verdict.

A few minutes before 5 p.m., Drinkwater put the question to them formally. "Have you arrived at a verdict?"

"Yes, my Lord," the foreman replied.

"Are you unanimous?"

"Yes, my Lord."

"On the charge of first-degree murder, how find you?"

"Not guilty."

"On the charge of second-degree murder, how find you?"

"Not guilty."

"On the charge of manslaughter, how find you?"

"Not guilty."

The courtroom erupted.

About the Author

Jim Bennett was born in Daniel's Harbour, Newfoundland. Upon graduating from Memorial University, he joined the financial planning industry. After an award-winning, fifteen-year career in Newfoundland, Nova Scotia and Alberta, he entered law school, graduating with an LLB from Windsor and a JD from Detroit.

He practiced law, mostly contested matters, in Ontario until 2002, when he returned home to Daniel's Harbour and opened a law practice.

In 2011 he was elected to the Newfoundland and Labrador House of Assembly where he served for four years. He did not run for re-election in 2015.

Today he writes and practices law. Jim is married to Ontario resident and former Cabinet Minister Sandra Pupatello and divides his time between both provinces. *Degrees of Guilt* is the first of what he hopes to be a series of novels that allow readers to explore human motivation through the world of fiction, often set in Newfoundland.